"Evie Dunmore's debut is a marvel. Set against the backdrop of the British suffrage movement, *Bringing Down the Duke* is a witty, richly detailed, historically significant, and achingly romantic celebration of the power of love and the passionate fight for women's rights. A stunning blend of history and romance that will enchant readers."   —*New York Times* bestselling author Chanel Cleeton

"Evie Dunmore's *Bringing Down the Duke* dazzles and reminds us all why we fell in love with historical romance."
                    —*New York Times* bestselling author Julia London

"Miss Dunmore is a literary force to be reckoned with. She's single-handedly forging a new historical romance era and I am here. For. It."   —#1 *New York Times* bestselling author Rachel Van Dyken

"Simply superb! Evie Dunmore will wow you."
                    —*New York Times* bestselling author Gaelen Foley

"One of my all-time favorite historicals."
                    —*New York Times* bestselling author Maisey Yates

"*Bringing Down the Duke* was one of the best books I've ever read—absolutely adored it. Dunmore had me in tears, had me holding my breath . . . the emotion and passion made the book ache and sing."
                    —*New York Times* bestselling author Jane Porter

"Dunmore creates pure magic with this charming, romantic novel featuring a strong, stubborn heroine and a sexy, slightly broken hero. Full of romance, humor, and heart, all revolving around the fascinating dynamics of the suffragist movement, it's one of my favorite novels of 2020!"
                    —*New York Times* bestselling author Jennifer Probst

"Funny, smart, and a fantastic read! *Bringing Down the Duke* was absolutely brilliant!"

—*New York Times* bestselling author Corinne Michaels

"What an absolutely stunning, riveting, painfully gorgeous book! It's not only the best historical romance I've read in a long, long time, it's one of the best books I've ever read! I adored it!"

—*USA Today* bestselling author Megan Crane

"With just the right blend of history and romance (and a healthy dash of pride from the British suffragists that would make Jane Austen proud), I was hooked on Annabelle and Sebastian's story from the very first page. I can't wait for the rest of the League of Extraordinary Women novels!"

—*USA Today* bestselling author Stephanie Thornton

"Evie Dunmore's *Bringing Down the Duke* delivers the best of two worlds—a steamy romance coupled with the heft of a meticulously researched historical novel. . . . Readers will be entranced watching Annabelle, a woman ahead of her time, bring the sexy Duke to his knees." —*USA Today* bestselling author Renée Rosen

"Evie Dunmore has written a story we need right now—strong, smart, and passionate, featuring a heroine who won't settle for less than what she deserves and a swoony hero who learns to fight for what really matters. With her debut novel, Dunmore has instantly become a must-read for me."

—*USA Today* bestselling author Lyssa Kay Adams

"Charming, sexy, and thoroughly transportive, this is historical romance done right." —*Publishers Weekly* (starred review)

"Dunmore's beautifully written debut perfectly balances history, sexual tension, romantic yearning, and the constant struggle smart women have in finding and maintaining their places and voices in life and love, with the added message that finding the right person brings true happiness and being with them is worth any price. A brilliant debut."
—*Kirkus Reviews* (starred review)

"Chock-full of verve, history, and passion."
—*Library Journal* (starred review)

"Full of witty banter, rich historical detail, and a fantastic group of female friends, the first installment in Dunmore's League of Extraordinary Women series starts with fireworks as Annabelle and Montgomery try to find a path to happiness despite past mistakes and their vastly different places in society. Dunmore's strong debut is sure to earn her legions of fans."
—*Booklist* (starred review)

ALSO BY EVIE DUNMORE

Bringing Down the Duke
A Rogue of One's Own
Portrait of a Scotsman

The Gentleman's Gambit

The League of Extraordinary Women Series

EVIE DUNMORE

BERKLEY ROMANCE
New York

BERKLEY ROMANCE
Published by Berkley
An imprint of Penguin Random House LLC
penguinrandomhouse.com

Copyright © 2023 by Evie Dunmore
Readers Guide copyright © 2023 by Evie Dunmore
Penguin Random House supports copyright. Copyright fuels creativity, encourages diverse voices,
promotes free speech, and creates a vibrant culture. Thank you for buying an authorized edition
of this book and for complying with copyright laws by not reproducing, scanning, or distributing
any part of it in any form without permission. You are supporting writers and allowing
Penguin Random House to continue to publish books for every reader.

BERKLEY and the BERKLEY & B colophon are registered trademarks of
Penguin Random House LLC.

Library of Congress Cataloging-in-Publication Data

Names: Dunmore, Evie, author.
Title: The gentleman's gambit / Evie Dunmore.
Description: First edition. | New York: Berkley Romance, 2023. |
Series: The League of Extraordinary Women series
Identifiers: LCCN 2023019636 (print) | LCCN 2023019637 (ebook) |
ISBN 9780593334669 (trade paperback) | ISBN 9780593334676 (ebook)
Subjects: LCGFT: Romance fiction. | Novels.
Classification: LCC PR9110.9.D86 G46 2023 (print) |
LCC PR9110.9.D86 (ebook) | DDC 823/.92—dc23/eng/20230512
LC record available at https://lccn.loc.gov/2023019636
LC ebook record available at https://lccn.loc.gov/2023019637

First Edition: December 2023

Printed in the United States of America
1st Printing

Book design by Laura K. Corless

Dedicated to my Tayta,
who led the dabkeh ahead of her time

The Gentleman's Gambit

Chapter 1

Applecross, Scotland, July 1882

In a world run by loud people, quiet was a scarce commodity. Catriona was willing to pay for it and she knew all the ways to acquire some solitude. The one thing she couldn't do was store it in her veins for later use —a pity, because tonight at seven o'clock, a stranger would invade her home.

For now, she had sought refuge in the cool waters of Loch Shieldaig. The lake of her childhood home filled her ears with the heavy silence of a tomb. She floated on her back, her bare white body stark against the black depths, her arms outspread as if trying to embrace the blue expanse of sky above. Now and then a wave lapped over her face, leaving a brackish taste in her throat. Had she known her father would invite a guest to the family seat, she would have thought twice about coming up to Applecross for the summer. One assumed that a remote castle was free from the distractions that lurked back at Oxford: sociable friends. The suffrage cause. The lingering awkwardness of an unrequited crush. Where could she work on a book in peace if not here?

The visitor's presence would make her feel alien in her own dining hall. She'd do her duty and play hostess, of course. At five-and-twenty, she knew the protocol: hold his gaze, smile slightly, and put her comfort last. Ask light questions about his travels and research plans, all while discreetly observing his plate and wineglass in case the footmen failed to anticipate his needs on time. She did have an eye for detail. Luckily, most people did not. Few ever saw the true emotions behind her mask. The visitor, too, would be none the wiser that she was wishing him away.

The breeze stirred and sent shivers across the loch, and the cold entered her bones, urging her to return. She swam with practiced backstrokes, her mind inattentive as her body knew the route to the eastern bank by habit. No one ever visited the small crescent of shoreline where she had left her clothes. The spot was shielded by a rare patch of forest, and only sheep and old gamekeeper Collins knew the path, neither of whom posed a threat to the daughter of Alastair Campbell, Earl of Wester Ross.

Gooseflesh rose on her wet skin when she emerged from the water. She strode to the forest edge quickly. Her clothes were still laid out on the boulder, secured in place by a thick volume of Virgil's *Aeneid*. With clammy fingers, she picked up the book and her spectacles. Then she noticed it: the presence to her right. She froze.

A man.

A man was blocking the entrance of the forest path.

Ice shot through her stomach.

She clutched the Virgil in front of her modesty; her spectacles clattered to the ground. He was five yards away. Watching her. Her heart was racing. He had already seen her . . . he had seen everything. She turned to him fully with the treacle-slow motion of a bad dream. His contours were fuzzy, but conclusive enough: still young, strong features, broad but lean shoulders in a fitted coat— he was in fine fighting form. Not good. *And he was still staring.* With an age-old expression of awe. As though he had unexpectedly stumbled through the doors of a cathedral and felt ambushed by the dizzying heights and the dusty taste of the eternal. It would have given her pause, except there was a pair of binoculars resting against his chest. A white-hot sensation rushed to her head.

"What do you think you are doing," she snapped, the words shooting out cold and clipped.

The man came alive as if he had been released from a spell. He turned his face away.

"You . . . are a woman," he said, sounding vaguely stunned.

"Astutely observed, sir," she said, incredulous.

He made a noise in his throat, like a surprised chuckle.

The pulse pounding in her ears near drowned out her conscious thinking. "Of course you're amused," she said. "One would expect nothing but low humor from a cowardly Peeping Tom."

He twitched, as though it cost him effort to not whip his head back round to her. "I was not . . . peeping."

"So you did not, while walking along the ridge, spot me in the water, use your binoculars to ascertain that I was indeed an un-clothed woman, and then creep all the way down through the forest to spy on me?"

Her tone had sharpened with every word and by the end, he should have lain on the ground in neat slices. He stood quite intact if a bit befuddled. His head tipped back on a soft laugh.

"That sounds like a lot of trouble just to see an unclothed woman," he said. "You are very charming, miss," he added, "but it's nothing I have not seen before."

Her cheeks stung as if she had been slapped.

"Then why," she cried, "are you still standing there—oh!"

Her startled gasp did make him look back at her, just as a trans-lucent shape flew toward him on a fresh gust of wind. Hell. Her untethered underclothes, fine like cobwebs, had taken off in the breeze.

"Blast." She lunged forward and slammed her palm down on a remaining stocking. She cast a quick glance sideways. The man was straightening from a crouch with her chemise caught in his fist, as if he had swiped it from midair like a large cat. He eyed her pantaloons next—they had landed in a shrub, and it had to be the pantaloons because there were blurry pink ribbons, doing a saucy dance.

"Don't touch that," she wheezed.

He raised his arms over his head. "I won't touch."

Her chemise fluttered in his hand like a white flag.

"You really ought to take your leave now," she suggested through gritted teeth.

"Absolutely," he agreed. "See here."

He turned around, seemed to survey the nearest tree, and then he deftly tied her chemise to the trunk by its decorative cords.

"Voilà," he said and spread his fingers. "You shall never see me again."

Without a backward glance, he strode into the forest at a fluid pace.

"Nearly gone now," he called out before his elegant form disappeared around the bend.

She stayed hunched over the boulder, barely able to swallow around the shock still clogging her throat. The path remained empty and the forest quiet, as if the man had never been here at all. Oh, he had been quite real. His roaming gaze had left a smoldering trail across her body. She had refused to flail and twist to cover her breasts; he had already looked his fill anyway and it would have probably given him satisfaction to see her squirm.

Eventually, she picked up her spectacles. They had survived the fall intact. She put them on, and Castle Applecross slid into focus on the plateau on the opposite bank, its old stone towers sharply delineated against the clear sky. She was rather far from home here, on the other side of the loch. Sudden energy surged, and she rushed to take her chemise down from the tree. What a neat, pretty bow the creeper had tied, *voilà!* Would it be safe to walk home? He could be lurking in the brambles and pounce after all. She looked back at the castle, half a mile across a rippling surface. The decision was made quickly: she chose the risk of the water over the man. Back at the boulder, she put down the chemise and pulled her shawl from under her gown instead, wound it round her head, and secured it with her hatpin. She gave the Virgil an apologetic pat. "I shall fetch you later."

The loch engulfed her body like a large cold fist.

When she staggered onto the shoreline below the castle, her arms and thighs were burning with exhaustion. The plateau enclosed the beach like a protective wall, so she took some time to regain her breath. Wrapped in the plaid, she hurried up the crumbling steps her ancestor had once hewn into the side of the rock face. Overgrown vegetable beds and a tumbledown cottage blurred past on her dash to the castle walls. She slipped through the side entrance into the dimly lit wine cellar, then up the cobwebbed spiral staircase, one floor, two, three. On the final landing, she threw her shoulder against the servants' door, until she burst into her chamber.

A scream rang out.

MacKenzie was pressing a fist to her chest, her wide-eyed gaze fixed on Catriona as if she were one of the castle ghosts. "Milady. I near jumped out of my skin."

Catriona padded past her on numb feet to the rocking chair with the tartan throws. She sat and huddled into the blankets while her former nanny-turned-lady's-maid surveyed her with a hand on her sturdy hip. After thirty years of service in the Campbell household, MacKenzie was accustomed to remarkably eccentric behavior, but parading around in nothing but a plaid was a novel, unacceptable development. *Sorry, MacKenzie.* Crossing the loch with the added weight of waterlogged undergarments would have been rather too reckless.

Before MacKenzie could inquire about her clothes, Catriona asked: "Do you know if the earl has employed a new gamekeeper?"

MacKenzie's consternated expression changed to concern. "A new gamekeeper," she repeated in her thick brogue. "I hadn't realized you let the old Collins go."

Catriona rocked with the chair. "I would never."

Neither would her father, come to think of it. Then why the binoculars on that man?

She couldn't feel her face. The hexagonal room on top of the south tower, despite thick wall tapestries and sprawling Persian carpets, was never warm, and the fright from being watched was still lodged in her chest like an icicle.

"You must make haste," MacKenzie said, and nodded at the copper basin in front of the hearth. Steam was swirling lazily into the cool air. "His lordship's guest has arrived."

"What—already?"

The clock next to the chamber door said it was not yet three in the afternoon.

MacKenzie pursed her lips. "He's arrived early. Poor manners if I may say so—everyone's in a tizzy. But the tub's ready for you."

"Good grief," Catriona muttered. A sudden change in schedule made her feel queasy on the best of days. "Oooh," she then said. "Oh no. Oh dear."

She felt so weak, it was as though her heart had stopped.

"Dinna fash," came MacKenzie's voice from a distance. "The earl has just returned, he was at the Middletons'—they are separating, the Middletons, have you heard . . . but his lordship is back, and he's entertaining the young gentleman until dinner. All's well."

All this was easy for MacKenzie to say, because she didn't know about the stranger at the loch.

"He rolled his *r*'s," she moaned.

"Huh?"

She buried her face in her hands. "This is bad."

"If you bathe now, you should be ready soon enough," Mac-Kenzie said in the soothing tone she used on the unwell.

Catriona looked up at her, feeling dizzy. "Did our guest take a walk after his arrival?"

The math was damning: two strangers on the same day in remote Applecross was highly improbable. Had she not been so shocked, and so set on him arriving at seven, this would have occurred to her it was happening.

"I don't know if the gentleman went for a walk," said MacKenzie. She opened the top drawer of the dresser next to the fireplace to take out a stack of towels. "Once Mary told me he was here, I saw to the bath and laid out your clothes."

While MacKenzie's back was turned, Catriona rose, dropped the damp plaid, and climbed into the heat of the tub.

"What's he like?" she forced herself to ask.

MacKenzie placed the towels on the footstool next to the tub and straightened with a soft grunt. "I haven't seen him," she said. "Mary said he's brought a trunk full of wine and he carried it from the carriage all by himself."

She should have asked questions about the man when the earl had announced a visitor, but, frustrated by the news, she hadn't. She knew he was an expert on Phoenician high culture from the Levant, Mount Lebanon more precisely, with several terms at Cambridge among his credentials. He was one of the numerous international scholars interested in an exchange with Oxbridge academics, and, apparently, just the person Wester Ross needed to assist with cataloging some of the Eastern artifacts back at Oxford. *Voilà.* What if he had said *wallah*—Arabic—and not *voilà*—French—and in the heat of the moment, she had misunderstood? The penny would have dropped sooner. *Wallah, you shall never see me again.* Well. Well, they would see about that.

"What a day," she said tonelessly.

"I'll be back to help do up your hair in half an hour," MacKenzie said. She walked to the door with a slight limp that had certainly not been there before.

Catriona contemplated this as MacKenzie's steps faded away, momentarily distracted from her scandalous situation.

While her father diverted time and attention toward hosting academic guests, the castle was crumbling around them, weeds conquered the grounds, and the people in charge of maintaining it all were increasingly plagued by their own ailments. An attempt at a land sale with neighboring Baron Middleton, which could have eased the strain on the Campbell purse, had fallen through in the spring. No wonder her thumbnails were bitten to the quick. In the end, it was the earl's and her responsibility to run Applecross, but they were as bad as each other when it came to managing the stewards and accountants. Usually they justified their neglect with their cerebral brilliance—who had time to look after ledgers if one could add to the production of knowledge or advance women's rights instead? However, lately, she was failing at it, the brilliance. On her desk below the window loomed a stack of books. She had already scoured it top to bottom for inspiration. After co-authoring countless papers with Wester Ross, she had been keen to finally write a book in her own name, on a topic of her choosing, but a curious blank yawned where passion should have been. Writing without that passion was like squeezing water from a stone; weeks had passed and her well was still running dry. She had no noble excuse left for letting Applecross fall into ruin.

She grabbed the floating flannel and ran it over her arms and neck. She gave her shamelessly ogled chest a good scrub. She was neither a waif nor voluptuous, but her breasts were sizable in relation to her frame. Plain gowns concealed this. Now a man knew. On her left nipple, the silver studs of her piercing caught the red gleam from the fire in the hearth. Had he noticed the intimate piece of jewelry?

For a moment, her hand lingered on the wet, warm curve of her breast. She exhaled and put her head under water.

Her thick black hair was still damp when she made her way to the ground floor an hour later. She had pinned her bun so rigorously that her scalp ached, but she barely felt it—the moment of truth was upon her. At the sound of male voices coming from her father's study, her stomach hollowed. *Smile, how do you do.* Heart pounding, she entered the study. Her father stood just to her left in front of the wall-mounted bookshelf, and his tall frame fairly concealed the guest on his other side. Both men had their heads bent over an open book in the earl's hands.

Her father turned to her, and, in a familiar motion, he took off his glasses. "Ah, Catriona. How delightful. I hadn't expected to see you before dinner."

"Father." It came out thin. The stranger at the earl's shoulder had dark, curly hair. Still young. Broad but lean shoulders.

The earl stepped aside. "May I introduce our guest? I present you Mr. Elias Khoury. Mr. Khoury, my daughter, Lady Catriona."

The stranger's surprise was a palpable pressure on her skin. Her eyes felt hot. They exchanged a fleeting glance, as if looking at each other properly risked igniting the room in the way a match lit an explosive gas.

As the silence spread, the earl looked from one to the other.

Elias Khoury placed his right hand over his heart. "My lady."

His voice was raspy. Hers was gone, her throat squeezed shut. The moment their gazes had connected, an old recognition had hit her belly like a shock wave. His eyes were like the sky where it met the Scottish sea, a liquid mosaic of blues and greens, streaked with the golden rays of a starburst pattern. In their depths glinted, unmistakably, a spark. *The* spark. She had encountered it before, three times to be precise, homed in three different human shapes. Each time, it had caused her misery. Now it had found her again. In her father's new colleague. It didn't help that he was handsome—clean-shaven, his complexion tanned and smooth, with a symmetry to his angular features that would have delighted a da Vinci. It *certainly* didn't help that he had already had his hands in her undergarments.

Chapter 2

His grip on Scottish lore was shaky, but any lingering doubts Elias might have had were gone: the selkie was not a selkie. The enchanting creature from the lake was a human woman, clearly horrified to see him, and the daughter of the professor he intended to charm. Grand. At first, he looked away, as though she still weren't properly covered. As though it would make him unsee . . . curves. Skin shimmering like moonlight. Wet black hair, cascading down to shapely hips in a tangle. His nape felt hot and pulsed as if he had done himself an injury. Catriona. She was real. She was *here*. And he couldn't unsay any of the words he had said. *It's nothing I have not seen before.* God take him now.

"Mr. Khoury comes highly recommended by Professor Pappas," Professor Campbell said, ruthlessly ignoring the awkward atmosphere that filled the study. "He will be in charge of classifying Leighton's pieces in the Ashmolean."

Lady Catriona took an audible breath. A perfunctory smile appeared on her white face.

"How do you do, Mr. Khoury." Her tone was well-tempered, as if she hadn't already made his acquaintance. His name had rolled off her tongue effortlessly. "I hope your long journey was uneventful?"

"Too uneventful, I'm afraid," he replied as smoothly. "I arrived rather too early, which must have inconvenienced your staff. My apologies, ma'am."

His jaw was tense. If she but whispered a word to her father, his mission here would come to an end before it had begun. She was difficult to read, standing there all bloodless and still as a column. Gone was the nymph. A pair of round spectacles perched on her fine nose. Her features were regular but unremarkable except for their quietness, which gave her an oddly timeless appearance. In her high-collared gray dress, and with the parting of her sable hair as precise as if drawn with a knife, she was the picture of a bookish, British spinster. Still alluring if one liked his women aloof and invisible. Which, to date, he had not.

"I was over at the Middletons' when Mr. Khoury arrived," the earl told his daughter. "Fancy that."

"Oh dear," she said. Her eyes were like pieces of glass, clear but without expression. "I hope you found ways to entertain yourself, Mr. Khoury."

"He took matters into his own hands," the professor said, only now closing the book on Byzantine mosaics he had been showing Elias. "He took a walk to explore the grounds. Apparently, he's an avid birder."

"Lovely," Lady Catriona said in a bland tone.

Elias clasped his hands behind his back and said what he should have said three hours ago: "I had hoped to spot a white-tailed eagle, hunting over the lake."

"Ah, unfortunately they're all but extinct, even as far north as Applecross," said Professor Campbell with a frown. In contrast to his daughter, the earl's face was mobile and expressive. The lines fanning from the corners of his intelligent gray eyes said he had a habit of smiling and squinting. "I never asked whether you did spot anything interesting?"

The lady's posture became tense like a bow ready to sling arrows.

"No," said Elias. "Nothing, nothing remarkable anyway. Anything I might have seen I would have certainly forgotten by now."

The earl blinked. "Uhm. Well. You had a long journey. Was it four days, five days?"

"Five, to Britain, sir. Another two to Applecross."

"That's a whole week. Scrambles the mind. Would you prefer to rest in the smoking room until dinner? My collections will be right here when you feel refreshed." The earl nodded at the shelf, which was stuffed with yellowing tomes about bygone eras of the Levant.

A relaxing smoke would do him good right now, but a true scholar would probably prioritize looking at old books, and so Elias said: "I could never be too fatigued for a book about Roman empires."

Wester Ross's eyes promptly lit up. "I quite agree." He surprised Elias by turning to the lady. "Would you care to join the discussion? Byzantine wall mosaics, sixth century."

She immediately shook her head, but her lips moved soundlessly for a moment before the words came out: "I must work on my book."

"Very well," the professor said. "You do that."

"I'll have Cook send up refreshments," she said, her gaze sliding warily to Elias. "Do you prefer tea or coffee, Mr. Khoury?"

Liquor, please, because this situation was ridiculous. Ironically, it could have all been avoided, had he not tried to be punctual to demonstrate his reliability and trustworthiness. Since the British thought that Eastern people had no grasp on time, he had told Professor Campbell an arrival hour that allowed for a few minor disasters during the journey. Everything had run perfectly on schedule, and he had made an early entrance like an overzealous Prussian. The housekeeper had jumped around on stiff legs like a startled goat. Then, the naked woman, who turned out to be the lady of the house.

"Tea, please," he said, because that was what the earl would choose.

"Send up a pot, my dear," said the earl.

The lady dipped her head. Elias found he was staring at her rather too intently, as if his eyes had severed the connection to his rational brain and tried to soak up her dreary appearance before she vanished. She flashed him an unexpectedly sharp look in return; it cut through his very English suit with surgical precision, as though she were about to study his inner anatomy including all his schemes and secrets. For a beat, he felt like the one in the nude. He smiled at her, pretty shamelessly. Her lashes promptly dropped, and a blush scorched her cheeks. She left quickly. Professor Campbell's speech was an indistinct background noise. How the hell were they to sit through a week of dinners together? Without attracting suspicion from the earl? He could well control himself, only a boy or a fool would jeopardize a business deal over a woman, but the lady . . . she was a dark horse, unpredictable.

Later, on his way to dinner, Elias formed an opinion on Castle Applecross. The estate was a textbook example of mismanaged "old money," a tableau of fading glory typical for some of the grander families in Britain these days. In his guest room, the wind blew straight through the closed windows. The bare stone walls of the corridors gave off a chill that would creep into one's bones come winter. And while the décor and furniture were sturdy and costly, all was a little dusty, a little cracked, a little scuffed around the edges from being passed around for a century or two. On a low table in the main hall, a game of chess sat abandoned, two moves away from checkmate. In the dining room, a candle-studded wagon wheel hung above the long table instead of a chandelier. The place still had potential, but the inhabitants barely seemed to maintain themselves: the Earl of Wester Ross, one of Europe's leading scholars on Mediterranean archaeology, needed a barber, and his olive tweed jacket had been mended in multiple places. His absent-minded air suggested he wouldn't even notice it if moth holes were on full display. In his immaculately tailored dinner attire,

Elias was glaringly overdressed next to his host, but then only the local gentry had the privilege of wearing patchy jackets with impunity—everyone else would be judged as lowly bred or poor.

Lady Catriona was seated opposite Elias, cloaked in an old plaid and stoic silence, her pale face tinted golden by the evening light. It wasn't overly surprising that she had joined them instead of feigning an indisposition. At the lake, she had faced him with the fatalistic courage of a queen on the brink of a battle.

"How are you enjoying Scotland thus far, Mr. Khoury?" asked the earl. He sat at the head of the table to Elias's left and was eating the first-course soup with a hearty appetite.

"I enjoy it very well," Elias replied. "In my homeland, I can see the sea from the mountains—just like here, on Applecross."

"Mm." The earl nodded with his mouth full. "You ought to feel right at home here, then."

He wouldn't go as far as that.

"Was that a Jacobite flag I saw on my way to the dining hall?" he asked instead. "It was in a frame above the main staircase."

"Ha!" Wester Ross looked pleased. "Well spotted. Don't let the English know. Or our fellow Campbells."

"I have limited knowledge about Scottish history," Elias said. All he knew came from a book he had hastily acquired in Marseille while on his way here. Had he skipped the chapter on sea lore and selkies, he might not have stood and stared at the earl's well-formed daughter like a pervert. He cleared his throat. "I thought the Campbells famously supported the government against the Jacobite rebellions."

"Indeed," said the earl. "However, two Campbell leaders joined the Jacobites, and my family descended from one of them. I reckon that's why we call this windy peninsula our home, rather than a grand place in Argyll." He chuckled. "Now, the flag is from the first rising, nearly 170 years old. We keep it; it's an archaeologist's innate affection for bygone things, I suppose—and"—he looked at

Elias over the rim of his spectacles—"a reminder of the troubles between the Highland people. Turning on one another when a greater enemy was always right at the gates? Don't repeat foolish mistakes, says that flag."

Elias wondered whether the earl and his daughter were Catholics, like the Jacobites. He sensed cautious blue eyes on him then, stealthy as kitten paws. His skin warmed all over with awareness. He glanced at her, his gaze brushing hers as carefully as fingertips would test the heat of a stove top.

Lady Catriona pulled her plaid more tightly around her shoulders. "Where in Mount Lebanon are you from, Mr. Khoury?" she asked.

She had mastered the art of looking at a person while avoiding their eyes by a hair.

"From Zgharta," he replied. "A mountain village two hours from the coast, from Tripoli."

She nodded as if familiar with the geography. "Did you leave from Tripoli?"

"No. From Beirut to Marseille. From there, railroads, carriages, then a ferry to Dover."

"Was your journey affected by the aggression in Egyptian waters?"

He wasn't often uncertain what to say, but he was now.

"The British navy began shelling Alexandria last week," she added, misreading his silence when he had understood her very well.

"My journey was not affected," he said at last.

Discussing politics at the table of strangers was a taboo and it was surprising that she had broken it. What made a British lady if not her flawless mastery of etiquette? She actually seemed disappointed for a moment, as though she had wished for him to engage. She picked up her spoon and turned to her soup. He drank some wine so he wouldn't say something reckless to regain her attention.

"I'm delighted that you brought a whole crate of this vintage," remarked the professor. "A most excellent red." He raised his glass toward Elias. In the old crystal goblet, the wine glowed like liquid rubies. "What winery was it, you said?"

"Château Ksara. From the Bekaa."

Lady Catriona had not yet touched her glass.

"Catriona, have you heard," the earl said, "they found an industrial-sized wine press near Sidon, in Tell el-Burak. Phoenician. Almost three thousand years old."

She glanced up. "Aye, I've read the article."

"Nothing escapes her attention," the earl told Elias, his eyes shiny with pride. "She never forgets a thing, either."

Clearly, appreciating the daughter's bookishness would flatter the earl. Elias took the opportunity to look at her with impunity. "Ma'am, earlier today you mentioned that you are working on a book."

She visibly tensed. "Aye."

She kept spooning soup into her mouth until her father asked: "Have you made any progress?"

She pressed her lips together. "I need a wee bit more time."

"What are you writing about?" Elias prodded.

"I don't know yet," she said in a flat tone. "I don't know what I'm writing about."

"It takes time for a good thought to ripen," the earl explained. "Pluck the fruit too soon and it shall be hard and bland." He refilled his glass. "We support genuine scholarly exploration in this house, and rumination and percolation are part of the process, even though to the untrained eye it may look like idleness. Wouldn't you agree, Mr. Khoury?"

"Certainly," he said, and, to keep the attention off his nonexistent processes: "Have you written a book before, Lady Catriona?"

"Not one," she said with forced calm.

Her eyes were hidden behind the fiery reflection of the candles in her glasses. Perhaps it *was* her eyes shooting flames at him.

"Not one?" The earl regarded her with a furrowed brow. "You wrote a whole anthology."

"Have I?"

"Aye, the one about women in positions of power."

"Papa, I never finished it."

"How curious—that must have slipped my mind."

Her stoic expression gentled. "Well," she said. "You're preoccupied with greater things."

"Time passes so quickly, and I forget sometimes."

Footmen detached from the walls and collected empty bowls. The main doors opened, and two more footmen arrived with the next course. A draft went through the hall until they left again. For a while, no one spoke, the silence punctuated only by the clink of heavy old silverware on fine china plates, the opening and closing of tureens, the cork popping off another bottle of wine. Elias politely praised the blandly seasoned lamb shanks.

"Have some more," the earl insisted. He studied his daughter, who mechanically picked meat off a bone with her knife. "You never finished that anthology," he said. "I remember now, but I still don't understand why."

Lady Catriona put down her cutlery and reached for her wineglass. Her plaid fell open at the front, revealing a low, square neckline and the elegant, winged lines of her collarbones. Elias raised his gaze to the wall behind her and focused on the portrait of a grim-faced Scotsman. He imagined he heard her soft throat work as she swallowed. He was stretched on some resplendent torture rack where the lure of her fine skin pulled him to one direction and basic manners to the other.

"The book was pointless," she said at last. Her glass was almost empty.

"Now, now," her father protested, "your work is always excellent. Why not tidy it up, rather than begin something new?"

"Father, let us not bore poor Mr. Khoury with my failed academic endeavors."

"I could not be bored by you," Elias said. *Damn.* "By your conversation."

The lady gave a soft huff. "Very well," she said. "A few years ago, I began drafting an anthology about powerful women since antiquity."

"Powerful women," he echoed. "Such as?"

Her chin tipped up in a silent challenge. "Such as Elissa of Carthage."

"Eh," he said ruefully. "A Phoenician princess."

"I wrote the book with the intention to support women's suffrage," she continued.

"We are suffragists in this house," the earl explained. "We advocate for a woman's right to vote and to be coequals with men in all spheres of life, particularly in marriage."

The daughter's carelessness around politics at the dinner table was encouraged by the father, then. Personally, Elias would have steered the conversation back to proper subjects like wine or the weather, but when in Rome . . .

"Our opponents argue that women ought to be kept out of the public sphere and remain rightless in our own homes because we are too emotional and too irrational to govern ourselves, least of all the political fate of a nation," Lady Catriona went on. "I thought—quite naïvely—if only there were sufficient proof, black on white, that women have been capable leaders and scholars for millennia, then there would be no basis for such arguments."

"This sounds logical rather than naïve," Elias remarked.

A humorless smile curved her lips. "The trouble is, Mr. Khoury, that people aren't interested in either logic or facts, not when it's at cross-purposes with their convenience and convictions. I soon realized that too many husbands in Britain would feel greatly inconvenienced by the presence of an equal in their own home. They would dismiss my work."

She radiated a quiet intensity now, drawing the eye like the one bright spot in a dim room.

"You can't predict whose minds your work might touch," he said.

"Possibly," she allowed. "But the past is a good predictor of the future. The issue isn't a lack of proof of women's abilities, but rather an unwillingness to recognize our contributions. You see, women are a popular subject of study already. Male scholars are quite obsessed with us. Have women a soul, they wondered in ancient Greece, and they still wonder whether we're capable of rational thought, whether these humans who aren't men are good for anything beyond procreation."

Elias choked a little on his own spit.

"So much theory and guesswork," she said with a shrug, "when instead, they could simply ask us and listen to what women say. But that would be too radical, I suppose."

He cleared his throat, but his voice was still rough: "You hold men in low regard."

She tilted her head, as if considering it. "No," she then said. "I find the human species as a whole rather disappointing."

A laugh escaped him. "Equal misanthropy for all," he said, "fair and just."

He was shaking his head at her, intrigued and disturbed. Her intention was to repel him; *Have I shocked you yet?* said the look in her eyes. Color was cresting high on her cheeks, and her full lower lip was stained red with Ksara wine. His heart thumped far too fast against his chest. The woman from the lake was back. She was a mountain river in winter: an icy burn, a mighty current under a quiet surface. A man might find himself in troubled waters if he attempted to navigate her without a plan. Too bad that he had an innate urge to figure out the solutions to a challenge. He locked his gaze to hers.

Don't exert yourself, he messaged back, *I'm no threat to you.* He would dream of her body for the foreseeable future but he didn't press his attentions, and she was entirely unsuitable in any case . . .

"Wonderful," the earl said, his voice shattering the mounting tension like a thunderclap, "a very stimulating exchange."

With a hot jolt, Elias realized he was leaning toward the lady and that his hands on the table had inched that way, too.

"We appreciate a vigorous discussion at dinner," Wester Ross went on, "and I rarely see my daughter so at ease with guests."

The man was so enthusiastically mistaken that the cogs in Elias's brain briefly malfunctioned. He made a noncommittal sound while reassuming proper posture.

"This is fortunate," the earl said as he looked between Elias and his daughter, "because I have a proposition for the both of you."

Lady Catriona froze. Elias's mind blanked.

"Middleton offered to reconsider the land sale today," the earl told his daughter.

"Oh," Lady Catriona said after a small pause. "Such news."

"It appears he has separated from Lady Middleton."

"MacKenzie mentioned it, yes."

"I suspect he needs more funds, to maintain the Lady Middleton living separately from him down in London."

A pucker formed between Lady Catriona's brows. "What does it have to do with Mr. Khoury and me?"

What indeed.

The earl sounded serious. "I shall have to deal with the Middleton business, so I suggest you accompany Mr. Khoury to Oxford in my stead."

"What?" The lady said it out loud, aghast.

"You know everything I know, and the fellows at St. John's hold you in high regard," her father said. "You could introduce Mr. Khoury, instruct him, assist with the classification of the artifacts, even. I shall follow as soon as possible."

Her mouth quivered. "Can the dealings not wait," she managed.

The earl took off his glasses and rubbed his eye with the back of his hand. "Middleton plans to go overseas and he's in quite a hurry. A new woman, I reckon. Excuse the gossip," he said to Elias.

Normally, Elias would have let the elder man, the local, the host, make the suggestions, but Lady Catriona's hand had curled into an agonized, white-knuckled fist on the table.

"It's no trouble for me to stay at Applecross longer than planned," he said to Wester Ross, suppressing a surge of frustration. To gain the professor's trust and assistance, he needed to spend time with him.

The earl slightly bowed his head. "I appreciate that. However, I would be absent from the house for days at a time, as the legal business requires travel to Glasgow, possibly London, and we don't wish to give the neighbors something to talk about, do we. Especially not when Lady Middleton is about to infiltrate London society."

"Of course not," Elias said reflexively, though it was beyond him how traveling with the daughter should be any less scandalous than staying alone with her in the castle. "If Lady Catriona prefers to stay at Applecross, then I shall go to Oxford by myself," he suggested.

The earl smiled. "I appreciate the offer, Mr. Khoury, but much of your work takes place in the Ashmolean—I believe you would be more comfortable and your studies more efficient when someone associated with the university assists you with navigating the bureaucratic hurdles and idiosyncrasies."

Neither the earl's tone nor his posture had changed, but it was quite clear that Elias would not be left unsupervised in a room full of treasure. The earl was scruffy but not stupid. He had moved mildly like a pawn through most of the conversation, only to do an unexpected promotion to queen. Check.

Elias returned the man's smile. "As you wish."

They both turned their attention back to Lady Catriona.

She appeared to look right through them.

"Well, it all appears to be decided," she said after a brittle silence.

"There's another option, my dear," the earl replied. "I accompany Mr. Khoury as planned, and you negotiate with Middleton. Including the honorable Charles."

She stiffened. "No," she said softly.

"I thought not," the earl said under his breath. He signaled one of the footmen that they were ready for the final course.

Lady Catriona ate her dessert with minute bites, her back rigid as a fence post, because she had been given a choice between plague and cholera: Elias, or Mr. Charles. Who the hell was Charles?

Before the last plates were cleared, she took her napkin off her lap and stood. "Please excuse me," she said to no one in particular. "I ought to look after the lambs."

She left, her stride so quick that her dark head bobbed with every step. The thud of the mighty doors falling shut behind her echoed through the hall.

Wester Ross turned to Elias, his weathered face unreadable. "You have my word that she is a worthy representative for me at Oxford," he said. "She is my best man."

Oh, but she was a woman, too, Elias thought. *And she loathes my very presence.*

He had to find out where the Campbells kept their sheep.

Chapter 3

A Brutus couldn't have betrayed her more viciously. Catriona was quietly fuming as she strode to the stable. One moment, Wester Ross extolled the virtues of intellectual percolation, and the next, he tossed her schedule aside to send her traveling with a man who knew the exact shape of her breasts. She had suffered through dinner with her insides churning from a powerful emotion, and now she was to be stuck with him for days?

Her burning cheeks cooled a little when she entered the sheep stable. The familiar smell of straw and wool grease and the bright *baas* of the spring lambs solidified the ground under her feet. Old Collins was leaning against the whitewashed wall of the last pen, talking to Will, the stablemaster. The men had finished sorting the lambs into different pens; some animals would be sent to the market tomorrow, the others would be shorn and released back into the hills.

She stood next to Collins and surveyed the flock.

"Middleton wants to purchase the old borderlands in the west," she said.

Collins regarded her from the shadow of his greasy brown cap. "Aye."

So there had already been talk.

"Do you think it necessary?" she asked.

Regret pooled in the gamekeeper's blue eyes. Few Scotsmen willingly sold land. Will raked five fingers through his blond hair when she looked at him.

She blew out a breath. "I see."

At least having her academic plans disrupted was for a worthy cause, then. It was always the worthy causes that impeded her own work, wasn't it.

Will gave her the weekly report about the lambs. Wool prices were falling again. Would the land sale indeed be worth it, or just postpone the inevitable? Except for the borderlands, the estate was entailed and there was little more to give. She absently rubbed her throat. Any sensible woman in her position would have laid down her pen a while ago and set out to snare a rich industrialist for a husband. Any sensible father would have long urged her to do so.

The stable doors opened with a squeak, and they all turned to look down the aisle. Mr. Khoury's well-built figure appeared on the doorsill. Heat scalded her stomach. Her gaze flitted over walls and rafters before settling safely on MacKenzie, who was hard on Mr. Khoury's heels as he approached.

"You have found our stable," she said, aware her voice sounded like an automaton's.

He tilted his head, a faint smile on his lips. "Mrs. MacKenzie was so kind to accompany me every step of the way."

As any decent chaperone would, sir.

She crossed her arms over her chest. "You have an interest in sheep?"

"In fibers and textiles," he said smoothly. "My family is in the silk trade."

"I thought you were a scholar."

His eyes flicked toward the lambs in the pen. "I suppose I'm the, how do you say, the black sheep of the family," he said.

Interesting. Such self-deprecation was hardly commonplace in his culture. He must have paid attention to English habits up at Cambridge.

Mr. Khoury shifted his attention back to her, and his direct gaze sent warmth washing down her legs. These kaleidoscope eyes had seen . . . everything.

"May I touch them?" he asked.

"What?"

He nodded at the pen. "The lambs."

"Oh. Yes, of course. If they'll have you."

He held his hand into the pen and made some soft hissing sounds, *bzz bzz bzz*. In profile, his features were as appealing to her as in portrait. His strong nose befitted an emperor. His thick dark hair was clipped close to the sides and back of his head but kept longer on top, and a stray curl fell into his brow when he looked down.

"Collins, William," she said. "Why don't you go and enjoy your evening."

The men mumbled their acquiescence and left. MacKenzie visibly dug in her heels; she was here to stay. This was a problem because what Catriona had to say to Elias Khoury was not for a chaperone's ears. Meanwhile, Mr. Khoury's strange method had lured a lamb. He was cooing words of praise in Arabic while his tanned fingers expertly scratched the curly coat. Unexpectedly, he looked at Catriona, his eyes gleaming aquamarine with some genuine enthusiasm. Like the sun-kissed surface of the sea. Oddly terrified, she glanced away.

"It's good wool," he said in an appraising tone.

Her cheeks were overwarm. He pronounced *wool* like a Frenchman. He sometimes intoned like one, too; she didn't need her linguist training to notice. He was too sophisticated to be in her stable, with his proud nose and French vowels and English suit, though his languid posture said he was a man at ease in his body anywhere. It made her acutely conscious of her ugly, thick-soled boots, how awkward her arms felt in any one position; of her monotone voice, the twinge of pain when she tried to hold his gaze. *Bloody spark.*

She pulled back her shoulders. "Mr. Khoury. Are you truly a bird-watcher?"

Since there was no escape from MacKenzie, she had addressed him in Arabic.

Mr. Khoury relinquished the lamb and faced her with an alert expression. "Eh." *Yes.*

MacKenzie huffed with disapproval at the switch of language.

Catriona ignored it. "So your presence at the lake this afternoon was purely coincidental?"

His dark brows arched high, as if her audacity to mention the unmentionable had shocked him. He raised his hands. "I swear," he said, "I watch birds of prey."

"I see. Still. We ought to address our situation."

Mr. Khoury glanced at MacKenzie, who had resorted to ignoring them, too.

He came a little closer. "I came here to speak to you. I'd spare you this journey if I could."

His rich scent teased her nose, warm and woodsy like afternoon sunshine on a dry summer day. It had muddled her mind throughout the entire meal earlier.

She adjusted her glasses. "You have seen me in a terribly compromising position," she said, stating the obvious. "We ought to pretend it never happened, but happened it has, and we both know it. We know it's an outrageous situation."

The corner of his mouth tipped up. "Indeed. Where I'm from, we'd be married by now."

A wheezing sound came from her throat.

He moved his hands in a soothing gesture. "A joke," he said. "Forgive me."

His tone was suspiciously light—there was some truth lurking in this joke.

"Luckily, all that is required of us is to journey to Oxford together," she said coolly, feeling color creep up her neck. "I shall introduce you to relevant places and gentlemen there, and then we shall keep our distance."

"Of course," he readily agreed.

"I wish to leave the day after tomorrow."

He had traveled a week to come to Applecross, but he didn't blink. "As you wish."

"Lastly, I would prefer that we travel in separate compartments at all times to avoid the awkwardness of tiptoeing around our situation." *Tiptoeing* she said in English.

Mr. Khoury nodded, but now it looked as though he was biting his cheeks to trap a grin.

His debonair demeanor was unsettling. Was she acting overly missish? It was easy for him to feel this way, she supposed. *It's nothing I haven't seen before.* Was there a Mrs. Khoury back in Mount Lebanon, or was he just a rake? He radiated the vitality of a healthy, active young man, but the fine smile lines around his eyes suggested he was past the age of five-and-twenty. He was likely married, and the thought made her already queasy stomach plummet. Pathetic. As if this man's marital status made any difference to her. A meaningful silence ensued, until a needy *baaa* from the pen ruptured the tension. The lamb was still there, watching Mr. Khoury with its ears twitching back and forth. This, too, seemed to amuse him. He was probably used to shameless bids for his attention, one more reason to utterly ignore him. It felt as though *his* attention remained trained on her back like a poised arrow as she stalked off.

His presence stayed with her. She was brushing out her hair for bed in her dimly lit tower room, and her face still burned as though she had spent too much time in the sun. Her stomach kept clenching with a diffuse, anxious anticipation. She knew this feeling. It had happened three times before, starting with Charles Middleton and ending with her best friend's brother-in-law, Lord Peregrin. Three times was enough to make a pattern, and the pattern said romantic attachments were not for her. In fairness, it wasn't a romantic attachment she thought of when picturing Elias Khoury's competently stroking hands; rather, something deep inside her stirred, like a forgotten captive in a cell when the light came in. As though her passion were still alive and there was hope that she hadn't yet kissed her last kiss. This needed to be stomped out quick. False hope was one of the cruelest, most time-wasting tricks humans played on themselves.

She put her brush down on the vanity table. In the mirror, her face was a placid, pale shape. A slight tension between her brows was the only indication of internal upheaval. This was why people thought of her as cool and collected, when in truth she just had a faulty transmission between her emotions and her facial muscles. It hid a multitude of sins.

Behind her, MacKenzie stopped transferring hot coals from the hearth into the bed warmer and glanced at her.

"It'll be lovely for you to see your friends again at Oxford, no?" she said placably. She knew Catriona did not take sudden interruptions to her work schedule lightly.

"I suppose," Catriona said, and opened the jar with lavender crème. "I miss them, of course. Unfortunately, it crushes all hopes I had for writing the book."

"Why is that?"

"My friends are in Oxford because our campaign requires exacting coordination until Parliament reconvenes and hears our bill." She dabbed cool crème onto her cheeks. "Which means the moment I'm back, they will coax me into endless cake feasts and suffrage work."

Between that and assisting Elias Khoury, she could kiss her ruminations goodbye.

MacKenzie frowned. "I thought the Duke of Montgomery put the Property Act through the House of Lords just a few months ago? What more suffrage work can they possibly give you now?"

"The House of Lords was a grand hurdle, but there are still the MPs in the House of Commons. Unless we convince them to vote in our favor by the end of the summer, all our work of the last years was for nothing. Lucie *will* find a task for me."

And because the Cause was most important, and Lucie, Annabelle, and Hattie were the sisters she had never had, she would crumble and try to fit too much onto her plate.

MacKenzie was shaking her head; in her opinion, women's suffrage was a fancy idea by the gentry, for the gentry. She closed the lid of the bed warmer and came to her feet.

Catriona rose. "Hold on."

When she tried to take the pan from MacKenzie, the older woman made a brusque motion with her head. Catriona stood by empty-handed while MacKenzie swished the bed warmer round under the covers. Every year since MacKenzie's fiftieth birthday, Catriona had offered her early retirement, and it always elicited the same response: a polite *Thank ye* and a glance that said *and who'll look after you then?* MacKenzie lived in the Shieldaig village, but whenever Catriona came to stay, she returned to the castle during the week unless one of her daughters had a new baby. To this day, MacKenzie seemed to have trouble separating nine-year-old Catriona, newly bereft of her mother, from the adult woman she had become.

"I must practice my Arabic," Catriona said. "Mr. Khoury suits me for practicing."

It was an apology and an explanation for excluding MacKenzie from the conversation in the stable earlier.

MacKenzie arched her brows without comment.

Their carriage left the courtyard at dawn, with a yawning Mac-Kenzie on the opposite seat in the role of chaperone. The air inside the coach was cold and damp. Both women were dressed in robust gray tweed dresses and coats to protect them from coal dust and chilly air during the two days of travel. Catriona nestled deeper into her plaid as the castle grew smaller in the rain-streaked rear window. *Deep breaths.*

"What a strange fellow this Mr. Khoury is," MacKenzie remarked, her lined face turned to the misty landscape outside. "To insist on riding up there with the driver, in this weather."

Mr. Khoury was indeed up there, with a wet face, somewhat protected from the elements by a borrowed waxed topcoat. As agreed, he was keeping out of Catriona's space. It had to be the preferable option for him, too, she told herself. Never mind that hospitality was sacrosanct in Arab culture, and that between Wester Ross changing plans and her stipulations, they had provided him with a visitor experience from hell.

MacKenzie fixed her with a gimlet eye. "Mary says he drinks wine," she said. "I thought Turks don't drink wine."

"His homeland is part of the Turkish Ottoman Empire, but he is no Turk," Catriona said.

"But he speaks Arabic," MacKenzie said. "You said it's Arabic."

"Aye, and Turks speak Turkish. In any case, I understand Mr. Khoury is a Maronite—a sort of Catholic." As a Catholic herself, it gave her some insight into his creed, though both she and Wester Ross had fallen in with the agnostics years ago.

Her companion made a face. "A Catholic, with an Arabic name?"

"Khoury is the Arabized version of *curia*, which is Latin for *priest*. His name literally means priest."

"It's very odd," MacKenzie insisted. "A Catholic, from Arabia."

"He's from the Levant," Catriona said with a yawn. "The region borders the Mediterranean Sea and is home to places like Antioch, or Bethlehem, Jerusalem . . ."

Confused silence.

"MacKenzie," Catriona said, "where do you think Christianity originates?"

MacKenzie gave a nonchalant little sniff as if she had comprehended this all along.

"Mr. Khoury's people date back to the days when the different branches of the faith first formed, and they didn't adopt the Arabic language until the ninth century, when it was clear that the Muslim conquest was there to stay and Arabic became the lingua franca," Catriona said, warming to the topic. "They still kept speaking a form of Aramaic, called Syriac, which . . ."

The flicker of alarm in MacKenzie's eyes was impossible to miss—an unsolicited linguistics lecture while trapped in a carriage wasn't her idea of a grand pastime.

". . . which means, Mr. Khoury may drink however much wine he likes," Catriona concluded lamely.

"I'll take a wee nap," said MacKenzie.

Catriona opened the upper part of the carriage window, letting fresh, wet air stream into the compartment. For a few miles, they rattled along the pass in silence, climbing up the only way out of Applecross, a narrow road winding through a vast, green sweep of land. Sheep dotted the surrounding slopes. Occasionally, the silver surface of a loch sparkled in a dip between the hills. One day, much of this land would have been hers. Now they were preparing a sale to the Middletons.

When they reached the high point of the pass, MacKenzie woke from her snooze. "It's been almost ten years," she said after a bleary look outside. "More like nine years I suppose, that Wester Ross sent us away the first time, in this weather."

Catriona tightened her shawl. "I remember."

Wester Ross had sent her away from Applecross because of her foolish behavior over Charles Middleton, romantic failure number one.

MacKenzie reached for the tea flask in the provision basket. "I heard he's newly engaged."

"He is, yes."

He had flaunted the announcement in the *Glasgow Herald* a month ago. Accompanying Mr. Khoury to Oxford was preferable over negotiating land deals with Charles, because that would require facing him, and she'd be left in no doubt that he had grown into a perfectly happy, well-adjusted young man, while she, well, she was still herself.

They reached the coaching inn in Glasgow during sunset, after a long train ride on a crooked railway route. If Mr. Khoury held a grudge over his various al fresco rides, he hid it well—he climbed off the shuttle carriage looking remarkably bright-eyed and un-rumpled. He helped both Catriona and MacKenzie descend, and he stayed back to oversee the handling of their luggage. Catriona and MacKenzie went ahead to secure accommodation. Inside the old inn, the air hung heavy and stale like cheap cigarette smoke. The reception desk was located halfway down the narrow corridor, beleaguered by a queue. Off-key singing and braying laughter came from the taproom; a frantic atmosphere poured through the open wing doors that revealed an intoxicated crowd of locals. The queue at the reception desk was moving slowly; they would be trapped in the noise for a while.

"All upper-floor rooms are booked," the lass behind the desk told the couple first in line.

MacKenzie made a disgruntled sound. "A room upstairs would be better," she muttered.

It would have certainly been safer. They should have stayed at a hotel in town.

The entrance door opened again, and Mr. Khoury appeared. Just then, the noise from the taproom swelled, and three men stumbled out into the corridor, thick-necked fellows, rolled-up sleeves, gaslight glancing off their bald heads. They approached the reception desk. Catriona looked straight back at the counter. Intent gazes still roamed up and down the length of her body, making her skin contract uncomfortably. The men squeezed past behind her back in meaningful silence. Until one of them smacked his lips. Rude. Her right hand made a fist in the fabric of her skirt. It was so loathsome, being selected for casual entertainment, but the harassment was too subtle to address outright, they'd say she had imagined it. A movement in the corner of her eye drew her attention back to Mr. Khoury. He was stalking along with the predatory deliberation of a big cat, his narrowed gaze singularly focused on the men as they disappeared down the other end of the corridor. A chill spread up her neck. He seemed like a very different man to her now, all charm gone. He must have sensed her staring, for his gaze met hers and his black expression vanished.

"Demoiselle," he said, his mouth smiling. "The luggage will be brought straight to our rooms."

He positioned himself next to her, his shoulders effectively blocking any lewd backward glances. A tension in her neck loosened, as if her body knew that it was safe in the shelter of his.

She was breathing again, inevitably inhaling his pleasant scent.

Judging by the escalating noise, the taproom was in for a brawl. The woman in front of them finally received her keys.

Mr. Khoury lowered his head, closer to her ear, and said: "Ask for two adjacent rooms."

At once, MacKenzie's round shoulder budged between them. "And why should milady do any such thing, young sir," she demanded to know.

He straightened and looked back and forth between them. "In

case there is any trouble," he said. "You knock on the shared wall to alert me."

"Trouble," MacKenzie drawled. "What trouble? This is a proper, civilized, Scottish establishment."

A roar and the sound of breaking glass burst into the corridor, followed by a cheer. Shouting ensued. Something or someone had been tossed through a window. MacKenzie looked on stoically, pretending to not have heard a thing.

An ironic gleam lit Mr. Khoury's eyes. "Well, then," he said. "Should any *civilized gentlemen* show at your door, I'm at your service."

Catriona gave a vague nod, her knees a little soft. The way he peered down at her was ambiguous, as if he was contemplating a flirtation. The inky double rows of his long lashes framed his eyes like a lining of kohl. It could have looked feminine, but in his face, it didn't. A moment ago, when he had fixated on the three men, his right hand had moved to his left hip with instinctual ease. He was almost certainly armed under his coat. She requested two adjacent rooms.

The chamber was cold, and the bed linen might or might not have been fresh. Now and then the floorboards shivered when people stomped past in the corridor, jerking Catriona back to being wide awake. She had locked and bolted the door, but the bolt fittings were a little loose. Perhaps she should start carrying a pistol like Lucie.

MacKenzie rolled over, making the mattress shake. "Verra cheeky of Mr. Khoury to request his room to be next to ours, just like that," she said.

"His intentions were honorable," Catriona said to the wall.

"Fat good would it do us, though," MacKenzie grumbled behind her.

"What can you mean?"

"Would he know how to brawl with a Glaswegian? He's a scholar. The heaviest thing he lifts are big auld books."

A scholar who moved like a soldier at the sign of trouble. It rankled.

"My money would be on Mr. Khoury," she said softly. "He's certainly the most unscholarly scholar I have ever encountered. Something odd about him there."

"Don't study him too closely," said MacKenzie after a pause.

"Good night, MacKenzie."

Her cheek was warm against the pillow. She had pictured him on the other side of the thin wall. Would he undress for bed and lie on his back in just a clinging cotton shirt? Did he keep his shoes on like an actual soldier? Her body was tense while she tried to blot out the forbidden images. She rarely had the impulse to touch people and she preferred to not be touched, but with those sparkling few it was different. Between waking and dreaming, her fingertips were curious about him, about the feel of his soft-looking lips, his lashes, the texture of his hair. She ought to be politer to him, more mindful of her behavior. She was a lady, after all, and he had never set out to embarrass her. Tomorrow, she would try again.

She dreamt he stood outside the door, arms crossed over his chest, boot heels planted into the ground as he searched the surrounding vastness with his narrowed gaze, and it was not clear whether he was keeping her safe or keeping her captive.

Chapter 4

The next morning, the southbound trains were delayed, and the platforms of Glasgow Railway Station were crowding with waiting passengers. Elias glanced at his watch, and when he tucked it back into his waistcoat pocket, Lady Catriona looked up from the watch she wore pinned to her bodice.

He said: "I have to send a telegram," just as she announced: "I'm going to the telegraph office."

The transparent mesh of Catriona's travel veil couldn't hide her flash of dismay. Her chaperone, Mrs. MacKenzie, lowered her brows at him, as if he had done it on purpose.

He gestured in the direction of the telegraph office. "Please. You go, ma'am."

Lady Catriona laced her gloved fingers into a knot. "Our train might not be delayed long enough for us to take turns. The office is at the other end of the station."

"It is, yes." During his stop in Glasgow on his way up, he had sent a telegram to Nassim in Manchester, to inform his cousin that all was proceeding smoothly and that he'd be at Oxford in ten days' time. Well, plans changed.

The lady straightened her shoulders. "Shall we go, then," she said, surprising him. "MacKenzie, would you mind watching the luggage cart? We shall be right back."

MacKenzie's mouth turned downward, rightly so. This wasn't proper. Normally, Elias would have insisted the lady take her turn as good manners dictated, and his telegram wasn't truly urgent. However, last night, he had also decided to keep close to her during this journey, to hell with their agreement to stay apart. Damn her father. What man sent his daughter across the length of a country with no one to protect her but an older woman? A country where people had made a sport of not holding their drink? It went beyond eccentric, it was negligent.

"Very well," he said. "We go."

He heeded a respectable distance between them as they crossed the station, but he was precisely aware where her body was in relation to his. He smelled her, too; she wore lavender, a disappointingly plain scent, but the clean fragrance filtered through the mist of soot and brake oil like a fresh breeze on a sweltering day. It carried the subtle note of her skin, which he shouldn't notice, nor enjoy.

They joined the neat queue for the telegraph clerk desk. The lady shifted on her feet and surveyed the room with hunched shoulders.

"It's rather noisy, isn't it," she said, pulling at her shawl.

His brow furrowed. People were coming and going, and there were the taps on the telegraph keys, but it all seemed quiet and orderly to him.

"I shall notify St. John's College," she went on, "so your lodgings should be prepared when we arrive. And I'll send word to the curator of the Ashmolean—is there a particular day when you should like to meet him?"

"As soon as possible," he replied. "Thank you."

"Not at all. I suggest I introduce you to the dons tonight at the college dinner."

Her tone was polite but distant, and her eyes met his only

sporadically from behind her veil. She had sealed herself off from him very effectively while she was standing right by his side. A gentleman would have left her alone in her fortress, yet here he was, his muscles humming with the desire to scale the walls.

He made an advance. "What is your position with the university? Are you a tutor?"

She moved her head between a shake and a nod. "I'm faculty, by way of being my father's assistant. Sometimes, I teach classes for the female students."

"In archaeology?"

"Rarely. I'm a linguist."

"Your Arabic is very good," he said, a fact that had preoccupied him since their chat in the stable. "Why did you learn?"

They moved forward in the queue, and she glanced left and right, as if to ascertain that no one took notice of them conversing.

"When I was a girl, I saw a print with Arabic calligraphy in my father's study," she said with some reluctance. "It was intrigue at first sight."

He was intrigued, too. "Who taught you? Wester Ross?"

"Books."

"Books?"

She pushed her glasses back up with the tip of her index finger. "At first, yes. Wester Ross eventually hired a tutor so I could apply what I had learned. I spent a few months in Egypt with my father in the seventies, too. You seem amused, Mr. Khoury—I assure you I took learning the language quite seriously."

His smile widened. "I just wondered," he said, "is it very lonely, being so clever?"

She had sounded neither proud nor coy, as though she didn't consider it a notable accomplishment that she had taught herself a complex language that was completely different from her native tongue. It was just something she had done. She looked at him wide-eyed now; his comment seemed to have startled her.

"That was a joke," he clarified.

Her fingers plucked at a fold in her skirt. "I reckon I sound terribly formal when I speak it."

"You do. Like a newspaper article. Do you understand my dialect well?"

"I do. It's lovely. Your pronunciation, too."

"Is it?" he asked idly.

The blush on her throat was instant. "I mean the echoes of the Aramaic substratum. What I mean is, from a linguist's point of view, it's interesting." She lifted a hand to her cheek. "I also noticed some French underlying your English."

He would have preferred to hear more about how lovely she found his dialect.

"I learned French long before I studied English," he confirmed. "I attended a Jesuit school in Paris when I was a boy."

An unexpected discomfort constricted his chest the moment the words left his mouth: a bewilderment that he had shared private, superfluous details about his person with her. Her eye contact was shaky, but she had still listened to him with a gravity that had simply drawn the words from him. The compassionate tilt of her lips said she sensed that Paris had not made for a happy time in his life. For a moment, their gazes clung and probed deeper. It was the sort of connection that left a piece of insight behind in each other, a deepening of mutual understanding that couldn't be undone. He glanced away. He had come to Britain to take things away, not to give something of himself.

Someone loudly cleared their throat behind them. The queue had moved on, and they had allowed for a gap to form.

When it was his turn at the clerk desk, he sent a telegram to Nassim:

Dearest cousin

Plans have changed. Inshallah I am in Oxford tonight already.
Your affectionate cousin

Eli

Their train soon rumbled south. Elias had found a place in a coach just behind Catriona's coach, and his fellow passengers kept to themselves, so he looked out the window where the gentle landscape of the lowlands slipped past. In the distance, plumes of smoke rose over industrial structures. He was preoccupied; his prolonged absence would impact the business operations in Beirut and his uncle wouldn't be pleased, though this was Uncle's status quo in any case. In obtrusive intervals, he thought about sex. Usually, the fantasizing was diffuse, smooth bodies of women he had never met, faces he couldn't properly see, but today, he thought of the nymph by the lake. Her skin had the luster of pressed silk in the sunlight. In his imagination, she was pleasantly surprised to see him. She leaned slightly back against the boulder and smiled at him, and he went to her. He ran his palms over her softness, from her throat to the enticing curve of her bottom, thoroughly, leisurely, until he felt her body loosen and her breasts were heavy in his hands. He tasted her rosy lips, still wet with lake water. He wrapped her long black hair around his fist and took his place between her thighs. He steered his mind away then, because a rude feeling heated his cock, and these tight Western trousers hid nothing.

He opened his satchel, where he kept his chessboard, carefully wrapped in cloth, and *A Comprehensive Work about the History, Nature, and Culture of Scotland*. He found his last page in the book and sank himself into passages about the fertile soils of Fifeshire, about

Scottish inheritance laws and political treaties. He studied the chapters about sheep pastoralism with great intensity, as if there were clues to a treasure hidden between the lines.

Under a pale blue sky, the train rolled into Oxford's railway station shortly before six o'clock in the evening. At half past six, Elias had settled in his new lodgings at St. John's College and was unpacking his suitcases. He washed and shaved. At seven o'clock on the dot, Lady Catriona knocked on his door. She stood at a distance when he opened, as though she had just taken a step back. The ugly tartan shawl still hung around her shoulders, though she had changed into a blue dinner dress. She held an envelope in her hand. Behind her, the chaperone hovered, a little droopy after the long day.

"How do you find your accommodation," the lady asked politely. She had snuck a decidedly less formal glance at his sharply tailored black-tie attire and now her face was a little pink. Interesting. He stepped aside to reveal the bright, spacious reception room.

"The accommodation is excellent," he said.

It was a grand flat, reserved for visiting fellows or students from abroad. An oak table stretched under the room's chandelier, long enough to seat half a dozen guests for dinner or card games. A row of diamond-panel lead windows with stained-glass flower vignettes lined the outer sandstone wall like breakable paintings. Next to the fireplace, a door led to a bedchamber with a small antechamber. The antechamber was fronted by a narrow stone balcony with views over the grounds, where Elias planned to smoke in peace and feast his eyes on lush, well-tended green in the middle of July.

Lady Catriona's attention snagged on the fireplace. His neck heated. On the mantelpiece sat several large, airtight jars with olives, skinned apricots in sugar syrup, and bright pink pickled turnips in brine. Stowaways in one of his trunks. His family was convinced that there was no food abroad.

She held out the envelope. "I took some notes for you—the times when the scouts come in the morning to sweep and light the fire, when they collect laundry, and the locations of shops and pubs with decent lunch offers in the vicinity."

He took the letter from her hand. "Very helpful. Thank you."

He placed the list onto the table, next to his chessboard that he had set up for later in the evening. He caught her staring at the board then, a little like a hawk before it swooped. Remembering the unfinished game of chess on the table in the great hall in Applecross, he asked: "Do you play, ma'am?"

She looked away quickly. "Not in a while. I'm afraid we must make haste. The dons like their food and start dinner punctually."

His quarters were located on the upper floor of St. John's Canterbury Quadrangle, a two-hundred-year-old building with musty corridors, steep flights of stairs, and the particular crookedness brought on by the weight of centuries. Lady Catriona navigated the way with telling ease. Her lodgings had to be in the same building since her father was a don at St. John's. But, Wester Ross wasn't presently in residence. He had left his daughter alone in a quadrangle full of men.

In the cloisters, they encountered a group of dons in academic dress who greeted her respectfully in passing.

"Will they turn me away for not wearing the gown?" Elias asked. He was only half joking. At Cambridge, formal dinner had required academic regalia of everyone.

Lady Catriona shook her head. "They shall make an exception, given the circumstances of our arrival."

"You're not wearing one."

They entered the Front Quadrangle. "Women aren't permitted to wear them," she replied. She kept her eyes on their destination, presumably the doors to the dining hall.

He slowed. "I thought you were faculty."

MacKenzie near bumped into him from behind and she gave a displeased snort. The chaperone was taking "to be on someone's heels" a little too literally.

Lady Catriona cast him a sidelong glance through her spectacles. "I have a position here thanks to my father," she said. "Allowing me to wear the academic regalia would take it a step too far, wouldn't it?"

This was almost certainly a trap. "Would it?" he asked, tempted to see it snap.

"Now, if women were allowed to properly matriculate and sit the same final exams here as the male students, they might be deserving of the gown," she mused. "But, according to leading physicians, such educational exertion will cause swelling to the female brain, damage to her reproductive organs, and usher in the collapse of society. Hardly worth the ephemeral glory of wearing the academic gown?"

"I see," he said dryly.

He was used to ribald, provocative women well enough—he had lived in close quarters with French bohemians for years—but this here wasn't seduction; rather, the opposite. He had encroached with casual conversation, inching across the line she had drawn in the sand in the sheep stable, and she was warning him off. She had said *reproductive organs* to his face.

During the dinner, his eyes kept returning to her. She was engaged in discussion with her dinner partner, a gray-haired professor, a few seats down across the table. She obviously wasn't shy. She was selectively reserved, and the innate insouciance of a moneyed lady shone through in her interactions with men. Perhaps unsurprising, as she and her father were a law unto themselves in their Dickensian castle, with only curmudgeonly staff for company. Their roots reached deep into the Applecross rock plateau. It fascinated Elias. He had told her he was from Zgharta, which was only half-true—his mother was indeed from the mountain, but his father had grown up on the coast. Mountains and sea were indomitable forces; they molded their inhabitants rather than the other way around. His mother's people had become inward focused and embodied the fierce stubbornness required to turn rocks into fertile gardens, while his father's side had kept their eyes on the horizon, curious, mobile, counting strangers as opportunities rather than as threats. His parents' blood now mixed in his veins. Two souls resided in his chest. It had left him a born negotiator, successfully adaptable to most places, but on the other hand he was neither fully here nor there. Lady Catriona struck him as her own center of gravity. She would be the same peculiar woman in London as in Beirut.

Her eyes met his across the table, solicitously. He was a guest, after all.

He wondered whether her passion for justice extended beyond her cause for women's rights. Was she aware that Mr. Leighton's antiquities in the Ashmolean were wanted back in the Levant? Would she care? It was Wester Ross who had to care, since it was his introduction to Mr. Leighton that Elias needed. But Wester Ross wasn't here, and until the earl returned, he'd better keep his distance from the daughter. Elias was, in fact, not an expert on Phoenician antiquities—and Lady Catriona's eyes missed nothing.

Chapter 5

"There she is!" Hattie squeaked the moment Catriona stepped foot into her friend's drawing room at Oxford's Randolph Hotel.

Three smiling young women rose from the sofa as one and rushed to her. There was a crush of silk and satin skirts when their arms hugged her tight, and she endured being kissed and squeezed while she breathed in the familiar scents of flowers and vanilla. When they let go, she adjusted her spectacles with a sheepish grin.

"I'm terribly pleased to see you, too," she said.

"When I received your message yesterday, I screeched," Lucie said, her gray eyes bright like polished silver. "I never screech."

"I can confirm that she did, indeed, screech—happily, of course," Hattie said, and her red curls bobbed around her face as she nodded. "Have you had any breakfast? Come, sit down, dear, have some tea."

"And have some lemon cake," Annabelle suggested as her gaze covertly searched Catriona's face. Catriona touched a hand to her cheek; yes, she might have forgotten to eat regular meals at Applecross while trying to summon a topic for her book.

She took off her gloves and sank into the soft armchair where she usually sat during their informal morning meetings, when it was just the four of them and an étagère full of cakes. Hattie's drawing room was large enough to accommodate twenty or more people, however, and judging by the rows of chairs facing the blackboard and speaker's desk, they had hosted a suffrage meeting recently. Lucie's hasty handwriting was scrawled across the blackboard:

*Amending the 1870 Married Women's Property
Act—victory imminent?*

*The Matrimonial Causes Act of 1878 & Writ for
Restitution—the next battlefield!*

Hattie kept her rooms at the hotel since she had another year left in her studies of the fine arts, and she divided her time between Oxford and her marital home in London. The evolution of the room mirrored the nationwide growth of the Cause: when Oxford University had admitted female students for the first time three years ago, only a handful of local women had joined them here for debates on suffrage; the banner above the mantelpiece had been taken down after every meeting; the speaker's desk was kept hidden in a wardrobe. Since Hattie had married and her husband supported the Cause, they now had a permanent, well-equipped space for planning revolution. Meanwhile, suffrage membership numbers across Britain had swelled, more chapters had formed, and there were talks about organizing local chapters in a national union. Maintaining the current momentum, however, seemed to hinge almost entirely on whether the House of Commons would pass the Property Act amendment in late summer.

Catriona eyed her eager-looking friends with some trepidation. If they were counting on her full availability for the Cause, she would have to disappoint them. If they planned on drawing her into the social scene, dinners, charity, occult séances, or whatever the fashion, again, her time was scarce.

Hattie poured her some tea. Annabelle heaped frosted cakes onto a plate with silver tongs, looking elegant and willowy in a dusky pink gown and with a gleaming coil of hair falling over her shoulder. Lucie, icy-blond and dainty in a snug blue dress, put her elbow onto the sofa arm and studied Catriona with an expectant expression.

"Now," she said, "what brings you back into our fold, my friend?"

She might as well have said *my lost sheep*. As the leader of the chapter, Lucie had taken Catriona's retreat to Applecross during a "heated phase" rather personally. The problem is, Catriona had explained to her, there is never not a heated phase with the suffrage movement, so, good day.

"I'm to help Wester Ross's new colleague from abroad to acclimatize here," Catriona said, careful to keep her tone and expression neutral. The last thing she wanted was to explain anything at all about Elias Khoury.

"Trust some crusty old gentleman to interfere with your summer plans," Hattie said, and wrinkled her upturned nose, "but it's our gain—your clever head was much missed."

She placed cup and saucer in front of Catriona with a soft *clink*, and Catriona glanced at her friend's sweet face and thought, *If only you knew about the monkey circus inside this head*.

"Have you changed your hair?" she asked instead.

Hattie touched her coiffure warily. "No?"

Odd. Something *was* different. The warm brown eyes, the sprinkle of golden freckles across the nose were the same. A subtle new fullness to Hattie's cheeks, perhaps?

"We do need your clever head," said Annabelle. "But first—tell us, how is your book coming along?"

There was genuine interest in Annabelle's voice, probably because she was a classics scholar who knew the pains of academic writing, and for some reason that made it worse.

"It's quite unwritten," Catriona said flatly. "I'd rather we talk about the Property Act."

"I see." Annabelle gave her a commiserative smile. "Tell me more later, if you wish."

Ten months ago, Annabelle had become a mother. She could have been at her estate in Wiltshire this moment, looking beautiful while mothering the cherubic heir to the Duke of Montgomery, and most people would agree that with that alone she was fulfilling her highest, if not only, purpose. Instead, she was at Oxford for the day, supporting revolutionary causes and taking interest in her friends. Catriona couldn't have adored her more.

"As for the Property Act," Lucie said, and smoothed back a strand of hair that had slipped from her chignon.

"Right," Catriona said. "I'm all ears."

"I'm not prone to optimism, as you know," Lucie said, "but there is hope. Montgomery won us an important battle when he pushed the bill through the House of Lords, bravo. However, as I told the chapter the other day"—she nodded at the blackboard—"while there's still no coequality between husband and wife, still no full access to our own property after marriage, the current Property Act gives us more than nothing. I now keep seeing the gentlemen in charge pointing to those crumbs and saying, *Behold, we gave you some rights, why must you keep demanding more, you greedy girls?* I cornered MP Warton in Westminster last week to talk some reason into him, and you know what he said? To my face, he said: 'It would behoove you to be patient, and to consider how your demands undermine the harmony of the British family.' Patient! After two dozen years of lobbying without any success? And what about his poor wife? He doesn't even try to hide the fact that he thinks his domestic harmony hinges entirely on Mrs. Warton's legal subjugation."

Catriona had stopped stirring her tea. "Did you say anything back?"

"Yes, in the words of our formidable Frances Cobbe," Lucie said smugly. "I asked him whether he was aware that under coverture, personhood of a woman who commits murder is dealt with by the law in the same way as it deals with the property of a woman who commits matrimony—she loses it all."

Catriona smirked. "Brilliant."

"Beautiful," Annabelle agreed.

"I hope he was lost for words, the silly sausage," said Hattie.

"He was perfectly self-righteous and therefore, he felt unduly harassed," Lucie said, her cheeks reddening as the scene still seemed to play out again before her mind's eye.

"The current act does allow working women to keep their wages, though," Hattie pointed out.

Lucie cut her an arch look. "What of it?"

"I'm just noting that it wasn't entirely useless."

"You sound just like him," Lucie said darkly, "like Warton."

Hattie's brows flew up. "No, I don't?"

"It's a slippery slope."

"You sound a little tense, my dear."

Catriona took a bite out of her lemon cake. A burst of zesty flavor, and then it melted in her mouth. She sighed. The night had been short, but tea and sugar eased her out of her stupor. She had better be alert—an appointment with Elias Khoury was next. She mustn't say anything outrageous again like she had last evening on the Front Quad, but when he fixated her with his sea-sky eyes, she wavered between being frozen stupid and unleashing verbal havoc. *Is it very lonely, being so clever?* She cringed. It wasn't just his eyes, it was his *jokes*, proper spears to the gut, targeted as if he knew her secret soft spots.

"I'd love to petition my share of MPs," she said to Lucie. "The truth is, though, I'm trying to write a book and dealing with MPs like Warton will be quite distracting."

Lucie gave her a lazy smile. "Then it's a good thing that what I have in mind for you doesn't involve any traveling or canvassing."

Fiddlesticks. "Do tell."

"Allow me to introduce our newest campaign," Lucie said, and pointed at the blackboard again. "The Matrimonial Causes Act of 1878."

Catriona ate the last bite of her cake. "That act allows wives to petition for a separation in case of maltreatment, doesn't it?"

"Correct."

"What has it to do with our Property Act campaign?"

"It has to do with the safety of women," Lucie said, a little stern. "I worry that *if* our Property Act amendment is passed with all our demands, it will enrage quite a few husbands—and their wives might bear the brunt. We ought to remain one step ahead."

Catriona licked frosting off her bottom lip. "I don't quite follow yet."

"Assume you are a wife, and you're unsafe in your home," Lucie said. "You can apply for a separation. The problem is, more often than not, Mr. Magistrate will reject your application. Now, if a wife could keep her property thanks to our amendment, she could just keep what is hers and leave anyway, right?"

Catriona nodded.

"Wrong," said Annabelle. "If a spouse leaves without a legal decree, she can be ordered right back home."

"Precisely," said Lucie. "And how does a husband do that? He takes out a Writ for Restitution of Conjugal Rights against her. And if she refuses to comply with that writ?" She stabbed the air with her spoon. "She might go to jail."

A slow, sinking feeling was weighing down Catriona's stomach. This was hurtling right at her and evading it would make her feel terribly guilty.

Lucie promptly confirmed her suspicions. "I was hoping you could lead the effort against the writ for restitution."

Her jaw wouldn't move, and so she just sat and stared in silence.

"Just think," Lucie continued, eyes gleaming, "with our new amendment in place and this ghastly writ gone, wives could just make a run for it. They now have the means, and the freedom. Stuff the magistrates."

"I shall consider it," Catriona said at last. A faint pulse was ticking in her ears.

Hattie and Annabelle were glancing back and forth between them, clearly sensing her reluctance.

"Excellent." Lucie, who had the social grace of a derailing locomotive, looked well pleased. "It should be no great trouble. Just drafting a first letter. As soon as possible."

A soft huff of disbelief came from Annabelle. Letters to men in power required days of complicated legal research and sophisticated rhetorical arcs. The sender, in this case Catriona, would receive foolish replies that would enflame her enough to write rebuttals.

"I'm certain there's someone more suitable for this position than I," Catriona said.

Lucie's gaze narrowed slightly. "You are one of our best. Hattie, Annabelle, and I are fully occupied with conquering the House of Commons for the Property Act, as are the other chapters. Hattie also has her hands full with her Friendly Society."

"Which Friendly Society?"

Hattie brushed crumbs off her skirt. "A new one," she said. "I'm creating it as we speak—it's for the benefit of northern factory women who are in the family way."

"That is news."

"We are trying to establish a temporary payment for the months before and after birth," Hattie explained, "so that pregnant women may stay home and rest without losing pay. Aoife Byrne and Miss Patterson are helping me with the details."

"That's a fine and worthy cause," Catriona said, gloom in her voice. Her desire to contemplate vague academic ideas undisturbed sounded more self-indulgent by the minute.

"Blackstone and I are hosting a dinner on Friday to advertise the initiative," Hattie said. "I never sent you an invitation since you were in Applecross, but now you're here—join us!"

"Gladly," she said tightly. "Are there any charitable causes where I could lend a hand, too?"

Hattie was beaming. "Yes, I'm so relieved you ask."

"I—"

"The Lady Margaret Hall fire drill exercise is tomorrow morning, and I can't join in," Hattie pressed on. "I'm—I'm indisposed, and they are missing members because of the term break."

"Why is there a drill during term break?"

"To keep the brigade well-prepared? I felt rotten, having to cancel," Hattie said. "If only I could offer them a replacement. Lucie is already standing in for Lady Henley."

Catriona shifted around on the upholstery as her legs became restless. "What time?"

"Eight o'clock."

At least it wouldn't split her day down the middle and render it useless.

"I shall replace you," she ground out. "This one time."

After their meeting ended and they had said their goodbyes, Catriona rushed down the grand staircase to shake off some of the tension in her limbs. She would have to research the Writ for Restitution of Conjugal Rights. In addition to dealing with Elias Khoury, and supporting the women's fire brigade, and attending a London dinner on Friday.

Her resolution to stay away from all distractions was going so well.

She was about to leave the hotel foyer when quick footsteps sounded behind her on the polished floor.

"Catriona."

Hattie had dashed after her and her face was pink from the effort. She pulled Catriona aside, out of earshot from the bellboys.

"There's something you ought to know—" She paused and worried her bottom lip with her pearly teeth.

"You have found a new spiritualist and want me to attend a séance with you, don't you?" Catriona said. "The answer is no."

"Goodness, no," said Hattie, and scrunched up her face. "I don't dabble in that . . . anymore." She ducked her head. "Lord Peregrin is in residence at St. John's. He's back for the summer, doing some work in the archives. I thought you might wish to be prepared. In case you cross paths."

Catriona's belly hollowed at the sound of his name. A name that had been entwined with nervous nausea and daydreaming for too long to not have an effect.

"It's fine," she assured Hattie. "I knew he'd be here." It was one of the reasons she had left in the first place. There was no chance of bumping into men who made her feel awkward in Applecross. Or so she had thought.

Hattie gave her hand a quick squeeze. "That's good, then."

"Say, is there anyone who isn't aware of my silly crush on him?"

"Yes," said Hattie, "Lord Peregrin."

If only. "Do you remember when he called me a 'good chap' to my face?"

"Oh well, that was ghastly."

"I'm surprised he didn't give me a few hearty slaps on my back, from lad to lad. He knew. He was kind enough to make the situation clear at once."

"Not at once, though," Hattie remarked. "Only after you had helped him hide from his brother for months."

". . . I suppose."

"Lord Peregrin is a boy," Hattie said earnestly. "A charming, clever boy, but boys have nothing to recommend them over proper men."

Catriona grimaced. Hattie was a few years younger than her, Peregrin's age to be exact, but since her marriage to Mr. Blackstone, she took on an almost maternal air sometimes, like a plush ruddy mother hen eager to spread protective wings. It was odd to be at the receiving end of such care when one was older and almost certainly more twisted.

"Let's meet at the St. John's porter's lodge tomorrow morning," Hattie suggested. "We could go to the fire drill together."

"I thought you can't attend the drill."

"I can't handle the equipment," Hattie said with a shifty sideways glance. "I can, however, bring provisions and good cheer."

"Very well. Are you certain you haven't changed anything about your appearance?"

"A new hat," Hattie replied, which solved nothing, because Hattie always had a new hat. Today's headwear was amethyst velvet that matched her dress, decorated with silk flowers and imitations of various foliage.

Catriona walked back to St. John's College barely perceiving her surroundings. Her weeks were now overfull. Of course, liberated womanhood would benefit her academic ambitions, too. In a cruel paradox, the whole process of getting women liberation left very few hours for said ambitions. For the last five years, she had split her time between co-publishing with Wester Ross, hoping to build a reputation on his coattails, and the Cause. She had corresponded, picketed, fund-raised, and written essays in support of women's rights. She had studied the voting records and convictions of men of influence to better persuade them, and she had traveled between Oxford, Manchester, and London more times than she could count. But there were suffragists who traveled to the United States to foster the Cause, and those who had decided to forgo marriage and motherhood or broken with their parents just so that they could campaign without distraction. Her sacrifice was paltry in comparison. But when was enough actually enough? Twelve years ago, the Manchester chapter had achieved the current Married Women's Property Act after a decade of relentless politicking.

It had reined in some of the most oppressive stipulations of coverture, but as Lucie said, it was still crumbs, and any attempts to improve the act further had since failed. So, here they were, over twenty years' worth of effort later, still fighting. A lifetime was dust in the wind when pitted against the centuries-old machine of laws and mores that kept women chained in place. Sometimes, tending to her personal interests instead of someone else's counted as an act of sabotage against the machine, too. Or so she told herself.

In the porter's lodge at St. John's, white-haired porter Clive was staffing the desk and his smile indicated he was pleased to see her. They had a little chat, about the weather—an abnormal amount of rain this month; how quiet it was during term break; they'll be back soon enough—the same routine they had trotted out for the last decade whenever they encountered each other in the lodge. Finally, Catriona asked whether there was any mail for Wester Ross or her.

Clive looked under the counter. "No, ma'am. Doesn't look as though there's anything in your pigeonholes, either."

She surveyed the wall with floor-to-ceiling mail compartments. The Campbell pigeonholes were indeed empty. Casually, her attention drifted across the names at the bottom of the compartments to the row with the letter *D*. *D* as in Peregrin *Devereux*. Her gaze caught on the name and her skin tightened. Chances that they would cross paths here were high. Peregrin was assisting Professor Jenkins, a friend of Wester Ross and fellow don, with a digging endeavor in Greece. He would eventually attend a dinner in Hall or amble into the porter's lodge, his top hat at a careless angle on his sun-bleached hair, the spark in his hazel eyes . . . He would address her . . . When he did, what would she say? *Hullo, old boy?* Without warning, a lump blocked her throat. Oh dear. Slowly, she backed out of the porter's lodge, avoiding Clive's curious eyes. An emotional flare-up, like a reoccurring rash, nothing more . . .

She walked out onto the Front Quad and air hit her clammy face. Her breathing came in shallow gusts now, her gaze bounced off the enclosing walls of the quad with a strange sense of disorientation. Peregrin might be on the premises right at this moment. Perhaps he was behind one of the upper-floor windows, looking down onto the quad. She was exposed like an awkward deer on a clearing . . . Heat swept down her back. Her impulse was to cut right across the circular lawn to reach her lodgings. The flagstone path around was much longer, endless. Her pace picked up. She dashed into the Canterbury cloisters, on tiptoes like a thief on the run. Heart drumming, she slipped into the Campbell flat and slammed the door behind her. The wooden surface of the door was cool against her cheek. She focused on that cool spot while her chest rose and fell, rose and fell. MacKenzie, alerted by the sound of the door, entered the vestibule from the study with an unfinished piece of knitting in hand. The Scotswoman did a double take, and then her face smoothed back into a neutral expression. "I fetched a tea tray from the kitchens," she said. "It's in the study, on yer desk."

Obviously, MacKenzie was thinking to herself how every Wester Ross Campbell generation had an odd one, and how it was a pity when it happened to be a girl. *I know, MacKenzie. I just can't help it sometimes.*

She removed her hat and checked her sweaty reflection in the small mirror next to the door. Ugh. She licked her teeth, loathing the dry feeling in her mouth. In half an hour, she had to look like a normal person and take Elias Khoury to the Ashmolean Museum. A great dissatisfaction weighed down her body. She was Lucie's best lieutenant when it came to writing a legal letter. She excelled at debating an MP face-to-face. But, look at her now, a name on a letter box had left her flailing like a motherless fawn. She was quite tired of being the odd one.

Chapter 6

The knocks on his door were loud and erratic and came twenty minutes earlier than the agreed time. Definitely not the Lady Catriona. Muscles tense, Elias strode from his bedchamber toward the racket, then paused and listened intently for a moment.

A muffled voice: "Yalla, Eli."

He opened the door in disbelief. He was face-to-face with Nassim.

"He he he, look who's here," his cousin cried, dropping his valise with a thud and flinging his arms open wide. He pushed into the room, and the men embraced.

Elias bussed Nassim's cheeks. "My dear. You madman. What are you doing here?"

He hadn't expected his cousin for another week, but here he was, with overlong hair and the wide smile that turned his hazel eyes into squinty half-moons. Elias hadn't seen him in a year. He squeezed his cousin a little tighter.

Nassim clasped the back of his head with one hand and looked him up and down. "You are in good health?"

"I'm—"

"How is Tayta?"

"She's very well, and—"

"And Layal, and—"

"Thriving. They miss you. You shouldn't have come here just to see me."

Nassim tsked. "You wrote *plans have changed*. You are leaving Scotland after what, one day, two days . . . no explanation, nothing. Perhaps it was a cipher for *trouble*, how would I know? I had to come and see. I do have to meet for business in London tomorrow—instead of seeing you on my way back, I see you on my way there, it's no trouble. What about you, how are you; you look terrible."

"Yiii, leave me be."

"I swear. Like a naked mole—where's your beard?"

He patted Elias's clean-shaven jawline. Elias pulled away. A beard would immediately announce him as a stranger here; removing it was an intentional decision because he wanted this artifact deal done quickly. Nassim looked fashionable; he wore a royal blue Italian linen suit with a burgundy silk cravat, and *his* beard was still intact, gleaming and expertly trimmed.

Elias flicked Nassim's golden cravat pin. "And what are you, a catalog model?"

The sound of a throat clearing drew his attention back to the corridor.

A white-haired college porter still stood waiting, stiff and overlooked like a forgotten umbrella. He had a handcart loaded with a wooden crate by his side, and he wore a well-mannered Englishman's expression of *annoyed*. Elias thanked him profusely and hoisted the box into his arms. He closed the door behind him with his heel.

Nassim was prowling the length of the room and randomly touching different surfaces. "So are you," he prodded, "in trouble?" He looked delighted about the prospect. He was too energetic for having left his post at Manchester Port before dawn. "Ah, put it there, put it there." He waved at the fireplace.

Elias set the crate down with a *thump*.

Nassim came over to loosen the crimps on the lid. "We have a new import-export at the docks," he said. "I doubted they have food here. Voilà, they don't—I stopped at two bakeries on my way here from the railway station, and they don't have any bread."

"Grand," Elias said as familiar jars appeared. Red bell peppers in olive oil; more apricots. A bottle with mulberry juice. At least four pounds of pistachios.

"I'm not sure how you'll eat any of it without proper bread," Nassim said while he built a food pyramid on the mantelshelf.

"I'll manage," Elias replied.

"But how."

"I could use this old Roman invention they keep in the college kitchen."

Nassim paused and frowned. "An invention?"

"They call it—a fork."

His cousin slapped his arm.

"I can't accept all of this," Elias said. "It's too much; take it back, eat it yourself."

"Nah, you keep it," Nassim said, looking mildly offended. "I'll go home in a month. I restock at the source."

Restock, and liaise with Uncle Jabbar about business, no doubt. The potential prospects and troubles for the silk trade with Britain in light of the British tussle with Egyptian nationalists and Ottomans over Egypt. Focus on Lyon and let the French deal with the distribution in Europe, Elias would have advised, but his uncle's ears were rather closed to his opinions. Jabbar liked to keep him on the fringe of the family business, quite literally, by assigning him positions in Britain, in Lyon, in Beirut, important positions, but outside the innermost circle of decision making.

"They'll find you a wife this time," he told Nassim instead. "So watch out."

Nassim jiggled the bag with pistachios. "Listen, I'm ready. How is your French girl?"

Elias shook his head. "I came from Beirut. Francine was in Lyon."

He also hadn't seen Francine since leaving Lyon two years ago, but he knew she would have laughed at being called a girl.

"No one in Marseille, then?" Nassim asked, winking so hard it looked like a spasm.

"You're shameless," Elias said darkly. "Too nosy."

Nassim stepped back to admire his handiwork on the shelf. "You may ask me about my sweethearts," he said, using the English word *sweethearts*. Despite overseeing their British operations for the past seven years, his accent was still strong.

"As for my business here," Elias said. "There has been a delay." In few words, he explained that the Scottish professor would be away for at least a fortnight.

Nassim's strong brows pulled together. "What will you do in the meantime? Have you learned any more about that Englishman?"

"Mr. Leighton? Not yet." He knew the collector's family had made their wealth through textile trade, and he seemed diplomatically well-connected throughout the Levant.

"I tell you what he is," said Nassim, his lip curling with contempt. "He's the son of a dog."

"He may be unaware of what he's done."

Nassim scoffed. "Of course. And he'll just give everything back once he knows. If you believe that, why don't you write it down, on a sheet of ice."

The skepticism was justified; even a pragmatic optimist like Elias could admit to that. Leighton helping himself to priceless Levantine artifacts was part of a wider problem that had affected the Ottomans, the Chinese, and the Persians for a while now: foreign travelers and academics were relieving their territories of their antiquities. Matters had gone out of hand lately, with entire pantheons disappearing and then resurfacing on estates in Europe and the United States, and Ottoman officials were losing their patience. From Egypt to Asia, talks were held, appeals were made, a system of fees and licenses had long been introduced. Yet on it went. The soil of the Levant alone was a layer cake of imposing structures and skilled craftsmanship, produced by half a dozen high cultures over the course of five thousand years. Put a spade in the ground, the newspapers in London claimed, and you might just hit a Byzantian mosaic, an Assyrian obelisk, or intricate Phoenician jewelry. How could a visitor from Europe resist such an exotic treasure trove? A British collector was shortchanged at home; except for the few things the Romans had built, there had only been sticks and mud until recently. So he helped himself, during grand tours or at official digging sites, or he purchased pieces from locals who had realized how easily they could turn old stones into food on their tables. Two years ago, Münif Pasha, Ottoman minister of education, had opened a museum in Konstantiniyye, center of the caliphate, in an effort to prove that one was fit to care for one's own antiquities. Elias had read the minister's speech in the newspaper during another dull hot summer afternoon at the Silk Office. *Until now, Europeans have used various means to take the antiquities of our country away,* Münif Pasha had lamented, *and they did this because they did not see an inclination toward this in us.*

Elias had mocked the *our country* part because the Ottomans had taken Constantinople and many provinces from the Byzantines, and while the House of Osman had reigned for centuries now, most of the pilfered artifacts predated their rule by millennia. As the current stewards of the region, the Ottomans were certainly entitled to worry about the situation, but Elias had witnessed their inconsistency: with Ottoman approval, countless pieces had left their provinces in Greece, the Levant, and Egypt, while the native populations had watched their heritage being packed up and shipped west. Besides, a museum wouldn't help their cause—the foreigners took artifacts not because they cared, but because they could.

"You can come to the museum with me," Elias told Nassim. "In fact"—he glanced at the beleaguered clock on the mantelshelf—"we're expected there now."

"Very well," Nassim said brightly. "Let's look at the loot."

Elias smoothed his cravat. "The professor's daughter will meet us at the lodge."

Nassim paused. "A daughter."

"Behave, will you."

Nassim went to the fireplace and plucked one of the jars with apricots off the shelf.

"What are you doing?" Elias asked, his hands gesturing confusion.

"A gift for our hostess," Nassim replied. "I shall say they are from our grandmother."

"Come on, you can't be serious?"

"I have good manners," Nassim said, "unlike you. These are excellent apricots."

"I have a brain—you don't give a lady a pound of fruit to lug around."

Nassim cocked his head, a calculating look in his eyes. "She's pretty, isn't she."

"Her appearance is none of your business."

Nassim smirked. "Brother, you protest too much."

Elias grabbed his walking stick from the commode. "You want to carry the jar around the museum like a donkey, or make her carry it?"

Nassim gave a harassed groan and put the jar back. "It would have been polite, and she would have been charmed," he said, "trust me."

The lady and her chaperone were already waiting in the gothic archway when Elias and Nassim entered the Front Quad. She did not look charmed. Her quiet oval face seemed ghostly against the dark background, and she didn't brighten upon seeing Elias approach with a stranger in tow. In a confusing contrast to her solemn mood, she wore a blue silk dress so snug, the curve from the dip of her waist to the flare of her hip could make a man dizzy. Not helpful, this dress, not in the slightest . . .

Elias introduced Nassim. His cousin pushed out his broad chest.

"Enchanté," he crooned as he took Lady Catriona's hand, and Elias, not easily incited to violence, wanted to slap him upside the head.

Faced with two charged males, one posturing, one brooding, Lady Catriona didn't seem to know where to look, and so she was staring right between them with a pained expression. Behind her, MacKenzie crossed her arms over her chest. *Imagine bringing apricots into this situation*, said Elias's sideways glance, and Nassim pulled up his shoulders in a shrug.

The Ashmolean was located nearby, a short walk up the street to the Lamb and Flag public house where Elias planned to have lunch with Nassim, then a few minutes down the Lamb and Flag passage, which brought them to Parks Road. The museum was held in the contemporary neo-gothic style on the outside.

"It was built for the natural historical artifacts from the first Ashmolean on Broad Street, when that became too small," Lady Catriona explained when they entered. Their voices echoed in the empty hallway. "Currently, it's also a temporary home for private collections waiting to be classified."

Both Nassim and Elias dipped back their heads to take in the sweeping construction of glass and pointy iron arches of the main hall. The towering cast-iron pillars were fashioned into tree canopies on top, and the vertical, airy architecture seemed more suited for a cathedral than an exhibition room.

"Impressive," Elias admitted.

"The pieces in the original collection were donated to the university in 1677," Lady Catriona said, "by a namesake of yours, Mr. Elias Ashmole."

Her tone had been matter-of-fact, but as they looked at each other, they both appeared to realize the same thing: that she had his Christian name on her mind enough to draw this connection, and that she had just blithely announced it to three people. A dull pink color crept over her face.

"I just thought it was curious," she said.

"It is," Elias said generously. "Perhaps it's destiny that I'm here."

"Ha ha. This way to the curator's office—oh dear." She had almost walked into one of the surrounding stone columns.

MacKenzie muttered something under her breath.

Elias thought it best to fall back a little. Nassim cut him a bemused look. *Destiny?* he mouthed. *Shut up*, Elias gestured back.

The curator was a quiet, balding man of middle age who thankfully asked few questions about Elias's qualifications. He gave Elias a map of the premises and a university badge to wear on his lapel, and he explained the importance of the ledger at the reception for signing in and out. Afterward, Lady Catriona took them to a side chamber at the very back of the museum.

"Here you are," she said, and swung the door open wide. "Mr. Leighton's collections."

Elias remained rooted to the spot in the doorsill. His mind processed the scene before him in fits and jumps.

Behind him, Nassim verbalized what he felt: "Ya imme, shou heda!"

Indeed, what was this mess. The room was windowless except for a large domed skylight, through which the sun beamed down in a broad shaft like a stage lamp. Two marble sculptures loomed in the light: twin heads of bulls, thousands of years old, monuments to the ancient Phoenician gods. Each marble was the height and breadth of a small horse. Behind the bulls, against the wall, piles of smaller artifacts jostled for space on long shelves.

Elias turned to Lady Catriona. "How were these bulls transferred into this room?"

"Hm, I believe with horse carts from the railway station," she said. "Then they must have laid tracks from the museum's back entrance to this chamber and used a manually propelled handcart. That's how they usually transport the big pieces inside."

"Ingenious," Elias said smoothly.

"Similar pieces are stored around the museum, so the proximity greatly facilitates any cross-referencing exercises."

"Sensible."

"Do you require any further assistance?" She looked hopeful that he wouldn't.

He declined, and she and her chaperone took their leave.

After the door had closed, Elias and Nassim locked eyes.

"Damn," Nassim said. "They are bloody big."

Elias nodded. "They are sizable."

"How will you take them?"

"Take them," Elias repeated. "Inshallah, they shall go out the same way they came in."

Nassim made an annoyed gesture. "You want to lay railway tracks across this floor? No one would notice?"

"Nassim."

"Tell me you have a plan to take them if need be."

Elias bit his bottom lip in a warning. "Shout louder, will you."

"So, if the Englishman refuses, you . . . will just come back with empty hands?" Nassim's eyes looked ready to pop from their sockets.

Elias moved his hand up and down. "My dear. Don't speak bad things into existence before I even have an introduction to the man."

"Ha."

"I ask Wester Ross for an introduction. Then I meet Mr. Leighton. Depending on the outcome, we think about how to proceed. That is the plan."

Nassim hissed. "I bet he will say he had a license. License, what license—give a filthy official enough baksheesh and you have a license; it doesn't give the Englishman the right to take these and put them into this stinky museum."

"We shall see about that."

"What's there to see? They are ours, enough!"

"The ownership of an item after three thousand years isn't always clear," Elias pointed out. "Everyone involved in commissioning, making, and purchasing it, is dead. My sponsors merely own the land where these were taken."

Nassim stared at him for a long moment. "Fine," he finally said. "You want to say these things."

"It is what they will say."

"But what is *very* clear is that these"—Nassim glared at the bulls—"are neither Ottoman, nor English. Also, don't pretend you haven't done it before."

"I have done what before?"

Nassim's voice dropped low. "Smuggled such things."

Elias turned his walking stick back and forth between his fingers. Here, they would probably call his odd jobs *smuggling*. Personally, he would call it *assisting with repatriation* when required. His missions tended to come about spontaneously, when he was approached by people who knew he was fluent in the languages of the thieves and educated in their customs. Often enough, his negotiation skills in combination with sponsor money saw pieces returned. In the cases where money didn't talk, well, perhaps he might have shared the floor plan of a mansion or a warehouse and marked locations of artifacts with an X. He might have deliberately ignored it when his cargo ship carried something other than textile products back east in the darkness of the hull. But he never took payment; he dealt in favors and he gained trust—essential for strong relations between men of business. The family who sponsored the bull mission were merchants, on the cusp of entering a joint venture with him, so if they wanted artifacts from Sidon returned to Sidon and asked him for help, he was at their service. His ambition in life was to build his own business stronghold and reduce reliance on the family enterprise before he turned thirty, and if he were a proper smuggler, who would trust him?

He studied the nearest bull, who returned his scrutiny with the patient expression of those who had watched the rise and fall of various empires.

"He's laughing at us," Elias said, "isn't he."

"He is," Nassim confirmed, and dutifully unleashed a stream of insults at the bull that involved his cock, cocks in general, and all of the bull's dearest relatives.

Elias put a hand to his forehead, his thumb against his temple.

"Listen here," Nassim said. "I'm by your side. Whatever your plan. Just, *a* plan would be helpful?"

"Any plan," Elias said, "would have to involve the local networks. I'm not well enough connected here yet for a major operation."

Nassim's expression turned brooding.

"I shall see if anyone in France would fit," Elias said.

"Yes. And people here at the docks will know."

"They ought to be higher up in society," Elias replied.

Nassim's face brightened at that. A grin split his face. "Of course. That's why you did it. And I doubted you."

"What are you talking about?"

"Come on. The lady," Nassim said, his grin widening. "It did surprise me."

Her bespectacled face flashed before Elias's eyes. "Nassim."

"You are seducing her," Nassim said; the appreciative look in his eyes said *You fox!*

"Seducing?" Elias drawled.

"It's *destiny*," Nassim mimicked with a dainty wave of his hand. "It struck me as odd, you trying to flirt with her; she seems very stiff, very English."

"She's Scottish," Elias said in a flat tone.

"Well, it's the same," said Nassim with some impatience. "But she seems unused to flirtation, so I reckon you'll win her favor easily . . ."

"Stop insinuating that she would be free with her favors," Elias said a little too quietly, and whatever Nassim saw in his face made him go still.

A still Nassim was a rare sight, but behind his eyes his quick mind was jumping to outrageous conclusions about Elias's reflexive protectiveness of Lady Catriona's honor. Elias, for his part, preferred not to dwell on this at all.

Nassim leaned a shoulder against the bull and tilted his head. "I was complimenting the power of your charm, not insulting the lady," he offered.

Elias rubbed a hand over his eyes. "Tell me. What would seducing her accomplish?"

"So," Nassim ventured, carefully, sweetly now, as a devil sitting on a man's shoulder would. "A woman in love does foolish things. She overlooks things. She explains things away. She likes to help, to make you love her more."

"Foolish things," Elias repeated. "Such as: help me with a heist that would besmirch her father's reputation, the very reputation on which her own ambitions hinge—don't touch it."

Nassim withdrew his finger from the bull's nostril. "Be that as it may, if the Englishman refuses to do business, we will need someone from their side who does cooperate."

He wanted to say that she wasn't on another side, but he wasn't a fool. Not entirely, yet.

"Look," Nassim coaxed, "if you haven't done the sweet talk on purpose, I believe you"—clearly he did not—"but it might soften her just the same. You know how quickly one becomes delusional when love beckons; it wouldn't even be your fault if she jumps to conclusions."

This sounded like a half-veiled reminder of Elias's own, now abandoned, delusions about love. There had been a brief but ecstatic interlude, which had resulted in his de facto banishment from the mountain. It was why he was here in this room, he supposed, on his own mission, pushed into establishing himself without much family assistance.

Seduce her.

It was true, her assistance, in whichever form, could only help.

"Shame," he said, softly, as if to himself.

Nassim shrugged. "Sacrifice something minor to win the whole game. I've seen you do it often enough."

"Yes, when playing chess, idiot."

The lady wasn't a wooden pawn on a board. Besides, she did not wish to be seduced. Compliments and poetry wouldn't woo her, this he knew instinctively, and learning her personal preferences required closeness in the first place . . . Nassim was smiling faintly. The silence had been too heavy with Elias's weighing of his conscience against his ambitions, and they both seemed to know which way the balance was tipping. It didn't feel as deplorable to him as it should. A part of him was clearly influenced by his unholy desire to see more of her.

"If I did it," he said, "it would have to be within the bounds of propriety."

"Of course, Eli," said Nassim. "Of course."

He probably imagined it, that the air still smelled of lavender.

The clean scent filled his mouth and teased his tongue as though he had already taken a bite from the forbidden fruit.

Catriona arrived at the Campbell flat with drooping shoulders. After showing the men around the museum, she had spent the day at various libraries, selecting research material for her new suffrage task that should be ready for her to read by tomorrow. Her body felt as though it had been encased in lead. Too many people for one day. Fleeing imaginary Peregrins this morning hadn't helped.

"If anyone calls on me, I'm not home," she told MacKenzie.

Listlessly, she stood in the door to the study. Bookshelves covered the walls from floor to ceiling, except for the doors leading to the bedchambers. On the right side of the room, two Chesterfield armchairs flanked the fireplace; to the left, two desks stood below the windows facing the walled garden. On her desk, a stack of empty pages loomed. She ignored it on her way to her bedroom.

She freshened up over the washbowl. Her reflection looked very young and very old in turn as it contorted on the moving surface of the water. Time had been acting strange since Elias Khoury's arrival. Time did in fact not provide a solid barrier between haunting past events and present day; it could crumble or turn to glass. All it took was a particular disturbance. First, the arrival of Mr. Khoury, who had reminded her that her desire wasn't dead. Add Hattie's remark earlier that Peregrin had spurned her only after he no longer needed her, and the lid on her personal little crypt had cracked open. Hattie was right. When the Duke of Montgomery had tried to impress Peregrin into the Royal Navy several years ago, she, Catriona, had helped Peregrin hide. She had conspired against an English duke without giving it much thought, because it had been the right thing to do; she would have assisted Peregrin regardless of his feelings for her. Peregrin, however, had gone on his merry way later, thinking he had her spinsterly crush to thank for her care. It added insult to injury to have her intentions misjudged so severely.

She patted her chest dry in front of the age-speckled mirror. Soon, she could at least leave Elias Khoury to his own devices. When he was gone, the past would go back where it belonged, too. As she picked up her hairbrush, her eye caught on the reflection of her smallpox vaccine scar, a penny-sized white circle with uneven edges, forever marking her upper arm. She touched it with her fingertip. If only one could inoculate against stupid emotions as one could inoculate against a virus. Her brows pulled together. She scraped her nail over the scar, then pressed it slightly. Perhaps one could do that. Could she temper her erratic reactions to nerve-racking encounters with small, deliberate doses of exposure? Because acting like a thunderstruck cow was costing her both her nerves and her dignity.

A sudden knock on the door made her jump. Caught in the act, was she. MacKenzie stuck her head into the room. "Will ye be having dinner?"

Catriona slipped her arms into a fresh chemise. "Give me a moment."

In the corridor, on her way to Hall, she noticed the envelope on the mail tray.

"What's this?"

"This," MacKenzie said in a slightly sour tone. "Our Turkish visitor called and left it for you."

"His name," Catriona said absently, "is Mr. Khoury. Why am I only seeing this now?"

"I forgot it in my apron pocket earlier."

Shaking her head, Catriona opened the folded note.

His handwriting was beautiful; fluid and sweeping, imbued with the memory of the Arabic script.

To the Lady Catriona,

May I challenge you to a game of chess—I shall set up the board every day at 1 o'clock, in St. John's Common Room.

Always your faithful servant,
Elias Khoury

Chapter 7

She had burned his invitation. Not immediately, mind you; it had lingered on her desk until midnight. Hence, she had barely managed to convince MacKenzie to stay home for the matutinal fire drill. MacKenzie had perceived her holding on to the letter, and her chaperoning sensibilities were on high alert. But, the morning was cool and rainy, and anyone with a stiff limb should stay in. On her way to St. John's main gate, Catriona passed several dons holding glistening black umbrellas. Too late to turn around and fetch her own; Hattie was already waiting in the college archway, her voluminous purple velvet cape announcing her from a distance. A large picnic valise stood at her feet. Oddly, she had her arms crossed over her chest and was in the company of an equally stiff-looking Lucie.

"You all seem rather cheerful this morning," Catriona said, glancing from one to the other as she rubbed her spectacles dry on her plaid.

"Catriona, you're a rational, impartial person," Hattie said, her face serious under her pink hat. "Tell Lucie that wearing white on her wedding day if her groom wants it so is perfectly fine, even *if* the queen made it popular?"

"Och." Only a small cup of tea was sloshing in her empty stomach, not enough sustenance to enter a quarrel over fashion with Hattie. Or with Lucie over weddings.

"Ballentine has an opinion on your dress?" she asked Lucie.

Lucie raised a fine straight brow. "Astonishing, isn't it," she said pointedly.

"I should have been so lucky," Hattie said. "My mother chose my wedding gown, a beastly thing, and my groom didn't know me and couldn't have cared less. He has made up for it quite nicely ever since, of course," she added with a pleased little smile.

Lucie gave a snort.

Catriona stepped aside to let two dons pass on their way out of the college.

"Is something else the matter," she tried, "because both of you are a wee bit too sensible to squabble over something as petty as a dress at such an early hour."

Hattie paused. She gave Lucie a wary look. "Is there?" she prodded. "Something else?"

Lucie's gray eyes narrowed. "We're late. Let's stop a cab."

Hattie gasped. "So there is. Lucie, what is it? Tell us."

Lucie had made to walk out onto St. Giles. Both Hattie and Catriona stayed put. Lucie glanced back, and with an annoyed sniff, she returned to them.

"Fine," she said in a low voice.

Hattie stuck her head closer.

Lucie furtively looked left and right. "It's Ballentine."

"Oh no," Hattie said, and put a hand on Lucie's elbow. "If he's mean to you, we'll have a word with him."

This was a puzzling development. Ballentine, Lucie's fiancé, was known for two things: looking too beautiful for his own good and offering fierce support to Lucie in all that she did.

Lucie brushed a damp strand of hair from her cheek. "Remember I agreed to marry him as soon as the Married Women's Property Act is amended?"

Catriona nodded.

"He has been taunting me about it lately."

"Goodness," Hattie said, frowning. "Why would he do that? What does he do?"

"Well. Ever since Montgomery pushed the bill through the House of Lords, I catch him looking at me. Smirking."

"That sounds sinister," Catriona remarked.

"It gets worse," Lucie hissed. "He hums—he is humming the Bridal March. And then he pretends that he didn't when I . . . What?"

"Nothing."

Hattie's shoulders had begun to shake beneath her cape.

"You're laughing."

Hattie put the back of her hand against her brow and raised her gaze toward the vaulted ceiling. "Woe is me," she cried softly. "My terribly, terribly handsome, titled, and charming fiancé, whom I love, is greatly looking forward to marrying me."

Lucie gave her a brooding stare. "I might actually have to marry him now," she said. "I might be a married woman, and soon. So many laws still need amending, abolishing . . ."

"Ooh," Catriona said, understanding dawning, "is that why you're so keen on having this writ for restitution crushed all of a sudden?"

"Of course not," Lucie snipped. "That writ should have never existed in the first place."

"Good grief," said Hattie. "Lucie, you can't wait for the world to be perfect before you commit to him. The law won't protect you from having your heart broken by someone you love in any case— they have that power regardless."

"That's solved, then," Catriona said with sudden impatience. "It's not about the dress, it's about Lucie's cold feet. Shall we hail a cab?"

"Absolutely," Lucie said.

Hattie looked put out. "But that's worse," she said. "Cold feet are serious."

Catriona adjusted her plaid. "Has anyone here expected Lucie not to have cold feet? Raise your hand."

No hands rose.

"Well, then," Catriona said. "Anyone seriously expecting Lucie to not marry Lord Ballentine when the time comes, raise your hand."

She looked closely; not even a twitch of a finger was in sight. Lucie's fine lips had flattened into a hyphen. Hattie looked reluctantly impressed.

"There," Catriona said. "Are we all ready to hail a cab now? What's in this valise, anyway, Hattie?"

"Biscuits and scones for the firefighters, fresh from the Randolph kitchen."

"That's kind of you," Lucie said, her frown easing.

Hattie smiled, mollified. "You know I like to feed people."

Everyone's mood seemed somewhat restored. If only she could reason her way out of her own situations as easily, thought Catriona.

They formed a cluster on the pavement with the biscuit valise between them, taking turns in trying to hail a cab. It was morning traffic, and, in this weather, all cabs seemed to have been snatched up by tutors spilling out of the colleges along St. Giles.

"Why don't we walk," Lucie suggested. "It's better to arrive late rather than never."

"I can't carry this for a mile," Hattie said, and pointed at her valise. "It's a lot of biscuits."

The doors to St. John's opened and released another man with a flipped-up collar and an umbrella onto the pavement. Catriona's body recognized the outline of his shoulders before her brain did. By the time his cursory glance became a double take, her belly burned as if it had been jabbed with a hot poker.

Elias Khoury stopped and tipped his hat. "Lady Catriona. Good morning."

His friendly smile beamed like a small sun on this dreich day;

it nearly cleared the fog off her glasses. The heat spread up her throat into her cheeks. Lucie and Hattie had gone curiously still. They wore their polite, public faces while they took him in with eagle eyes. She supposed he looked dashing in his austerely cut camel's-hair coat. His scent had taken on an earthy note in the damp.

"Erm," she said. "May I introduce Mr. Khoury—he is a visiting scholar and an esteemed guest of Wester Ross."

"You certainly may," Hattie said with a meaningful little undertone.

Catriona glared at her, furtively. "Mr. Khoury," she said. "Lady Lucinda. Mrs. Blackstone."

"It is a pleasure to meet you, Mr. Khoury," Hattie chirped, pronouncing his name *Cowree*. "Shame about the weather this morning."

"We say it's good for the land, ma'am," he replied, a wink in his voice.

"Oh, so do we," Hattie said, looking far too pleased.

Elias Khoury relaxed his stance, one knee slightly bent; it seemed he was settling in for a chat. Just great. Catriona watched him from under her lashes, how easily he conversed with her friends, smiling with his eyes as though he had known Hattie and Lucie much longer than two minutes. Would he mention his chess invitation? Her stomach dropped. A gentleman wouldn't mention it. Had she contemplated last night to go to the Common Room today at one o'clock? Possibly. Beating a man at chess was a straightforward social interaction. A decent game could be as short as ten minutes and one didn't even have to hold a conversation.

"You're catching us on our way to the fire drill," Hattie said with a regretful glance. "It isn't a full drill, actually, because those happen unannounced just before dawn . . ."

Elias's dark brows expressed alarm. "A fire? Where?"

"Not a fire," Lucie explained. "A drill to fight the fire."

Hattie nodded. "At Lady Margaret Hall. A women's college. We are a few women short, but Catriona is coming to our rescue. She handles the hose like an actual fireman."

Catriona cut her friend a look of disbelief.

Mr. Khoury's eyes had gone wide for a moment. "Ah," he said. "Why aren't *actual* firemen handling . . . the, erm, equipment?"

"Women students have the candles, the open fires, the gas lamps in their rooms," Hattie said. "We must know how to respond to a fire because before the town brigade arrives, the dormitories would be burned to a crisp."

And everyone in them were the unspoken words. Mr. Khoury's frown deepened.

"The women's halls are built too far from the town center," Lucie explained. "To preserve propriety. It's usually impossible for the town brigade to reach a women's college on time."

Hattie gave him a winsome smile. "If one must perish, it's best to do so with one's reputation intact, wouldn't you agree?"

His bewildered expression turned thoughtful. "Is there a handbook?" he asked. "About your drill."

Hattie and Catriona exchanged a glance. *I haven't a clue,* said Hattie's small shrug.

"Perhaps we can help if you tell us what you need it for," she remarked.

Mr. Khoury's posture was more formal now. "My family is in the silk business. Many young girls work in the factories, and their accommodations aren't easily accessible, either. I'd like to see your practices; perhaps I notice something that could help improve the safety at their dormitories."

"We will find you the handbook," Lucie said at once. "Right after the drill."

Catriona's shoulders softened. It sounded as though they would now all take their leave; the *Good morning*s were already in reach, and then she would be able to breathe again . . .

"I have an idea," said Hattie. "Why don't you join us, Mr. Khoury, and see for yourself?"

Oh no she didn't.

"I'm certain Mr. Khoury is busy," Catriona said to Hattie.

His expression was unreadable. "Will there be another drill? I was on my way to the museum just now."

"Not anytime soon," Hattie said. "The museum, however, will be there this afternoon."

It was decided—Mr. Khoury would attend the drill and take any lessons back to Mount Lebanon, and Catriona couldn't say a word against it because only a monster would deprive working girls of improved fire safety.

Hattie was on a rampage. "I own a camera," she said, her cheeks glowing with enthusiasm. "I could document everything for you, sir. Why don't we fetch it?"

"You do that," Lucie said. "Catriona and I will go ahead, if we ever manage to stop a cab."

"Allow me," Mr. Khoury said, and he stepped onto the street, blithely maneuvered traffic, and hailed a closed brougham carriage over.

"I hadn't seen that one," Lucie muttered.

"It's easy for him, he's taller than we are," Catriona muttered back.

Through the small back window of the coach, Catriona watched Hattie and Elias Khoury cross the street to the Randolph Hotel. He carried the valise, and his gaze was focused attentively on Hattie's face as though he was riveted by their conversation. Hattie was a married woman; she could walk and ride alone with men with impunity. One of the few perks of married life.

The brougham joined the stream of vehicles moving toward Summertown. Catriona and Lucie sat next to each other, both forward facing and steeped in brooding silence. The interior of the coach smelled like old carpet. At least it was spacious and quiet.

"She said *hose* in front of a man," Catriona finally said, "didn't she."

"She did," Lucie confirmed. "When she described how well you handle the hose."

"Thanks."

When they pulled up in front of the student accommodation of Lady Margaret Hall, she paid the driver of the brougham double to stay put in case the rain continued and they needed a ride back. Despite the damp conditions, two dozen students had already assembled round the emergency meeting point in front of the college's dorm. The captain of the brigade was a sharp-featured girl whose voice carried without the help of the megaphone.

"Today's maneuver is focused on equipment testing and maintenance," she announced, "so expect to use the chute, all water wagons, and the hoses."

"No bucket lines?" someone asked, although there were a number of buckets in plain sight on the lawn before the house entrance.

"We shall certainly practice the bucket lines, just not inside the building. We begin now. Subcaptains, lead your brigades."

A groan went through the group. Bucket lines were considered exhausting yet boring. Catriona liked them; there was a meditative rhythm to grabbing a new bucket while passing one on, quick yet careful to not spill a drop. While they were lining up, one of the girls took the whirling ratchet from the captain's basket and ran a lap around them. *Krrrrr krrrrr . . .*

"We're all quite awake," Catriona told her when she passed a second time.

Krrrrrr went the ratchet in her face, rattling her teeth.

"It's more authentic this way," the girl said with a laugh.

Grab, pass, grab, pass, all while fantasizing about snatching the ratchet and dismembering it into tiny pieces.

A cab stopped near the brougham just as their exercise ended.

"Who is that?" asked Ratchet Girl when Elias smoothly descended from the vehicle. Realizing they had an attractive male spectator, she doubled her noisy efforts.

Catriona plonked her bucket down and strode to the engine room, her face hot under a sheen of rain and perspiration. The engine room homed the pump wagon, which was heavier than an ox when full. She waited until the wagon crew arrived to roll her vehicle into the open. Outside, the wheels sank into the softened lawn. Shoving and pushing, she helped move the wagon, one foot, another foot. The soles of her boots slipped on the wet grass. She looked up to take a deep breath, her pulse in her ears. Nearby, Elias was holding his umbrella over Hattie while she was setting up her plate camera. He glanced over, and her heart gave a *thump* in her throat when his brilliant eyes met hers. She dropped her gaze and joined the last push to maneuver the wagon into position. In the dorm in front of her, several girls stuck their heads out of an upper-floor window, awaiting rescue. A chute appeared among them and while they let it unfurl to the ground, Catriona unspooled the hose. She instructed her crew to pump. Elias Khoury was of course right there, watching. It made her aware of her every move; her own limbs felt cumbersome. The hose stiffened in her grip when the water came in; it pushed back like a living thing in a fight, and she dug her heels into the ground to take control. Water gushed out and hammered the building façade, spraying the brigadiers below the evacuation window. Shrieking ensued, but the hands of the different teams soon worked together as if directed by a conductor. Catriona's breathing calmed. Hattie was right, she excelled at handling the equipment. She *liked* pitting her physical strength against it, to feel the force of the water, to channel it purposefully.

Had she been much younger, fifteen or so, she would have relished Mr. Khoury watching her put out a fire, confident that he'd find her skills charming. These days, she knew better; a spurting hose in a woman's hands was quite shocking, and men usually found nothing alluring about a lady mastering manly tasks. Boarding school and an equally painful season in London had made perfectly clear what type of behavior must be performed to charm a man in want of a wife—and to her, it was a performance. Growing up, she hadn't witnessed romantic interactions between spouses, since Wester Ross had remained alone. While she knew how to act—coy, cheerful, moderately clever—whenever she had tried it, it felt like she stood there in a clown costume and everyone else could see the costume, too. She had never aspired to master it better. For a long while, she had just kept hoping for someone who would find her charming as she was, but the few men who seemed intrigued were her father's age, which did not appeal to her.

At the evacuation window, the first girl climbed into the tube. She plummeted down, a bulge in the canvas like a fish in a pelican's throat, until she was spat out moments later, laughing and disheveled.

When the drill was over, and all equipment cleaned and returned to its positions, the subcaptains distributed towels and biscuits. As Catriona dabbed her face dry, she watched Hattie emerge from under the dark cloth of her camera. She had taken a photograph of Elias standing in front of the dorm. She had taken another one of him earlier, with his right hand on the pump wagon. Now he was saying something to Hattie that made her flip back her head and cover her mouth with her hand. She was giggling, and there was nothing performative about it. Catriona balled up the towel and tossed it straight into the nearby basket. A circle of curious girls was forming around Elias. She stayed back; her face still felt damp and sticky.

"Are you riding back into town with us?" she asked Lucie, who had supported the ground team for the chute. Lucie's house was located on Norham Gardens, only a short walking distance from the college.

"I'm going home," Lucie said, and snapped open her umbrella. "Boudicca needs feeding."

The mention of Lucie's little black cat eased the tension in Catriona's neck. "Give her a treat from me."

"I'm taking her to London tonight," Lucie said darkly. "She loathes the pet carrier."

"Then I shall see you next at the Blackstone dinner on Friday?"

"Yes." Lucie glanced across the lawn to Elias, who was picking up Hattie's camera. "I hope your father's colleague won't eat too much of your time until then. Tally-ho, my dear."

Elias carried the camera to the waiting brougham, and Catriona watched this with alarm. Surely, surely he would not climb aboard. He didn't. He briefly chatted with Hattie at the carriage door, then turned and walked down the road at a leisurely stride. He was returning to town on foot.

Hattie bounced back to Catriona, her eyes suspiciously shiny. Beneath her flouncy cape, she vibrated with poorly repressed excitement.

"You secretive thing," she whisper-squeaked as she looped an arm through Catriona's. "*That* is your father's colleague?"

She moved her chin to the direction whence Elias was disappearing.

"Aye."

Hattie's fingers dug into her wrist. "Why didn't you tell me that he was young, charming, and terribly handsome?"

"It hadn't occurred to me that this was relevant information."

Hattie eyed her with fox-like cunning. "So you agree that he is terribly handsome?"

"Hattie, it's an objectively verifiable observation that he is handsome, nothing to get silly about."

"He cares about working girls' safety," Hattie said, and sighed. "His eyes are like gemstones. His facial structure makes me want to paint in the classic style again."

"Dear oh dear."

"I shall ask him to sit for me," Hattie said. "As a young Apollo."

"You do that," Catriona said, "if you want him to think you're properly unhinged."

"Hmph. He had no objections to being photographed."

Elias Khoury's face, eternalized on a bromide plate. A memento that would remain long after he had returned to the East. Hattie was very skilled; she would capture the confident tilt of his head and the expressive eyes . . . She hardly needed photographs to remind her. Her memories tended to be as sharp as any picture. Her blessing and her curse.

"Do what you must," she told Hattie. "I don't mind either way."

"I invited him to the dinner," Hattie said. "May I write you down as his table partner?"

She stopped in her tracks, instantly dizzy. "You have what?"

The enthusiasm slipped off Hattie's face. "I . . . invited him to the dinner on Friday. I know it was rather too ad hoc, but he didn't seem to mind."

Some of the students were approaching them, so Catriona swallowed her reply, but she must have made a face of abject horror.

Hattie looked distraught. "It appears I made a gaffe," she said. "I thought that since he's an acquaintance of your father's, and you know how Blackstone is invested in the arts and used to deal in antiques . . . so Mr. Khoury would fit in very well. It hadn't occurred to me that you have reason to object. I do apologize."

Catriona grabbed her hand. "It's all right."

"I shall uninvite him."

"You can't—and there's no need."

Hattie always meant well, and her reasoning was sound— Blackstone was indeed knowledgeable on antiques thanks to his past life as an arts dealer, and it also wasn't fair to deprive Elias Khoury of stimulating company. The man's one crime to date was catching her with nothing but a volume of Virgil shielding her privates, something he couldn't undo if he tried.

The brougham driver glanced down from his seat, looking as pleased as a wet cat. "We'd be ready, then, ma'am."

Three of the students crowded the open carriage door, their

damp, upturned faces hopeful. "Are you headed toward town? May we come along?"

Ratchet Girl was among them, still looking exhaustingly cheerful under her frizzy fringe.

"I'm afraid we're at full capacity," Catriona replied, and they laughed and climbed aboard, thinking she was joking because it was a four-wheel carriage that could take four girls, five if they squeezed together. Squeeze they did. The carriage lurched forward. Catriona stared out the rapidly fogging window. Someone's knees were touching hers. *Deep breaths.* Hattie was chattering with the others about nothing of consequence, and so a lot of meaningless words quickly filled up the small space. She pulled her shawl as tight as it would go, compressing her body underneath.

Relief was fleeting. Halfway down Norham Gardens, it became clear that one of the girls had a returning cough. *Cough cough cough.* Persistent, dry, erratic. Catriona moved jerkily on her seat. Just as bad as the ratchet, it pulled her out of her skin. The *krrrr* had whittled her noise tolerance for the day to the bone. *Cough cough cough.* She swallowed around the tightness in her throat. It wasn't far to St. John's. She could last. Just to the end of this road, then they'd take a left onto Banbury Road, and then it was barely half a mile. They overtook a man who was striding along on the pavement. A wheel hit a pothole, and Hattie's elbow bumped against hers. She wanted to melt into the carriage wall. Dissolve. Disappear. It was the brunette girl on the opposite bench, the cougher. Criminal, to leave a house with a cough and without lozenges. Noisy *and* inconsiderate. There she went again. *Breathe.* The air was thick and wet like liquid. They turned the corner onto Banbury Road . . . salvation was near . . . *Cough!* Loathing burned through her, hot like hell. At the next cough, she would scream. She stood up and hit the coach roof. A collective gasp . . . The carriage slowed . . .

Hattie cried, "Catriona?"

She pushed the door open, causing screams of surprise. One, two, three long seconds, and finally the vehicle ground to a halt. She took the plunge, and pain twinged in her knees when her boots hit the street. Air. A cool spray of rain on her face.

"Catriona? What is it?"

Hattie was in the carriage door, gathering up her skirts. Catriona raised her hand and shook her head.

"I'm all right," she said.

She stepped onto the pavement, unbalanced as if caught in a bout of vertigo.

The coach stayed put, as did Hattie in the door, still contemplating whether to lower the ladder.

"I'll walk," Catriona called at her, and waved, a little desperate. "Just go."

Her breath was a solid block in her throat.

"Demoiselle?"

The male voice cut through the cotton wool in her head. No. Not him. Not now.

Elias approached from the direction from which the carriage had come. His dark brows swooped.

"Shou?" he asked, and spun his hand in an inquisitive gesture. "Are you all right?"

His concerned gaze glided over her like fingers searching for an injury. He'd find nothing, and even if she explained, he wouldn't understand.

Hattie was still hovering in the open carriage door, concern plain on her face.

"Just go, please," Catriona said through her teeth.

"Are you certain?"

"Very, very certain."

"Very well," Hattie relented. "Call on me."

Thump! The door closed and the carriage joined the traffic again.

Catriona's lips felt swollen and sore like one big insect bite.

"I'm taking some air," she told Elias, who stood rather close. "It's a fine day for a walk."

The expression in his eyes became oddly gentle, and she realized he was holding his umbrella over her. A lazy rainy rhythm drummed on the protective shell.

"I'm wet anyway," she said. "Look."

"May I walk with you," he said, politely, but something in his posture made clear that it wasn't a question. His steady gaze was an anchor in surroundings that still felt flat and inanimate like paper cuts. She nodded.

They walked slowly, or perhaps the earth was just rotating away under their moving feet. The leaves of the trees glistened with a harsh luster.

"Forgive me," came his voice, faintly amused. "Are you breathing?"

She wasn't. She gave him an aggrieved sideways glance. "How would you know?"

"I can sense it."

She was trying. Her breath kept stopping in her throat. It would resolve itself eventually.

"It helps if you put your hand here and breathe against it," he said, casually, as though he weren't putting his hand low on his flat stomach and drawing attention to his body.

Imagining pressure low against her belly, she inhaled right through the blockages in her throat and chest. He seemed to have sensed that, too, because his silence sounded smug.

"Surprise," she muttered. "Gentleman explains breathing to a woman."

He gave a shocked little laugh. "If it's any consolation," he said, "I learned this technique from my grandmother."

Mentioning his family to her was a sign of great goodwill. Perhaps he didn't think her completely bonkers. Yet.

"Your grandmother is a wise woman," she said, mortification creeping in.

"Yes. She is a . . ." He frowned. "She helped deliver babies." He angled his free arm, quite expertly, as if he were cradling an infant.

"A midwife," Catriona said.

"A midwife, yes. When I was a boy, I carried her bag. So I learned."

"She let you into the delivery room?"

He gave her a startled look. "No, no. The breathing I showed you, it helps first-time fathers, too—far away from the delivery room."

"I see. What else does your grandmother suggest in such a situation?"

He smiled at that. "Petting a cat."

They walked on, her breathing against the pressure of her hand, him content to just keep her company. The ground firmed under her feet. The air had flavors again, the smoky sweetness of domestic coal fires and Elias's scent. She snuck a glance at him, but he was focused on finding a good spot for crossing the road as St. John's came into view on the other side. He wasn't under the umbrella, she realized; he was holding it fully over her head and kept a respectful distance. Droplets had formed on his brow, and his dark lashes were in clumps. If she invited him under the umbrella, he would refuse. She could ask to hold on to his arm, and he'd feel obliged to offer his support, bringing him close enough to share the shelter of the umbrella. But she would have to touch his arm. His biceps would brush against her shoulder. They would look like a couple, taking a stroll.

He made to cross the road, then paused, eyeing her. "You aren't feeling faint, are you?"

"No," she said.

She hoped he would keep his other questions unsaid. *Why did you jump into traffic? Do you do this often? Are you raving mad, by any chance?*

I'm not mad, she wanted to tell him, *I just can't be trapped in crowded spaces with erratic noise patterns.*

On the last stretch to St. John's entrance, their pace seemed to slow as if by an unspoken agreement. Eventually they did arrive and faced each other. Just like that, they were both under the umbrella. Her belly clenched nervously. Looking up at the underside of his jaw shouldn't feel so exciting.

He glanced down at her with a friendly but casual expression. "I'm afraid I shall have to look after my cousin now," he said. "He leaves for London after lunch."

"That's quite all right."

Had he expected her to want lunch with him?

A tutor emerged from St. John's and looked at them, then up to the sky, then back at them, an odd expression on his face. Obviously, the drizzle had ceased, and yet she and Mr. Khoury were still standing under the umbrella. A cold sensation dripped down her back. Lo, Lady Catriona, looking cozy with a young man with no chaperone in sight. She stepped away.

"Mrs. Blackstone has invited me to a dinner on Friday," Elias said, his gaze following her.

May I come was what he was asking.

"You'll have fun," she replied. "She hosts the most enjoyable parties. Lots of games."

Yes, you may. Who was she to deny him a dinner after he had helped her breathe.

Another smile played over his lips. "I hadn't taken you for someone who enjoyed games."

She thought of his chess invitation, catching fire on her grate. She blushed.

"Good day, Mr. Khoury."

Back at her desk, the cold wouldn't leave her bones. She flipped through the pages of Virgil's *Aeneid* without comprehending the text. She was picturing a curly-haired boy on another continent, the pink soles of his feet slapping dusty yellow soil as he ran out on an errand with his midwife grandmother. He had lived an entire life story before becoming a character in hers. Would he forget this little chapter here in Oxford once he left again?

Her watch said it was half past eleven. Would he play chess today, and if yes, with whom? It could have been an excellent occasion to test her hypothesis about emotional inoculation. A deliberate infection to control future responses. Who better to practice with than him? He had seen her without a stitch of clothing; if she learned to feel unbothered with him, she could manage it with anyone. In case the experiment did go pear-shaped, no matter—he was leaving Britain before the summer was over.

In the end, she did not go because her motives were unclear—was she hoping for self-improvement, or was she hoping for something else entirely? She couldn't have *something else*. She had just flung herself from a moving carriage over a cough. The noise, the entrapment, the *people*. And what was marriage, and the inevitable family life, other than an entrapment in a small, crowded space with erratic noise patterns? Even if all the laws of Britain changed in a woman's favor, she would still be stuck inside her skin. People would always exhaust her eventually. So she remained at her desk, reading, acutely aware when the chapel clock struck twelve, then one.

Chapter 8

She walked to the Bodleian the next morning to begin the campaign against the writ for restitution in earnest. A blustery wind had cleared the skies, and she entered the library still holding on to her hat. The librarian had her stack of books and journals pertaining to the writ ready, and then he briefly became reluctant to release the requested Home Office reports into her female hands. The Campbell name held enough authority here to overrule his compunctions.

The Upper Reading Room of the Bod was largely empty, few students were present during term break. None of the usual glances followed her as she steered toward a desk. She sat down quietly and opened the first journal, a freshly sharpened pencil at the ready for note-taking. Opponents of the Cause rarely changed their mind based on facts alone, but when they found just a single fact wrong in a petition, they used it to bash the credibility of the Cause itself. Hours later, she had a pile of notes, and she was parched. She went to the fountain on the floor below. The water was nice and cool in her throat, and she lingered a moment while her mind whirred and shifted recently acquired information around. The writ for restitution was a vile piece of legislation. It claimed lives; apparently, a woman from Suffolk had perished in prison because she had refused to return to her marital home as decreed. Catriona curled her hand, still damp from the water, over her nape. They built women's colleges far from the ribald town centers and surrounded the dorms with walls that were topped with broken glass, but there were no walls to keep a woman safe in her own home.

Approaching noon, she had a first draft to lobby a generic man of influence:

Dear Sir / To the honourable /

I'm appealing to you today on the matter of a policy that abjectly affects the safety and dignity of married women in Britain: the Writ for Restitution of Conjugal Rights.

The Matrimonial Causes Act of 1878 allows a wife to apply for a legal separation from a physically abusive husband. Nothing demonstrates the necessity for such a law more clearly than The Report on Brutal Assaults, *compiled for the Home Office in 1875, which showed that according to court records, over the course of five years, over 6,000 cases of the worst possible offences had been committed against women by their own husbands. This equates to 1,200 cases a year, or over three cases a day, a figure which does not include common assault (which is estimated to be 25 times higher than the figures reported to the Home Office).*

However, wives still find their plea for a separation frequently rejected by a magistrate, and the moment a wife takes her fate into her own hands and separates without a legal decree, she is guilty of desertion. Her husband may take out a writ for restitution against her, and a wife forfeits all access to her own children and property if she ignores it and might be made to choose between the gaol or an unsafe home.

Therefore, abolishing the writ for restitution is keeping in spirit with the Matrimonial Causes Act, which you have supported / which your noble friends supported / . . . It could in fact be considered a necessity for making the act fully operational.

The letter felt concise and factual to her, which meant it was too blunt. She would have to soften it and dress it with a bow; make it appealing to a man's sense of honor or his vanity so that he would consider saving the damsel instead of becoming defensive on behalf of his entire sex. The prettifying would deplete her more than a whole day of research ever could. Annabelle would have to help her; Annabelle was naturally tactful and too pragmatic to indulge in Weltschmerz.

She left the Bod shortly after noon and went across the street to Blackwell's to treat herself to a cup of tea and a scone. Her place next to an upper-floor window provided good views over busy Broad Street below. Carts rumbled over cobblestone; people were running errands. A nanny led two children on strings. All of these busy people had a mother somewhere. Her mind drifted to the inevitable, the man who stalked her dreams these days. How would Elias Khoury treat his wife behind closed doors? For the wife's sake, she hoped he was truly as calm and charming as she had perceived him during her embarrassing carriage episode. Much like the Catholics, Maronites were not allowed to divorce.

She reread her draft while nibbling on the scone. Why did women do it, marry? Pecuniary pressures and the need for respectability drove most of them down the aisle, but there were plenty of independent suffragists who said *I do*. Look at Lucie. No one was safe. Elissa of Carthage, grandniece of Jezebel, had outfoxed a tyrannical king, founded a city, and ascended to be its queen, only to end herself because her lover had left her—as Virgil recorded: *But the queen, long since smitten with a grievous love-pang, feeds the wound with her lifeblood, and is wasted with fire unseen. Oft to her mind rushes back the hero's valour, oft his glorious stock . . .* Rome's greatest enemy, still obsessing over a cad.

She put her glasses up on her head and rubbed her eyes. She knew why she did it, fall in love. She knew, and annoyingly, it didn't stop her. She had deciphered the pattern a few years ago, while tutoring Peregrin on hieroglyphs: bright, charming, carefree, if not careless, he had instantly appealed because he embodied something she lacked. People like him danced through life and radiated light, while she carried a dark void inside her. She stayed well away from the edge, but the awareness that her own mind had the potential to swallow her whole never left. A Charles or Alexandra or Peregrin never ran such a risk. There were limits to their depths. At first, she had thought if she peeled back their layers, she'd eventually uncover familiar abysmal complexities, but much like an onion, some people's layers were the substance, not the cover for a core. She couldn't help but like it. She'd burn herself on their flame for the promise of some easy warmth. Some closeness. Some fun.

She put down her scone when a grim vision struck her: What if this inclination never went away? What if all the intellectual prowess in the world would never close the void? Forty years from now, she might be an acclaimed professor, but also a perpetually nervous elderly lady who tittered when a young charmer helped her from the carriage . . .

The decision was made very quickly, then. Perhaps she had already made it days ago and she had just been too anxious to give marching orders. She looked at her pocket watch. If she hurried, she might make it back in time for a chess match.

"I'm not certain this is wise," MacKenzie muttered when they arrived at St. John's Senior Common Room.

Catriona paused with her hand on the doorknob. "You know what they say, MacKenzie?"

"I'm sure ye'll tell me."

"There are three kinds of stories: a man goes on a journey; a stranger comes to town; and a man hunts a whale."

MacKenzie put on her polite you-are-the-lady-and-I-am-but-a-simple-woman expression.

"Where are we women in this?" Catriona asked. "Women rarely leave town. Our stories tend to begin with the arrival of the stranger."

"Yer hunting plenty of white whales in yer study," MacKenzie said under her breath. "There's yer story, no need for an entanglement with an outlander."

An *entanglement* was the opposite of her desires; immunity was the aim.

"We are just playing a game," she said, and opened the door.

The Senior Common Room was a calm space with dark wood paneling and low-legged leather furniture. The sweetish smell of coal fire and the low murmur of male voices permeated the air. Elias Khoury was the only man she saw. He had chosen a table in a bay window nook and was in the process of setting up opposing armies with practiced efficiency. At her entrance, he looked up. A pang of feral excitement hit her belly. He stood. When she arrived at the table, the corner of his mouth tipped up.

"You have decided to play," he said, his voice low and husky. His eyes were more green than blue in the soft light. Thinking of him as an experiment helped to hold his gaze, as if someone else was doing it in her place.

"I have," she said. "Prepare to be checkmated."

Chapter 9

Lady Catriona surveyed the table he had prepared. "We don't have a clock."

Her tone was matter-of-fact, but the nervous blush on her cheekbones stood out like two pink flags. Elias found the contrast very charming.

"Will my pocket watch suffice," he asked, "or are you planning on winning by drawing it out for sixteen hours?"

She looked alarmed. "Which game was that?"

"Howard Staunton versus Pierre St. Amant, in 1843."

"Sounds exhausting."

"It rang in the era of chess clocks."

Her lips quirked wryly. "I can't think why."

He smiled, and her color deepened. Being here was costing her. And yet she had come. He knew why *he* was here—he had entered the Common Room with a plan of seduction:

- checkmate her in ten instead of five moves to draw out their time together
- refrain from overt, flowery wooing because this would not charm her
- steer the conversation to a topic that roused her passions—it might put her in a passionate mood

A limited strategy, and he hadn't expected to deploy it. Notwithstanding her reaction to his chessboard the other day, she had not shown for the first few days. *What, then, is* your *intention behind this visit now, Lady Catriona?*

He pulled out the chair for her, then arranged seating for the chaperone.

"You look very fine today, Mrs. MacKenzie," he told the Scotswoman. "Would you care for a drink?" He gestured at the well-stocked shelves of the bar at the back of the room.

MacKenzie regarded him with a reproachful frown. "No, thank ye. We're not in the habit of drinking so early in the day here."

He gave her his politest smile. She pursed her lips and whipped spear-sized knitting needles from her bag. All righty.

"I'll have a sherry, please," came Lady Catriona's calm voice from behind his back.

He didn't let MacKenzie see his grin. The path to the lady led past this stalwart woman.

When he returned to the table with a tray, Lady Catriona had removed her gloves, and she was wearing her spectacles on her head as though they were a pair of sunglasses.

She gazed up at him when she took the sherry glass off the tray. "Thank you."

He stood holding the tray, head empty, trying not to stare down into her bare face. Her eyes were enchanting, a clear, deep cerulean blue, the kind silk-makers used to imbue a gown with hints of heaven.

When he sat down, a distracting heat was simmering low in his body. "I suggest fifteen moves per hour for time control," he said, his voice a little scratchy.

A nod. "Very well."

She had placed a little notebook and a pencil in front of her. She was taking this seriously; she would keep track of their moves. Her fingers, curled around the sherry glass, looked naked, like her face.

Her gloves, white leather with pearl buttons, lay snugly on top of each other at the edge of the table. Elias sucked in a breath and placed his pocket watch next to the board. His seduction plan should have included provisions for defense, not just attack.

"I use algebraic notation," he said with a nod at her notebook, because in Britain, they used descriptive notation, which he had never bothered to internalize.

"That's fine," she said. "I use algebraic, too."

"Ah," he said. "How come?"

A small hesitation. "I used to play with a German."

"I see." The thought of some stiff German count playing away with her in close quarters annoyed him. "Please. Choose your color."

"Dark," she said easily.

He turned the board around, putting the black army in front of her. She studied the board for some time in perfect silence.

"It's beautiful," she said at last. "A work of art." The fingers of her right hand twitched, as if she imagined touching it.

Her appreciation unexpectedly grazed a tender place in his chest. The board was one of his most prized possessions. He never parted from it. He knew its details with his eyes closed: the filigree patterns on the pieces, fine as if carved with a needlepoint. The squares were set with the precision of a watchmaker's hand, the white ones shimmering iridescent with mother-of-pearl; the dark ones intricate inlays of differently shaded kinds of wood. He could still smell the piney scent when he pressed his nose to the board. He still saw his father's patient fingers on the pieces, moving them toward victory. The chessboard had been a wedding gift to Elias's mother. *Your mother could play so well, her cousins refused to play with her . . .* His parents had enjoyed playing together; his father had taken pleasure in his wife's wit. The memories Elias had of them sitting together, looking connected and content in their own private cosmos, included the chessboard.

"It's an heirloom," he said, surprising himself.

Lady Catriona glanced up with soft eyes. "Did someone in your family make it?"

He gave a nod. "My paternal grandfather. Shall we begin?"

He opened with a pawn move to d4. Lady Catriona immediately moved her knight, Nc4, and he fortified his left flank with another pawn, c4. She planted a pawn on e6, and only then did she scribble the status into her book. Her responses to his moves had been rapid; she clearly knew the opening. They were on the verge of a proper chess match rather than a flirtation.

He leaned back in his chair to slow them down.

"Have you had a successful morning?" he asked, launching Point Number Three on his plan, the passion. "Women's revolution is on its way?"

She rolled her pencil between her thumb and index finger. "I can't quite tell whether you are mocking me," she said.

"I wouldn't dare."

Her fingers were slender and straight, and the backs of her hands looked unnaturally smooth as though she spent all her time indoors. Her fingernails were noticeably short, though, and ink smudged the side of her middle finger like a bruise. There was a bump, from always holding a pen. In its own way, it was a working woman's hand.

"Tell me," she said, "how is the situation for women's rights in your homeland? For married women?"

"Ah. It's simple," he said. "When the time comes for marriage, the head of the house gives the bride to whoever offers the largest number of camels. There she goes." He clapped imaginary dust off his hands.

MacKenzie's clicking knitting needles fell silent. Lady Catriona regarded him without blinking. "But you don't really trade in camels in Mount Lebanon," she said haltingly.

There went his banter, rolling out of sight like a tumbleweed. *Well done, Abu Charm.*

"It was a joke," he said. "There are few camels indeed. More importantly, Lady Catriona, we don't just barter women to the highest bidder."

"You don't?" she said. "Interesting. I thought that custom was universal."

On the board, he moved another pawn, to g3.

"As a rule, rights depend on the community," he said. "Muslim women in Ottoman territories have been entitled to purchase, inherit, and bequeath property since I can remember. They run businesses. They don't usually take their man's name. Then there is the matter of wealth—the more fortunate we are, the more value we all place on a woman's education."

"I may have read about that."

He looked up in time to catch the faint smile on her lips. Of course she knew already. She had simply tested his reaction to these facts. She was thinking two moves ahead, both on and off the chessboard, it seemed. It did however reveal that she had a degree of personal interest in him, too.

"Perhaps Britain will progress that way one day, thanks to your campaign," he said in an amicable tone.

She moved her mouth as if she had tasted something sour. "We have reason to hope," she said. "Scotland already passed a good Property Act a few years ago. England shall follow."

She sent a pawn to d5, a juicy little bait for his pawn on c4. Did she really think he'd fall for that?

"On the mountain, our revolutionaries are our factory girls," he said. "The amila. They remind me of your suffragists."

She slanted her head at an attentive angle. "How so?"

"They ignore convention and strike fear in the hearts of the elders."

"*Amila*," Lady Catriona repeated.

"Female factory worker," he translated.

"I admit I fail to see how performing manual labor in probably poor conditions equates to women's liberation," she said earnestly.

Her bluntness kept catching him off guard. How to improve working conditions in the factories was indeed one of the points of contention he had with his uncle.

"It's not straightforward," he conceded. "You need to take a long view."

He moved his bishop, Bg2, leaving her pawn well alone. She countered with her second knight to c6. Interesting. He ought to seriously focus on his next move.

"The girls used to care for the silkworms at home," he said instead. "It's always been important work—the mountain economy depends on the worm—but it was domestic work. Then the entire French industry fell into trouble some twenty years ago when their worms caught a blight; the French pack them too tightly, they don't care well for them. In the mountains, we keep them in a nice, ventilated room, and they are hand-fed mulberry leaves by the girls. When silk production moved from France to Mount Lebanon and our people began building their own factories, they asked the girls to come in, to process the cocoons, too."

He was talking with his hands now, but Lady Catriona was focused on him, riveted as though he were reading her her fortune. It could keep a man talking, such an interested face.

"So now girls board with girls from other regions, instead of only knowing home," he explained. "They exchange new ideas and earn a wage. They don't have banners or agendas, but it still changes what women do and how families function. These girls will raise the next generation one day. The hand on the cradle, as you say here."

"Are the girls allowed to keep their wages?" she wanted to know.

"Oh yes." He grinned. "They drive a hard bargain with factory owners, too—threatening to collectively go and work for the competition. It works like a charm."

He had memories of a fuming Khalo Jabbar feeling bested by a bunch of thirteen-year-old girls in braids. His uncle came from a generation where women were quiet and lowered their gaze to the floor in the presence of a man, but the amila were loud when they spoke with one voice. A late retribution on behalf of the first cohorts of girls in the factories in the sixties, Elias thought. With his keen eye for opportunity, Jabbar and other men of business had collected the many orphans after the civil war to harness their destitution for profit. The new generation, however, had both roots and teeth.

"Why don't the men go into the factories?" Lady Catriona asked.

He scoffed. "No man wants to work under a foreman. And they can't all be the foreman."

"I see. But what of the girls' honor?"

This sobered him. No father liked to send his daughter to work outside the home under a stranger.

"The problem is," he said, "that you can't eat it, the honor."

"No," she agreed, "you can't."

"So when hunger knocks on the door, the concept becomes . . . malleable."

He tapped his fingers on the table. Hunger was never far from Mount Lebanon these days, though it shouldn't be that way. Twenty years ago, the mountain economy had eagerly gripped the long arm of Western capitalism; the looms were running day and night and the volume of silk thread shipping out of Beirut had shot up exponentially. And yet many peasants found that their debt cycles and dependencies were getting worse. Meanwhile, as the truce endured, villages grew instead of being decimated by clashes. Prying enough food from the rocky slopes, from the dead lands, had always been a challenge even for the skilled, and the number of mouths to feed increased by the day. So the girls went into the factories, and the men went abroad. Steamers were waiting in the ports of Beirut and Sidon to carry away boatloads of sons and husbands, and sometimes independent women, pushed by limited opportunities and pulled by the promise of freedom and fortune. They left for Egypt or the United States, but also to Brazil, Cuba, the Caribbean. The roofs of Zahlé and Zgharta turned red with expensive Italian tiles and new mulberry groves spread over the mountains, courtesy of remittances.

When émigrés returned, with their pockets stuffed with money from work as lowly as peddling, they usually took a bride and left with her, but not before infecting more young men with travel fever. Khalo Jabbar began looking at his squadron of sons and nephews with a warning eye when these men came to the village. *If you leave, don't bother to return.* Jabbar needed them with their boots on the ground on Mount Lebanon, in the factories, in the Silk Office, and in the Church, to build his own little empire within the empire. Had there been parents to whom Elias could have sent his fortunes, he would have been very tempted to conquer exciting new horizons. As it was, his parents were gone, and their land was left. So he stayed.

His chess partner was watching him with her bottomless gaze, clearly waiting for more.

"And this"—he waved his hand—"is how the peasant girls bring revolution."

"You approve of it," she observed. "The revolution."

"I like a revolt, now and again," he replied. "Keeps a system healthy."

He liked playing chess with her quiet eyes on him and her scent in his nose, French lavender and delicate female skin. Unsurprisingly, he had no clue where to move his next piece.

She placed her hand next to the chessboard, notably closer to his side of the table.

"Conversing with you is very educational," she said in a low voice. She sounded a little breathy, too.

His gaze narrowed at her. She blinked, but she didn't look away. On the table, her hand trembled but stayed put. Her behavior was different today. Why *had* she come? He leaned forward slightly, as if having a closer look at her face, the gentle curve of her jaw, the pale rose of her lips, would reveal her secrets to him.

Above her prim lace collar, her throat moved visibly. "That was a compliment," she said. "I'm . . . enjoying myself."

It was his task to provide the compliments. She turned everything upside down.

"You enjoy being educated?" he probed.

Her lashes quivered. "Learning is my passion."

"I have many interests," he said. "It would be my pleasure to share knowledge with you, though I wonder what there is left to teach a polymath such as yourself."

"Plenty, I assure you."

"Such as?"

"Birding?" she suggested.

His muscles tensed as if hit by an electric current. A vision of wet skin and untamed hair flashed before his eyes and superimposed on the woman in front of him. Unwanted desire stirred in his groin. He tried to keep them separate, the naked goddess and the lady, to behave properly in her company. Now she had blurred the lines. Perhaps not consciously. Her soft lips had parted in shocked surprise, as if "birding" had grown wings and simply flown out of her mouth.

He tutted. "You don't need a chess clock to fairly keep to the time," he said, "but your other tactics are . . . questionable."

Her cheeks positively glowed with mortification. "What I meant is," she tried, in her cultured voice, "I understood you are an expert at it and I'm not . . ."

"I didn't think you were," he said soothingly.

Red-faced, she fussed with her pen.

"Perhaps milady would like to take a break," MacKenzie said in a marked Scottish brogue. "Take some fresh air."

The chaperone was looking from one to the other with her knitting needles angled menacingly toward Elias. She clearly wouldn't hesitate to make shish taouk, a kebab, out of him, right here in the Common Room.

"Fresh air is an excellent idea," Lady Catriona said. "It's a wee bit hot in here."

She grabbed her gloves, then searched the table for something until she remembered that her glasses were on top of her head. She put them back on her nose and stood, so he rose, too. She kept her eyes on his cravat.

"We should continue this game," she said, "another time. Good day, sir."

"Allah ma'ik," he said, gentle sarcasm in his smile. *God be with you.* He had never seen anyone look so stiff and yet so flustered at the same time.

She left with a very straight back and the plaid taut across her shoulders, leaving him standing there with his diffuse arousal. The other men in the room were glancing up from their books and card games when she passed, but there was little male appreciation in their eyes. Partly, this was understandable. A woman's allure was made of more than her feminine form and the silkiness of her skin; it came from her softer, coyer, more playful way of moving, speaking, and glancing, which conveyed a liquid adaptability to circumstance. The women who turned heads exuded these qualities like a scent, and it was obvious that none of the fellows here could smell it on Catriona. She didn't reflexively bend to please; that instinct seemed lost on her. A sudden swell of proprietary satisfaction heated Elias's chest from the inside. Poor fools, these men, they would never know. She was a vision under her clothes. Her blood ran fast beneath her skin. Playful eyes had their charm, but the full attention of her serious, intelligent gaze could give him the illusion of being the only man in existence. He had to be greedy or vain to like this as much as he did, feeling seen, having her to himself, but so everyone had their Achilles heel.

A few of the chaps who had played cards at the bar came over to study the chessboard.

"Catalan opening?" a young blond man with whiskers asked, steepling his fingers as he surveyed the field. He had tried to play with Elias the day before, but he had declined and played against himself—in case she showed up.

"Yes, Catalan opening," he confirmed.

"She countered well."

"Mm."

He recorded the few moves they had managed in his notebook. He had too many pawns at the front. He should launch his first knight next, putting pressure on her advancing knight and indirectly, her queen. If she was clever, she'd move her bishop, Bb4. Then what? A pawn, a3? In which case she could claim the first kill: his attacking knight with her bishop . . . he scratched the back of his head. He couldn't have beaten her in five moves, he realized, not while explaining the Levant's political economy. *Not even had you been fully focused*, whispered a little voice. He laughed under his breath. He rarely had to work for a win at chess these days. *Seduce her.* Seduce her without honorable intentions, without buying her gifts or using his body for her pleasure and protection . . . All he could use was his wit, and here it was, in black and white, that she wouldn't be easily impressed. She might, in fact, turn the table on him. The fiery energy of a challenge surged through him, compelling him to move his body. He packed up quickly. This game had only just begun. Something fundamental seemed to depend on him winning it now.

Birding. There was no rational explanation why she should have said that. It had just happened. Her darker side must have taken over and made choices.

"What's the haste," complained MacKenzie, who was huffing after her as she strode toward the arcade.

Remembering MacKenzie's limp the other day, Catriona immediately slowed—an effort, as she'd rather put distance between herself and the scene of her crime.

"Apologies," she said, and looked her companion up and down with some concern.

MacKenzie's frown eased. She smoothed the front of her jacket. "Milady," she said, and halted entirely.

Oh dear. That was her chaperone face. And tone.

"I'll say it here and now," MacKenzie began. "I feel it's not appropriate for you to play chess with the young man."

She balked. "It's chess. In a public place, and chaperoned."

"It's not the chess," MacKenzie said with a speaking glance. "It's whatever else is being played. The gentleman was rather flirtatious."

Catriona's brows pulled together. "We discussed the effect of international capitalism on women's position in society."

"That's right." MacKenzie nodded gravely. "Sweet music to your ears."

Her first instinct was to protest some more, but a lady must not protest too much. *Birding.* The simmering heat in Elias's eyes still warmed her face. It had sparked a tingling sensation in her lips, too, as if they had been keen on more scandal right away. She dropped her fingers from her mouth.

"I appreciate your counsel," she said to MacKenzie. "But there's nothing to worry about."

The first round of emotional inoculation hadn't quite gone to plan, but it hadn't been a full-fledged disaster, either. She had actually enjoyed herself when Elias had explained about the silk workers with an ease and level of detail that revealed a depth of knowledge. Briefly, her body had forgotten that it wanted his body. She had felt at ease, calm but intrigued, a very pleasant state of being. Things had gone wrong only when she had tried to be flirtatious, because he obviously outclassed her by miles on that terrain.

When she was back at her desk and had settled her nerves, she made a decision. She would try again rather than abandon the experiment. She would accept Mr. Khoury as her table partner at the Blackstone dinner, and she would dust off the red gown she kept in the wardrobe in St. John's for the rare occasions she cared to put herself on display. As long as she didn't try to be charming, the dinner would go brilliantly.

Chapter 10

How much time do I have left?" Lucie asked without looking up from the bridal magazine on her office desk.

"You have . . . four more hours," came the reply from the sofa, and the silky-smooth voice of her intended made her sneak a glance after all.

Tristan Ballentine was in shirtsleeves, stretched out on his back, his feet on the sofa's armrest. With his right hand, he was holding up a manuscript a hopeful writer had submitted to London Print; his left hand rested lightly on Boudicca the cat, who had rolled up in a perfect black circle on his stomach. A great place for a nap, as Lucie could attest—when one had time for such a thing. Hattie's Friendly Society dinner was tabled for five o'clock, but half of Lucie's correspondence was still unwritten. The Property Act would not amend itself. Yet her desk was cluttered with fabric samples. She pushed the magazine away.

"I should have recruited Catriona to help with the amendment lobbying instead of starting a new campaign," she said. "Shall we cancel the dinner?"

Squinting, Tristan turned his head toward her, and his hair

gleamed like freshly polished copper in the sunlight that fell through the dormer window. "What's the matter, darling?"

Even with a squint, he was beautiful. He would have no trouble looking bloody magnificent, whatever he wore at the altar.

"Where's a meddling mama when one needs to plan a wedding?" she groaned.

"Your mother offered," Tristan pointed out. "You refused any assistance."

"A mama other than mine," she amended. "I should gladly have someone else arrange this wedding and all its details, and that includes the dress."

A lazy smile spread over Tristan's face. "So many different shades of white," he said.

She scoffed. "I shall have a red one made, that much I know. I just can't decide whether scarlet, ruby, or crimson."

"Red," Tristan repeated, his usually blasé expression . . . disturbed? It was gone again in a flash, but it sobered her like a dash of cold water.

"You truly want to see me in white, don't you," she said slowly.

Tristan put the manuscript down on his chest. "You look grand in red."

Suspiciously diplomatic.

"I don't think I have ever heard of a groom so invested in the ceremonial details," she said. "The wedding might not take place at all if they reject our amendment yet again."

"They will pass it. I'm not that invested, by the way."

"White, like a chaste darling angel?" she prodded.

A shrug. "Rather like a sparkling ice queen."

"Sparkling."

"If you had it embroidered with diamonds. Or crystal if you insist on being economical."

She speared five fingers into her hair, dislodging her chignon.

"White and sparkling. Sir, for the past two years, you have sub-jected me to every carnal indecency imaginable and we are living in sin. We are doing sinful things in this office flat because we can't officially share a house. There's not a shred of innocence left between us, so decking myself out in the color of purity strikes me as ridiculous."

Tristan seemed too stunned to speak.

"I . . . subjected . . . you," he then drawled. "Subjected. Are you certain of that, princess?"

"I'm certain I never did anything of the sort before you barged into my life," she said, sounding smug.

His gaze darkened. "Mm-hm, and yet what we did last week was entirely your idea."

Heat flashed in her cheeks. "All right—"

"And the lovely young man in Italy—"

"That ought to confirm my choice of red," she said. "Scarlet sounds just right."

Tristan chuckled quietly. The motion woke Boudicca; irritated, she raised her head and noisily shook her black ears.

"Forgive us, Your Highness," Tristan told her, and stroked the cat from head to tail until she settled again. "Wear whatever you wish," he said to Lucie. "I'd wed you if you arrived in rags."

"Perhaps a compromise," she thought out loud. "Red and white. Stripes."

"Like a peppermint," Tristan told Boudicca. "How refreshing."

They both looked at her, man and cat, wearing twin expressions of polite disdain.

"Blimey." She buried her face in her hands.

Tristan put the manuscript and Boudicca onto the floor. He strolled over to her desk and pulled the pencil she still clutched from her fingers, leaned on the chair's armrests, and pressed his silky mouth to hers. He kissed through her muffled protest until she softened and sank into the upholstery. When he pulled back, her lips were glossy, and his irises had the golden hue of honey.

"Our lovemaking may be filthy, but our love is pure," he said, his voice turning tender. "Take that into account when you make your gown choices."

Longing washed over her in a warm wave. "You truly want this wedding," she whispered, "don't you."

"Yes. Your cold feet won't make a difference to me wanting this, I'm afraid."

"I don't have cold feet."

She would never understand how a man with such a quicksilver mind and a penchant for chaos mustered such infinite patience for her rigidity and stubbornness.

Tristan kneeled before her, his body effectively caging her in the chair.

"The wedding is a formality," he said, his eyes searching hers. "I look forward to what follows: calling you my wife. My viscountess. Seeing my ring on your finger, being officially entitled to give you everything, protect you with all that I have whenever you want it or need it . . . Sharing a home with you. Seeing you make use of the freedoms afforded to married women."

He had told her this before, but it felt good to hear it again. She played with a lock of his soft hair.

"And what freedoms they are," she said. "I can hardly wait to openly flirt with other men and to dance with anyone but my husband."

His gaze became heavy-lidded. "I pictured you moving around freely in the public arena for your work."

She caressed the shell of his ear with her thumb and rubbed the edges of the diamond stud that pierced the lobe. "Perhaps we're swapping minds after two years together."

"Oh, we are undoubtedly a terrible influence on each other. You

have become a little lecher, and I am an upstanding man of
business."

Her mouth fell open. "A lecher!"

"Yes, and it delights me to no end."

The mock efforts to push him away were unsuccessful; he just
grinned and leaned closer. She let him because he delighted her,
too. He had taken London Print to new heights with good decision
making. He was making good decisions in the House of Lords,
too. And he loved her and the cat so very well. She pressed back
into the upholstery. "I want it to be perfect," she blurted. "This will
be the only wedding I'll ever have . . . I want us to remain perfect
afterward, too."

Tristan's expression became intent. He cupped her face in his big
hand. "I want to take another twenty minutes out of your schedule."

"Oh."

He lowered his head and his lips brushed against her cheek.

"I want to do a sinful thing with you in this office flat," he
whispered, close to her ear. His other hand was under her skirt,
palming up her silk stocking to the sensitive spot at the back of her
knee. "I want to subject you to a few carnal indecencies in this
chair."

"But—"

His fingers circled over the soft inside of her thigh.

"But the cat . . . oh . . ."

A while later, they were on the sofa, she stretched out on top of
him, her cheek against his bare chest.

"It's never just *twenty minutes*," she said, her sated voice discred-
iting the complaint.

He caressed her neck, touching lightly with his fingertips. "I
love you," he said.

The corners of her eyes were damp with sudden emotion. She
kissed the hard ridge of his collarbone. "And I love you. So very
much."

"That's settled, then." His stomach growled. "Let's not cancel the dinner," he added.

"We can't," she agreed. "Hattie would be so cross." She raised her head. "Before I forget: she has invited a gentleman from abroad. He has no connections here, so she asked us to be nice and make conversation with him."

"I can be nice," Tristan said, and he surveyed her flushed face and rumpled hair.

"Hattie has designs on him," Lucie said. "I think she'd like to match him with Catriona."

Tristan made an amused sound. "That's silly. Lady Catriona doesn't want a man."

"Neither did I, yet look at us now."

He looked, very thoroughly, so she leapt off him as if he were an electric wire. She collected her clothes, aware of his eyes on her behind whenever she bent over.

"Lord and Lady Lech, that's what I shall put on the wedding invitations," she muttered, while he lay there looking smug and Boudicca came back out from under the desk.

Chapter 11

⟳⟳⟳

Elias spent the hours before the Belgravia dinner on his stone balcony in St. John's. A breeze carried the smoke of his cigarette away. To the sounds of the lawn croquet below, he read a letter from Nassim. His cousin was still offended about the vagueness of Elias's heist plans and had put himself to work on the matter while in London:

> *I learned the name of a man here who knows people,* he wrote. *Should the cattle thief prove incorrigible, tell me. Once we have extracted the oxen, we use our cargo route from the port here to return them to their proper stable. Of course, it will cost a lot but do not worry, we'll negotiate.*

Reckless Nassim. Enough scholars here at Oxford could read Arabic, and his attempt at an encryption was awful.

> *As for the tartan blankets you have gifted me, they are fine for me but don't give them to the girls and Tayta unless you want them to throw a shoe at you. The colors are nice and bright but the fabric, this wool, is "ruff as a badger's arse" as the British would say, rather harsh on the skin. I suggest you take a day and go to London's Savile Row and spend a lot of money on cashmere for the women. Also,*

stock up on shortbread in these pretty tin boxes—purchase them at
Liberty, not Harrods. It pains and surprises me but I'm beginning
to think you know nothing about women at all . . .

Elias exhaled smoke from his nose. Nassim meant well but had
no clue. He had acquired the woolly blankets in the Shieldaig village because cousin Layal would find them quaint. She *liked* quaint
and he knew she liked tartan because she had told him so. She'd
like these blankets because they said he had paid attention to her
preferences. He had learned this art of mindful gift-giving from
Francine, who might or might not be still in Lyon. He held the
corner of Nassim's letter against the glowing tip of his cigarette and
wondered what type of gift Lady Catriona would enjoy. He had
spent the day at the Ashmolean, trying to match the jumbled pieces
in the bull room to his inventory list, but his mind had kept straying. Catriona. In the span of a week, he had seen her brave like a
goddess, blush like a wallflower, leap from a carriage like a mindless rabbit, and play chess rather too well. What gifts would suit
such a woman? The letter in his hand curled and went up in a
single flame. He watched the potentially incriminating lines singe
away until they were safe, black flakes of ash.

A diffuse restlessness hummed in his body as he dressed himself for the Blackstone dinner. He couldn't shake a sense of caution
about accepting the invitation. There were good reasons for attending: one, to advance the charm offensive on Lady Catriona, and
two, every dinner was a potential gold mine for new business acquaintances. What gave him pause was that according to his wife,
Mr. Blackstone had once dealt in antiques, and the circle of such
dealers in Europe was small enough for people to know of one another. Elias had never heard the name Blackstone during his in-
volvements, and since he was at best an incidental actor in the dark
web on the continent, there was no pressing reason to avoid the
man. And yet, some instinct warned him to step carefully tonight.

———

He should have listened to his gut feeling. Too late now; he was already in Blackstone's richly decorated reception room, shaking hands with the man. While the name Blackstone had never come to his attention in artifact circles, there had been talk of "the scarred Scotsman." His host had greeted him with a faint but undeniable Scottish accent. A scar bisected Blackstone's upper lip and his nose had been broken at some point. Elias stared at the bump on the man's nasal bridge a bit too intently while memory fragments, deemed irrelevant at the time, resurfaced and clicked into place.

The Scotsman's dark brow rose. "Would you care for some refreshments, Mr. Khoury?"

He motioned a waiter with a champagne tray closer and picked up two glasses. "Mrs. Blackstone is sorting out some issue with the cook," he told Elias. "She's very pleased that you are joining us at such short notice."

"My pleasure," Elias said, already composed again. He had heard of Blackstone. Blackstone wouldn't have heard of him.

There were perhaps thirty people in the reception room. A musical quartet played soft classical tunes in one corner, and the sweet fragrance of hothouse roses wafted over from antique vases. A painting depicting the abduction of Persephone took up the wall above the fireplace and presided over a notably animated group of guests. The blond Lady Lucinda was part of the group, but a woman in blue with severe hair was nowhere in sight. He imagined Catriona's face, should she find out about his past dealings thanks to Blackstone tonight, and an emotion tightened his chest. It felt suspiciously like guilt. He had nothing to feel guilty about. Wester Ross had absconded to sell his land before Elias could disclose his perfectly honorable intentions to him.

"The champagne is from the Montagne de Reims," Mr. Black-stone said, his pronunciation terrible. "Do you reside in France by any chance, Mr. Khoury?"

Elias met the sharp gray gaze over the rim of his glass. "No. I'm based in Beirut."

"It's a booming city, I understand."

"It is."

"Mrs. Blackstone says you're an expert on artifacts?"

"She's too gracious," Elias replied. "I understand you deal in antiques?"

Blackstone's face remained a mask. "Not in years. My wife showed me the error of my ways over a pair of Han vases. My interest is in modern British paintings now. You're welcome to visit my gallery in Chelsea."

"I look forward to it."

"Good, good. Ah, there she is."

Mrs. Blackstone's curly red head had appeared at the door. Next to her was Catriona. Elias lowered his champagne goblet before it met his lips. She wore red. A deep, rich shade of claret that appeared almost black. The velvet hugged her figure as seamlessly as though she had been poured into the fabric. A stiff little collar closed snugly around her neck, but the bodice had a cutout that exposed a generous triangle of smooth skin from the hollow of her throat to the tops of her breasts. Heat licked over the surface of his chest. Their eyes met in a flash of raw appraisal, and her composed posture quavered.

Mrs. Blackstone tugged her toward the men, chattering about a kerfuffle in the kitchen.

"Do have another drink or two, and some fruit," she urged Elias, a hand on his sleeve. "Goodness, at this rate we'll all be sozzled before the first course." She touched her husband's arm. "Dear, a word?"

The pair moved over to the sideboard.

Elias turned to Catriona just as she faced him, and his shoulders

loomed over hers. He couldn't bring himself to step back. Her dark
hair was gathered up in a pile of soft ringlets, and a curl had come
loose and grazed her left cheekbone. The flower-scented air suddenly felt heavy in his lungs. Her breasts were rising and falling
rather rapidly against the velvety neckline, too. He dragged his gaze
up again and was met with another surprise.

"Golden glasses," he said huskily.

She touched a fingertip to the delicate earpiece. "Indeed," she
said primly, but her chest turned pink. "Shall we join the others?"
she asked, her gloved hands moving nervously over the front of
her gown. The group near the fireplace was perusing them with
not-so-covert glances.

"Certainly." He offered his arm.

She hesitated before placing her hand on him. It settled on his
arm light as a bird, but her touch resonated through his body, distracting him from the introductions.

"Have you written down your observations from the drill?" Lady
Lucinda asked him, her clear gray eyes moving over him with
friendly interest. She stood improperly close to her fiancé, Lord
Ballentine, a tall, red-haired viscount who exuded deviance despite
his perfectly polished appearance. An Irishwoman with cropped
curls, Miss Byrne, kept her arm linked with an angelic-looking
blonde—Miss Patterson—and she made good-natured complaints
about the delay of the food. The Duchess of Montgomery, a remarkably beautiful woman who appeared to be unaccompanied,
wanted to know more about his research, what he had read at Cambridge. He told her he had read archaeology and ancient history.

The duchess's green eyes lit with interest. "You studied under
Professor Babington, then."

"I did," he confirmed. "He's a friend of Professor Pappas, an
acquaintance of mine in Beirut."

Catriona had taken her place in the circle and added nothing to
the conversation now that she had introduced him. She could have

been radiant, with her red gown and lustrous black curls. Women commanded a room with less. Yet her presence was barely felt. She had folded herself up as tightly as a jasmine blossom after sunrise.

"I once had a fascination with Greek pottery," the duchess said, and a private smile tugged at her lips. "Is pottery your field of interest?"

It wasn't. Cambridge had been a chance opportunity entirely. He had been sent to Britain with Nassim to establish the family office at Manchester Port instead of causing trouble on the mountain. Once in Manchester, he had soon realized that if his family wished to do business with the British, he had to associate with the upper classes. Oxbridge seemed like an effective inroad into otherwise inaccessible circles, because neither his family's wealth nor his noble pedigree rolled out a red carpet for him on this island. An adolescence spent assisting the French archaeologists in Jbeil as a translator and his connection to Professor Pappas had allowed him to enroll under Babington's tutelage. For a time, shared lodgings and lectures were a good enough equalizer for young gentlemen from different backgrounds. He had been invited to grand homes where he had learned more about English mannerisms and values during debauched costume parties than a cultural handbook could have ever taught him. Too soon, Uncle Jabbar had found out that he had abandoned post without permission, and halfway through the second year, Elias had found himself in the office in Lyon.

"We shall have hors d'oeuvres in a moment," Mrs. Blackstone announced. She had arrived with two fair-haired young gentlemen, one on each arm. With rosy cheeks and high foreheads, the chaps were precisely the type of company Elias had kept at Cambridge. Their confident bearing implied that they were well-acquainted with everyone in the group.

"May I introduce Mr. Tomlinson and Lord Palmer," Mrs. Blackstone said to him. "Mr. Khoury is our guest of honor from Mount Lebanon."

Lord Palmer's finely drawn face brightened. "From Mount Lebanon," he exclaimed, making heads turn in their direction. "An ally from distant lands. To your health."

He raised his goblet. Judging by his shiny eyes, he had already toasted to enough people's health this evening to cure many ailments in England.

Elias tipped his glass toward his. "And to yours. As it is, London is allied to the other party."

Palmer swallowed his drink and went red in the face. "Oh dear," he said. "I appear to have stuck my foot in."

British gentlemen, as a rule, avoided knowingly causing offense, so Elias took none. In his experience, though, it made for great awkwardness later should a conversation continue under such false assumptions. When the British had seen the Maronites ally with the French for more leverage under Ottoman rule, they had reflexively allied with the other mountain community, the Druze. Whenever Paris had a foothold in any one region, London had to have one there, too. Europe's power balance was a precarious thing. They stopped at nothing to maintain it, especially not where the gateway to India was concerned.

"You're with the French, then," said the other young man, Mr. Tomlinson.

"I'm with the mountain," Elias replied, not suppressing his frown.

"Either way, I understand everyone is friendly now," Lord Palmer said. "You seem a good sport. It's never personal anyway, is it? The trouble is, we can't just let France have it all; the froggies would be hopping all over the region like a plague the moment the Ottomans are all a-cock. And mark me, they will be a-cock."

His friend Tomlinson raised an eyebrow at him.

Palmer glanced around the circle. "What. They are hemorrhaging territories. Whoops, there went the Balkans."

"Palmer, don't be a bore," drawled Lord Ballentine.

"You can't say there are ladies present," Palmer replied, "as every lady present here is keener and more knowledgeable on politics than I shall ever be."

"My brother-in-law had business in the Levant," Tomlinson said. "It's easy to become confused—lots of higgledy-piggledy politics there. Shouldn't trouble us here on this fine evening."

"Not at all," Palmer said generously. "We are well familiar with such troubles here ourselves in any case, nothing to be shy about."

Mrs. Blackstone wrinkled her nose. "Such troubles? What troubles can you mean?"

"Don't encourage him," said the Irishwoman, Aoife Byrne. The blond lady next to her patted her hand.

"King Henry the Eighth had a bad habit of cutting things off, including the pope," Palmer said with a flick of his long fingers. "It caused us a few centuries of religious wars."

Elias finished his champagne, thinking what a long evening this was going to be, when Catriona spoke up.

"You surprise me, Lord Palmer," she said, her tone rather cool, and there was a slight edging away in the circle, which normally followed the entry of someone grand. "Do you truly believe that Henry the Eighth split from Rome for religious reasons?"

Tomlinson blanched. "Uh-oh," he said. "I know that voice. I know that expression." He clapped his friend on the shoulder. "Sorry, old boy. You are about to feel stupid."

Palmer's neck turned blotchy. "Is it too late to take back what I said and to claim the opposite?"

"Henry the Eighth created his own church to consolidate his power and to refill his coffers with former monastic lands," Catriona said. "He was playing perfectly rational power politics. I should think the same applies to most all conflicts elsewhere."

Lord Ballentine stopped a waiter. "Brandy, for everyone," he ordered.

"Isn't everything about power in the end," Mrs. Blackstone suggested.

"Absolutely," Lady Lucinda agreed.

"With all due respect," Palmer said to Catriona, thus announcing he was about to make a patronizing statement, "when Bloody
Mary reigned; when they shuffled royals back and forth during the
reign of Queen Anne; when the Jacobites rallied to return a Catholic prince to the throne two hundred years after the fact, were they
not motivated by a higher sentiment?" He raised his gaze toward
the ceiling with some reverence.

"Leaders wage war over power," Catriona said, unmoved. "The
fairy tales they spin to rally the common soldier is of course quite
another matter."

She fixated on Palmer through her gold-rimmed glasses, but
everyone was looking at her. She stood tall and unmissable. This
was her element; she was unfurling, one quick petal at a time, and
a wiser man in Palmer's position would beat a retreat before she was
in full bloom. *Breathtaking* was the word, Elias thought.

The lord promptly turned to him. "Mr. Khoury," he said in a
conspiring tone, "didn't your brethren form an alliance with the
Holy See, around the time when King Henry went on a stampede?"

Now everyone was looking at Elias. This was the Campbell
dining table all over again; where Catriona went, parlors seemed to
turn into coffeehouses and political circles.

"Well," he said. "At the time, the pope was the strongest ally we
could secure to keep the Ottoman Turks out of our business."

"Sounds rational enough to me," Tomlinson remarked.

"Incidentally, it was a Druze prince who forged this connection
for us," Elias added. "His name was Fakhr al-Din."

"Astonishing," said Palmer. "Here I thought all that trouble in
the sixties was about your people and their people not standing
each other."

Elias looked him in the eyes. Lord Palmer raised his empty
goblet to his lips.

"Our communities used to live well together, often in the same villages," Elias said softly. "The alliances we had are old. They made us stronger against the Mamelukes, and later against the Turks when needed."

"I daresay I had no clue," Palmer said, sounding apologetic. "I'm merely a humble reader of newspapers, not a diplomat. Forgive my ignorance."

Not even the diplomats had a clue what was happening on the ground, and they did not have to, as their influence was entirely divorced from their competency. Catriona's blue eyes moved over him warily; something must have shown on his face. He could have just left it at that. Had Catriona not been in the room, he probably would have. He looked at Palmer. "I understand that English maps depict the . . . higgledy-piggledy politics of our region along sectarian lines," he said. "As such, you can't tell that different mountain communities once shared villages and alliances."

The waiter arrived with the ordered brandy tray, and several hands reached out to grab fresh drinks.

"Are you suggesting we have the wrong map?" Lady Lucinda asked, looking genuinely interested.

"I suggest your map doesn't tell the whole story. But it looks clear and simple, so there's that." It also made people in the Near East look like creed-addled fools.

Palmer opened his mouth as if to make another quip but then he thought better of it.

"Would you tell us the whole story, Mr. Khoury?" Mrs. Blackstone asked. "If you please."

Nods all around.

He couldn't. He didn't even know where to begin, how far back in time to go. For the last thirteen hundred years, Maronite alliances had shifted like quicksilver depending on what would best preserve their autonomy under the empire of the day: Byzantines, Muslim Arabs, crusaders, Mamelukes, or Ottoman Turks, they all had been friend as well as foe at different points, well, all except the Mamelukes, who had been hell-bent on eliminating mountain dwellers of all creeds rather than just taxing them. Now, if the pope was key to maintaining self-rule, yes, one would try to win him as an ally. However, had the Emperor of China proven more effective, Elias reckoned the local chiefs would have tried to make a deal with him.

Catriona had quietly receded back into the circle, but Elias felt her attention on his very skin, invisible yet physical like the warmth of the sun on one's face.

"I'm afraid I can't tell you the story of the maps," Elias said. "We didn't draw them; they were drawn up in the forties by an Austrian prince and a British diplomat. I know it was their solution for our peasant revolt, but it was a revolt against ruling elites of all denominations, so how would drawing new borders and shuffling us around depending on creed solve an economic issue? It did the opposite, I think, hence the 'trouble' in the sixties, but the maps stuck. *C'est tout.*"

The silence in the circle assumed a different quality. Ice clinked against the rim of a glass. Lady Catriona was looking at him with a frozen face, as though she had seen a ghost. Damn.

"Quite the story," Tomlinson said, nodding. "About the maps."

"The story is called divide and conquer," Lord Ballentine remarked. His tone was smooth but a cynical glint stirred in his eyes.

"A true and tested tale since the Romans, I'm afraid," said the beautiful duchess.

"I'll spoil the ending for you," Ballentine said to Palmer. "Usually, it is a takeover by a rational third party."

"I say."

Elias looked at the viscount more closely. "I believe the prime minister at the time did say that we were in need of a 'vigorous hand and a powerful head.'"

"It never ceases to enrage me," said Lady Lucinda, gesturing with her glass in hand. "The whole 'not rational enough to manage their own affairs' trick."

"Goodness," said Mrs. Blackstone. "It enrages women everywhere."

"That's how it goes," said her friend. "First, you deny someone the capacity for rational thought, then you establish control over them with a clear conscience."

"Sweet bulldog," said Lord Palmer. "Let me grab one of those hors d'oeuvres. Ladies, as always, a pleasure." He left, carefully balancing his strides as if in a daze.

Mrs. Blackstone thanked Elias for sharing his perspective, then she seemed to switch from political activist back to her role as hostess, a little sheepishly, and tried to steer the conversation to a lighter topic. Catriona was studying the pattern of the rug. Elias took a few deep breaths through his nose. He had never been so careless with his opinions on a stranger's territory before. She was doing something to him, and he couldn't say he liked it.

During dinner, it was as though there were a pane of glass between their chairs. Her conversation was so polite it almost felt insulting. From the end of the table, Mr. Blackstone's penetrating gray gaze raked over him in irritating intervals.

When the dinner concluded, Mrs. Blackstone issued them into the drawing room for some "fun and games." Catriona seemed part of the group moving toward the parlor, but she never arrived in the room.

"She loathes games," Mrs. Blackstone told him in passing with a knowing glance. "She's in a nook somewhere, reading a book."

He pretended to not know why this should be of relevance to him. Playing with him once didn't mean she wanted an encore. He couldn't shake the feeling, however, that he had caused her change of mood with his debate in the reception room. After two rounds of some strange posh game, he went in search of her.

Chapter 12

She drank the first glass of Scotch too fast. A lulling warmth spread through her limbs, so she poured another. *First you take a drink, then the drink takes a drink*, she thought darkly. *Then, the drink takes you.* She was nestled deep in the armchair and about to finish her not-so-wee second dram when the door to Blackstone's library opened.

"Lady Catriona."

A zing of excitement hit her bloodstream, more potent than the Scotch. His face was cast in shadow but she recognized the outline of his solid torso and his curls, backlit by the light in the corridor. She carefully put her tumbler down on the side table.

"Mr. Khoury. Are you lost?"

There was a brief, amused pause.

"As it is," he then said, "I have just found what I was looking for."

Her belly swooped as though she were descending on a swing.

The posture of his silhouette looked rather formal. "Why aren't you joining the games?"

"What are they playing?"

"When I left, it was Squeak, Piggy, Squeak."

"Such fun." She would need another drink or five to enjoy that.

"Forgive my directness," he said at last, "but I had the impression that I offended you in the reception room earlier."

They were conversing across a large room.

"Please, do come in," she said.

He stilled. A gentleman did not spend time alone with a lady, behind closed doors.

"The door has a lock," she added.

He considered it. She picked up her tumbler and indulged in another hot mouthful of vintage Springbank.

He entered and closed the door. Darkness fell. The lock snicked shut, and measured footfalls approached while her eyes readjusted to the dim light of the gas lamp on the nearby drinks cabinet. The hollow feeling in her belly spread up, between her ribs, a feeling close to nausea except it was thrilling.

Elias halted behind the Chesterfield sofa opposite her armchair, effectively keeping a barrier between them. He arched his brows at the glass in her hand.

"Whisky?"

"Are you terribly shocked?"

"Do I appear shocked to you?"

She studied him. The sooty glow of the lamp threw the sculpted angles of his face into somber relief. His charming disposition, usually so close to the surface, had given way to something impenetrable. Perhaps there was a trace of gentle mockery.

"I was wondering," she said, "when you go birding, do you snare the birds?"

He huffed, surprised. "Not usually, no. I observe."

"That's kind." She nodded at the bottle on the table. "May I offer you a dram?"

He declined.

"You prefer arak," she guessed. The drink of choice in his corner of the world.

A half smile. "I do. Though I enjoy a Scotch, too, now and again."

Just not with her, alone, in the dark. She understood. His unhurried demeanor on the brink of potential scandal made her feel as hot as the liquor; it simmered in her throat, her thighs, the tips of her toes.

"I suppose given the choice between sucking on a piece of peat or a piece of sweet anise, any right-minded person would choose the anise, and hence the arak," she mused. She held up her empty tumbler. "Scotch, I understand, is an acquired taste."

His voice deepened when he said: "Many of the best things are."

"Hm. Why do you think that is?"

"It takes a certain maturity to appreciate complexity."

The air seemed to swelter over her skin. Outside the faint circle of light around them, surroundings melted into the night.

"I wasn't offended earlier," she finally said, softly. "Not in the slightest."

Elias's lips relaxed into their usual fullness. "I misread, then."

He hadn't misread anything. Watching him speak in the reception room had been devastating. She hadn't realized how much she fancied him until she had felt hidden hopes shatter inside her chest. Even numbed by Scotch, she still felt the sting of the cuts. She had misread *him*—he was nothing like the crushes of her past. He wasn't just layers of sunshine. He knew pain, and he articulated it. Behind his easy smile lay the vast landscape of a serious, inquisitive disposition, and an urge had gripped her to crawl into him to see . . . everything. She suspected he could follow into the black depths of the human mind but withdraw again before he became lost. A unicorn, light and dark, humorous yet sincere. Sadly, he had spelled out in brutal clarity how much divided them: nothing short of the current world order. Did he loathe being here? Did he loathe her?

Any moment now, he would turn around and leave the library. In a few weeks, he would leave the country and she would never know him. She would never know *what if.* A twinge of panic stung behind her ribs.

Elias stepped around the sofa. "Would you accompany me back to the drawing room?"

She could do that. Or she could drink more and fall asleep in the armchair, head spinning.

"Very well," she said, and came to her feet slowly. She had poured her drink rather too generously.

He was by her side. "Allow me."

When she placed her fingers onto his arm, his gaze flicked over her and briefly lingered where her red dress molded snugly over the swell of her breasts. Her exposed skin prickled in response. He had already averted his eyes again, his jaw set in a tight line. Beneath the fine wool of his sleeve, his muscles were hard under her palm. She let him guide her into the dark part of the room, holding on unseeing, delaying him with small, slow steps. Her heart beat a painful, heavy rhythm: *Say something, say something. Anything.*

At the door, he purposefully found lock and key in the shadows. She slid her hand down his arm until her palm was flat against the cool wood of the door. She was dizzy with daring.

Elias kept looking straight ahead. He didn't seem amused.

"We could stay awhile," she said thickly.

His hand was still on the doorknob, so close to hers that her little finger felt the warmth of his.

"We can't," he said. His voice was rough.

He didn't withdraw his hand.

"I should like to talk," she said.

He faced her with a sardonic glitter in his eyes. "Talk, my lady?"

He had leaned in and his stirring scent enveloped her, rich cologne and cotton warmed by his body.

"Yes," she choked.

On the door, he spread his fingers, just a fraction. Enough for the tip of his little finger to touch the side of hers. Her breathing hitched. All her attention pooled in the spot of sensitive skin heating against his.

"I'm listening," he murmured.

A soft roar filled her head. *I'm drawn to you when I shouldn't be. What is in your heart? Do you ever think of us?*

"When we first met, at the loch," she said. "Did you like what you saw?"

Silence.

Still, she felt it, how something in him shifted. It felt elemental, like a sudden calm in the air, like a lull in the waves crashing against a shore.

Heart hammering, she lifted her gaze to his. His eyes were dark, and he held her gaze steadily. Then he lowered his head. A paralyzing heat flooded her.

His cheek was next to hers, and his warm breath fanned intimately over the side of her neck.

"More interestingly," he whispered against her ear, "did you like that I was watching?"

A pulse began to throb between her legs.

She turned her face toward his, slowly, slowly.

"I wanted to hit you with my book," she breathed, her lips an inch from his mouth.

A glint of teeth as he smiled. "Good."

He let his thigh press casually against the front of her skirt.

Her lips parted on a gasp.

"When I first saw you," he said, "I thought you were a goddess. I would have worshipped you, on my knees."

His voice came from a distance. The luscious pressure of his leg between hers heated her blood, turned her sweet and liquid like melting sugar. Their noses were almost touching; they were breathing each other's breaths, liking it, and shivering from the significance of it. They fit. Intimacy would be instinctual, their hands, bodies, lips, sliding and locking together smoothly even in mindless erotic urgency . . . Elias made a low sound in his throat. She registered it almost after the fact, when the fleeting, soft contact had already left her lips again, that he had kissed her on the mouth. He faced the door, his chest rising and falling as if he had exerted himself.

She touched her lips.

"We must leave now," Elias said.

He kissed me. We have kissed.

"Yes," she said, sounding a little faint. "I shall go ahead."

She was in the corridor when Elias grabbed her by the wrist. His eyes were stark in his face, a turbulent, liquid green-blue, and it looked as though he was on the verge of announcing something of great importance.

He gave a small shake. "I hold you in high regard," he said, low and urgent, "we can't—"

She pulled her arm from his clasp. "I understand." In truth, her head was empty. The familiar lethargy following the explosion of her senses was washing over her, and it would take a day to arrive at a conclusion about what had just happened. "Let's join the fun and games, shall we."

In the drawing room, she drank sherry with her friends and paid him no attention, but her carefree performance was for him— *Look, I can be fun!* And the kiss was nothing! She won the pantomime contest for her group, and when she feigned excitement and cheered, conscious of Elias watching her with hooded eyes, she thought that her immunization experiment had careened out of control like Frankenstein's monster.

She woke the next morning in one of Blackstone's guest rooms. The sunlight streaming through the chintz curtains was thick and golden, announcing noon. She sat on the edge of the mattress, her head drooping as if too heavy for the neck while she took stock of last night's consequences. Belly: queasy. Head: achy. Sensibilities: deceased. At her core hovered a secret glow, a small ball of light where her soul kept his kiss. Oh God, they had kissed. She buried her face in her hands. It would be easy to blame the Scotch for the escapade, but the Scotch only peeled back the thin veneer of civility which normally concealed her darker side. *I would have worshipped you, on my knees.* Her body turned weak and pink and she sank back into the sheets. She kept touching her mouth. How did one return to normal after such a thing? To date, everyone she had kissed, she had never seen again soon after. But Elias was very much around. What was worse, seeing him again, or not seeing him again?

To her relief and great disappointment, Elias wasn't among the guests milling around the late breakfast buffet.

"He left after we closed the drawing room," Hattie told her while Catriona spooned scrambled eggs onto her plate. "He said he had taken a hotel room near Victoria Station to catch the first train back to Oxford."

"Mr. Khoury is free to go where he pleases."

"Indeed," Hattie said, sounding . . . somewhat shifty.

Catriona lowered the spoon warily. "Is anything the matter?"

"Actually." Hattie leaned closer. "There is something Mr. Blackstone should like to bring to your attention."

Premonition fell over Catriona like a shadow and took all warmth from her body.

"Is it about Mr. Khoury?"

Hattie nodded.

Last night's whisky churned in her stomach. She put down her plate. "Take me to Blackstone."

"I meant to tell you after you had eaten," Hattie said mournfully.

They should have told her last night before the intoxicating feel of Elias's body had become irrevocably imprinted on hers.

Blackstone met them in a quaint, linden-green reading parlor. Impossibly, he looked more brooding than usual.

"Last night, I had a cable sent to an old acquaintance in France," he told her. He pulled a yellow paper slip from his jacket pocket— a telegram. Catriona felt a curdle of fear. Blackstone's "old acquaintances" were usually synonymous with his unsavory past.

"When Mr. Khoury introduced himself," Blackstone went on, "I thought I had heard his name once before, in the context of an incident involving some artifacts. It's unusual to my ears so it's not a name I'd forget. I sent a note to see if there was anything to my suspicions. An hour ago, I received a reply."

He held up the telegram.

"What has he done?" she asked quietly.

Hattie took her hand; her soft fingers felt hot against Catriona's cold skin. "There is no concrete proof," she said, "but several years ago, a Mr. Khoury was involved in the theft of some antique jewels."

"Jewels?"

"From a French count's private collection," Blackstone added.

"You wrote to the count?"

Blackstone shook his head. "I'm not acquainted with him, and I doubt he'd make the connection between Mr. Khoury and the theft; it was rumors in the, erm, unofficial networks; people had caught wind that there might be a new mole in town, from the east. It was a hefty theft, so the news of it reached London."

A mole. Someone who pretended to be one thing when he was quite another. Someone who inveigled himself skillfully with his target until he had what he wanted. Deep inside her chest, the bright glow sparked by their kiss went dark. The corners of her mouth had turned down as the pain stabbed through her, and she became aware of it. She turned her face away as she struggled to right her expression.

"It could have been another Khoury," she said mechanically. "It's a common name in his region."

A memory flashed, of Elias looking not at all scholarly as he prowled along a narrow, smoky corridor in a Glasgow inn, priming to take on three men at once. Swallowing hurt. She had known something had been off about him.

"It wouldn't have been proper to detain him without proof," Blackstone said and gave an apologetic shrug, "and he had left before I received this reply."

"Oh, detaining him would have been an inexcusable affront," Catriona agreed. She turned to the door.

Hattie grabbed her arm. "What do you mean to do?"

Catriona looked from her to Blackstone. "He's in Oxford right now. Alone. With access to . . . everything." A cold energy rushed through her. "I must go at once."

"Not on your own, you mustn't," Hattie said with an anxious frown, her grip tightening.

Blackstone quite agreed. "I'll accompany you."

"How kind, but you still have a house full of guests."

In the end, it was agreed that Carson, Hattie's personal protection officer, would accompany Catriona back to Oxford.

She barely registered the train ride. The whispers wouldn't stop: this was why Elias had kissed her, to burrow closer, as a mole would. She literally held a key to the Ashmolean. It was why he had asked her to play chess. She remembered her breathless arousal when his thigh had been notched between hers and she wanted to crawl out of her skin. *Did you like that I was watching . . .* Cruel creature. Granted, a man was innocent until proven guilty. Accosting him with a protection officer would be irreparably insulting in case he was innocent. She must keep a cool head; she would, she always did when in a crisis.

At the Ashmolean, the artifact room looked untouched, but the clerk's ledger showed that Elias had signed in from ten o'clock until noon. Was Elias Khoury even his true name? Or was it a lie, like his kiss?

She went to the St. John's porter's lodge, Carson in tow, keeping very calm. Porter Clive staffed the desk and gave out the spare key to Elias's lodgings without hesitation when she requested it. The vein in her neck drummed while climbing the narrow stairs to his flat.

"In the utterly unlikely event that you hear a commotion, please be quick," she instructed Carson when they reached the door. "For now, please stand down."

Carson was not pleased with this.

Undeterred, she knocked. "Mr. Khoury?"

Silence.

She knocked again and when no one answered, she turned the doorknob and found it unlocked. The flat's reception room was empty. However, the chessboard was on the table, and Elias's hat and coat hung on the garderobe. At least he had not yet absconded back to Beirut with lord-knows-what in his luggage. Perhaps he had gone down to the kitchens.

She turned back to Carson. "Please stand guard at the landing. If you hear someone approach, fetch me."

She had to be quick. On tiptoes, she slipped past Elias's collection of food jars and through his open bedroom door. Again the room felt abandoned. However, his now all-too-familiar scent hung over the bed. Briefly, misery twisted in her belly, an irrational sense of loss. *Nothing would have ever come from it anyway.* She pulled out the drawers of his dresser. Neatly folded clothes. She shook out the book he kept on the nightstand—no hidden compartments. She would know what she was looking for when she found it. Nothing under his pillows. He could be returning up the stairs this moment, his long strides quickly eating up the length of the corridor . . . Under the bed was a valise. It scraped across the floorboards when she dragged it out, and her skin prickled with alarm. With trembling fingers, she unlatched the lid. A gasp escaped her as her eye caught the menacing sheen of metal—a powerful revolver, a knife, and a sheathed scimitar lay side by side on tartan blankets. Heart pounding, she shut the lid and made to push the valise back under the bed. She froze. A sound had come from the antechamber. She swallowed her scream when the door was yanked open and Elias loomed in the doorsill, his handsome face dark like a thundercloud.

She stared up at him, her right arm still stuck under the bed like a naughty paw in a jar of sweets. Recognition flashed in his eyes, then turned to bewilderment.

"What are you doing?" he demanded. His voice was cold, how disturbing that he could sound so icy.

Her own voice failed her.

He took a step toward her, and she shot to her feet.

Chapter 13

⸻❧⸻

Lady Catriona scrambled upright, a hand stretched out toward him as if to ward off a wild creature. It briefly stopped him in his tracks.

"What are you doing here?" he repeated, his tone a little calmer. Her face was frozen, like a doll's. She had been snooping, no doubt about it.

She backed away, into the reception room, and he followed, matching her step by step.

"I should like to ask you the same thing," she said, her arm still up. "What are you doing here, Mr. Khoury?"

She placed an odd emphasis on his name, drew it out as if it were a question. The penny dropped then. He could practically hear the Scottish burr—*Are ye based in France, by any chance?* The room suddenly seemed very bright. The outline of her body in her gray dress was unnaturally clear, as if someone had cut her out from an illustration with sharp scissors. *Damn your father, Blackstone; damn your entire history.* He could deny everything. The trouble was, he had no idea what exactly she knew, and he hadn't a habit of lying.

He stopped stalking her so that she'd stop running.

"It was careless of you to come here alone," he said.

She hovered, warily. Her eyes were cool. "A protection officer is just outside in the corridor—a large, mean, ruthless one."

Not quite so careless, then. He gave her a thin smile.

She crossed her arms over her chest. "You don't deny that you're guilty of something?"

"I'm guilty of a number of things, Lady Catriona; it doesn't give you permission to search my chambers."

Her chin tipped up in defiance. "Your name has been associated with . . . events in France," she said. "If Khoury is indeed your name."

Barely a week, and his mission was on the verge of turning to shit.

He took a deep breath. "It is my name, yes. Do you know how many Khourys exist?"

"I'm aware," she replied quickly. "There's circumstantial evidence, however, and your arsenal of weapons hardly helps your case."

"An arsenal," he said, taken aback. "Every gentleman owns a revolver and a sword—what is so particularly offensive about mine?"

"They . . . seem rather oversized."

Incredible. He bit back an inappropriate comment about his oversized weapon. Under his indignant stare, her gaze dropped, and caught on his feet. Her expression turned slightly embarrassed, probably because he was only wearing socks.

"Forgive me," he drawled. "I hadn't expected visitors."

He had been on the balcony, smoking and minding his own business, when he had heard something scrape across his bedroom floor.

She touched her glasses, the awkward way, not the about-to-say-something-clever way. "The situation is that a few years ago, a Mr. Khoury took some antique jewels from a French count," she said with some reluctance.

The count. He knew immediately. She noticed the recognition in his eyes, and a mix of pain and anger chased across her face. Her lips compressed into a tight line. Last night, her mouth had been soft as a rose under his. Nymph and lady had been one, at last. His blood had burned with the urge to taste her, to lick her fine skin from throat to toe, to bury his fingers in her hair and to pull the lush strands free. They could have been anyone in the dark, just a man and a woman indulging in carnal pleasure. *Did you like what you saw?* It had been the whisky speaking. That was why he had stopped. He had considered it during the train ride back to Oxford this morning, why he had stopped when all he had wanted was to take more, to give more, and it had disturbed him that her intoxication had made him hold back rather than any of the other reasons why making love to her would be a foolish thing to do. Apparently, he hadn't learned his lesson back in Beirut. Apparently, he'd still take stupid risks for an unsuitable woman.

He studied her, gauging her mood, which was so unnaturally well-contained in her rigid body.

"I could explain about the count," he hedged. "But what if you decide you don't like it? You would call your officer, and we would have a mess here." He indicated a circle on the floor with his index finger.

"Please," she said, softly now. "Please explain."

"First, tell me," he said. "Do you believe that stealing loot back from a looter is theft?"

Her brow creased. "I don't think so, no."

"*Alors*," he said. "I didn't take the jewels, but I assisted in their taking. And the count, he was a grave robber."

"What?"

"Egyptian tombs." He shrugged. "The French and the English have a competition over emptying tombs along the Nile. They have become better at it than the local robbers."

Catriona had placed her fingers over her mouth.

"He also had two mummies," he said. "They like those, too." Something compelled him to add: "Not as much as the English, though. They hold mummy unwrapping parties here, don't they?"

She dropped her hand. "I have heard of that, yes." Her voice was flat.

He nodded slowly, his brows raised. "Is it true that people here are eating them, the mummy parts?"

She made a soft gagging sound. "Not in decades, to my knowledge."

"Hm."

"I don't approve of such a thing," she said, her cheeks flushing with color.

"You mean cannibalism?"

Her face looked drawn now, as though she hadn't slept in a week. "You are displeased, understandably."

"And here I thought you might have a taste for the macabre."

"Possibly," she shot back, "but not for sensationalism at the expense of piety."

"A very modern attitude," he conceded, but then she was a modern woman. "As for the count: the Egyptians who wanted the pieces back said he had removed them without license. They approached me after all attempts at negotiation had failed; they knew that I had associated with his lordship over silk business. I returned to his house for another dinner, scouted the location of the pieces, and handed someone a precise map of the place. Perhaps I told them the time when the guards on his property were changed, too."

He had shared far more with her than she needed to know, it felt like bludgeoning her with the truth. She processed it all with a blank expression but her shoulders were hunched, in the way a falcon tightly folded up its wings against a storm. It cooled the heat in his head. Wounding her was the last thing he had wanted. She was a woman he had kissed and wanted to kiss again, and his protective instincts seemed flagrantly unconcerned with the more adversarial parts of her position.

"What have you come to take from here?" she finally asked.

"Everything," he said gently.

She sucked in a breath. "Leighton stole all of these pieces?"

He twisted his hand, like a shrug. "My sponsors say he didn't have permission, and some of the pieces have been taken off their land. There are many more artifacts on these shelves than on my inventory list, though, and I don't know their history."

"My father would never permit work on stolen artifacts," she said, and her nostrils flared in a sudden show of emotions. "He requires proof of license for everything."

"I know. He has a reputation for being an honorable man, which is why I thought he was the right man to give me an introduction."

She raised a hand to her face and rubbed her left temple. "You became acquainted with my father because you want him to preside over your negotiation with Leighton?"

"Yes. I require a patron and a meeting with Leighton."

"The professor who recommended you to my father, did he know?"

"Professor Pappas," he said. "No, he didn't know the details of my cause."

She again crossed her arms over her chest, but now it looked as though she was hugging herself. "Are you . . . a scholar at all?"

"I'm a man of business."

"I see." A lump was visibly moving down her throat. "And what if my father introduced you, and your negotiations turned out to be unsuccessful?"

"Inshallah, they will be successful," he replied.

She smiled, a sad, knowing smile.

They took stock of each other. Officially, until last night, they had owed each other nothing. No words had given shape to whatever feelings they might have harbored. And yet, everything felt different now, as if the ground was splitting between them, and against all better judgment it made him want to grab her and hold on tight.

"I should like to continue this conversation over a cup of tea," she said, her tone all business now. "Would you join me at the Eagle and Child in an hour?"

Her request caught him off guard, but it sounded like an honest invitation, not a trap. She wouldn't await him at the pub with Scotland Yard, ready to remove him from British soil. On instinct, he said yes, he would meet her.

An hour later, she arrived in the tearoom of the old pub on St. Giles, accompanied by Mrs. MacKenzie instead of the protection officer. She had changed into a new dress—muted green taffeta silk with a velvet collar and black buttons. It occurred to Elias that she had still worn her gray travel attire earlier, so she must have hurried from Blackstone's house straight to his bedroom to spy on him. With hooded eyes, he ordered her a tea tray, thinking that only an idiot would make an enemy of this woman. Reversely, she could make a formidable ally, just as Nassim had predicted. Nassim, however, had counted on her to be weak-minded, when it was her strength that would make her an asset.

Mrs. MacKenzie was seated at a table right next to theirs, focused on her knitting. Catriona vigorously stirred sugar cubes into her tea.

"I just had a wee chat with Professor Jenkins, one of the dons at St. John's," she told him as she caused a maelstrom in her cup. "In the abstract only, of course. As I suspected, the charge of plundering doesn't apply in your case because Leighton hasn't taken the artifacts as spoils of war."

He took one of the thin cucumber sandwiches that had been served with the tea.

"Legal route would be a waste of time and money," he said. "I studied the precedents."

She glanced up at him with the teacup at her bottom lip. "Precedents such as?"

"Such as the Parthenon marbles Lord Elgin took. A fellow Scotsman."

"I'm not certain how that compares."

"Are you familiar with the case?"

"I'm not an archaeologist, Mr. Khoury. I'm a historical linguist who occasionally uses her language skills outside of the theory."

"Eighty years ago, Elgin chiseled off half the frieze of the Parthenon in Athens," he explained. "The Ottomans allowed it because the British had helped them beat back Napoleon. Now, since the moment the Ottomans relinquished control over Athens, the Greek government has been asking London to return the pieces. How many years is that?"

"Fifty years," she said easily.

"Eh, almost fifty years of asking for their things back. The Greek have a case: no one can produce the original firman that would prove Elgin had special permission to chisel stones off the walls. They argue that the Ottomans hadn't had the right to give away Greek heritage in any case, license or no license—they say it's theirs."

"I can see why they would."

"Many people said it. The British Parliament wasn't impressed with Elgin. Your Lord Byron called it an act of 'poor plunder' at the time. The Greeks had local advocates here, yet where are the marbles today?"

Catriona gave a grave nod. "Still in London."

He opened his hands. "See. This case now, is weak in comparison. The bulls are from a coastal city, which is under Ottoman administration. Leighton might have a permit from an official, and the British government obviously recognizes Ottoman rule. Legally, I see no case here. Our options are money, or perhaps, honor."

A pensive expression passed over Catriona's face. "The Ottomans have ruled over your region for three hundred years," she said.

He scoffed softly. "Nominally, yes."

"I'm just wondering," she said, her eyes narrowing, "after how many centuries does the occupier become the people of a land?"

He leaned back. "Is that a serious question?"

"I always feel serious about my questions."

Of course she did. "I understand that Scotland fell under English rule two hundred years ago."

"Not quite two hundred," she corrected. "It happened in 1707. Through a treaty, the Treaty of Union."

"A treaty, very civilized. Tell me, how English do you feel after not quite two hundred years of *union*?"

Her mouth quirked, conceding a point. "I don't. Although part of my maternal line was English."

"Three hundred years," he said with some impatience. "They always stay on our coast for two or three hundred years, then they leave, or the next conquest drives them out. In the meantime, the locals don't just vanish."

"I suppose not. Not entirely anyway."

"We become entwined, yes; we might take the language, but we give it our dialect; we take a custom or a dish but alter it to suit us. Sometimes, we intermarry. It's good for survival, good for business. Life goes on, *c'est la vie*. But when people don't feel free or at least prosperous, they only bide their time. Governing locals who don't much like you is costly, and a few centuries don't erase the old ways. As long as one native is left alive, so is the history."

She smiled, rather somberly. "And history becomes a legend."

"*Sach*," he conceded, "the truth."

It occurred to him that she had observed him throughout the conversation without any great reaction on her face or in her tone, as though information passed into her brain undistorted by the filter of personal emotions most people had installed in their ears. It made him feel as though he could trust her to distill her thoughts on any matter into something close to an objective assessment. He rarely felt this way about someone. Whenever he did, it meant he had found a person whose judgment he truly valued. His eyes were suddenly hurting as if he were angry; it had to be anger because his body was tense and he felt the urge to do something physical to relieve the pressure. He put his hands flat on the scarred table. Years ago, when he had caused a rift in the family thanks to his obsession with an unsuitable woman, Nassim had asked him: *Why her? Yes, she's beautiful and the family is noble, but many other women offer the same?* Elias had answered truthfully: *Because I want to know her thoughts and I know she wants to hear mine.*

You have exchanged three sentences!

It was in her eyes.

Lord. Women are women, they're not your friend, that's what men are for.

Elias had disagreed; in marriage, he had wanted something like his parents had shared. Laughter. Companionship. A haven in a stormy sea. Later, when less lovesick, he had decided his memories of his parents' relationship must have been the figment of a seven-year-old boy's imagination, embellished in retrospect. Making this decision had put his restlessness at ease. Any woman would do, then, once he was settled enough to marry well. It had eased the pressure off having to find *the one*. It was pure coincidence that he hadn't married yet; he was quite rich now, yes, but he was busy.

"I must meet Leighton as soon as possible," he said in a low voice. "Wester Ross should preside over the meeting."

She glanced left and right from under her lashes, then she put her teacup down and leaned forward. Her face was close now, her eyes so limpid, she couldn't have hidden a scrap of insincerity.

"I shall assist you," she said. "Within my means, I'm at your service."

A part of him had anticipated it. A part of him knew her. Color had returned to her lips, the pale pinkness of an apricot blossom. If he leaned just a little closer, too, her mouth was almost near enough to kiss. She must have read it on his face, because her expression abruptly shuttered and she rose.

"I shall see you in the Common Room, tomorrow, same time as

always," she said, her posture infused with a determination he hadn't perceived in her before. Now she seemed a hundred miles out of his reach while standing right in front of him.

Unexpectedly, he met her later in the day when he returned to Leighton's trove in the Ashmolean. The quiet figure in front of a shelf caught him off guard. She was alone. She did not turn around when he closed the door. Silence cloaked the marble bulls and the dusty air sweltered beneath the skylight, as if the chamber had been placed under a large looking glass.

He joined her in surveying the shelves, standing a little closer than was proper.

"All of this," she said, still taking in the jumble of statuettes and necklaces, stone fragments, and slabs of mosaic.

"A lot of it," Elias said. He opened his satchel and pulled out the inventory list, a careworn document of several tightly written pages. "There seem to be about twice as many items here than are on my sponsor's list. These ones for example, they are not from our shores."

He pointed at a pair of Sumerian sculptures that stared back at them with frozen indigo eyes.

"Neither is this," she said, and picked up the fragment of a glazed blue tile with a bright vegetal pattern.

"Persian," he said.

"Absolutely, Persian," she agreed.

Briefly, they glanced at each other in inconvenient, mutual appreciation. She returned her attention to the crowded shelves.

"It's as though he raked a net from the Caspian Sea to the Mediterranean and took all he happened to catch," she said. "Without much care, either."

Her voice was thick. She was running her gloved thumb over the still fresh edge of the broken tile in her hand, carefully as if stroking it better. His head went strangely empty, seeing this. His next coherent thought was that he had forgiven her for snooping through his belongings and for slandering his perfectly sized weapons.

"Oh, don't," she said when she noticed he was reaching for the freshly pressed handkerchief in his waistcoat pocket.

"You're sad," he said. "About the tile."

She carefully placed the fragment back onto the shelf. "Ashamed, rather. It might seem laughable to you."

"I'm not laughing, am I."

"It's just that this tile was intact for a thousand years until a random human came along," she said. "Imagine lasting a millennium only to be broken after all. By someone to whom you are entirely exchangeable."

He couldn't say that he had ever thought this way, but whatever she read in his face encouraged her to keep talking.

"There's a belief among the Celts, that the ruins of a house still home the spirits of those who once lived there." She angled her head as though she were asking someone a question. "Perhaps I believe it still," she said. "Perhaps that's what makes me feel sad, because my father presides over this mess, when he should innately be mindful about it. And I paid no attention, either."

Habibti, he thought.

He raised his hand to touch her pale cheek. "I'm lucky to have met a daughter of Celts, then."

Her breathing hitched. She took a small step back.

"Sir," she said in a low tone. "I must ask you to stop this."

He lowered his hand and curled his fingers. "Stop what."

"Your flirtations. They are not necessary." Her jaw set at a hard angle. "I would have assisted you anyway. You obviously have a righteous cause."

His face heated. He felt both caught and falsely accused. "I require no particular reason to flirt with you."

"I'm well aware that I was your pawn sacrifice," she continued, calmly, as if he hadn't spoken. "Ensorcel the earl's daughter to secure her cooperation, wasn't it? Her feelings are a small price for retrieving stolen artifacts. And you know, I do agree with that." She nodded. "I would have done the same, in your place."

Pressure built behind his eyes. She was misconstruing last night so terribly that he had a physical reaction to it, but yes, there had been a ploy to seduce her, too.

He gestured, impatiently. "Believe me that kissing you—"

"Please," she said, cutting him off. "Pretend *that* never happened."

She missed his stare by a hair: the stubborn, avoidant look of an animal that tried to defuse aggression by avoiding direct eye contact. He shook his head, as if that would clear his mind. It had been muddled since last night, since trying to figure out how to finish what they had started in the library. The decent way to do it involved asking the earl for his daughter's hand; but, given the circumstances, it was also the most outlandish way, and so he was still in a state of nonconclusion.

"Tayyeb, tayyeb, habibti," he finally said. "As you wish."

He would still be in the Common Room every day at one o'clock with a chess game they had yet to finish.

Chapter 14

Saturday afternoon, Catriona wrote an urgent note to Wester Ross to see her in Oxford in case he happened to be in London the coming week. The sooner justice was done, the better. As an added benefit, she would never have to see Elias again. *I require no particular reason to flirt with you.* Her smile was so dry, her lips might crack. He wasn't the first to use her for her brains or connections; everyone she had fancied before him had done it and patterns were nothing if not consistent. There was a cruel irony in finding herself reduced to the very thing she had worked so hard to cultivate, her academic position. It was as though a woman could have either a brain or a heart, and whichever way, she was allowed only half a life.

She spent another hour copying her letter of appeal about the writ for restitution for a fresh batch of men of influence. This, at least, was time and effort well spent on worthy work, and her moving pen kept the ghosts at bay. Unfortunately, her first wave of correspondence had elicited only two kinds of responses so far: silence, and utter nonsense. After signing the last letter, she tapped her pen against the rim of the ink bottle and put the cap back on. She sat in her chair and stared into the walled fellows' garden outside the window behind her desk. Her breathing was slow and careful. With her hands idle, her ghosts drifted closer. She could make out Charlie. Charlie had been the first to hurt her the way she had just been hurt again.

Charles, son of neighboring Baron Middleton, had called on the Campbells to see the hieroglyph stone. She had been ten, he had been twelve, with a slim build and silky blond hair that framed his finely drawn face in perfect waves. She had seen him on occasion since nursery days, but that day, when he stood in the library waiting in vain for Wester Ross, she had really *seen* him. A sensation had fluttered low in her belly. It had been a familiar feeling but only from reading about particularly beautiful, valiant characters in one of her novels. It had made her want to hide from him, but when it became obvious that her father had forgotten about his visitor, she had crept from her reading place and offered to take him to see the hieroglyphs.

The stone was kept in the artifact chamber adjacent to the library. Catriona knew the room like the back of her hand. She had played here at her mother's feet, pretending to be an archaeologist, too, between the rusting swords from the Danes, the Roman coin collections and cracked amphoras from Bath, and headless marbles of unknown origins. This was her nursery, and she gladly opened it for Charlie.

He seemed more interested in the antique weapons on the east wall. Of the stone, he said: "It's rather small, isn't it."

"I suppose," Catriona said.

"What does this one here mean?" Charlie pointed at a symbol at random.

"I don't know," she admitted. "Papa hasn't taught me yet."

"Does it really come all the way from Egypt?"

"Aye. An Egyptian colleague from Alexandria loaned it to my father."

"Wicked."

"When I'm grown up, I'll be an archaeologist, too," she informed him.

Charlie smiled at that. "You can't."

"Why not? I know Latin and Greek quite well already."

"But you're a girl." There was no derision in his tone, it was just a fact of life.

"So?" she said. "My mother used to dig." Her voice broke a little when she said *mother* out loud. Mother was buried for nearly a year now.

"True," Charlie conceded. "But Lady Wester Ross—well, you know what they say about her."

She hesitated. "What do they say?"

"That she wasn't a mother-woman," Charlie said, his fingers tracing hieroglyphs in no particular order. "And you want to marry one day, don't you?"

"Of course," she said reflexively.

Mother-woman. Charles must have overheard the term from an adult conversation; perhaps the staff had gossiped, perhaps his parents had during a carriage ride to or from one of the castle dinners. *Mother-woman* would become lodged in her brain like a piece of shrapnel.

Charlie gave her a lopsided smile. His eyes were the color of new moss. A spark glinted in their depths like a tiny sun. "We should marry one day, Kitty. It would make one grand estate out of our two."

She stood in stunned silence, not knowing where to look, or what to say, in the face of such an awesome announcement. Her belly fluttered with clear excitement, though. Yes, she would love to marry such a golden boy.

"What are those funny swirls?" Charlie pointed at the framed parchment on the wall above the stone.

Relief flooded her. This, she knew how to answer. "That isn't swirls, that is Arabic script. Look. This here, this is the first letter, called *aleph*. In Greek, it's the letter *alpha*. In our Latin alphabet, it's been shortened to just *A*."

"I know alpha," Charlie said, amused. "I'm at Eton."

Eton. She envied him his attendance at the prestigious school, there was nothing like it for girls. Admittedly, though, she didn't like the idea of leaving the castle.

"Now look at this parchment," she said, and pointed to the print next to the Arabic one.

"Looks like a child finger-painted that one," Charlie scoffed.

"It's a print of the Phoenician alphabet," she explained. "The first ever alphabet. It was invented in the Levant. The first letter is called *aleph*. The second, *beyt*. Aleph-beyt, alpha-bet, you see?"

"Astonishing," muttered Charlie, his gaze straying toward the wall with the armory.

"Papa says these letters are based on Egyptian hieroglyphs, but much simplified," she pressed on. "*Aleph* is the word for *ox*, so it's probably based on the hieroglyph that depicted an ox head. But because the Phoenicians created a consonantal alphabet, it connected the written to the spoken word and could be adopted and adapted by other languages." It felt as though her mouth were propelled by a steam engine; her lips were moving without a conscious command from her brain, and she couldn't stop. "It's the foundation of our Latin alphabet, too. If you turn our *A* upside down, you can still see the head of an ox with horns."

Charlie looked inward, obviously envisioning an *A* upside down, and then he turned to her with a smile spreading over his face. "You're so clever."

He gave one of her braids a playful tug, and her face went warm.

"I ought to send you letters from Eton about my tutorials," he said. "My Greek tutor is a beast. My Latin one, too. They are all miserable."

Her heart clanged against her ribs. Letters, just for her. Home was empty since Mama had gone. Her father was still physically present, but he was as vacant as the castle, and he no longer taught her Latin and Greek. Her governess was a nuisance, thinking she knew best when she clearly wasn't very intelligent; she accused Catriona of being brash just because she asked questions. It would be lovely to have someone think of her enough to write her letters.

"Yes," she said. "You may write to me."

His letters came every fortnight, and she answered, three or four pages to one of his. She composed essays for him, sometimes translation, for it was like play to her while he seemed to struggle. When he came home during the summers, his arrival felt as though Persephone were rising to the surface after her months in the underworld: the rooms were warmer and the colors burned brighter when he walked through the entrance. Life fell into a rhythm where Charlie's letters and visits constituted the emotional high points. The year she stopped wearing her hair in braids, her governess suggested a boarding school, and Catriona resisted. She'd never miss Charlie's visits, and while her father was absent-minded, she felt his loneliness bleeding through his patchy suits, and nothing would remove her from the castle in case he should want her company. Wester Ross indulged her and finally hired proper tutors. Her knowledge became far superior to what Charlie had acquired at prestigious Eton, but she loved him anyway. She loved him for his quick wit, his spontaneous laugh. He made her think life could be a light, easy thing after all.

When he was sixteen, Charlie became wide-shouldered like his father. He carried his new manliness with confidence; she, however, spent days staring at her own changing body in the mirror, unsettled by the uncontrollably burgeoning bits. There was a mismatch between the image she held of herself and her reflection, for this new body was deemed unsuitable for her passions, the swimming, the digging, the visceral hunger for knowledge. She was becoming stuck in the kind of body that had killed her mother while she had tried to bring new life into the world. All the pliant softness was the embodiment of weakness, if not a death trap. When she went down to Oxford that year, her father's colleagues noticed the new body, too, and her skin crawled under their perusal with a fierce annoyance and an unfamiliar sense of shame. The changed appearance changed the way she thought about Charlie, too. She now imagined doing unspeakable things with him, straight from the books her father didn't know she had been reading.

When he turned eighteen, he wrote of the grand tour he had planned before shuffling off to Cambridge: *Wouldn't have passed those awful entrance interviews without you, Kitty Cat!*

Not a word about a proposal. Hot tears ran down her cheeks while she penned a reply that sounded utterly delighted for him. During the party for his departure, she stood pressed against the wall of the small ballroom at Middleton House down in London, watching him whirl pretty girls across the dance floor. Sometimes, his eye caught hers, and he smiled. Shortly after midnight, she asked a footman to pass Charlie a note. She waited for him in the library. There, the disaster happened. First, he didn't seem too keen to see her, he kept glancing past her, his gaze searching. "Did you send the note? Asking me to come here?"

A question stirred at the back of her mind: had he expected someone else?

"It's just a goodbye gift," she said, and pulled the book from her extra pocket in her skirt.

Charlie turned it over in his hand. *"Ivanhoe?"*

"First edition of the first volume," she said, sounding too keen. He smelled of Charlie and exertion, an intimate mix that caused the edges of her vision to blur.

His smile showed teeth. "Splendid."

He seemed tense, ready to bolt from the potential scandal of being here alone with her. She closed the gap between them with

one determined step and rose to her toes. His green eyes were un-
familiarly close and wide. She pressed her mouth to his. Warm and
smooth. Like the sturdy petal of an exotic plant, tasting of rum and
tobacco. His hand was on her waist, and, stirred by the warm pressure, her new body made sense in this moment, too. Next, she
stumbled forward into nothingness. Charlie had retreated abruptly.
He had put the back of his hand over his mouth and his pale eyebrows were arching high in shock.

Mortification set her face on fire. "I'm sorry."

He dropped his hand. "Well, that was a little forward," he said
with a flustered laugh. "That's all right," he added quickly. "Too
much punch, hm?"

The forced lightness in his voice made him sound alien.

Her mouth was dry as desert dust. "Yes," she said. "I had a bit
much."

"Whew," Charlie said, still in this jaunty new tone. "Well,
good. I was worried there for a moment." He gave her a conspiring
look, which she met with a blank expression.

He ran a hand over his hair. "Goodness," he said. "I would have
felt like an utter cad, had I ever given you the impression that I, ah,
harbored romantic inclinations toward you."

Something sharp cut right through her chest, the feeling so
horrifying that she glanced down to see if a knife hilt was sticking
out from between her ribs. She saw the swell of her breasts, encased
in white tulle. She was wearing this fluffy thing for him. A cold
sensation rose inside her, all-consuming like the tide of an icy sea.
She couldn't seem to see very well.

"No," she said, looking at him, trying to clear her vision by
blinking. "You never gave the impression."

"Well, that's a relief," she heard him say. "Little Tipsy Head.
You were my best chum up there in that windy place, you do know
that, don't you?"

Chum. Chum?

Steps sounded outside the library. Charlie ducked and stilled.

"Let's get out of here," he hissed when all was quiet again. He dropped the *Ivanhoe* on a side table.

"You did say we should marry," she said when his hand was on the doorknob.

His head jerked round to her. "What?"

Her mouth smiled, making light of it. "In the artifact room. The day you came to see the stone from Alexandria."

Charlie frowned. "Why, I was nine years old when I said that."

"Twelve. You were twelve."

His confused expression did not change, and she understood that whether nine or twelve, he had been a child and only an imbecile would put stock in the word of a child.

"You said our estates would have made one grand estate," she added, loathing herself as the words came out of her mouth.

Charlie's inane smile returned. "Indeed, they would have made a grand estate. But aren't you married to your books in any case?" He cracked the door open and listened into the corridor. "Come. Let's go back. Do me the honor of a dance?"

She couldn't move. One step out of this room and she'd fall into an abyss, a world without Charlie. *I can change*, she wanted to say. *I will sew my book pocket shut. Just don't leave me, don't leave me. You are my only friend.* She followed him down the corridor. A group of his friends, brimful with punch, poured around the corner and absorbed them. Somehow, Charlie and she became separated.

She never remembered how she returned to the Campbell town house. Her mind was racing round like a mad rat in a cage. Had there been a magical phrase that could have set the wheels in motion in her favor? A gesture she could have made to change his mind? She should have told him that she loved him. Her journey to Applecross passed by in a fog, and the days blurred together while she lay on her bed in the tower room, next to his letters. She had been useful to him. *Chum*. As a woman, she was deficient in his eyes, missing some vital component to be considered for the wife role. Her uncertainty in how to be in such an ill-fitting body was apparently visible to outsiders. It confirmed it: something was wrong with her.

Her father came to her room and sat in the chair while she had her face buried in a pillow. He wanted to know if Charlie had done something to her, something he ought to discuss with Charlie's father. No, he had done nothing. He wasn't interested.

"It feels as though I'm dying," she sobbed. "I wish I were dead."

The earl was shocked. "Child, such violent emotions are not normal, not healthy."

He would know. She had heard him howl the night Mama and the baby had died.

The next day, Wester Ross told her she would attend a boarding school in Switzerland.

"It's an etiquette school for ladies," he added when she was too stunned to speak. "Your mother wasn't here to guide you. Mrs. Keller and her teachers will help you to become a proper woman."

She glared in disbelief. "I'm not going there."

He gave her a gloomy look. "It would break my heart to force you," he said. "However, don't think that I won't."

An iron band seemed to snap around her chest, and it tightened until all air was squeezed from her. She fell back onto the bed.

"If I were the only person in the world," she said to the ceiling, "how would I even know I was a woman? Who would tell me? Who would make me? I would just be me. Why can't I just be me?"

The earl was quiet for a moment. "An interesting hypothesis," he then allowed. "But no one is ever just themselves."

It occurred to her that he looked old; he was barely forty but there were grooves bracketing his mouth and his dark curls were shot through with gray. Perhaps that was why she had relented. She still had left Applecross feeling betrayed, with two dramatic conclusions in her luggage:

1. Love was cruel.
2. Men were misery.

When she found her way back to Wester Ross a year later, she was rather more disillusioned than before. It had turned out that men had no monopoly on causing misery. Or perhaps it was a fault within her person, that her oh-so-clever brain had a blind spot when it came to reading the person she adored. It didn't matter, though, because fixating on a man and marriage had been a childish thing to do for someone like her. She needed peace, not love. She needed freedom, not the status conferred to a wife.

Voices carried into the study. A group of St. John's fellows strolled past the windows in lazily billowing gowns. They were taking a turn in the garden before going to dinner. Catriona put a hand on her stomach, trying to determine whether she was hungry. She supposed she could eat something; but she might see Elias, or perhaps Peregrin. Under her hand, her stomach felt hollow. Listlessly, she sorted her campaign letters into a tidy stack. Avoidance was her preferred method of dealing with her romantic disappointments— she had never set foot in the Middleton town house again, and she had never called on Alexandra after she had left boarding school, even though her old friend resided in Chelsea with her diplomat husband these days. It seemed her world would just become smaller and smaller over time as she'd have to avoid more and more places and people. On the one hand that sounded comforting, quiet and safe, just her and good books and cozy blankets, on the other hand, it didn't seem right, not yet, not like this. Solitude that wasn't freely chosen was no better than loneliness.

Perhaps she shouldn't abandon her experiment entirely. Perhaps she ought to try to salvage what she could. There was no point in practicing feeling normal in Elias's presence, but she could certainly practice not giving a damn.

Chapter 15

Monday's suffrage meeting, just as Catriona had feared, was delayed in favor of forming a circle around the cake table to discuss Elias Khoury. Hattie had shared the turn of events about his true identity with Annabelle and Lucie after Catriona's hasty departure from Blackstone House.

"So, the trouble is that the licenses Leighton presented were issued by a corrupt official?" Lucie asked, two steep lines of concentration between her brows.

"I'm not certain he even had a license for everything that's in that room, though the official was likely corrupt, too," Catriona said. "However, even if the paperwork was perfectly in order, the point Mr. Khoury raises is whether an imperial administration is ever entitled to give away indigenous artifacts."

"I'm not a lawyer," Annabelle said in a serious, subdued way, "but I know that looting cultural treasures has been frowned upon since Cicero."

"Pillaging is officially forbidden since the 1874 Brussels Declaration," Catriona said, "but this wasn't a war, and Mr. Khoury is determined to strike a deal in any case rather than rely on the law."

Hattie, who had followed the conversation from her couch while nibbling on a sugar cube, raised her hand. "I'm the first to say give art back to where it belongs, but wouldn't the pieces be safer here? No one will make things disappear from the British Museum anytime soon."

Lucie frowned but nodded.

"Perhaps," Catriona said, "but why are these pieces ours to safe-keep when the people who had them taken from their ancestral lands want them back? A bit patronizing, isn't it."

Hattie blew up her cheeks. "It's not just any art, though, is it; it's from the cradle of our civilization."

"So, when England was at war with France for a whole hundred years, would you have appreciated it if someone from the Mongolian Empire had come over and decided to relocate Stonehenge? Because the stones would be safer there since no one messed with the Mongols at the time? And they'd give us a pat on the head when we said thanks but we'd rather keep them? It wasn't even Anglo-Saxons who put the stones in a circle, but we're all rather attached to them today anyway."

A broody little silence ensued.

Annabelle decided to refill their teacups for the third time. "I suppose we all agree that we ought to assist him," she said. "Have you any ideas yet?" she asked Catriona.

"Mr. Khoury and Leighton ought to be introduced as soon as possible," she said. "I wrote to my father. He cabled back this morning saying I should arrange for a dinner here with everyone at the end of the week."

Wester Ross had plans to be in London, in his solicitor's main office. She hoped it wasn't an appointment to break an entail on the estate to sell off even more, but it was not something she could presently worry about.

"I'm so relieved that Mr. Khoury isn't the villain in this piece," Hattie said, and lolled into the upholstery like a lazy cat. "For a moment, I was worried I was losing my touch. To think I could have left you to promenade alone with a scoundrel . . ."

"Promenade? When? Where?" Lucie asked, looking at Catriona with suspicion.

"The day of the fire drill," Hattie said. "When Catriona, erm, left the carriage to walk."

"Good lord," Catriona said, mildly disturbed. "You were trying to matchmake."

"Ha," said Lucie. "I knew it."

Annabelle gave Catriona an inquiring glance. "What have I missed?"

"Nothing," Catriona said. "Shall we begin our meeting? I have some fun letters here." She pulled the replies to her writ campaign from her pocket.

Hattie put her chin in her hand and regarded her with an annoying twinkle in her eyes. "Don't you like him?"

"No," Catriona said, feeling a muffled disturbance, her emotions, her shame, the memory of a kiss, trying to break from their icy shell. "I mean, it doesn't signify whether I like him or not."

Her red face was all it took for Hattie to keep prodding: "If you liked him, and you *were* looking for a match, hypothetically speaking, of course . . . would you consider him a good prospect?"

They all leaned forward slightly, luring her with curious glances to spill everything, the same way looking down a plunging rock face might induce the unreasonable urge to jump. They had comforted one another through enough scandals by now, their loyalty and discretion were true and tested, but somehow it was different when it was one's own scandal. Catriona took off her spectacles and polished them a little too vigorously with her shawl.

"It would be a terrible idea," she said.

"Because he's a foreigner?" Hattie asked with a small frown.

She shook her head. "Because I am me," she said, "but you're right; imagine if I were to marry an Eastern man—the gossip would be gross. His family would feel just as unimpressed, I believe."

Annabelle made a sympathetic noise. "There would be talk," she agreed.

"Such a thing can be overcome," Lucie pointed out. "Annabelle married a duke, and Hattie married, well, she married Blackstone. Ballentine used to make literal headlines with his antics. Look how well it all worked out for us in the end."

Catriona regarded her with her mouth open like a fish. "You?" she managed. "You are trying to hypothetically marry me off? Since when?"

Lucie gave an embarrassed shrug. "I think my own wedding preparations make me look at everything from a matrimonial angle," she offered. "It's quite disgusting."

The angle also seemed to give Lucie tunnel vision. For all their faults and scandal, none of her friends' matches were unprecedented in society history, when she, Catriona, couldn't think of a single case where a lady of her station had married outside of a European house. She put the glasses back on, and Annabelle's pensive face came into clear focus.

"I don't want to press you," Annabelle said with an apologetic smile. "But I'm curious—why exactly would it end badly? You have only ever been good for us, you see. I'm just trying to imagine how you could be bad company for someone you care about."

Catriona felt sudden pressure in her throat, like a big bite had become lodged.

"You don't have to tell us," Annabelle added.

"No, it's all right." She looked down into her cup, into the calm unicolored circle of her breakfast tea. "If I were to marry, I would only marry someone I loved," she finally said.

"Of course you would," Hattie exclaimed.

"I would still need time to just be inside my head. You know that I don't eat or drink at regular times when I'm focused on something. I wouldn't care about going to bed before midnight or hosting a social event and I would walk around thinking about the page I should write or translate whenever I'm not at my desk. Don't tell me a husband wouldn't come to resent this. He would begin voicing perfectly reasonable demands about my availability, about keeping a schedule, about acting like a regular wife. I would feel guilty. I would resent him, too, but because we love each other, we try. In the end, I would have to choose between the happiness of the man I love and living in a way that suits me, which is dreadful; either way we are probably so enmeshed by then that ripping his soul from mine would leave an open wound. We would both be in worse condition than we were before. I therefore see no reason to hypothetically entertain the idea of marrying Mr. Khoury."

Her friends were stunned, she could tell. They weren't really moving, not even blinking.

She raised her cup to her lips again.

"Given how much I just talked," she said between sips, "it could of course leave you with the impression that I *have* considered it."

"Not at all," Annabelle assured her.

"Never," Hattie agreed, but she was gripping the edge of her seat now, looking ready to burst.

"That was the longest I have ever heard you speak," Lucie said, sounding awed.

"You have played out an entire marriage in your head and divorced the man before you even attempted courting," Hattie cried.

Catriona put her cup back onto the saucer with a *clink*. "Why are we fussing over my nonexistent marriage to a stranger?"

"Right," Lucie said. "Let the poor woman be, Hattie. I'm ringing in our meeting now. Whoever wants to talk about anything other than our agenda shall have to leave the room."

She looked sternly at Hattie, whose room it happened to be, and opened her satchel, allowing Catriona to exhale with relief. It was hard enough keeping her face empty without having to spin romantic fantasies about the man she was trying to erase from her brain.

Lucie produced a sheet with a neatly drawn table containing names, some of them already haphazardly crossed out.

"Since our last meeting, we have spoken to two dozen dithering MPs, and in conclusion, it was a success," she announced. "If we continue at this rate, we might have an amendment before the year is over." She knocked on the surface of the table.

The point was agreed, and it was Catriona's turn to present.

"I sent my first appeals out last Friday." She nudged the two letters she had placed on the table. "My results are disappointing."

"Those are quick replies," Lucie remarked. Quick replies were usually written with tempers running high.

Catriona opened the first envelope. "Essentially, this one says: don't be silly—the writ protects women from being left abandoned and penniless by errant husbands. No man would pay maintenance unless he faced jail."

"Tosh," said Lucie, "as if there weren't other legal means available than this writ to correct such a man."

"I think this one here is closer to the crux of the issue," Catriona said and opened the second envelope. "Listen to this: *The Writ for Restitution of Conjugal Rights has a purpose*," she read out. "*If a wife could abscond on a whim, then who is to guarantee that she will honor her vows? A capricious bride could change her mind as soon as the day after the wedding and leave, thus condemning an innocent, upstanding man to years of celibacy as well as depriving him of the opportunity to father children. I am honouring your query with a response because I admired your academic work about the Theodosian Walls of Constantinople. I have much respect for a woman who has a man's brain. However, a word of warning: when a woman fails to pair her intellect with the softer inclinations of the female sex, she is in danger of becoming a harridan or unsexed altogether. My regards to Wester Ross, I should like to meet him at the club when he is in London next.*"

For a long moment, they looked at one another blankly. The muffled sound of nearby traffic filled the room.

At last, Hattie said in a grave voice: "The Theodosian Walls of Constantinople."

They burst out laughing, so uncontrolled and high-pitched that it sounded like screaming.

"Capricious bride," said Annabelle, wiping tears from the corners of her eyes, and just when the fresh shrieks died down, Lucie choked out, "unsexed," and they doubled over again.

"I wonder what it would feel like," Annabelle said when calm had been restored, "how I'd feel if I woke up every morning filled with such brass-necked audacity."

"Invincible?" Hattie suggested.

Perhaps I would consider marriage then, Catriona thought. *I could just close the door to my study whenever I needed and trust he would love me for being good at what I do, not for what I can do for him . . .*

She glanced at the pocket watch. In two hours, she'd face her most recent disappointment in the Common Room. His attractive face appeared before her mind's eye, and her body remained quiet, as if numb.

Chapter 16

H e had, very casually, looked at his pocket watch at five min-utes to one, then he had moved the chess pieces into their positions of the last game. When the door to the Common Room opened a few minutes later, he kept his eyes on the board for a moment as though his body hadn't just buzzed with awareness.

She wore a soft blue color today. This touch of gentleness was deceiving, he quickly realized. Up close, she felt as cool and remote as she did two days ago, when she had told him to keep his hands to himself.

"Ma'am. Mrs. MacKenzie."

Catriona's small smile didn't reach her eyes. "Thank you for setting up the game."

Her voice was smooth as glass, without a particle of emotion, good or bad. She returned his scrutiny with a placid expression that filled him with vague unease.

He walked round her to assist with her seating. Her hair was in a loosely pinned braid, and two dark curls had escaped from the updo and nestled in the tender indent of her nape. The chaperone was watching him eye up the lady's exposed neck. He pushed the chair under the lady's bustle.

She put her spectacles on top of her head again, but it seemed her gloves stayed on today.

It was his turn, and his least self-destructive move was to put his pawn in a3. As he had predicted after their last round, she immediately eliminated his knight on c3 with her bishop and was now behind enemy lines. It made him feel vindicated—at least during this game he knew what was inside her head.

She looked up at him. "My father will be in London midweek," she said. "We could have dinner with Mr. Leighton on Thursday or Friday, depending on his availability and preference. I could cable to him today to invite him."

"That's rather short notice," he pointed out.

She nodded. "Nothing wagered, nothing gained."

"You haven't told your father the reason, have you?" he asked in Arabic to lock out the chaperone.

"No—I understood you wanted to discuss the matter with him face-to-face, prior to the dinner."

It still impressed him, how effortlessly she switched between the languages. He launched a fresh pawn to destroy her pillaging bishop.

"As for Leighton," he said, "in his invitation, we tell him that we want to share our progress with the classification. Nothing yet about my proposal."

"As you wish."

She studied the board rather briefly, then switched her king with her rook.

He narrowed his eyes. "Interesting."

She seemed unflustered by the compliment, just graciously inclined her head. *Blush*, he willed her, *or say something strange. Say nothing at all, if you must, but act normal.* This was normal, he then realized—for probably the first time, she was acting perfectly in line with protocol. He contemplated his small army, wanting to do something reckless. An awareness of the greater picture was a must in chess as well as in life; to plan any possible scenario in too much detail, however, risked overlooking actual realities. Catriona probably lived life that way, though. He could just see her do it, classing people as pawns, knights, kings; intuiting their moves and switching her responses on and off accordingly. He brought his bishop into a position that would allow him to take her knight and penetrate deep into her ranks in a few moves' time.

"What do you think about using some bait to lure Mr. Leighton to the dinner," she asked. "We might need it, at such short notice."

"Do you have anything in mind?"

"I could suggest an exhibition in the British Museum."

He paused. "Take the pieces to London?"

"Aye. Such an opportunity would flatter the vanity of any collector."

"You mean to just suggest it to him, or to actually do it, if he agrees?"

A small shrug. "If it came to it, I could certainly schedule an audience with the curator of the museum through Wester Ross."

The fine hairs had risen on his nape. If the pieces were on a train, they were mobile. Anything in transit was vulnerable. He knew an opportunity when he saw one even if the use of it was yet unclear.

"It is a good idea," he said evenly.

"Wonderful." She took one of his frontline pawns with one of hers and gave him another meaningless glance. "I'm afraid I must go now. Shall we play another day?"

He suppressed the urge to put his hand on top of hers to keep her from getting up and leaving. She was still hurt, and he couldn't fix it, not while her chaperone was staring on, anyway. With a tight smile, he bid her a good day. On her way out, she stopped to chat with a white-haired, rosy-faced fellow who sat reading a book in a chair near the entrance, and the curve of her cheek said she was smiling throughout the conversation. A hot stab of irritation went through Elias, and he realized he was glaring at an old man. For some time after she had left, he kept sitting at the little table, frustration prickling under his skin like an itch he couldn't reach for scratching. Obviously, his desire to make up with her went far beyond general courtesy. He still wanted her. *Bury it, forget it.* For now, he had to endure her assistance, which grated on him enough—his instinct was to be of use to her, not put her to work—but soon, they would part. Then he would find himself a lover, one with a wide smile and richly perfumed hair, and he'd drown out the memories by focusing on his business.

She returned the following day, wearing a plain green cotton dress and a purposeful expression.

"I received a note from Leighton this morning," she told him. "He is joining us for dinner here on Thursday. They will want to look at the artifacts."

Thursday. The day after tomorrow. This was good news.

"Let us discuss the exhibition during the dinner," he said after she had taken her seat. "After dinner, Wester Ross could tell Leighton that we found that some of the pieces are not properly licensed. Then, I suggest possibilities for a return."

Lady Catriona kept her gaze on the board, where their armies were on the cusp of serious mingling. "We shall do that," she said.

After a pawn move each, he did steal her knight with the previously well-positioned bishop. She avenged the knight by unleashing her queen for the first time. The maneuvers took them over twenty minutes, during which her delicate scent distracted him, and then she again put an end to it and excused herself for the day—as though she could only bear him in small doses. She did turn back to him as if on second thoughts.

"Mr. Leighton will bring his niece, a Miss Regina," she said. "Apparently, she's an avid amateur archaeologist."

"Ya Allah," he muttered.

The corners of her mouth quirked. "I thought I'd warn you."

He chanced it, then. "Stay for another move," he said. "We will not finish this game otherwise. I might well be gone next week."

A quietness came over her. "Ah," she said. "I'm afraid I can't."

"Your book," he said. "You are working on it?"

"No. It's the suffrage business. I ought to be back at my desk and contemplate tactics."

"I see."

"Nothing but contrarian replies to my letters so far, if the gentlemen deign to reply at all." She had to be frustrated indeed to confide in him of all people instead of stalking off.

"The victory will be yours," he said.

Her lips parted, as though his encouragement had taken her by surprise. "You sound rather certain."

"You make good decisions," he said, and nodded at the board. "Many would be checkmated by now."

She made a small, cynical sound, like an *mmm*. "Wouldn't it be lovely if the real world were a chess game," she said. "All black and white and logical."

"I think that would be terrible," he said.

"Well, I'm glad I don't bore you," she said with a last glance at the table. "I haven't played since boarding school."

"Then you are, unsurprisingly, greatly talented."

She tilted her head to the side, dismissing it. "What is chess other than memorizing patterns."

"It's a lot of patterns," he said mildly. "Thousands, in fact."

Her false smile was back in place. "True. But I find we always gravitate toward playing the same tried and tested games. Unfortunately, I can't seem to forget a pattern once I have seen it. Good day, Mr. Khoury."

Chapter 17

Elias disliked Mr. Leighton on sight. There was nothing particularly offensive about the man's appearance to merit this reaction; Leighton had a perfectly inconspicuous middle-aged English face, thin lips, thin nose, tufty sideburns. A remarkably fine coat hung off his wiry build. His train from Birmingham had arrived with a two-hour delay, which meant they couldn't take a tour of the artifacts as the dinner was about to begin, but this was hardly the man's fault. *It's his eyes,* Elias decided while they shook hands; they stood a smidgen too closely together and held a mocking anticipation, as if anything could be a joke.

"It's such a shame that our train was delayed," said Miss Regina, the niece. She was a pretty brunette with a wealthy girl's pearlescent complexion, her alert expression indicating a bright mind. "I was rather looking forward to seeing the pieces."

"It's a pity," said Leighton, not sounding particularly perturbed. "Our Syrian expert here shall have to tell us all about them instead."

He smiled at Elias, revealing teeth with brown tea stains. Above the college quadrangle walls, unruly clouds were piling high into the sky; already, an evening chill lay in the air, as if summer had briefly run out of breath.

"If you please," Elias said, and gestured toward Hall. Leighton fell into step with him, as Miss Regina seemed to have attached herself to Catriona. The women followed them closely.

"I am such an admirer of yours," came Regina's young voice. "I devoured your handbook on Egyptian hieroglyphs. Oh, I know it is published under your father's name, but rumor has it that it's all from your pen."

Catriona's reply was too soft to decipher.

"I aspire to follow in your footsteps," Regina went on. "If my parents allowed me to come up to Oxford, I should be the happiest woman in England—I can feel my spirits rising just by looking at these marvelous old buildings!"

Next to Elias, Mr. Leighton chuckled. "My niece is very passionate about her education," he explained. "I daresay she's keener on seeing my latest acquisitions than I am."

Elias slowed. "You haven't seen the pieces yet?"

"I haven't," replied Leighton. "They were in crates when they arrived, and I didn't stay for the unpacking. Except for the bulls—splendid creatures."

They entered the dining hall. The long rows of student tables were empty but the perpendicular High Table was busy with dons, among them Wester Ross.

"I had been under the impression that you had extracted the pieces in person," Elias said, his voice sounding normal enough.

Leighton looked surprised, his upper lip curling with amusement. "Me? Oh no. I haven't ventured into that part of the world in years—not since I gave up the trade post in the region. The food doesn't agree with me." He shamelessly patted his stomach. "My brother is an attaché in Damascus. His son—Regina's brother here—embarked on a grand tour this spring and I sponsored him in exchange for some souvenirs. Ah, Wester Ross—it's a pleasure."

Souvenirs.

He focused on pulling out Catriona's chair. They were facing the wall behind the table, aged ebony wood paneling and rows of old portraits in heavy frames. Leighton, Miss Regina, and the earl were seated facing them, with a view over the hall.

While the Latin prayer was being read, Elias looked down at his hands. Over the monotone incantation, his heating temper cooled a little. He heard Catriona's breaths, flowing softly in and out. He tried not to look at her; she wore a snugly fitted satin gown with a tartan bodice that attracted him.

The first course was a root vegetable soup with parsley garnish. After a few spoonfuls, Mr. Leighton turned his attention back to Elias. "What do you think of the local fare, Mr. Khoury?" he asked. A bit of green was stuck to his canine tooth.

"I find it better here than at Cambridge," Elias replied.

Leighton made a pleased moue. "You're a Cambridge man. What college?"

"I was at King's."

"My nephew, the one I mentioned earlier, Wilfred is his name, was up at Trinity. Wilfred Leighton."

"I'm not familiar with the name, I'm afraid."

"Either way, you're well accustomed to the English cuisine, then," Leighton mused as he dabbed at his lips with his napkin. "No nasty surprises for you here, I hope. Though I have a theory, namely that the attack on the midsection affects Westerners traveling east rather than vice versa. What do you think, Wester Ross?"

Wester Ross looked surprised, but he duly studied his soup through his round spectacles. "Well," he then said, "these parsnips certainly look universally agreeable to me."

He raised his spoon toward Elias in a bizarre little toast.

"Sahtein," Elias said, his smile showing too many teeth.

Miss Regina's attention drifted over him, increasingly insistent, so he looked at her. A blush crested on her cheeks.

"That was Arabic, wasn't it," she said.

"It was, yes."

"What does it mean?"

He turned to his table partner, who was notably too quiet. "Perhaps Lady Catriona will tell you. Her Arabic is very good."

Catriona stiffened slightly, but she obliged. "I'm not familiar with all the words in Mr. Khoury's dialect," she said to Miss Regina, "but I assume it means 'enjoy your food.'"

"Yes," Elias said, "that's the meaning."

Miss Regina was looking back and forth between them with poorly concealed intrigue.

"In Egypt, one would say 'bil hana wa ashfa,'" Catriona added.

"Such a difference," Miss Regina said, and shook her head.

Around them, footmen quietly prepared the table for the second course. White and red wine was poured.

Just when Elias had picked up his glass, the young woman leaned in.

"Mr. Khoury."

"Miss Regina."

She lowered her voice, as if to impart a secret or something unsavory. "Is it true what my brother tells me—even the more educated people in your region are often illiterate?"

Ah. "It's true," he said after a pause.

"A pity," she said, a crease between her brows. "I thought there were many schools. Universities, even."

"There are, of course, but there is a great divergence between spoken and formally written Arabic. It's not the same as an English speaker learning to write English."

"How peculiar."

"It's hardly unique," Catriona said unexpectedly. "Think of the difference between classical and vulgar Latin—people in all provinces could speak vulgar, or common, Latin, but few could write the classical form."

Miss Regina gave her a polite smile. "Of course." And, to Elias: "What about watches? Wilfie said you don't have them because so few people can read the time on a clock?"

He carefully put his wineglass back down. "I have no trouble reading a clock, ma'am."

"You wouldn't," she said quickly, and moved her hand across the tablecloth. "But you are different."

"Ah," he said, "I'm quite the same."

Her cheeks dimpled; she thought he was joking because he was a Cambridge man and wore an academic gown from Ede & Ravenscroft. She should see him at home. He wouldn't repeat the mistake he had made in Blackstone's reception room and explain things, how keeping time was bound up with modes of production and that industrialization was fanning outward from Europe, or that mechanical clocks had first been invented in the West and their hourly gong in public places disturbed prayer time in the East, all good reasons why people still relied on other ways of keeping time.

"The people who work the land don't have watches because the time on a clock is irrelevant for successful farming," he said to Miss Regina.

She nodded slowly. "I suppose they simply feel the time," she said, "as they are so attuned to nature—they are still one with the land. It is something we have lost here, with most of the workers now in factories. Some days I worry Marx was right and the poor souls will become part of the machinery."

"Good lord," Catriona muttered under her breath. Elias cut her a warning glance. The last time she had exuded such coldness, she had lectured a hapless nobleman in front of his friends. She was supposed to charm these ones here, to facilitate, diplomatically—

"Mr. Leighton," she said, her voice so low that one had to pay attention to hear her. "We were so pleased that you accepted our invitation at such short notice."

Leighton waved his hand in an appeasing gesture. "The pleasure is mine. I had thought to myself, just before your invitation arrived: these pieces belong in a museum. As it is, the rooms for my private collections are becoming a little crowded, too."

"What a well-timed coincidence," Catriona remarked.

"It shall be a loan, of course, but I'm contemplating a very long loan indeed," Leighton amended. The parsley bit had attached itself to his front tooth. "As my wife and my niece here inform me, when a man is in the position to do so, sharing the heritage of humankind with the broadest possible audience is his moral duty."

Both Miss Regina and Wester Ross nodded. Elias forcibly relaxed his jaw, trying to shake the feeling that his negotiation was unfolding in front of him like an absurd stage play.

"Now, tell me more," Leighton said to Catriona. "What do you have in mind for the exhibition? The bulls ought to take center stage, of course. I envision an entire room just for them."

Catriona inclined her head as if impressed. "We could certainly try to interest the curator in this idea."

Leighton lifted the lid off the terrine on his plate. "Yes, yes, that would be splendid."

"It would of course be truly revolutionary," Catriona continued, "if you considered a museum closer to the audience where the pieces were found."

Subtle, thought Elias.

Leighton appeared confused. "What can you mean?"

"I mean that locals would have to travel quite far to see their own heritage displayed if the pieces were exhibited in London," Catriona ventured.

Miss Regina blinked.

Leighton chuckled. "Ha ha, I like your humor."

"How so?" asked Wester Ross.

This gave Leighton pause. "Sir," he said. "Surely we all agree that all the world *is* in London." He smiled at Catriona. "I assure you, the natives don't care where the pieces happen to be." He sliced into the rosy beef on his plate. "It is us who recognize the significance of these artifacts, why else do you think they had just been lying around until we secured them? To the locals, why, even a

Roman temple is just another source of building material for walls and huts. Isn't it, Wester Ross?"

Elias said nothing. A dangerous heat was quickly creeping up his throat.

The professor took off his glasses. "Roman temples still exist in the region, some astonishingly well intact, to my knowledge, hence not all have been turned into huts just yet," he said. "There is also at least one large museum in Constantinople. But Mr. Khoury is right here, perhaps he can enlighten us."

"Oh, that museum," Leighton said. "I have heard of it. Unfortunately, it seems to be filled with an absurd collection of rubbish."

The professor rubbed the bridge of his nose. "I'm surprised to hear that."

"I have it on good account," Leighton assured him, and skewered a bite-sized piece of meat with his fork. "No, no, they should be grateful for every statue we preserve on our expense. Just look at the bulls. Witnesses of ancient high cultures, marvelous craftsmanship, I think it would be a shame to see them pockmarked by the cross fire of the next petty local strife."

"There always seems to be trouble in the Near East," Miss Regina said. "Such a pity."

"It is. British naval ships shelled Alexandria into the ground just the other week," Catriona said. "I can't imagine the structural damage."

Elias pressed his right knee into her skirts. *Don't*, it said; *we are at an impasse*. Indeed, a charged stillness fell between the dinner guests. Leighton eyed Elias while he chewed his beef. He licked around over his teeth behind closed lips, then said, "Where did you say you were from, Mr. Khoury?"

It took a moment to override his pride and answer. "I hadn't said. I'm from Zgharta."

Leighton gave a shocked little laugh. "I say. Fancy that." He shook his head and looked around as if to share his astonishment with an invisible audience. "Your people caused us quite the trouble," he then said, and wagged a finger at Elias. "Threw a christening in my family into disarray, if you can believe it."

Elias perceived the admonishing, pointing finger through a rapidly thickening red mist. He saw Miss Regina tilt her head and move her lips, but only Leighton's reply reached his ears again.

". . . hence, all was quite settled," Leighton explained, "when the governor of this young man's district decided he disliked the new order after all. Bey Karam was his name, well, Karam was a hothead and thought he knew better than us, and the Ottomans, the French, and the Austrians put together, and he went and bedeviled the Pasha with some mutiny. Naturally, the Pasha sends in the army to restore order on the mountain yet again, but, in a strange turn of events, Karam beats back the army with just some ragtag band of villagers—an embarrassment, for the Ottomans, that is. Next, the French ambassador and our foreign office are inundated by Ottoman complaints, and one another's complaints . . . the Austrians stuck their noses in again, too. That's why your father missed his boat to your sister's christening—he was entangled in crisis negotiations."

Miss Regina put her fingers to her lips. "Goodness," she said to Elias. "How fateful that we should all meet here today."

He pushed back his chair and stood. Catriona's upturned face was an anxious white blur.

"Do excuse me," he said. "It seems the food doesn't agree with me after all."

He left with long strides, a vein pounding in his throat.

Catriona sat staring down at her plate. Elias's exit pulled at her insides as if he had her vitals on a leash, and her distress would show on her face.

"Interesting," she heard Leighton say. "Felled by mere parsnips. I recommend ginger tea to restore the young man."

"Ginger cures many ailments," said Wester Ross in a neutral tone, but to anyone who knew him it was clear he was not amused.

"Not in time to report his progress on the classification, I fear," Leighton said with a sniff.

Catriona pressed the edge of her knife against the slab of beef on her plate. A rivulet of blood seeped from the meat into the gravy. Her forehead pulsed with some strange fever but her thoughts were clear and sensible: to save face for everyone, to not burn bridges, to conceal her private feelings from prying eyes. Her body demanded only one thing: to see him. It beat through her with the bright insistence of a church bell. *Go see him.*

"What do you think about positioning the bulls in a long corridor," Leighton suggested, "one on each end, facing each other."

Where was Elias going? Would he stew in his room? Return to twist Leighton's neck?

The whirl of faces and voices surrounding her made her dizzy, so she closed her eyes for some respite. In the dark, she felt it more acutely, the angry heat of his body still smarting on her own skin. He had been bloody furious.

She put down her cutlery. "Excuse me," she said, and gave a little wave when her father and Leighton scrambled to stand up. "Please, do carry on. I shall only be a moment."

The dining hall, first quad, second quad, narrow staircase, all passed in washed-out colors. Fateful moments always caused a shift in her material setting, as if a veil had been pulled from her eyes, or perhaps the reverse, her ever-vigilant senses turned inward with a singular focus on what actually mattered.

She was yards from Elias's flat when the door abruptly opened. Her stomach did a flip, and her hands flew to her middle. Elias stilled upon spotting her, one hand braced against the doorframe, but the force of his momentum still moved over her like a gale.

They regarded each other. Both wordless. Both aware of the ragged sound of their breathing filling the shadowed corridor.

Elias gave her a nod. "Ma'am."

She stood as if nailed to the floor. He felt different. He had cast off his smile, the fine shoes, and the dinner jacket. Instead, he was broody, booted, and cravatless. His shirt fell open below the throat down to the first button, revealing dark hair on tan skin. She glimpsed the glint of a fine gold chain around his neck.

"You're going out," she said, attempting a casual tone.

"I am," he replied.

Now she noticed his binoculars, slung over his right shoulder. "Birding?"

"Yes."

He walked past her, his arm an inch from brushing her shoulder. The scent of male anger clung to him, sharp and salty. It didn't deter her, she followed him.

He stopped and turned back, and the set of his mouth was impatient.

"Birding," she echoed. "Right now?"

His eyes flashed. "It is that," he said in a low, hard voice, "or returning to the dining hall"—he pointed in the direction of it—"where I would . . ." He bit his lip, keeping the details of Leighton's demise to himself.

She raised her hands, as if to place them against his chest. "He's ghastly," she said. "I'm sorry."

This made him look at her with renewed interest. "Are you his family?"

She drew back. "Certainly not."

A shrug. "Then you can't apologize on his behalf."

Her heart was racing at the thought of him walking away, angry like this, possibly put out with her.

"May I walk with you," she blurted.

Elias slanted his head and his gaze traveled over her from top to toe. Something in his eyes sent a delicate shiver shimmying up her spine.

"You should go back," he said. "You are the hostess."

"These people are of no importance to me."

A hawkish expression passed over his face. "What of your reputation?" he asked. "Is that of importance to you?"

"What can you mean?"

He took a step toward her and peered down his nose. "I mean that somehow, we keep ending up alone together—in my bedchamber or poorly lit places."

Thoughts tumbling, she returned his reproachful look with a defiant silence.

Elias ran a hand over his chin, and the gesture felt more charged than a curse word.

"Madame," he began, but paused.

Footsteps sounded on the stairs leading up to this particular poorly lit corridor. They saw their thoughts mirrored in each other's eyes: Was the intruder coming, or going? It could be a college scout. A porter, or a fellow. It could be someone who would gossip about Lady Catriona being alone with the foreign scholar an awful lot . . .

Elias's hand was on her upper arm, his thumb pressing into the soft flesh beneath the stiff sleeve of her gown as he walked her backward. For a breath, he was thrillingly close, the exposed hollow of his throat right in front of her nose. Then they were inside his flat, and her back was against the door, which shut with a *slam*.

A stormy-blue gaze bore into hers. He was still holding her by the arm, his grip warm and overwhelming in its easy strength. She held very still, so he would keep holding on.

Outside, the corridor was silent.

Their eyes remained locked.

"Why did you follow me?" he asked.

His tone wasn't friendly, but his thumb stroked her arm, up and down, a slow, repetitive caress he seemed to be doing unawares. The surface of her skin warmed as if she had stepped too close to a fire.

"I wanted to see how you are," she said.

He gave a gentle squeeze. "Why?"

She licked her lips. "Because you are our guest."

A sardonic glint flared in his eyes. He kept his mocking gaze on her damp mouth while he took off his hat and placed it onto the commode next to the door.

"A guest," he said, dark laughter in his voice. "I see."

He clasped the back of her neck with a firm hand and leaned down. When his lips met hers, the lights went out inside her head. The hot, confident sweep of his tongue against hers was pure relief, like a deep breath, like letting go of a weight. She made a sound in her throat, lustful desperation, and Elias pressed into her, caged her against the door with one hand buried in her hair, the other flat on the wood. His body was hard, thighs, chest, shoulders, astoundingly solid. She had expected a man's embrace to feel different, but she couldn't have anticipated what it did to her. It made her offer her mouth when his tongue invaded deeper, it made her arch and quiver when he possessively palmed her breast. It wasn't so much his physicality that compelled erotic surrender but something more ephemeral, the hot ardor pulsing under Elias's skin that said nothing and no one would have kept him from kissing her, that he would have battled the very elements to feel her body in his hands. Sensing her yielding suppleness, he gentled, and she felt the weight of his arm around her waist to urge her closer. She touched the base of his throat, where his skin was warm and bare over firm muscle. His chest hair was surprisingly soft. Her fingertips grazed the metallic texture of his chain, followed it up to his nape. Emboldened, she grabbed a fistful of his thick, luxurious curls. With a low groan, Elias detangled himself and eased back. She blinked, breathless and disoriented. The light in the room blazed too brightly, anything that wasn't him seemed to have been burned out of existence. They were holding each other's faces now, both panting softly. He rubbed her swollen bottom lip with his thumb.

"Is this how you usually treat your guests?" he asked hoarsely.

His heart beat a visible rhythm on the side of his throat.

"No," she breathed.

His lips twitched with a mirthless triumph.

"What now?" she whispered an inch from his chin.

He released her and stepped away. An impressive erection strained against his trousers, and her head went empty again.

Elias took off his jacket and hung it in the wardrobe.

"Now you should leave," he said, glancing at her while he pulled off his gloves. "You can stay, too, but then we won't stop at kissing."

Chapter 18

Her ears hurt with sudden pressure. His scandalous announcement didn't seem quite real. Elias held out his hand to her, his expression calm, but the glitter in his eyes said *It is very real, darling.*

"Do you mean intercourse?" Her voice came out weak, as though it had lost its range.

A smirk. "No. My word on it."

"You're not married, are you," she asked.

"No." His eyebrows indicated disbelief.

Before her courage left her, she placed her hand in his. His palm felt warm and dry against hers. The flame in his eyes burned brighter.

"On my honor," he said, "I will have the sculptures back, one way or another."

She gave a tiny nod. "I know."

He would keep his vow no matter what happened next between them. She left her hand in his. His fingers closed around hers, and instantly the air seemed charged with something wild and unpredictable. A tug, and he pulled her into a twirl as though they were dancing, but he just wanted her with her back against his chest. Strong arms locked below her breasts, and the tight hold stimulated her aroused senses to a fever pitch. His heart was still drumming furiously, setting a frenzied beat in her own blood. He claimed her vulnerable neck in a hungry, open-mouthed kiss, and she let her head drop back against his shoulder on a soft moan. The sensation of his sleek tongue gliding over delicate skin seemed to melt her between her legs, and she had to shift to accommodate the swelling ache. The loosening of her bodice registered with a delay. Elias leaned his cheek against hers, and they both paused to take in the lush view, the exposed tops of her breasts framed quite prettily by the low-cut corset cover.

His ragged voice was next to her ear. "Beautiful."

He fingered the lacy edge of the cover, measuredly, like a test. Her breathing turned unsteady. Elias turned his face and looked her in the eye.

"If I do something you don't like, will you tell me?"

She nodded.

"Good."

His fingertips met silken skin, and he made a sound in his chest while his eyes fell shut. For a moment, she saw his profile in stark detail, every atom clear and magnified: his handsome cheekbones taut with desire, his thick lashes resting against his cheeks like dark crescent moons. He pushed his hand inside her corset. Her breath came through her parted lips now; it felt too decadent, looking on while he was shamelessly feeling her breasts. Glancing touches, then pinches to the sensitive tips, and she was on her toes, pushing her bottom into his groin. With a near audible *snap*, a leash on his restraint gave way. He turned her in his arms. Her feet left the ground. She was sitting on the commode, her hips level with his and her skirts bunched in his fist. His half-lidded gaze searched her face while he pulled up the rustling swathes of fabric. He would touch her, right where she was thrumming with need.

"Yes," she heard herself say, when she could have been sensible and stopped it. A smile flashed, and Elias eased her knees apart. Sensibleness ceded to a dreamlike blend of sensations: the cool rush of air over her most intimate place. Elias's hand, warm and heavy on the top of her bare thigh. He stroked higher. His mouth opened slightly when he slid his fingers over the slick opening of her sex. He rubbed, lightly, over just the right spot. Pure pleasure, bright and hot, spread through her thighs, and she caught her lower lip between her teeth to stifle a cry. He did it again, his fingers moving confidently now, up and down, slipping inside her a little, then back to tease the aching pearl on top. On and on. She realized, quite shocked, that he could take her to the end. The tension in her muscles was already thickening. His touch was skillful, reading her and adjusting; clearly this wasn't his first seduction, but he was breathing hard now as if pleasuring her was undoing him, too. He pressed his mouth back to hers and his hips replaced his hand, making her feel a hard protrusion through the fabric of his trousers. He moved, as though he was inside her. Her legs stiffened around him, her feet were pointing with the first shivers of bliss. Then she hissed, trying to evade the scrape of hidden buttons against her tender flesh. He slowed and murmured, soothingly, "Shhh, habibti." Somehow, he opened his trousers, and his penis was between them, thick and flushed.

She gasped. "No, not like this, we can't."

"We won't," he said softly, "we won't."

He hooked an arm under her knee and fitted himself against her.

"See?" He held himself perfectly still, just let her feel the warm, heavy weight of his arousal. When he moved again, skin on skin, they both moaned. This. This part of him was made with a woman's enjoyment in mind, hot and blunt and velvety smooth . . . he flexed his hips, again, and the tension spiked so hard, her vision dimmed. She gripped the warm cotton fabric of his shirt for purchase, and he glanced down at her, his gaze black; his throat sheened with sweat. He'd be like this in bed, above her, steadily moving back and forth between her thighs, filling her with frantic energy.

"It's as though we are doing it," she said, her voice high and strained.

"Not even close," he ground out, but her words derailed his rhythm. The commode began thumping against the wall, in time with his thrusts. It distracted her, right on the cusp, her toes were already curling. Her climax flattened from an impending explosion to a shallow ripple, a mangled flutter that made her whimper in frustration rather than relief.

Her lover had no such trouble, his release racked him moments later. He was perfectly silent but his strong body arched like a trapped creature trying to break its chains. While he slumped forward, eyes glassy and lips parted, he was reaching into his waistcoat pocket for his handkerchief.

The room resonated with silence. There was just the *thump thump thump* of her pulse in her ears. Her legs relaxed, and her heels tapped against a wooden drawer. Elias took a deep, shuddering breath next to her temple, and she realized she had not been breathing at all.

They looked at each other with twin expressions of disbelief, like possessed people after a successful exorcism, rumpled and askew. The musky-sweet scent of female arousal lay over the scene, mixing with an unfamiliar alkaline note.

Wordlessly, Elias cleaned his hand and buttoned his trousers. He smoothed her flipped-up skirts back down.

"I take the blame for this," he said at last. "But have you *any* sense of self-preservation?"

She gathered her gaping bodice at her throat and sat up straight.

"I trust you," she said. She glanced away. "I wanted it."

He balled the handkerchief in his fist and made an exasperated motion with his head. It wasn't about what she wanted, of course, it was about what was proper. It must be difficult to grasp for him, how the same woman who struggled to look him in the eye and make polite conversation had let him go under her skirts without resistance. Perhaps polite conversation just wasn't as true or as necessary as the sensation of his hands on her skin; there was a realness to their physical intimacy that made it natural and easy, unlike etiquette. The moment his mouth had met hers, she had reacted on an instinct that had been bridled since girlhood, and it had thrilled her to feel it so ready to charge, so close to the surface. A lifetime of elaborate, petty man-made rules could be swept away by something as base as an open-mouthed kiss. Her body was still buzzing like an electric conduit, all objects in the room had a rainbow halo. They had recklessly penetrated through to a real part of life.

Elias cupped the curve of her heated cheek in his hand.

"We will not do this again," he said.

They took measure of each other's damp faces and turbulent eyes, and without any more words being exchanged they both knew that they would absolutely do this again.

Chapter 19

The following day, she entered the Common Room at one o'clock, and the flicker of surprise in Elias's eyes said that he had not expected her to show. The urge to hide had been strong indeed, but the dice had rolled, the cards were on the table—they desired each other. At least that part was clear, and a clearly laid-out situation, no matter how outrageous, was always preferable over the agony of vague anticipation.

She did order a sherry today and sipped on it immediately. MacKenzie had seated herself extra close to the small table, and the determined click of her needles punctuated the tense silence. Elias's fiery anger seemed to have defused, but his hair flopped low across his brow and a broody resolve edged his mouth as he moved his army across the board. A pawn, f4, en route to box in her king, prompting her to position her bishop to prepare a countermove.

"I understand you no longer want my father to approach Leighton," she said. Elias and Wester Ross had met over an early breakfast before the earl had returned to London.

"Yes," Elias said. "This is correct."

His voice was bland. He would not reveal his next steps, that much was clear.

"Do you think it's pointless?" she asked nevertheless.

"Eh." *Yes.*

He launched his remaining knight, and she had no clue where he was planning to go with that move, either. She moved her rook from file *a* to *b*. She kept her gaze on the black and white squares so that only Elias's fingers moved in and out of her field of vision when it was his turn. She couldn't look him in the face without seeing his body arch with erotic abandon. She kept wondering how it would feel if he did this while she was straddling him, which was strange because it was not a position she imagined enjoying very much. Her brain often betrayed her like this, conjuring up comical or tawdry scenarios in moments when it was highly inappropriate. At boarding school, during the required attendance at mass, she had compulsively thought about kissing her crush, when she should have contemplated her mortal coil. Perhaps there was a connection, an unconscious attempt to counterweigh the scepter of mortality with another, tangible, life-bringing force. The schism between Elias and her after the dinner had felt like a death of sorts, too, like the loss of something rare before it had been given the chance to unfold. They didn't have the power to change the circumstances that made it so; they both were particles in grand churning systems that touched every facet of their lives and were slower to change off course than an ocean liner. What they had done on the commode struck her as rebellious now; while man-made rules budged even into those most intimate spaces, deciding who could legitimately mate with whom, at the end of the day the act was as old as time, universal across all living creatures, and defied regulation once the door was closed.

"It's bizarre, isn't it," Elias said, "how the world hangs together." He was surveying the positions on the chessboard, but his fingers drummed rapidly on the table, sounding like the hoofbeat of a tiny horse in full gallop. "Thousands of miles from Vienna and Paris and London, a small region in West Asia goes through a feudal revolution. Every day, such a thing takes place somewhere on the globe, and no one takes note. But when it happens within the borders of an empire Europe wants to maintain at all costs . . . it's no longer simply a local conflict. It becomes a crack that reveals that the Ottomans are losing their grip. And this can't be. France and Britain don't want to go to war outright over the Ottoman carcass, and they don't want Russia to have it, either. Austria-Hungary has no interest in a tipping balance unless it's in their favor. So the House of Osman must not fall, and the five greatest powers in the world gather round a shiny table to squash a local struggle. They sit in plush chairs in Versailles or Downing Street and meddle in a faraway strip of land where people don't even read the clock."

"It is bizarre," she agreed. "And overwhelming."

He did a castling, switching his king and kingside rook, which effectively put His Majesty on the presently safest spot on the battlefield.

She glanced at him.

He caught her gaze, and a crackling arc of tension sprang up between them. Oh, he was still angry. His eyes were an iridescent riot that could well tip over into revolution. A nervous heat spread from her chest all the way to her hairline.

Unexpectedly, he grinned, a rather mean grin. "Leighton mentioned Bek Karam," he said. "Do you know who betrayed Bek Karam in the end, after he beat the Ottoman army?"

"I don't, no."

He leaned forward. "Fellow Maronites."

"I see."

"As your friend said, it's all about power—all are scrambling for a slice, to the detriment of the whole. Bek Karam is in exile now. I doubt he will see the mountain again."

She couldn't think of anything appropriately profound to say. He probably thought her awfully cold.

On the chessboard, the situation looked like a text in a language she didn't speak.

"If we continue to play now," she said, "you will win. I can't seem to focus."

His mouth softened. "Are you asking for mercy?"

"I suppose. I'm aware it defeats the objective of this game."

He made a soothing motion with his hand. "I won't deny a lady. We reconvene, as you wish."

Don't deny me, she thought stupidly. *Kiss me again.* For a moment, neither seemed to know what to say. Last evening, her numbness after an overwhelm had proven useful: she had fixed her hair in front of Elias's mirror, and she had returned to Hall in time for pudding. She had reinstated a cordial relationship with Leighton and Miss Regina, and they had furthered their plans to put the Ashmolean pieces into the British Museum. All throughout, she had seen Elias's face, taut with dark desire as he rocked against her.

Elias's eyelids lowered. "Don't look at me like that," he said in Arabic.

She pressed her lips together, feeling caught. "Like what."

"Like you did last evening, in my room."

"I wasn't," she said, her tone convincingly prim.

MacKenzie's needles clanged like foils coming together. MacKenzie, who always seemed to be with her these days, always watching from under critical brows.

Elias made a cynical sound. "Your father was just here, at St. John's."

"Indeed." It came out in English. Did he mean to tell Wester Ross? Her heartbeat turned painfully unsteady; it felt as though a creature tried to butt its way out of her chest. Did he mean to go to her father . . . to do the honorable thing and ask for her?

Elias's gaze tracked the expressions on her face, and briefly, a cold emotion hardened his eyes. "I won't kiss you under your father's roof again," he said.

She exhaled. Found her way back into his mother tongue. "What does that mean?"

"I respect the earl." Said as though he implied that she did not.

He hadn't kissed her more in the Blackstone library, because he "held her in high regard." Her consternation showed in her prickly undertone. "Does that mean that when you kiss me, you disrespect me?"

"Some would see it that way."

"How do you see it?"

His face was inscrutable. "Does it matter, as long as those around us think like this?"

Yes, it did. She would like it confirmed that in his heart of hearts, he found their kisses above reproach and understood that she was her own woman. She glanced away, aware that she had already said and done too much. She had thrown herself at Charlie before, and she had all but propositioned Elias in the Blackstone library, then let him have his way with her on a commode. In the moment, it hadn't felt like self-degradation because the sincerity and depths of her feelings constituted their own virtue, but he was right, no one else would see it that way.

She emptied her sherry glass.

"This is not my father's roof," she said. "It's university property."

He smiled at that, softly, as if he understood her pain.

She returned to the Campbell lodgings with her focus shot to pieces. In the study, traces of Wester Ross's pipe tobacco still lingered in the air. He wasn't a habitual smoker, but the situation with Leighton had troubled him enough to light up last night. *What would you have me do*, he had asked her, puffing and raking his fingers through his hair. *I saw the firmans, the licenses, with my own eyes before I accepted work on the pieces, and the Ottomans are the official government of Sidon.*

It hadn't satisfied her. *You are one of Britain's leading scholars in archaeology. If you can't think of how to make this right, who can?* She hadn't told him that she'd set about fixing this particular case herself if he didn't. Wester Ross had asked her to be patient, at least until he had completed his deal with Middleton. Before he left, he had promised to present the idea to the curator in charge during his remaining days in London.

Behind her, MacKenzie entered the study with a tea tray.

"There's mail for you," she announced. Next to the sturdy teapot was an envelope. Catriona took the entire tray from MacKenzie. She carried it to her desk, then poured the tea so it could cool while she read. The letter turned out to be a reply to her writ campaign, not a note from Elias. Good. Excellent. She had a cause to support, and she owed it her full attention.

The letter's sender was an MP she had never met in person, but his profile was in her folder where she filed all relevant men of influence, and he had struck her as a promising candidate. His note, however, was not promising at all:

It appears that you have misunderstood how the writ is used in practice. The Writ for Restitution of Conjugal Rights is commonly taken out by females, as it statutorily entitles them to interim alimony from their husbands in the case of a de facto separation. It may be filed in the same way as a separation petition, but may be filed more speedily, namely the moment a roguish husband has left the marital home. To put it simply for you, this law benefits your sex. I advise you to not become distracted by whichever sensationalist stories you may have heard and put your considerable time and effort toward alleviating the truly vile conditions that plague our society.

Sensationalist stories. She placed the letter flat onto her desk and rested her eyes on the lovely, blooming garden outside the window. Very carefully, she sipped some tea. Her research in the

Bodleian had suggested that at least one woman had perished in prison, and some women had left the country to avoid incarceration. It was enough to merit her efforts, thank you very much. Today was Friday. On Monday, she would report her abysmal record to the others and ask Lucie for help. Under the desk, her legs were restless. The ghastly note in front of her should cure any sensible woman of the desire to kiss any man ever again, and yet an urge stirred, to see Elias and read the letter to him. He'd probably say something terribly astute that made her want to take her clothes off again. She shifted around on the chair in some luxurious physical discomfort and berated herself for her stupidity. What if Elias *had* gone to Wester Ross? She had played with dynamite when she had stayed in his bedchamber. She smoothed her hand, warm from the teacup, over her forehead. Ridiculous, that she had ever thought one could immunize against the effects of attraction with low doses of exposure—an attraction was not a virus, it was a spark. One spark was enough to set off an explosion. One spark could light an inferno.

A cool wind brushed over Port Meadow, carrying the dampness of the river. Elias lowered his binoculars and inhaled. He was sitting on the trunk of a fallen willow between a narrow footpath and the banks, his back turned to the leafy woods behind him. The Thames flowed past his feet with barely perceptible surface movement. On the other side of the water, the green blanket of the meadow stretched toward Oxford's spires and steeples. Cattle egrets dotted the plain with plumages as soft and white as cotton fluff. He had also noted several species of duck, a brown-breasted stonechat, and a bird he had had to look up in his English ornithology guide. It gave him no pleasure. Birding, like chess, required the concentration and attention to detail that muted and cleared the mind. Not today.

Catriona's face kept flashing before his eyes, how it had frozen when he had mentioned her father in the Common Room earlier. The bent of her thoughts had been obvious, possibly because one track of his mind, the hidden one that operated outside the realm of etiquette and reason, was preoccupied with asking Wester Ross permission to court her. It hadn't been a serious plan as much as a manifestation of his desire to have her, to finish what they had started with the kiss in the Blackstone library. And yet, her reaction had felt as sobering as walking into a wall.

He soon tucked his bird guide back into his pocket and jumped off the tree trunk. As he strode along the path at a punishing pace, he couldn't ignore how closely the situation mirrored his predicament eight years ago: an overwhelming desire for a woman, and all circumstances stacked against him.

He had just turned twenty and Khalo Jabbár had entrusted him with a good position at the port. The Silk Office had not yet existed but trade with Europe had reached great heights, so Elias worked long hours in the large warehouse, overseeing the export of silk thread to Europe and doing the inventory of the imports. From France came modern looms, from Britain processed textiles, finest cotton but also silks. It was the luxurious shawls and gowns that first lured the girl Nayla into his family's warehouse. Later, he found out that her family was in the trade business, too, and that she often accompanied her uncles to the port to have the first pick of new deliveries. The day she entered the front office in a group of aunties, Elias found himself face-to-face with the most beautiful creature he had ever seen. She was the moon, she was a jewel, sparkling bright. He knew the exact moment when she noticed him staring—startled, she turned away while pulling her gauzy veil across her lower face. After a second that lasted an eternity, she peeked back at him. Her large eyes were dark and liquid. Gazelle eyes. Pools of infinite mystery. She returned his gaze for a fraction longer than would have been incidental. A place inside his chest expanded violently, and he couldn't breathe.

When she returned the following week, his heart pounded so hard, he thought he was ill. It was a sort of sickness that spread between them through glances alone, and the anticipation building in the now meaningless hours between her visits fanned the heat to an unsurvivable fever pitch. The amount of gold on her neck and head and her style of dress indicated that her family was wealthy but Greek Orthodox, not a choice his family would readily approve. Still, he couldn't stop, it was too addicting to freely project the full force of a young man's passion onto her beautiful face. He became reckless, and left gifts for her in the silk showroom: a blossom, a flower, then flowers with messages on tiny scraps of paper tied to the stems. The ecstasy when she left him a message in return! She had written a single word: Nayla. *Nayla, Nayla, Nayla.* For a week, her name was on his lips like a prayer.

It all went wrong when Khalo Jabbar went to Damascus for some business involving cashmere goats. He was still traveling when Elias learned that Nayla's name was on a matchmaker's list. His interest in the girl hadn't escaped the more eagle-eyed of his colleagues at the port, and they wanted to either warn or tease him by letting him know the news over lunch. Any hesitation he had felt about proposing was instantly blown to bits; he was on his feet and walking before he even had a plan. The correct procedure would have been to wait for Jabbar and tell him that he wanted to marry Nayla. If in favor, Jabbar would have approached her guardian, and if in agreement, they would have asked Nayla to consider Elias. All this Elias knew. All he could think was that another man would snatch his princess from right under his nose—because Jabbar was looking at goats in Damascus. In hindsight, temporary insanity was his only explanation for what he did next: in midday heat, he walked up the hill to her family's mansion in Ashrafieh, and asked to speak to the head of the house.

Nayla's brother was puffing on an expensively imported Cuban cigar when Elias entered his study. The east wall behind the man's back was covered with icons in gilded frames, and the eye couldn't settle on a quiet surface anywhere; vases, silk settees, veined marble, and potted palm trees seemed to encroach. The contrast between the elegant décor and Elias's regular weekday attire couldn't have been starker. Still, he was heard out.

"It might offend my sister," the brother said after Elias had presented his case. "It might offend her, the idea of a husband who is not one of ours."

Elias had expected this, but at the end of the day intermarriage did happen and was hardly a crime. He had thought about such things since he was a boy who had had his life upended by a war, and his current conclusion was that more fractures would not heal the mountain and love was love; what mattered was respect, the will to cherish, to protect . . .

"She might ask for additional compensation," Nayla's brother added.

Ah. "How much would she expect from one of yours?" Elias asked.

"Two thousand in American dollars."

His face felt hot. That was almost the entirety of his investments. He offered two thousand five hundred.

The brother blew out smoke. "It is four thousand for you, and a thousand of that in gold."

Elias stared at the man. "Why?" he demanded.

"One thousand surcharge, and an additional thousand to compensate for the Zghartawi temper—hupp, there it goes."

Elias had shot to his feet, his pulse drumming with righteous outrage at being mocked.

His opponent crushed the cigar into the ashtray. "I don't want trouble," he said. "Go back to your village."

He went back to the warehouse instead, white-hot with anger. When Nayla visited an hour later, he managed to split her from the herd and pulled her into the supply room.

"Your brother refused me," he said in a harsh whisper. "I'm here to take you away."

She shrank from him, her gaze bouncing between his looming shoulders and the door he had locked.

"Nayla."

Her bewitching eyes were huge. "We can't."

Those were her first words to him. He clasped her wrist, and she gasped.

"Do you want to?" he urged.

She turned her head slightly to the side. "We mustn't."

"It's our only option."

"We could never return home!"

"I shall build us a home—better than here."

She was stiff and unmoving in his grip. "Please, think," she pleaded, exasperation repressed in her voice. "Do you truly want a wife who disregards her family's wishes so severely?"

Yes, yes, apparently that was what he wanted, if that was what it took to have her. Her cold demeanor suggested that she didn't share the sentiment. She seemed afraid, reluctant. In fact . . . if she weren't trapped with him, alone and at his mercy, she might be making a proper scene. The realization sank into his consciousness like a toxic cloud, withering any youthful delusions and virginal idealism to a husk. He released her abruptly. She rubbed her wrist with some exaggeration, but the look in her eyes changed from fearful to sad. "Elias," she said. He walked out the side entrance without a backward glance.

He left Beirut for the village to lick his wounds, but everyone at the mountain mansion was up in his business: the cousins, his aunt, the cats. His grandmother noticed something was wrong, so she personally brought him plates with cut-up fruit, but the sweet slices had an aftertaste of onion because someone hadn't changed the knife. He was packing a bag to go and find some peace when Khalo Jabbar returned—unsurprisingly, the news of Elias's doomed proposal had reached Jabbar through the grapevine on his way home. Instead of brooding undisturbed in a hermit cave, Elias saw his dignity flayed in his uncle's study.

"You want to marry, you come to me. Make any decision? You come to me—I am calm, rational," Jabbar shouted, his hands chopping air in every direction, "you, what are you? A heavy idiot! Your brain is an ornament! This is my life, I'm surrounded by donkeys." He stuck his head out of the study door and yelled for his sons, and when one of them dared to venture forth, Jabbar skewered him, too: "Damn your father, could you not take him to someone?" He pointed at Elias. "Here, I present you Majnoun Nayla, making us look stupid just because he glimpsed a woman."

His own temper boiling, Elias decided to become an émigré there and then. Anticipating this, Jabbar sent for him half an hour later and revealed that he was putting him and Nassim in charge of running their fledgling British outpost in Manchester. "Nassim's English is bad, and he is only eighteen," he said to Elias, "you should go with him and protect him from himself and the British."

His hand forced because he loved his cousin, Elias was on a boat to England a few days later, too far from the mountain to cause further furor but still bound to the family business. Clever Jabbar. In truth, he *was* clever; it took Elias a few more years to appreciate the blood, sweat, and cunning politicking Jabbar provided to make his clan untouchable in a place of revolving conquests, but, young and heartbroken at the time, that day he began to plan his exit.

"All great love stories are unrequited," Nassim told him on his first day of staring at the horizon from the steamer railing, "that's the hallmark of true love, the unrequitedness."

Elias, suffering from seasickness for the first time he could remember, told him to go away.

"Life is full of misery, and most is caused by women," Nassim offered the next morning.

On the third day, he arrived with a bottle of arak. Elias refused to drink it; the way past pain was right through the hot hell of it. Later, he learned that Nayla had been married to an Italian count soon after he had gone. To he who has enough money, a princess is his bride.

Elias entered the residential part of Oxford that bordered the meadow, a brooding expression on his face. These days, he possessed the means to woo the daughter of an earl, certainly one whose estate was in such pecuniary decline. He had worked hard for this position; he had put off finding a wife and focused on expanding, amassing, investing, driven in part by a fiery determination that he would not be denied again over his status. His hand clenched around the hilt of his walking stick. In an ironic twist, his wealth was rather low on the list of obstacles now. She was a British aristocrat while he wasn't even from her world; he would become persona non grata in Britain the moment he succeeded at taking the artifacts. She was also keenly aware that she wasn't free. Most women of his acquaintance, East or West, were kept in luxury and ruled their homes, which seemed to sufficiently dull the sting of any restrictions placed upon them, but Catriona was an activist and gilded bars probably still looked like bars to her. Was he equipped to manage with such an unconventional wife? Whichever road they could choose to finish what they had started, it led to chaos.

Once he reached the main street, he walked straight to Oxford's telegraph office and sent a message to Nassim. He would go to London on Monday to meet Nassim's contact. He would set a plan in motion that would bring home the loot. A few days away from St. John's might help quell the mad want ticking in his veins.

Chapter 20

Monday morning, clouds rushed across the sky and the wind tugged on Catriona's skirts from all directions while she walked to the Randolph Hotel. Her hairdo was loose by the time she arrived in Hattie's drawing room. She brushed the locks away from her face, annoyed by the untidy sensation. She watched Hattie and Lucie put the plates from the tea cart onto the table and felt a pang of dread. Her friends were quite observant, and she currently seemed to carry a massive sign above her head: *I have done very naughty things with a man!*

She had dreamt about doing it again, too, had taken everything to its conclusion in her sleep. In reality, he had said, *We will not do this again . . .*

"Catriona, why are you lurking? Join us," Hattie called, and waved her closer.

Nobody will know.

She entered with a stiff smile.

"Annabelle can't attend today because baby Jamie has the sniffles," Hattie related while she handed out cups of tea. "The poor mite."

Lucie and Catriona made commiserative sounds. Underneath her skirts, Catriona's left leg was bouncing. She couldn't seem to breathe properly. This wasn't just owed to her situation with Elias.

She had been around too many people for too long, taking in too many stories. If there weren't so many layers to her feelings lately, she would have recognized her exhaustion sooner.

"We don't have much to discuss anyway," Lucie said. She glanced over the documents she was balancing on her knees. "We are still advancing on the Property Act front—we've converted three more to vote in our favor last week. I suspect they sense a sea change and prefer to not be on the losing side. Only a few of the usual suspects will cause us trouble."

"Who," Catriona asked.

Lucie checked her notes. "Most notably, Sir George Campbell, and our old pal Mr. Warton. They are actively running a counter-campaign."

"Sir George," Catriona muttered. "Ghastly creature."

The man was loud and uncompromising at the Campbell clan meetings. She would never forget his thinly veiled criticism that Wester Ross seemed content with having a daughter for an heiress rather than taking a new wife and thus another chance at producing a son.

Hattie put down her biscuit. "Could they truly stop the bill again at the last moment?"

"They could delay it severely," Lucie said, "or weaken the wording, if they garner enough support for their proposals on the day of the decision."

Hattie made to pick up her biscuit again, then just left it on the plate.

"I'm so sick of them," she said softly. "I'm tired of them."

She reclined on the sofa and picked up her fan from the side table to cool her face.

Lucie arched a brow at her but turned her attention to Catriona. "What about the writ campaign?"

"Discouraging," she replied, thinking of the last letters she had read. "I think it requires personal visits, not writing. I might as well put it aside for now, until a team supports me."

"Is that so?"

"Yes. At this pace, it shall take the usual fifty years before anything changes."

Lucie's frown lines ran deep as she looked from Hattie to Catriona. "What's the matter this morning? Defeatist noises from both of you?"

"I'd call it realistic, to be honest, not defeatist," Catriona said.

Lucie huffed. "They *want* us to not even try. Don't fall for it."

"They also want us to spend our precious time on nonsense, and this feels like a waste of my time. It's not an unprecedented pattern: very few replies at all, and all of them negative."

Lucie made a face that said *Oh well, then*. "I trust your judgment," she said. "I just don't think you have tried long enough to make *this* judgment."

"I think the evidence is pretty conclusive."

"You do put a lot of stock into patterns," Hattie remarked as she flapped her fan. "There are advantages in being . . . open-minded."

"Extrapolating is a rational method," Catriona said with a frown. "It's neither closed- nor open-minded."

Hattie dropped back her head and made a guttural sound. "Human beings are not rational," she said. "They are . . . a mess."

Catriona's eyes narrowed. "You're still put out because I didn't want to marry Elias Khoury, aren't you."

Great. She just couldn't stop herself from sneaking in his name, could she? His face kept springing up before her mind's eye, short-circuiting the flow of her thoughts. *I won't kiss you under your father's roof again*. That was what his mouth had said, at least. A stubborn thought returned: that it wasn't truly over yet . . .

"Not at all," Hattie said in a docile tone. "I just feel it's important to think of some patterns as just that, a pattern—I wouldn't treat them like a crystal ball. And yes, yes, I'm aware I have consulted actual crystal balls before. How is Mr. Khoury, though? Was your dinner with Mr. Leighton successful?"

Catriona simply shook her head because her voice might come out an octave too high.

Hattie stopped fanning and pursed her lips. "Bother. I had hoped for some good news."

"Pattern of doom or not," Lucie budged in, "perhaps we find a compromise, Catriona. I could allocate two or three suffragists to the writ campaign to support you, seeing that the Property Act looks promising."

Catriona sat quietly in her chair, her body tense. *I don't want to,* she thought. *I want to just not see people for a while; I want to roll up on a bed and read a romantic novel and not think.*

"Fine," she muttered.

On the surface, she was present for the remainder of the conversation and nodded where required. Perhaps noticing the glum quality of her silence, Hattie took her hands in hers when they were saying their goodbyes. Her freckled face looked contrite. "I didn't mean to call you closed-minded earlier," she said. "It came out wrong."

Catriona made to assure her she hadn't understood it that way. Instead, she stared on while something clicked together in the depths of her mind.

"Of course," she said.

"What!" Hattie looked startled.

Catriona grabbed her upper arms. "Hattie," she said. "You are a genius."

"What?"

"You're right, a pattern is just that, a pattern. It describes a truth, but it isn't the truth—not the whole truth, anyway, not necessarily. I was distracted by what is there—when I should have also looked at what isn't there."

Hattie exchanged a glance with Lucie. "I understand nothing—that's a genius for you."

Catriona flapped her hands. "We are trying to abolish the writ so that wives can't be ordered back home by force, correct?"

"Correct," said Lucie.

"But where are the husbands who are forced back home? In theory, the writ works both ways."

Silence.

Lucie's mouth curved with mild disdain. "What sane woman would wish to force an unwilling husband back home?"

"I don't know," Catriona said. "I haven't a clue, but just picture it: a husband, languishing in jail, not because he refused to pay alimony, but because he refused to share a home with his wife again?"

"Well, well," Hattie purred. "How the tables turn. Parliament would shut down in shock."

Lucie was slowly shaking her head. "It would, but it's a hypothetical case—I can't think of ever having heard it applied this way round."

"Then we have to make a case," Catriona said, and began to pace. "A real one."

Hattie looked stunned. "You mean, setting a precedent?"

"Manufacturing one, rather."

"That would be brilliant," Lucie said absently; the wheels were clearly spinning behind her eyes. "Blimey, I adore the idea, but I can't see it happening in practice."

The urgent beat in Catriona's chest persisted. "We could try to convince a lady to do it. For a good cause. We've done it before; we've recruited a dozen lady investors for London Print."

"Yes, yes," Lucie said, pacing now, too, a hand on her chin. "But the investment consortium asked the ladies for money. What you suggest is asking a woman to stake her reputation."

Hattie's round shoulders sagged. "That's true. Drat. What notable lady would invite such a scandal into her life?"

"Exactly, and it would have to be a lady, or rather, a husband with a standing," Lucie said. "Otherwise, neither lawmakers nor the press will care."

"Let's try," Catriona said. "There must be one who is above petty slander."

"Petty slander?" asked Hattie. "'Ma'am, have you considered suing your husband into staying under your roof?' Imagine the headlines—if he chooses jail over her company, she'll forever be known as a proper dragon. That's not petty slander, that's . . ." She couldn't even find the word.

"I don't know any ladies who are unofficially separated," Lucie said. "However, we don't win if we don't risk. Let's ask in our chapter; someone will know of someone."

A knot formed in Catriona's stomach. A name had flashed across her mind, her brain already knowing before her heart was ready to admit to it.

Hattie and Lucie's chatter bled together into a faint, indecipherable roar.

"I know a lady," she said at last.

Lucie perked up. "Who?"

Catriona ran a hand over her face. Her palm was damp. "I can't see her doing anything like it. She might know someone else in her situation, though—birds of a feather flocking together and such . . . It's Lady Middleton—our neighbor, up in Applecross. She resides in London now."

"Lovely," Hattie said with an encouraging smile. "You are already acquainted."

"It's why I'm quite certain that we can't expect much help from her."

The real reason for her reluctance to even try was of course Charlie. The Middleton town house was an emotional crime scene. Memories lurked in the corners. Lady Middleton would have portraits of Charlie all over her walls, and she would look back at Catriona with Charlie's moss-green eyes . . .

Lucie clapped her hands. "Nothing wagered, nothing gained," she said. "Call on her, Catriona!"

She could have just kept her mouth shut. It would have been so easy.

"Hattie," she said. "Are you still planning to return to London today?"

Hattie's face brightened. "I am—on the eleven o'clock train. Do join me."

Unless she left with a friend, she would not leave St. John's at all; the plan had come about too sudden, and the destination gave her chills. If she accompanied Hattie, however, she could be in London in time for the afternoon slot reserved for social calls.

"She might see me already today—our families used to be close."

"Let's go together," Hattie said and clapped. "We shall have so much fun."

She put the back of her hand against her forehead. Surprisingly cool. Her breathing could be worse, too. Interesting. Perhaps her experiments with Elias had made her more robust after all.

Back at St. John's, she quickly packed her largest valise with her smartest dresses.

"I should like for you to stay here," she told MacKenzie while she piled clothes and cosmetics into the compartments.

MacKenzie handed her a stack of neatly folded chemises. "Staying with the Blackstones, are ye?"

Her gaze slid away. "Aye."

She would have dinner with the Blackstones. She would probably stay at her own house, however; not the Campbell town house, but her house, where she didn't even keep regular skeleton staff. The more she had thought about it on her way to St. John's, the better she had liked the idea of burrowing for a couple of days.

"It's no trouble for me, going to London," MacKenzie said. She smoothed her red hand over the fine undergarments before she placed a corset on top.

Catriona picked up her hairbrush. "I have kept you away from Applecross long enough."

MacKenzie was watching her with narrowed eyes.

Catriona stuffed the brush into a side compartment. "I want you to be well," she said. "Your leg seems improved, and I'd rather you rested now instead of rushing around the city with me. Hattie is a married woman. Her company suffices."

MacKenzie relented; despite their unconventionally close relationship, the only authority in Catriona's life was Wester Ross, and he shone with his absence.

A porter brought her valise and hatbox to the college's main doors. Catriona stepped into the lodge to leave a note for Elias. Barely through the doors, she halted as abruptly as though the ground had split before her feet: the man in question stood right there at the reception desk, chatting to porter Clive. He promptly turned his head toward her and their gazes clashed. Electricity crackled through the small room; it seared through her body and her knees sagged as though they had melted. Elias wore a finely cut wool jacket in dark navy, a perfectly respectable color and yet it made him look like a rake. It wasn't the jacket, of course, it was her awareness that behind closed doors, he had the hands, the mouth, and the audacity of a rake.

He politely dipped his head. "Lady Catriona." His voice was neutral. Impersonal.

Her stomach twisted.

"What a coincidence," she said. "I meant to leave this for you."

She awkwardly waved the envelope. He glanced at it with slanted eyebrows.

"Since you are right here," she went on, "I can tell you in person, obviously—I'm leaving for London. I shall be away for a couple of days. I trust you are well acclimatized by now."

His body had gone still. "So am I," he said. "Going to London."

There was, in fact, a large valise behind him, still on the porter's handcart.

"I left a note for you, too," he added.

It was true, an envelope was sitting in the Campbell pigeonhole.

Her poor heart was torn between sinking and somersaulting.

She turned back to Elias. "Are you taking the next train, by any chance?"

His colorful eyes flashed, confirming her suspicion.

A high-pitched noise rang in her ears. Was it destiny, laughing at her? Judging by the resigned look on his face, he was hearing it, too.

Fifteen minutes after the train had left Oxford's railway station, Catriona was ready to jump from the small compartment to escape the chaos radiating off Hattie. Her friend was sighing, fidgeting, placing her hands on her rosy cheeks.

Finally, Catriona fixed Hattie with a dark eye. "Go on. Out with it."

The freckled face was pure innocence. "Out with what."

"Whatever it is that is trying to burst out of your mouth about Mr. Khoury."

They were alone in the coach, which seated six, their travel veils thrown back. Elias was in the next coach, safely out of earshot. Still his presence was so *present*, he might as well have been seated right next to her. Had she really thought she could escape him by changing location? While he was so snugly ensconced under her skin? Hattie's eyes had near popped out of her head upon spotting him in their platform section. He had patiently answered all her questions—*Where are you staying? The Oxbridge Club in St. James's . . . For very long? Not too long, I should think . . . Oh, you must come to dinner! I would be delighted, ma'am . . .* He even had put his old smile back into place and it had felt glorious, like the sun breaking through November clouds.

"I have nothing at all to say about him," Hattie said.

"Clearly you do."

Hattie shook her head. "My body wants to chatter. I don't."

A relatable conundrum—Catriona's muscles were trembling from holding in all the turmoil. Part of her wanted to drag it into the open and rake it over with Hattie until the pressure in her body eased, but since it wouldn't lead to any conclusion, she kept choking it back down. She put a hand over her stomach and turned her attention to the landscape outside the window. She was seated with her back to the direction of travel, and the gentle summer-green hills of Oxfordshire were flying past as if in retrospect. Hattie took a novel from her pocket, a penny dreadful that probably had a happy ending.

"Hattie," Catriona finally said, her eyes on the green. "What do you do when something is pointless and yet you still can't seem to put it aside?"

Hattie lowered the novel, looking alarmed. "I think," she said after some contemplation, "if it keeps popping up, perhaps it isn't all that pointless."

Catriona scoffed, clearly in contempt of herself.

Hattie's gaze weighed on her. "You really like him, don't you."

The gentle, knowing tone loosened the knot blocking her throat.

She blinked rapidly. Next to the railway tracks, the shrubbery was a blur.

For a long stretch, the squeak and rattle of the train wheels filled the silence between them.

"Aye," she whispered at last. "I really, really like him."

For once, Hattie's impish face was somber. "Catriona, what will you do?"

Catriona shook her head. "I don't know. What do you do when your feelings don't match your options?"

Hattie made a self-deprecating sound. "You try to not go mad," she said.

The frenzied encounter on the commode flashed before Catriona's eyes. She was quite past the point of sanity. She rubbed her thumb over her index finger in a repetitive, soothing motion. She had had a clear plan in place for her life: Become a professor. Help fellow women realize their aspirations. Live in peace. Emotional turmoil was but a blip; every woman knew longing, and most learned to live with it. The misery of an unrequited crush had long been a familiar constant for her and in a way, it had been better than feeling nothing at all. *Look here, I do have a heart*, said that pain. But now . . .

"It's funny, isn't it," she said, "how we feel rather certain about something, and then it turns out we simply lacked a piece of crucial information that changes everything."

Such as finding out that unicorns like Elias existed, and that they might desire her, even if they felt that way despite themselves.

Hattie moved her lips while she pondered that. "I suppose we must never be too certain of any one thing."

"I like certainty," Catriona said. "I want certainty."

Hattie squinted at her. "Do you?"

"I thought that was obvious."

"Hm. You always struck me as quite open to changing your mind."

"Hardly."

"You are. It's true that you are a little on the rigid side, but look around—so many people won't change their stance on anything, regardless of evidence to the contrary. You do. No, it's true; I remember you having this conversation with Annabelle, how to know when an academic paper is finished, when there might be some evidence or a case you overlooked. You always search for more."

Catriona considered it. "I think," she said, "I think there is a difference between academic papers and people."

"Well, I hope so."

"The mind expands the more it errs and tries again. A heart just keeps breaking into smaller and smaller pieces."

Hattie's amused little smile slipped into an uncomfortably compassionate expression. "Oh, darling. I would hug you," she said, "but I know you don't like that."

Unexpectedly, a grin tugged at Catriona's mouth. "I feel well hugged right now, my friend."

After a pause, Hattie asked: "May I invite both you and Mr. Khoury to the same dinner at some point?"

She thought about it, her gaze flicking rapidly to keep up with the landscape rushing past. She nodded slightly. In just a few hours, she would see him at the railway station. A soft, erratic sensation fluttered in her belly, an emotion had just been let out of the cage again and stretched its wings.

He was already on the platform by the time Hattie had managed to open their unwieldy coach door. He helped Hattie down the step, and Catriona tried not to stare. Few men looked better in a hat when their hair was as nice as Elias's, but his hat effectively eliminated all distractions from his nicely structured face. It almost made her angry that he was walking around looking so handsome and that she just had to bear it. When it was her turn to alight, he offered his hand with a knowing flicker in his eyes—she had taken his hand like this only a few days ago, and they both knew where it had led them. The memory spread hot like lava through her limbs. His touch now was perfunctory; he let go at once. The warmth of his palm kept lingering while he was on his way to fetch their luggage.

Hattie sidled up to Catriona until their arms touched. "Mr. Blackstone is waiting for me."

At the platform entrance, the dark, forbidding figure of Hattie's husband stood out from the milling crowd. He lifted his top hat when Catriona caught his eye.

"You are welcome to join us," Hattie said in an even tone. "We could take you to your place, or you may stay with us."

At the other end of the platform, Elias oversaw the transfer of their luggage onto a cart. His stance was relaxed, his profile smiley as though he was exchanging a quip with the luggage clerk. The sun slanted through the roof's vast, arched end-screen behind him and delineated his form with a fuzzy golden glow.

Catriona squeezed Hattie's hand. "I shall manage on my own."

Hattie hesitantly squeezed back. "Then perhaps I should go to Mr. Blackstone now." She had traveled without luggage.

Catriona nodded. Hattie took her leave, casting a last furtive look back over her shoulder.

Elias arrived a minute later. He gave the clerk who had pushed the luggage trolley a coin, then glanced around. "Where is Mrs. Blackstone?"

The buzz of the railway station was unnaturally loud.

"Her husband picked her up," Catriona replied. "She left."

Elias's brows lowered. "What about you?"

"I have made my own arrangements. I have a house in Cadogan Place."

He searched the busy entrance hall with sharp eyes. "Someone picks you up?"

"No."

"Helps you with your valise?"

"I can manage."

He exhaled. The pause between them drew out.

"I should—" she began.

"Allow me to assist with your luggage," Elias said in a tense voice, "and to convey you to your house."

Her heart knocked against her ribs. It echoed in her ears. "All right."

Outside the station, he found them a hansom cab willing to take both their luggage and to drop them off in different districts for a surcharge.

They were wedged next to each other on the narrow seat, both facing the chaotic street ahead. His shaving soap, or perhaps it was an oil, edged out the mucky smell of the London fog. His arm bumped against hers now and again, causing small heat waves to lick at her center.

"You are in London for pleasure?" he asked, his eyes on the traffic. His profile looked stern. On the seat between them, the fingers of his right hand twitched, as though he would quite like to be the one holding the reins of the vehicle.

"I'm here for suffrage business," she replied. "How about you?"

"For business, as well."

Briefly, the reminder of his business made her whole body feel unpleasantly heavy. He was scheming to take the artifacts, and when he did, he would effectively be banned from Britain. Their time was so limited. She could not think of anything more to say until the cab came to a halt in front of her address. She owned the last in a row of terraced town houses, four stories tall and gleaming white, with a balcony fronting the entire first floor. Two white columns and a portcullis framed the black lacquered entrance door.

Elias followed her up the steps with her valise. When she picked out the key from her chatelaine rather than ring and wait for a butler, his confusion was palpable. He was wary by the time they entered the quiet corridor. The air smelled musty and undisturbed. The open doors revealed rooms with furniture shrouded in protective linen sheets. A fuzzy layer of dust covered the surface of the sideboard.

Elias put her valise down and his cutting gaze met hers.

"No one is here," he said.

"No." That was the point.

He spun his hand in a quizzical motion. "Your servants ran away?"

"I don't employ permanent staff here."

"You . . . will stay here . . . alone?" he drawled.

"Aye."

He picked up her valise again. "Let me take you to Mrs. Blackstone's house."

"What—why?"

"You cannot stay here."

"Well, I think I shall?" She sounded almost amused.

His eyebrows were moving up and down with disapproval. "Alone."

"Perfectly alone."

"You need meals," he said, "a fire in the hearth. Someone to stand guard." His free hand was emphasizing every sentence.

"I know how to set up a fire, but I don't need them in summer anyway," she replied. "The plumbing here is excellent, and there is a pub at the corner where I fetch meals."

"The pub, ya rabb." He glanced up at the ceiling with a harassed expression. "The pub we just passed? What if some drunk notices you? Follows you back here?"

His agitation had thickened his accent. The beat of her heart became unnaturally slow.

"I appreciate your concern, sir, but I know my own mind," she said.

She sensed what he would do before he did it: he looked up again, as if summoning divine guidance for how to proceed.

"Very well," he then conceded. "You know your mind."

"Thank you."

He put her valise back down.

"May I call on you," he asked, calmer now. "In the mornings. To put my mind at ease."

Her mouth made the decision for her. "You could stay."

She had said it so softly, she was not certain he would hear it.

Elias had heard very well. He stood still as a statue with her suitcase in his hand. Surprise etched his face, but the depths of his eyes were quiet. As though a part of him was not surprised at all.

"You see," she went on, "this isn't my father's house. It was always my mother's, and she left it to me. I'm under my own roof."

Chapter 21

~~~

She had retreated into the reception room and was waiting next to a shrouded armchair, her pulse thumping in her throat. From the corridor came the sound of the entrance door falling shut. Elias had returned; he had gone outside to pay the cab driver so the man would wait a little longer. He entered the reception room with a blank expression, but the details of his face stood out so clearly, she could have counted his dark lashes from where she stood. He halted in front of her, as close as a lover about to move in for a kiss. His warm scent filled her on her next breath.

"Now," he said, his gaze rather piercing. "Will you tell me why you have asked me to stay?"

She felt surveyed like some exotic creature, so she studied the nearest wall. He clasped her chin in his hand and turned her face back to him.

"You don't have to stay," she said.

"Oh, I know. But you surprise me. We are surrounded by eyes here—there is much at stake for you just by allowing me to enter this house."

"It's the middle of the summer," she replied. "Everyone is in the country. We have a back entrance, in the kitchen. I'm not out for a proposal, if that is what you think," she added.

"I didn't think you were," he said easily. "You wouldn't ask me to stay here, like this, if you wanted the position of my wife."

For a heartbeat, her insides felt hollow and charred. "Is that why you touched me in your room the other day," she murmured, "because you think I'm a strumpet."

He clenched his jaw. "No. That I did because I forgot myself."

Because he had been angry.

Something in his undertone compelled her to say: "I don't think I want to be, or rather, can be, anyone's wife, Mr. Khoury."

There was an infinitesimal pause.

"So you only want us to—" He gestured it.

Her arms hung limply by her sides. "All I know is that whenever I think of you leaving, I'm shaking inside," she said in a low voice. "I'm shaking as though I were falling ill."

He made a soothing sound and pulled her closer, until his thighs pressed into her skirts between them.

"Sometimes, I don't know what is inside your head," he said, his eyes searching hers. "You say outrageous things with the most unassuming face."

She wasn't unassuming. She had imagined their naked bodies entwined, sated and gleaming with spent desire.

"Is it truly so outrageous?" she asked.

Elias closed his eyes for a moment, then shook his head as if to clear his mind. "If you and I existed in our own world, all alone," he finally said, "then no."

She had all but missed their first kiss. The second had been angry, to demonstrate a point. This time, when he lowered his head, his mouth met hers slowly, molding their trembling lips together with deliberate care. Her eyes fell shut. The silky tip of his tongue glided over her sensitive bottom lip, and her breath left her with a sob. He used the moment to slip into her mouth. *Yes.* A soft groan, and his gloves dropped to the floor, and then he was holding her face in his warm palms. His thumbs were at the corners of her mouth, caressing the delicate skin as he deepened the kiss with gentle pressure. She kept her eyes closed to feel it all in the dark, the rush of his breath over her cheek, the intimate textures of him like the glassy smoothness of his teeth, the warm slickness under his tongue. She was warm and slick between her thighs, too, right where she felt the insistent heat of his arousal through the thickness of her skirt. When her hands clasped restlessly at the knot of his cravat, he broke the kiss.

The room was blurred around her. Elias kept the pad of his thumb against her lips, as if wanting to prolong the sensation of her mouth on him. Drunk on impulse, she licked him. He took a sharp little breath, which made her do it again, and he pushed the tip of his thumb into her mouth. At first, he held still while she explored the salty taste and unfamiliar feel of his skin against her tongue, and then he moved his finger in and out for a bit. She let him.

"Ah," he said, and pulled back his hand, his gaze fixed on her mouth. "Do you like it when I do that?"

She liked the look of his eyes swimming in molten desire.

"Yes," she breathed. "I like it."

He muttered something incomprehensible, then: "I shall think about your proposition."

Well, that was humiliating.

He took in her lowered head and burning cheeks.

"Heh," he said softly. "You know it's a bad idea."

She eyed him with caution. "But you don't . . . not want it?"

He thrust his fingers into his hair. "Not want it?" The way he looked at her, as though she were short of a few marbles. "You know that I want it, most any man would. Do you want me to take you on this couch here, or on this chair? I can do that, easily. This, though"—he wagged his fingers back and forth between them—"is not that easy."

Nothing ever was, with her. "Of course," she said. "I'm aware."

He glanced at the clock next to the door. It hadn't shown the correct time in a while, with no one here to set it regularly, so he looked out the window where the sun stood high over Cadogan Park.

"For now, let's not be hasty," he said. "Let me fetch my luggage. Then we will have lunch."

She nodded and took a step back, back into reality. "I'm afraid I must call on an acquaintance as soon as possible. It's why I'm here."

Once they slept together, it would probably rob her of her focus for her cause.

Elias's brow furrowed. "You want to leave, now—without eating any food."

"I'd rather be done with it right away."

He was skeptical but he made a motion with his hand that seemed to say *Do as you wish.* She wasn't hungry, in any case. The thought of doing it with him made her nerves jangle. The misdeed was taking shape outside of her head; a part of life she had written off seemed to become a reality for her after all, and her stomach spasmed with unintelligible sensations. If she didn't calm herself, she would be numb before the evening. First things first: the visit to Lady Middleton.

She went to the yellow bedroom to change into a day dress. The room was on the first floor and the bay windows overlooked the small park across the street. After Elias had brought their luggage to the room, she methodically removed protective throws from bed and armchairs, fluffed pillows, checked for traces of mice. She pulled the curtains half-shut, though the risk of anyone seeing in from the park below was negligible.

When she came downstairs, Elias was in the corridor, wearing his hat and overcoat again, and her heart briefly stopped.

"Is there a market nearby?" he asked. "Or a grocer."

She looked at the floor, disconcerted by the pang of panic she had just felt.

"There's a grocer at the end of Cadogan Lane," she said, "half a mile from here, I reckon. Why?"

"For the meals." A mocking glint lit his eyes. "Look at me, you're turning me into an errand boy. What else will you do to me, Catriona?"

He left through the kitchen door, the hat pulled low over his face.

Before setting out, she splashed her face and neck with cold water from the kitchen faucet. She was about to take a lover. Married women, country women, widows, they all did, but a woman in her position had to be mad to do it. The risks were enormous; a lady's name was such a fragile commodity and her only bargaining chip. It still seemed impossible to veer off this course now, just as a train that had jumped tracks would inevitably derail. She had been headed toward this point for a long time. Ever since she had left girlhood behind, sometimes, when she sat in the bathtub, she felt a sudden, breathless rush of dread at the thought that no other human being had ever seen her fully naked. Touched, yes, seen exposed in parts, yes, but never all of her. Beneath layers of expensive fabric, her firm middle, her thighs, her breasts, would wither away over the years and her finely turned ankles would swell with age, until the current her was irretrievably gone. There would be no photograph, no one else's memory, to preserve this version of her in time. It sickened her to even have this notion, that she did not really exist unless another person carried a lasting impression of her. The price a woman paid for her peace was oblivion, so to still crave space in another's head felt greedy and indecisive, almost weak. Elias, however . . . He wasn't just a random person. He had seen every inch of her, had broken down the barriers before he had even known her name.

She set the rustic oak table in the dining room, laid out cutlery, plates, and water glasses. There was no wine cellar, but in the kitchen cupboard next to the disused ice chest was the last bottle of Bordeaux. It did not compare to the wine Elias had brought from the Bekaa Valley, but it would have to do. The wineglasses were in the fine china cupboard back in the dining room. She arranged knives, forks, and plates until everything was aligned and evenly spaced. Now she felt settled enough to take on Lady Middleton. A note for Elias was left on the table, informing him that she would return in an hour, or perhaps two, depending on traffic.

During the cab ride to the Middletons' town house, she rehearsed the ludicrous story she had invented to win Lady Middleton for the Cause: she was doing research, because she was writing a novel. On her lap, she held the silver case for her calling cards, and she was opening it and letting it snap shut again, and again. She had weeded out the cards in the bedchamber earlier; she had too many because she rarely called on people. Thus, her cards were unfashionable, a batch from seasons ago. She should have had larger, more elaborate ones printed to secure an invitation in London homes. Charlie's mother was rather fond of *more is more*.

She ascended the once-familiar granite steps of the Middleton town house feeling sick. The last time she had stayed here for Charlie's leaving do, she had sworn never to return. Yet here she was, in the opulent entrance hall with the red carpet snaking up the main staircase and the dusty smell of dried flowers cloying the air. The old calling card seemed to have worked, though: Lady Middleton would see her on the spot, in the green parlor. Catriona handed her coat to a maid and gave up her protective shawl, too. She followed the butler swiftly. A social call lasted twenty minutes at most, so her time to succeed was limited.

The first thing she saw when she entered the green parlor was the painting. It took up the wall above the fireplace with a life-sized Charlie. Charlie and his bride. He stood next to a chair, posture erect, chest thrust forward and his right arm by his side. His left hand rested on the back of the chair, behind his bride's strawberry blond head. She was half in profile, adoringly gazing up at her husband-to-be, while Charlie stared straight ahead at the observer from under the familiar golden quiff. There was a barely perceptible tilt to his lips. Was he sneering? Smiling? Feeling constipated?

"A lovely pair, aren't they," said Lady Middleton. "We had it commissioned to celebrate their engagement."

She had risen from the sofa to greet Catriona. A broad streak of white wound through her neat coiffure, but she was still as nimble and sharply angled as when Catriona had last seen her, during the night of Charlie's ball. Her style of dress seemed to have reversed, however, had mellowed from stiff fabrics to lace and pastel. The interior of the room, too, was decidedly frothier than before.

"Indeed," Catriona said, belatedly. "It's a lovely painting."

Her forehead was already aching.

With a small, efficient gesture, Lady Middleton invited her to sit.

"You aren't married, are you?" she asked, her green eyes on Catriona while pouring tea.

"No."

"I thought not. I would have heard. Engaged, then."

"I'm not engaged, either."

"I expected as much. You never were the marrying sort, that was obvious before you were a debutante. Wester Ross is quite patient with you, considering."

Considering that she was the last in the line of her Campbell branch. She was here under false pretenses, so the false smile came easily, like part of a play.

"I'm just terribly pleased for Charles, ma'am," she said.

"Lady Sophie is a lovely gal," Lady Middleton replied, and placed saucer and cup before her. "Are you acquainted? No, I would not think so, she came out years after you made your debut. In any case, between Charles's and my consistent guidance, one hopes that she will eventually rise to the demands of her position as mistress of Middleton House."

Catriona's gaze crept back to the painting. What if it were her, on the chair, in the flowing white gown, looking up at him. Awaiting his consistent guidance. She felt empty at the thought. Not numb, empty. Charlie looked pleasant enough, but, disturbingly, he also looked just like any other young gentleman she might pass on the streets of London.

Lady Middleton leaned forward. "Now, to what do I owe the pleasure of your visit?"

On the other wall, the pendulum clock said she had twelve minutes left.

"Wester Ross and Lord Middleton are currently doing business together—"

Lady Middleton stiffened. "I wouldn't know," she said. "I don't concern myself with Lord Middleton's affairs these days." She gave Catriona a cool little smile. "It's quite refreshing."

"Ah. Congratulations."

That gained her an odd look.

"The truth is," Catriona said, "I was hoping you could advise me precisely on that matter."

"On what matter, dear?"

"The matter of separation . . . I'm wondering whether you could recommend me to a few ladies who live separately from their husbands."

Lady Middleton's expression became exceedingly bland. "Whatever for, I wonder?"

"It's a matter of . . ." Her tongue tied. It was too bad that words like *women's rights* and *justice* made most decent people terribly uncooperative.

"... it's a matter of research."

"Research?"

"For my novel. I'm writing . . . a novel."

"A novel. Oh. Well, you always were scribbling away at something."

Yes, at your son's term papers.

"It's a romantic novel," she lied with reluctance, "where the heroine and her husband separate, and then she tries to bring him back home with absolutely all means possible."

Lady Middleton drew back slightly. "I say," she said. "That sounds quite tawdry."

"No, on the contrary. The heroine, you see, she is trying to order him back with the help of a Writ for Restitution of Conjugal Rights."

Lady Middleton looked aghast. "That's bold—mark my words, it shan't rekindle her husband's tender feelings."

"It doesn't," Catriona said, sweat breaking over her brow. "She . . . she learns the error of her ways."

Lady Middleton's thin brows were still arching high. "I thought it was a romantic novel."

"It's quite . . . French, in its atmosphere"—she was rambling now—"and to make her story feel as authentic as possible, I must speak to ladies who would consider such legal actions, or a lady who might have felt passionately enough to do so at some point."

"I see." Lady Middleton rapidly stirred her tea with a tiny silver spoon. "I do meet a group of ladies in my position once a week. We have a literary salon. It is very pleasant. Intellectually stimulating."

"How wonderful."

"None of them would dream of acting like your heroine; I'm afraid there isn't a French lady among us."

"I suppose not," Catriona said, trying to think of something sensible to say while she was speaking. Charlie was smirking at her from above. The long arm of the pendulum clock ticked onward loud as a gong. Seven minutes left. Inside her gloves, her palms were sweaty.

"Wait," Lady Middleton said, and held up her hand. "There's one woman." She wrinkled her nose. "I'm thinking of a certain Mrs. Weldon," she said. "She isn't a regular member, she usually only attends the séances. Her husband left years ago, but I daresay she remains obsessed with him."

Obsessed sounded promising. Nothing less would make a woman risk her reputation. She would know.

"Why do you believe she is obsessed?" she asked.

Lady Middleton gave her a pointed look. "Not a meeting passes without a Captain Weldon this or Captain Weldon that . . ."

Captain Weldon? A giddiness gripped Catriona. There was her man of influence. This was too good to be true. Praise her stubbornly complacent face, because inside she was grinning like the Cheshire cat.

". . . even during the séances, it's him she asks about," Lady Middleton continued, "where he is, whether he plans to visit her. It's unfortunate, quite embarrassing. She has a lovely house in Acton, for which her husband pays in full, and I gather he pays her five hundred pounds a year, too. Captain Weldon would provide anything for her, anything at all. Some women are simply never satisfied."

"He seems dutiful," Catriona said. "Perhaps that's why she still regrets the separation."

"He keeps a fancy girl somewhere," Lady Middleton said curtly. "They all do. They always do. No, I believe she would feel less ireful if he cared nothing at all—in that case, a woman may blame the abandonment on his dishonorable character, whereas when he generously fulfills his obligations, then it must be a fault in her that caused the separation."

Perhaps neither party need be at fault at all; a bad match of temperaments was possible, too, but it was not her place to suggest this. With an eye on her swiftly disappearing minutes, she asked Lady Middleton for a written recommendation that she could present to Mrs. Weldon for an introduction. Lady Middleton obliged her, although her lips were pursed with disapproval while she wrote.

She presented the introductory card with a sniff. "Here you are. I shall find out Mrs. Weldon's address in Acton and send you a note."

Catriona slipped the card into her skirt pocket. "I so appreciate it."

Lady Middleton smiled haltingly. "Well. It was quite lovely to see you again, Lady Catriona. Our families have long been friends."

Distinct lines framed the lady's mouth, even when her smile had been switched off again. *I would have called this woman Mama, had Charlie wanted me ten years ago.* A whole decade. Sitting there on his mother's sofa, in his banal presence frozen on canvas, Catriona felt the weight of these years, like physical blocks pushing between her current self and the girl back then, until the two seemed worlds apart. She left Charlie's house feeling dazed. During the carriage ride, her thoughts were in such disarray, it was like thinking of nothing at all.

Elias's presence was palpable when she entered Cadogan House. Sure enough, his coat hung on the garderobe and his elegant walking stick was in the cast-iron umbrella stand. He might be upstairs. She took off her hat and gloves and placed them onto the sideboard. In the mirror, her lips looked pale and her eyes glassy, as if stunned. Hardly enticing.

When she approached the kitchen for some water, she heard a rhythmic clacking she could not place. The kitchen door was ajar. She entered and Elias looked up from a cutting board. Afternoon sunlight warmed the room and the air smelled unusually fresh, like cucumber and herbs. It was disorienting, as though the gray flagstone tiles, the wooden cabinets, the brass pots on the floating shelves were new surroundings. It was too unusual to see a man standing behind the cabinet at the center of the room, jacketless, a large knife in hand, chopping something.

"You know how to cook," she said, pretending not to notice that he was in shirtsleeves. It wasn't his well-tailored jackets that created his broad shoulders—his build filled out the cut of his soft cotton shirt perfectly.

He twirled the knife between his fingers. "No," he said. "I can't cook. But I know how to cut a tomato. We can't dine out together and your pub offers only fish and chips to take away. I need more than just beige food on my plate."

There was a basket on the cabinet countertop and something green and leafy was sticking out from it. Additional brown paper bags from the grocer's sat on the floor.

She halted next to the cabinet, awkward like a visitor in her own kitchen.

Elias's attention lingered on her bloodless face. "Are you well?"

She nodded. "I'm fine."

His head tilt said he didn't believe her.

"The place where I went today, it holds unpleasant memories," she said as he made to keep slicing. "I was hurt there, once."

He went motionless, the knife suspended in midair. "Who hurt you?"

His eyes had narrowed to the same assessing slits she had seen before in the Glasgow inn.

"It was a long time ago," she said. "Someone said something hurtful."

"Ah."

"It only took a minute or two for them to say it, but I can see now that the words stayed with me, for years. When I went to the house today, I was quite nervous. I wondered how I would feel . . .

and then, when it came to it, I felt barely anything. Not a fraction of the turmoil I had dreaded I'd feel."

Elias tipped up his chin. "That's good, *non?*"

His eyes remained alert, as though he was reading every nuance of her expression.

She moved her hands over her stomach. "There have been other incidents throughout my life that have caused me grief, and now I can't stop wondering how bad they truly were," she said. "In the carriage, I kept thinking, I kept thinking about how a part of me has wallowed in sorrow for years. How many decisions have I made because I was afraid of some dreadful thing that in the end would have never come to pass? How often have I said yes or no to something just to avoid a certain type of pain? I don't think I'm a coward; sometimes I even think I'm brave. But now I look at myself and I think, who would I be, today, had I never been so needlessly afraid? I'm . . . pathetically sensitive."

He tutted softly.

"Do you know how a tree changes shape to grow around an obstruction?" she asked, her voice hollow. "How it develops an unnatural bent, or ugly bulges?"

"I have seen these trees, yes."

"I'm wondering how misshapen I am," she whispered. "I wonder how bent out of shape I am from these attempts to exist around some fear, instead of just growing, straight and up, as I should have."

Elias was silent for a moment. He put down the knife. "A tree cannot be ugly," he said. "In nature, all that matters is to survive. A living tree is a good tree."

She felt like crying. In a normal tone, she said: "That's true." And, when it felt safe to keep speaking: "Does that mean you don't believe we have an essence?"

He exhaled on a huff, then he scratched the back of his head. "I think we have our own will; we can decide how to respond to others, but respond we must. When you live, you can't stay pristine. You can't remain a child. We come into the world through other people, so from the beginning, you are not a separate entity."

"*No man is an island*," she said, calmer now, "*entire of itself.*"

"See? You were hurt, so you became cautious," he said. "It's not unusual. We have a saying: 'He who burned his tongue on soup, blows on yogurt.'"

A small laugh burst from her, and it sounded surprised to her own ears, that she could have a laugh in her at such a time. His face brightened as he took in her smile. *I think I'm in love with you, Elias*, she thought, *really in love, differently from any love I ever felt before.* She closed her eyes and let the sweet devastation of it wash over her.

"I have seen you," came his voice, low and dark. "You're not misshapen. You are a beautiful creation."

She swallowed. "You flatter me."

"I haven't yet begun to flatter you, habibti."

He had moved around the cabinet and stood in front of her, his presence warm and solid like a rock out in the sun that she might rest against.

Their gazes fused. His scent, his certainty, the alluring pull of his leashed sensuality, entered her bloodstream, the same stealthy invasion every time he was close, until every part of her body filled with a keen awareness of him. His hand was next to hers on the countertop, but she felt it on her, curving around her waist as if their souls were ahead of their bodies and already embracing.

"Elias," she said. "Could you do something for me?"

His face tensed at the sound of his Christian name. "Eh, tikram ayounik," he replied.

For your eyes, literally, but it meant he would gladly give her whatever she'd ask for.

"Would you kiss me?"

A shaky breath escaped him. "See how bold you are," he murmured. "Not cautious at all."

He touched her waist, then slid his hand to the small of her back and urged her closer. His lips were soft against her forehead, awakening her skin with a rush of goose bumps from nape to toe. He inhaled, as if to savor the scent of her hair. They stood like this for a long moment while a tightness behind her ribs loosened, unspooled, until it dissolved into nothing. *No more fear.* Longing flowed like a warm current under her skin. She put her hand on his chest, and the ruthlessly contained energy inside jolted through her. Elias took a step back, and his eyes were sharp now with a singular hunger.

"Why me?" he asked.

She spoke without thinking: "When I'm with you, I don't feel wrong. I feel . . . I just feel."

His lashes lowered. "Let's go upstairs," he said huskily.

Chapter 22

Her clothes were dropping to the floor the moment she crossed into the bedroom. Elias had unbuttoned the front of her bodice on their way up the stairs, his arms coming round her from behind as they swayed toward the landing with their bodies pressed together. He was still behind her, unhooking her skirts from her bodice while she faced the bed. A pool of sunlight shimmered golden on the smooth counterpane. She had a strange sense of weightlessness, as though she consisted only of her breath and the rapid beat of her heart.

"What made you change your mind?" she asked.

"I haven't changed it," came his sarcastic voice. "I still consider this the worst decision I have made in a long time. I'm a fool to do it. Alas, I can't keep from touching you. My hands dream of your skin."

He was obviously aroused, but his fingers had been methodical with the buttons. Now the weight of her skirts loosened under his efficient hands. The layers of fabric and the bustle collapsed, down to her knees.

Elias moved around her and offered his hand with an air of chivalry, as though he wasn't about to strip her naked and lie on top of her. With his assistance, she gingerly stepped out of the pile of contraptions.

His passion-bright gaze burned over her face. "If there are consequences, of any kind," he said, "we make it right."

It wasn't an offer but a condition. Her mouth turned dry for a moment. She swallowed and moved her head a little; it could be a yes.

Satisfied, he eased the bodice off her shoulders, his thumbs skimming along the wings of her collarbone. The light touch sparked a tingling warmth in all her delicate pulse points, and she suppressed a moan.

"So silky," he said in a low tone. "Are you certain about this, Catriona? Because I will put my mouth on every soft inch of you. I have wanted to do that for a long time."

Hot color spread from her throat to the top of her breasts. He noticed, and his eyes went soft. "Hayeti," he said. *My life.* "Such a bad idea."

Her breathing was shaky. "We can regret it later."

The bodice fell away, and her freed arms rose into the cool air on their own volition. Elias smoothed the corset cover over her head and let it sail to the floor, and her corset swiftly followed. He was down before her on one knee, his hands under her chemise, his shoulders moving while he rolled down her stockings. Every glance of his fingertips against the sensitive back of her knees sent a small shock to her core, making her clench. He tugged at her pantaloons. "I remember these," he said, looking up at her with a wide grin. One of the pink ribbons was wrapped around his finger.

She was in her chemise, blushing and trembling. His smile faded and his eyes darkened. "Sit on the bed."

The bedsprings creaked. Sunlight lay warm like a hand between her bare shoulders. He undressed in front of her, cravat, cuffs and collar, then the waistcoat, revealing richly embroidered braces. *Who made these for you?* He undid the top buttons of his shirt and a sunbeam glanced off the gold chain around his neck.

Who gave you that? She lurched from one impression of male secrets to the next.

"This is happening fast," she said.

He pulled the braces off his shoulders. "Too fast?"

"I just thought this part would be slow. I can't seem to think."

The corner of his mouth twitched. "Good. For what we will do, you only need to feel."

His voice was like his movements, fluid and imbued with purpose. He dragged his shirt over his head and when he reappeared, his curls disheveled, she wasn't breathing. Strong arms, tapered torso, as if chiseled by an expert. He wasn't smooth like a statue; dark hair covered his tightly wrapped muscles. Instead of vulnerability, his naked body radiated power. She felt terribly soft in contrast. He smiled, a little crooked, and she realized she was gazing at him with her mouth slightly slack.

His gaze dropped to her breasts and now she felt them, tense and strangely full underneath her chemise.

"Will you take off your chemise for me?" he asked.

He liked telling her what to do in the bedroom. Perhaps he was testing her compliance, preparing her for other instructions. *Lie back. Spread your legs. No thinking.*

She stripped and sat back down.

His face went very quiet while he took her in. He looked almost shy, an echo of the reverence she had sensed in him at the banks of the loch. When his lips moved but no words came, she understood that her softness held its own power. The act would not be done to her. They would do it together.

Elias discarded his remaining clothes. He was highly aroused, his erection almost touching his flat stomach. A heavy heat pooled in her belly. Once he was inside her, not a thread would go between them then. *Mine*—if only for a moment.

He turned to the nightstand, opened the drawer, and took out a small vial and a sheath. It had been prepared, and he handled it smoothly.

"Where did you find those?" she asked.

He shot her a look from under his lashes. "Pharmacy next to the grocer." A soft snort. "The pharmacist warned me to exercise moderation in all things."

"Why, how many did you buy?"

"Plenty." He tossed the vial onto the counterpane and put his knee between hers onto the mattress.

She reclined, awed by the proximity of a naked man.

He hovered over her, feeling large and infusing her with his body heat. His addictive scent entered her on every breath and coated her taste buds like nectar.

"You need these now?" He was holding her face and tapped a finger against the rim of her glasses.

She shook her head. "I don't need them, no."

He took them off and lowered his face to hers.

A curl brushed over her forehead. His lips were soft like a butterfly's wing on her closed eyelids, and the tender, unfamiliar sensation drew a gasp of pleasure from her. He kissed her on the mouth, twining his tongue with hers, licking, tasting, teasing. Faintly, she was aware that her hips were moving, pushing up as if seeking the weight of his. Instead, Elias stretched out alongside her. He put a hand on her breast, but she was very aware of the hard, hot part of him that was pressed against her thigh. He plucked at her nipple, the one she had pierced, and lanced a stab of erotic pleasure low into her belly.

Her small cry made him smile.

He nipped the tightening bud with his teeth, and she arched against his mouth, shamelessly clasping the back of his head to hold him in place. He suckled, patiently, relentlessly, until she felt the sinewy caress of his tongue inside her. She heard herself say please. He picked up the vial; oil poured into his palm, then his slick hand glided between her thighs. For a beat, he went motionless, as if he wanted to savor the feel of her liquid heat against his fingers. *Please.* He stroked, light and quick. "You liked this the last time," he said, and her body contracted as it remembered the last time, the swelling pleasure, the need. Her breathing fractured. Oil melted into the downy insides of her thighs. Heat flashed, chased by chills.

She gripped his arm and stared up at his tense face. "I think I'm . . . I'm . . ."

"Spending?" he said gently. "Yes, that would be very nice." His fingers penetrated her, slipping easily in and out. She was riveted to the one tense point under the pad of his thumb, to the enticing friction that was winding the tension tighter and tighter. She needed it to snap, or else she might die. She grabbed his wrist. *Faster.* He obliged, his smile raw and dark. Ecstasy surged, sudden and powerful like a riptide, pulling her right into her own black center. There was nothing. Then only pulsing bliss, exploding outward, flinging her to the edge of a galaxy. She had barely emerged, dazed and still twitching in the sheets, when Elias ran his oiled-up hand over himself. The hot muscled length of his body settled on top of hers, then there was pressure between her legs. He gazed down on her with a hard look in his eyes.

"Are you certain?"

"I'm certain, yes."

Her body was sated; the void in her heart still craved to be filled. She raised her knees slightly, making a cradle for him between her thighs.

Elias's expression changed when he entered her. It was a look of surprise, as if an unexpected emotion had seized him when he felt her around him, as though he had forgotten whatever plan he might have had. Her own grip on the situation was slipping rapidly; a place inside her she had never consciously felt before opened and yielded to accommodate him. Another person was in her most intimate space. Her panting turned a little frantic. Abruptly, Elias went still over her.

She clasped his hips. "Don't stop."

He didn't move, his hazy eyes searching her face. "Are you fine?"

"I am."

"All right."

He lowered his head when his hips met hers, as if needing a pause. She gazed up at her lover, senses stretched and flooding with the salty smell of aroused skin, the heavy fullness inside her, the brush of soft chest hair against her breasts. They were doing this. He moved. Shallow thrusts, so careful. He wasn't fucking her, that whispered word no woman should know, printed only in magazines no decent person would read. The golden curve of his shoulder gleamed from his efforts to not do that, he was reining himself in. The intrusion of forbidden words made her slippery again, and her fingers danced over his back in gentle encouragement. Creaking mattress, guttural sighs. His chain touched her chin, then her nose when he pulled back. With a muttered curse, Elias pushed himself up on one arm and ripped the chain off, causing her to gasp with surprise.

He stroked her face with both hands. "It was annoying you, my darling."

"I'm—" His next thrust had brought a wave of warm pleasure, and whatever she had meant to say turned into a husky moan. It was all the encouragement he had needed. The reins dropped. His head fell back, the tendons in his neck strained like harp strings. He was engaged in an age-old rhythm, hunting down his own release, and she cried out with him because he was finding such pleasure inside her.

He felt heavy on her after and had his head ducked against her neck. His breath drifted over the damp skin of her throat.

"I thought it would take longer," she said out loud.

He gave a strangled grunt. When he looked at her, the afterglow of ecstasy was still bright on his face. "Because you underestimate yourself," he said. "Severely."

He parted from her with some reluctance. When he rolled back to face her, she was on her side, too, one hand tucked under her cheek, her other arm covering her breasts. Their gazes found each other and held. The silence filling the space was new, teetering and fragile like something freshly hatched. She had spent her life studying languages and now all the words she knew seemed too crude, too small, to embody what was passing between them.

Elias curved his hand around her shoulder, the warmth of his touch a welcome shock on her cooling skin.

"Ahlan," he said. *Welcome.*

"Hullo," she replied, a hesitant smile in her voice.

She knew his face well, his strong brows, the prominent nose, the nicely curved shape of his lips. Now there was more, a new rendering she suspected only she could see. *Now he looks like he's mine.* A small shiver raised the hair on her arms. She glanced down the relaxed length of his body. How comfortable he appeared in his skin wherever he went, in whichever situation. He wasn't the same color everywhere; he was pale where his trousers would cover him. She traced the demarcation line across his slim hip with a fingertip.

"Who are you really, Mr. Khoury?" she asked. "Someone else entirely? A farmer, perhaps, or a fisherman."

His eyes crinkled at the corners. "I'm often in the sea when I work in Beirut."

"You enjoy swimming?"

"I swim, yes, but usually we just jump off the rocks or the cliffs."

"That sounds rather dangerous."

"Not at all." He said it too casually for her to believe him. "But for a moment, you fly."

She understood the risks people took for that sensation. Her sated body still felt weightless enough to levitate. Just like that, he had taught her the difference between light and empty.

She eyed the angry red mark the chain had left on the side of his neck. "You broke your chain."

He pursed his lips. "We broke your spectacles, too."

"We did?" She made to raise her head.

"I shall fix them for you."

The Arabic language offered many romantic possibilities, at least eleven different words for love to precisely capture the various stages of the emotion, and perhaps, secretly, she had expected more elaborate verbal wooing from him. Yet here he was, making her swoon with a plain *I shall fix them for you*.

"I brought a spare pair," she said.

A languid smile. "The golden ones? I liked those." His eyes were admiring her again, and his hands were wandering, enjoying her skin without hurry. "Lovely," he said, stroking the slope of her breast, "helou kteer," *very beautiful*, when he traced the curve of her belly below her navel. He put a hot, possessive hand between her legs. "Petite chatte."

Her toes curled. "Little cat?"

My cat, said the look in his eyes. Her throat felt too tight.

He glanced over at the nightstand, then back at her. "How do you feel?"

"Perfectly well," she said, and he smirked because she had said it very quickly.

They made love slowly this time, under the covers, while he kept her cocooned in his arms. She learned that the blissful sensation at the end could come gently, like a slow warm tide, and make her cry. He wiped her tears away and told her it happened sometimes.

She had been impossibly arrogant, of course, to grab this particular slice of life for herself and to think that she would be its master. For a moment, her soul had found a matching power. As his thumbs touched the wet corners of her eyes, she knew he had etched a space for himself into her heart so deeply that the days without him would echo with his absence.

Chapter 23

In the silver-blue shadow of dawn, Elias watched her sleep. Her hair spilled over the pillows, dark and liquid like ink. She lay on her side, motionless, her breathing barely a whisper. His lover was a light presence, whether dreaming or awake. How had such quietness snuck under his skin, so quickly? Since his exodus from the mountain, he had led his life with intention: He kept things simple. He did not repeat mistakes. A fling was a fling. Yet here he was, with a disturbing emotion roiling inside his chest while he watched her simply existing. A crucial part of him, a spot where he kept his most loyal devotions, had hardened against her when she had rejected any commitment from him. Then she had lain under him, so brave and yet seemingly unconscious of what she was giving him, and it had nearly cracked him open again. The sheer depths of her emotion sanctified their transgression, or so he told himself. They would repeat their mistake many times before the week was over.

Outside, below the window, a carriage rattled over cobblestones. London was waking, his mission was calling. He picked up a loose strand of her hair and pressed it to his lips. It was soft but not sleek to the touch, like a coil of raw silk, its scent a heady blend of her essence and their lovemaking. Having to affect her with something that could cause her grief caused a physical resistance in his body, the righteousness of his cause did not change that fact. Against true passion, reason was like a drop against an ocean; it stood no chance. Carefully, he placed the lock of hair back onto the pillow. What he could do was to take care of the artifacts but to keep the business away from her for as long as possible, until his plan had a proper shape. She was still asleep when he left for the underground station, in an inconspicuous gray suit and a nondescript hat.

He met Nassim's man in a shady pub at the corner of Little Queen Street, a stone's throw from the Houses of Parliament. Soot dimmed the morning sun. The street itself was an odd demographic aberration in a moneyed district: dilapidated seventeenth-century houses were crammed shoulder to shoulder, and a foul smell rose from the brown puddles on the pavement. Not a slum like Drury Lane, but no gentleman would walk a child or woman down this street. The pub façade, however, faced the respectable Princes Street, and Elias had gone inside through the main entrance. His contact had entered through the side door from Little Queen, ten minutes past the time they had agreed on in their telegrams. They occupied a grimy table next to a window, out of earshot from the patrons who were having cigarettes and liquid breakfast at the bar.

The contact was a short, muscled Englishman of indiscernible age. His mustache was well-groomed and his clothes were plain but clean; he would not draw too much attention in either Little Queen or on Parliament Square.

"You 'ear this," he said in a conspiring tone as he leaned over the table toward Elias. "I's all Irish." He whirred his hand around in the smoky air. "Every single fellow in 'ere is Irish. It all started ten years ago, with them coming 'ere, now one in three fellows in London is an Irishman." The man's own accent was thick Cockney; he was dropping his *t*'s and *h*'s like hot coals. "They 'ave nofing to eat, over there," he added, tilting his head, presumably in the direction of Ireland. "No work, either."

Elias sympathized. Some people just seemed collectively condemned to be born into a small place to which they were greatly attached, only to leave it behind for London or America, driven away by foreign overlords or hunger.

The man ordered an ale, and Elias asked for tea, all while gauging each other with unreadable eyes. Allegedly, the man was a relation of a man who worked with Nassim, so there was a rapport by association. It had to suffice.

Their drinks were served quickly.

"I'm in need of a crew," Elias said after taking a sip. "Half a dozen men."

The contact licked over his mustache. "Are you."

"And two wagons."

The man's eyes narrowed. "You're aware that my acquaintance trades in logistics only?"

Elias knew the business of "logistics only"—meaning a low risk of someone losing life or limb during an operation.

"I'm aware," he said.

A noncommittal grunt. "Prices 'ave gone up for that, too."

He'd afford it. A matter of honor had no price. His options were limited, however: the only moment he could strike was the bulls' arrival in London. A man had to infiltrate the crew that was responsible for loading the antiques onto the train in Oxford, and several men would have to replace the workers sent by the museum to pick up the pieces at the London railway station. The London transfer would take place from train to carriage as officially planned, only that the carriages would speed to London Port, load their cargo onto a ship already running on all kettles, and sail back east. Simple in theory, rather complex in the execution. It also hinged entirely on Catriona following through with her plans to have the pieces transferred, and on her sharing the exact schedule with him even though it would cause her family a scandal. Catriona. He tossed back his tea, but the bitter black brew did nothing to wash her taste away; it had clung to him inside and out all morning.

"Wha' are you needin' it for anyway, cousin of Mr. Nassim," the Cockney wanted to know.

"Li watani," Elias replied. "For my homeland."

The man's dark eyes were quiet. "Awright," he said after a pause. "I've a name for you. If 'e likes you, 'e'll 'ave anofer name for you."

Elias would stake his fortune that the man at the very top of this crime pyramid was a local, with good connections to the Metropolitan Police and the mayor, and he'd reside in a town house in the most expensive street. It always was so. A note with an address was exchanged for a small but heavy purse, and the Cockney wished him best of luck.

After they parted, the only intelligible sensation Elias felt was a hollowness right behind his ribs. While his plan was successfully set in motion, its trajectory would carry him in the opposite direction of more private desires. Instead of going to the nearest telegraph office to send news of his progress to Nassim, he briskly walked the short distance to the Thames. The area was busy with working people. A few street boys immediately recognized him as a foreigner and buzzed around him, cheeky and annoying like flies, imitating his gait and asking if he wanted to see tricks. Westerners had a name for their city urchins—*Street Arabs*, owed to dubious ideas about the Bedouins, whom they considered homeless, roaming, and possibly thieving. Perhaps that was why Elias indulged the boys; he spun his walking stick and tossed a few pennies to the smallest in the group, and their gratitude was repressed under a thick layer of mockery. When he reached Westminster Bridge, a horse-drawn omnibus rolled past and the boys lost interest in him; they ran after the vehicle and tried to cling to it.

Elias stopped at the middle of the bridge and turned east to watch the river on its way to the sea. Gulls balanced above him, throwing their yearning cries into the wind, and the stink of bilge water hung in the air. A short distance ahead at the southern side of the river, the brown brick buildings of the wharves lined the banks next to clusters of bobbing ship masts. London. All the world was *not* here, Mr. Leighton, son of a dog, but it was still the richest city in the world. And the largest. It kept growing, too, stacking people atop one another and spilling over old borders at a quicker pace than booming Beirut. Despite death on every shadowed corner, the place was rapaciously alive, its hungry pulse reverberated through the railing under his hands in a cacophony of crowded omnibuses and busy cogwheels, of ship horns, steel hammers, and telegraph keys. Just behind him in the palatial building of Westminster, policies that shaped the world were made during strolls down a corridor. Where else other than America would an Irishman—or any man—go, if not here, where it felt as though anything might be possible?

The cruel irony that the displaced turned to the shores of the displacer was not lost on him, but the truth was that a home without a future felt like a graveyard to the young. A man only lived once. His mind was whirring, here on this bridge, examining potential opportunities, as it happened when he was immersed in a stimulating environment. El watan. The homeland. It had given him such rich and strong roots—and yet it kept denying him the full span of his wings. On the mountain, the head of the family had assigned him a role that left him treading water. At the coast, imperial soldiers roamed and might harass his kind at random, and retaliation could necessitate exile for the whole family. With the glint of the river in his eyes, a long diffuse confession revealed itself to him: that he did feel homeless. He knew very well where he came from, but where should he settle? Lately, whenever he was in any one location, he missed parts of the places where he was not. Nowhere was whole these days. He had accepted this about himself

almost unconsciously; given that his origins lay somewhere between mountains and sea, he had always been destined for the
places in between. It still left him feeling restless. A sense of *what
next?* had become a rather constant companion.

Except for last night.

His grip around the railing tightened. He saw the quiet form
curled up on the bed. The tears of bliss glistening in her eyes. In
the lucid moment a man knew after passion, he had rested his head
on her soft breasts and felt the rhythm of her heart against his
cheek, and a deep sense of peace, as though time itself had stopped,
had settled in his body. This was how it felt in his imagination:
home. Perhaps it was why London began to look like an opportunity, not because of its gigantic port and international merchant
class, but because of her. He stared into the glare of the sun on the
water without blinking, as if that would cure the brain rot. A moment later, he was striding back to the street, overtaking pedestrians and horse carts. The house might be empty upon his return;
she seemed like the type who would simply disappear when frightened. He stepped in front of a cab, causing the driver to holler at
him. He cursed the driver throughout the ride for creeping toward
Cadogan Place slow like a snail.

She emerged from the reception room silent like a cat while he was
still in the hallway, taking off his gloves. Her eyes were huge in her
face, and it made him think she was surprised to see him.

"You're back," she said. It sounded scratchy, as though she was
using her voice for the first time today.

"I never left you," he replied.

They regarded each other warily.

One moment they were separated by half the length of the
hallway.

Then they were not.

She was flat against him, chest to chest, her arms twining around his neck with an urgency as though he had come home from a battle. They groped haphazardly, gasping between kisses. He pressed her against the wall, his thigh wedged between hers, her bodice already on the parquet. It was a relief to feel her bare shoulders under his fingers. It wasn't enough. He scooped her up and carried her up the stairs. When he crossed the threshold to the bedroom, he realized he was holding her like a groom would carry his bride into her new home, and it was jarring like an off-key tune in an otherwise perfect harmony. Face-to-face with her, tasting her, feeling her glassy-smooth skin, his revelation on the bridge took on a different quality, because the woman in his arms was, in fact, reluctant to give more than her body. She could slip through his fingers like the wind. Instead of slowing the seduction to a more tender pace, his hands moved quickly. A button skittered over the floor, which made her laugh.

He was straddling her on the bed, trapped her nicely rounded hips between his thighs and pressed her deeper into the mattress with his weight.

She smiled up at him, a little uncertain but drunk on erotic arousal.

He slid his palms up over her ribs, and they groaned together when he filled his hands with the soft round weight of her breasts.

"I think of them every day," he said, squeezing lightly, then a bit rougher. "I imagine doing this."

She bucked underneath him. "I wondered if you imagined it."

"You did, hm?" He plucked at her mysterious nipple piercing. "You look prim on the outside, but you are very naughty inside your head, Catriona."

Her indignant gasp wasn't convincing, the flush on her cheeks said she felt quite caught out.

He slid his hand under her neck and ran his thumb over her throat. "What do you want," he asked.

She moved against him. The heat of her lap seeped into his skin, quickly unspooling his self-control.

"Tell me," he murmured. "There are many nice things we can do."

"I want you inside me," she whispered.

"I want that, too, but I think it might be too soon." They had done it three times since yesterday, surely too much for a novice.

She arched up a little, luring him with her hips.

"I think it's fine," she said in a soft voice, her blue eyes brilliant beneath drooping lashes, and it nearly made him slide right into her, precautions be damned.

He lowered his body over hers and kissed her on the mouth.

Her slender hands stroked down his back, then more tentatively over his behind. It drew a low, throaty grunt from him.

"She's fine," she said, sounding serious. "Really."

"Let me see," he said.

She was moving restlessly at first, choking back tiny noises when his mouth brushed her breast, her belly, the charming little dip of her navel. He kissed lower, and she went silent.

He kept her thighs apart with the breadth of his shoulders.

"She looks beautiful," he said.

"I'm glad to hear it," came the faint reply.

He trailed a finger through the fine protective curls, and her thighs clenched against his biceps.

"Just making certain," he murmured, already intoxicated.

He ran his thumb up and down the delicate seam, parting it slightly. At her hesitant sigh, he pushed inside her, then spread the wetness with the pad of his finger. She said his name, and it sounded anxious, seeking . . . He lowered his head and did it with his tongue. He indulged himself, taking long licks, his fingers digging into the softness of her hips. He was lost, so hard he could feel his pulse in his cock, and so he didn't immediately register her response. It dawned on him that he wasn't hearing or feeling affirmations of her pleasure.

He raised his head and searched her eyes across the tense plane of her stomach. She was looking up at the ceiling.

"Is it good for you?" he asked.

She lifted her head. Her face looked red and anxious. "I think so."

"I like it," he said, in case she doubted it. "Very much."

She nodded. "Go on, then."

When he lowered his head, he felt her thighs stiffen. She was bracing herself.

He paused. "You don't enjoy it," he said slowly, "do you?"

She put a hand over her eyes. "I don't know," she said in a small voice. "I'm familiar with the practice, I have read about it, women are supposed to find it wonderful."

He sat up, and so she raised herself up on her elbows.

"I don't care what your forbidden book says," he said. "If you dislike it, we don't do it."

"I don't dislike it," she said. "It's just . . . it's so . . ."

She drew up her feet and tried to close her knees. He shifted back to let her, resisting the urge to grab her thighs and keep her wide open to him. He clasped her ankle instead, just holding it.

"It's what," he nudged.

"It's wet," she said at last.

He ran his hand over his chin. "It is, yes."

She grimaced.

Difficult to think without much blood in his head. "You don't like it because it's wet? It's mostly you, by the way."

"I know, but the sensation distracts me. It doesn't really hurt, though, we can certainly do it if it pleases you. Goodness, I've made it terribly awkward now."

An unexpected surge of tenderness tampered his lust. A few of his observations about her, parceled away at the back of his mind, began to form a picture.

"You're very sensitive," he said. "I noticed. Your skin ripples when I barely touch you. You don't suffer noise well, either."

"I'm sorry." She made to tug the sheet over her breasts.

"Ah, ah." He gripped the sheet in his fist.

He brushed his lips over her knee, and a lustful sigh was the response.

He rested his chin on the spot he had kissed and watched her confused face. "There," he said. "You can't even help it."

He slowly ran his hand down her shin, and inch by inch, the tension seeped from her limbs. He raised her foot and pressed an open-mouthed kiss onto the lovely arch. She held her breath. He dipped his tongue between her toes. Her body bowed up with delight.

"Habibit albi," he said. "It's a gift, your sensitivity. It's a pleasure to pleasure you. Allow me to try."

He leaned over the edge of the bed and snatched her chemise off the floor. The garment was light as cobwebs in his hand. He spread the fabric over her thighs, and she held still, just watched him with attentive eyes. He put his mouth back on her, but now there was a thin layer of cotton between his tongue and her tender nub. His next lick created friction. She rewarded him with a breathy moan. When he tried a gentle suck, her fingers curled in his hair, tightening instinctively to hold him in place.

"Yes," he murmured, a glowing sensation spreading in his chest. "Show me what feels good for you."

After, she lay boneless in the sheets and a glow seemed to emanate off her skin. At last, she gave a languorous stretch and smiled up at him so widely, his heart gave a curious twinge.

"I think every woman ought to have a birder for a lover," she said. "You observe everything so closely. You seem to miss nothing."

He could have told her that every man who truly cared about a woman would observe her closely, but her ears might not be open to it.

He stretched himself out alongside her, deciding to take care of himself in a moment.

"Have you had many lovers?" she asked.

His face heated. "I don't like this conversation, my heart," he said. "It lowers us."

She brushed her hand over the blanket, embarrassed. "I'm not jealous," she said. "Just curious."

With a sigh, he rolled onto his back. "One," he said. "In Lyon."

She sat up and looked down at him. "One?"

Her puzzled face amused him. She looked so surprised at things he considered banal but wouldn't blink at something outlandish or complicated. "Have you heard of the free love movement?"

She squinted. "I don't think so."

"I thought you might have, since you're an activist."

"Our activism puts us under such scrutiny that we are a little less free in some respects."

"It's an idea from America, but I think the French bohemians practiced it already and the Americans just gave it a slogan."

"Well, they are an economical bunch." Said with a small smile.

"The idea is that people ought to choose their lovers freely," he explained. "Legal or religious blessings shouldn't be necessary to sleep together. Sharing a bed should end when the love is gone, not when a government decree grants it."

"Ah," she said. "Yes, I know it. We call this the Shelleyan way of cohabitation. It caused some trouble for some of our suffragists."

"My friend in Lyon likes these ideas."

"How interesting." Her tone was neutral, but her face looked as though she was of a mind to bite someone.

He lifted a hand and stroked her overwarm cheek with his finger. "See. You shouldn't have asked."

She leaned back, out of his reach. "It sounds as though only your friend's convictions prevented a marriage between the two of you."

He dropped his hand back onto the mattress. "You have stories in your head," he said mildly. "Her convictions made our arrangement possible. I don't pay for a woman's company and I had no plans to marry at the time."

In truth, he hadn't even planned on taking a lover. He had grown up thinking he'd share his body only with his wife. Then he had lost his mind over Nayla and after emerging from the stupor, he had decided that regular release and a habit of talking to pretty women who weren't kin would keep him from turning into an idiot again should the next pair of gazelle eyes glance his way. *So how has that worked out for you*, mocked a little voice as he eyed the bewitching naked Scotswoman next to him in the sheets.

"But you stayed faithful to her," she said softly, as if to herself.

He put a hand over his eyes. "I'm always places in between, Catriona. I live and work in two, three different countries, I keep changing between different clothes, cuisines, languages . . . I liked having one part of life in just one place."

Her face softened. "Right," she said. "I gather you won't follow this free movement with your wife, then," she added in a teasing tone.

His lips twitched, as though she had said something endearingly naïve. "No," he said. "My wife will be mine. And I hers. Until the end."

His words seemed to freeze her in place; her whole body went still as though he had triggered two equally strong but directly opposing emotions in her. Well. In the presence of a flighty creature, he just had to refrain from making loud noises and sudden movements to keep them from taking off.

Chapter 24

━━◦◦◦━━

They lay face-to-face, warmed by the morning sun slanting through the window. The scent of their sleep-kissed skin rose from the linen. It struck Catriona as significant that they were creating their own fragrance when they were together. She was new in the space they created. Softer, bolder. Recklessly happy.

Elias's fingertips were skating lazily from the dip of her waist to the curve of her hip and back again, leaving her in a state of relaxed arousal. She had no idea what time it was, only that it was still early enough to stay in bed a little longer.

He raised himself up on his elbow. "Habibt albi," he said. "When will you know a date for the artifact transfer?"

Her brain was slow at forming a response.

"The transfer," she repeated. "From Oxford to London?"

He nodded, his eyes dark and serious.

She tugged the sheet a little higher over her hip. "Well, we shall have to talk to the curator at the British Museum. We can try to do that this week. My father already sent word to him; he promised me he would."

He gave her waist an appreciative squeeze.

"I'm not sleeping with you to dissuade you from it, by the way," she said.

His hand stilled. "Dissuade me from what."

"Your quest. I want to assist you. I just . . . wanted to make it clear."

"Ah." His dark eyebrows looked sarcastic. "You think I would bed you if I thought you were doing it with that in mind?"

"No," she said. It was just that an urge kept gripping her: to explain whatever was explainable about her objectively reckless behavior. The thought that he might misunderstand her twisted her stomach.

Elias's palm rested warm and heavy on her hip. "Is it very strange for you, to be with me like this, and under such circumstances?"

"I know it should be," she said. "But it isn't." The strangest part was how very natural it felt to be with him; to be naked in front of him, and to say things like yes, she would sleep in his arms all night.

"Why," she asked, "is it strange for you?"

He made a vague motion with his head. "When the stakes are high, it's best to either do it right or not touch it. This is . . ." He searched for the word, then shook his head. "Listen, I'd ask you to not think about my issue with Leighton at all unless I need information from you, but I don't think your head ever stops thinking."

"Sometimes it does," she said with a sideways glance.

His eyes brightened with understanding. He gripped her chin and kissed her, his mouth delicious, and she wrapped her arms around his neck with sudden emotion. When he lifted his head, she was breathing hard.

"We don't have to talk about the artifacts," she said, "but . . ." She swallowed. "Please don't just disappear, when you are done."

He looked surprised. "I won't," he said. "I promise."

"Let's just not talk about it, then, not now." She threw back the sheet. "I shall make some breakfast tea. Then I must be on my way."

He sat up. "Where are you going?"

"To Acton." She had received Lady Middleton's note with Mrs. Weldon's address yesterday noon.

Elias caught her by her hand when she clambered off the bed. "You are going with Mrs. Blackstone?"

"No."

She could tell it made him uneasy; her going places on her own bewildered him.

"You could accompany me," she said on a whim. "I take the District Railway from Sloane Square; it goes through Acton in no time. No one knows me in Acton."

Interest sparked in his eyes. "And what are we to each other, in case someone does ask?"

"Cousins?" she suggested after some thought.

For some reason that made him smile quite diabolically. He pulled her back by her wrist, so she stood between his spread thighs with her knees against the mattress and her chest was at the height of his eyes. He shaped his hands around her breasts, looked at them thoroughly, then gave each a leisurely kiss.

"Get dressed, then, *chère cousine*."

The address on Lady Middleton's note led them to a handsome, detached double-fronted house, located on a leafy street a short distance from Acton's railway station. A flower wreath decorated the white entrance door and a tabby cat lazed on the steps next to potted plants.

Catriona lingered on the pavement. "It looks friendly enough, doesn't it?"

Elias wrinkled his brow. "The curtains are drawn."

"Perhaps to keep out the summer heat. In I go, then."

She sounded confident but her stomach had dropped a wee bit. She was trying to ascertain whether a perfect stranger might sue her spouse for a good cause, an outlandish endeavor even by her standards, and this house looked so respectable she might as well save herself the trouble of trying.

Elias tipped his hat to her. "I'll wait by the green bench a few houses down."

She walked up to the door with his gaze on her back, steadily nudging her forward. She clicked her tongue at the cat. She rang the bell. Footsteps sounded inside right away, though what followed was a clanging and rattling of metal as though several locks and chains were unlatched. At last, a burly man in a butler's livery opened.

Catriona handed him her card. "Mrs. Weldon is expecting me."

The butler studied her face with an inappropriately penetrating stare. Whatever inspection this was, she seemed to pass it, for he eventually stepped aside.

"Mrs. Weldon will see you in the library, milady."

The house was dim, as all curtains were indeed drawn, and the hallway smelled like burned herbs. They passed a shelf with dozens of crystals on display. The library was small, the effect of the low light compounded by black ebony shelving. An oxblood red velvet divan stood in the middle of the room. Mrs. Weldon balanced on her tiptoes, on a chair in front of one of the bookshelves, and for a moment she carried on with her inspection of the spines as though she were alone. She appeared like a regular middle-aged matron, fuller figured, with a soft jawline in profile, her graying hair in a plain chignon. Her dress gave Catriona pause—it was jet black but made of fine silk rather than crape or bombazine, so it could well be a fashion statement rather than a sign of mourning.

"Hullo there," said Mrs. Weldon. "Thomas, send in Suze with the tea, please."

She stepped off the chair with a huff, the book tucked under her arm, then looked Catriona up and down with curious eyes. "Well, don't you bring interesting company."

Catriona glanced back over her shoulder in case Elias had followed her on soundless feet. The hallway behind her was shadowed and empty. The butler had vanished.

"No, ma'am," she said. "Though my . . . companion is waiting outside."

Mrs. Weldon's gaze became oddly fixed. "That's not what I meant." She lifted a pale hand toward Catriona's head. "The veil is markedly thin around you. Are you certain you don't perceive anything?"

Catriona stood with her arms stiffly pressed against her sides. "Perceive what?"

Mrs. Weldon's hand made a flourish. "The presence of the unseen."

A chilly draft seemed to brush through the room.

Catriona shook her head. "I don't, I'm afraid."

The woman's tone turned businesslike. "Hm. Do you experience any visions or voices?"

"No?"

"But your intuitions or predictions come true rather often?"

"Often enough, I suppose—"

"Ah." The woman glided closer. "How about fellow humans—can you abide their presence? Or do most strike you as rather . . . loud?"

The situation was becoming more absurd by the moment.

Mrs. Weldon nodded slowly. "It's not the volume of their voices that bothers you, Lady Catriona, it is everything else they bring with them, the things unseen, the untouchable ones. Now, with some practice, someone like you could achieve remarkable things in the field of the occult. An open mind is of course required."

The skeptical tilt of her lips said she considered Catriona's mind severely closed. Nevertheless, she asked Catriona to take a seat on the red divan. The elegant piece of furniture was badly upholstered and sagged under Catriona's weight.

"I'm afraid there has been a confusion, Mrs. Weldon," she said. "I'm not here to inquire about the occult."

Mrs. Weldon stilled. She folded her hands in her lap. "Lady Middleton recommended you. She said you were a young lady undertaking research for a novel. Naturally, I assumed you were seeking out my expertise in intercommunication."

A hot pressure built behind Catriona's forehead. "The truth is," she began haltingly. "The research is about a lady who lives separately from her husband . . ."

Mrs. Weldon stayed her by holding up her hand. Her absentminded stare seemed to go right into Catriona's skull, and then her round face froze. Her eyes widened.

"Lies," she whispered. "That's not why you're here, is it."

"I'm afraid I don't—"

"You aren't writing a novel at all."

"Erm," said Catriona. "No, but—"

Mrs. Weldon shot off the couch and looked down at her with a sharp expression. "What is your purpose?"

Catriona seemed stuck to her seat.

"He sent you, didn't he?" the woman demanded.

"Who?"

"Oh, I curse the day I married him." Mrs. Weldon's hand curled into a claw. "The knave—the spiteful creature."

"No, I—"

The woman cried for the butler, who dashed into the room so quickly, he must have hovered right outside the door all along. A tall woman in a maid's cap and apron followed right on his heels.

Catriona rose.

Mrs. Weldon gestured wildly. "Please assist the lady to the door."

Catriona raised her hands. "Ma'am, it appears there is a terrible misunderstanding—"

"Out, out!"

The female servant moved between Catriona and Mrs. Weldon.

"Ma'am, kindly follow us outside," the butler said, moving in on her, too.

Behind him, Mrs. Weldon had buried her head in her hands, and her shoulders were shaking.

The house all but spat her back out onto the path, and the white door firmly shut behind her. She blinked into the sun as she stumbled toward the pavement. *What on earth?*

Elias took one look at her face when she approached, and he abruptly rose from the bench. "What happened?"

"I'm not even sure. The poor thing seems unwell."

He fell in step with her. "She's ill?"

"Not in that sense—she knew about my plans, somehow. She is a spiritualist."

"What's that?"

"Apparently, the veil is thin around me," she said. "She thinks I'd have a knack for communing with the dead."

"Yiii." He crossed himself.

"Her credentials were perfect: her husband is a captain—Parliament would be loath to send a military officer to jail, and he would probably prefer prison rather than spend time with her because I daresay she was odd."

Elias fell into a more leisurely pace, compelling her to slow.

"I understand it wasn't the success you hoped for," he said.

"It wasn't, it was creepy."

"There's an oyster bar near the railway stop," he said. "Am I allowed to take a female cousin there?"

She shot him a consternated look. "Female anythings may dine or lunch in most eateries these days, even entirely unaccompanied."

He grinned. "Do you mind the rustic fare? Come, let's have lunch."

She balked; how was she supposed to summon an appetite at such a moment?

Her irritation subsided quickly; this was a rare opportunity to share a meal with him, alone, outside her kitchen.

The façade of the oyster bar was painted fire-engine red; inside, the room smelled of brine and woodsmoke. Nautical lamps in different sizes lined the mantelpiece of the fireplace, the polished brass catching the light. A blackboard on the wall advertised a pint-and-oysters special. They were the only guests, outside the regular lunch hour. Elias requested a table in one of the two bay windows. It felt illicit, lunching in bright daylight with her lover in a public place. When the waitress arrived, Catriona hid her hand where a ring should have been under the table.

"We won't have the oysters in for another six weeks," the waitress informed them. "There's fish soup, and fish pie."

"What about champagne?" Elias asked.

"We have that, sir, a dry Perrier-Jouët."

He ordered a bottle.

Catriona took off her glasses and slipped them into her jacket pocket. Briefly, her surroundings blurred. Elias remained in focus; he was indecently good-looking and had mischief in his eyes. Champagne at noon.

"This excursion was a complete shot into the brown," she pointed out. "It hardly merits a celebration."

"It was a what?"

"Oh—it's a phrase to describe a failure. A shot gone astray, far off target."

He nodded, unruffled. "All the more reason for champagne." His lashes lowered a fraction. "Don't forget it's not even noon— this could become the best day of your life just yet."

The waitress arrived with a dusty champagne trolley, the neck of the perspiring bottle sticking up from a plain wooden ice bucket. When she made to pour the drinks, Elias told her he'd take care of it. He filled Catriona's glass with Perrier, then his, and he raised his goblet with a soft *Salute*.

The first sip was unexpectedly refreshing. Crisp and tart. The bubbles pearled against her palate.

"From what I gather, Mrs. Weldon isn't obsessed with her husband at all," she said after drinking some more. "She said, 'I curse the day I married him.'"

She related the bizarre events in the Weldon library in full.

Elias topped up her glass.

"It still sounds as though there was a misunderstanding," he suggested. "Your idea is . . . unconventional. It would confuse anyone at first."

She shook her head. "She seemed scared. I'd rather not trouble her. The poor woman, how dreadful, to be afraid of your own husband, in your own home, even when he's already gone."

Elias leaned a little closer. "I wondered about this," he said softly. "You said you don't want to, or can't marry. Why? Are you afraid?" he prodded. "To marry a bad man?"

She made a small sound, like a resigned sigh.

"Various reasons," she said. "You saw me jump from the carriage near St. Giles a while ago, didn't you?"

"I have already forgotten it," he said politely.

"I haven't. I feel crowded rather too easily."

He looked at her blankly.

"I need a lot of time alone," she clarified. "I require my own, quiet space."

He regarded her with a level stare. "Wouldn't you have your own wing of the manor?"

"Ideally, yes." She could feel the champagne bubbles in her brain. "The trouble is, I just can't hear myself well when I'm surrounded by people, and when the noise persists for too long, it feels as though I'm disappearing."

He mulled it over. "Send your husband away on business when he is underfoot."

She shook her head. "I worry it wouldn't end well."

"You are very certain about something you have never tried."

"Remember the book about powerful women I never finished writing?"

A nod. Her glass was full again, too. She narrowed her gaze at it, but she took a drink.

"I said I stopped writing because I realized the futility of the book for my political goals," she explained, "but the truth is, I also stopped because it gave me the morbs. It turned out that the women on my list were either backstabbed by their lovers or died bad deaths. Often both. Elissa of Carthage took her own life over unrequited love. Cleopatra, seduced by two men, then she poisoned herself; Boudicca, again, poisoned herself. Hypatia, flayed alive. Joan of Arc, first venerated, then executed. Elizabeth I—heartbroken over Lord Dudley; Isabella of France and Catherine the Great, just grim, how their kings betrayed them. I stopped after Tamara of Georgia—her husband came after her not once, but twice, with a rebel army. It's probably just the price everyone pays for power, but it's my impression that women who hold their own pay double, just because they are women. I see it in people's faces every time I hand them a pamphlet, or when I retreat for some solitude during a house party. When I exist for my own pleasure or have a conviction, it invites resentment. If queens across the ages can't have it all, what chance do I have?"

A complex emotion stood in Elias's eyes. "I think I understand," he said, "but not everything can be experienced through abstract analysis. Some things need to be lived."

He reminded her of Hattie, scolding her for her faith in patterns. "Unfortunately, real life can't be undone quite so easily," she muttered.

The waitress reappeared with two bowls of fish soup.

"Have you considered," Elias said when she had left again, "that you could marry a man who loves you?"

Catriona lowered her spoon, a downward smile curving her lips. "Hmm, I should have thought of that."

"You should have," he said, his gaze intent. "He would raise an army for you, not against you."

He had dropped his voice to a seductively smooth murmur, and it made her skin prickle more deliciously than the drink in her glass. Her fingers clenched, nervously. He kept doing this, flirting away with her as though she were a desirable siren rather than a bit odd. Was it the distance between their cultures? Did the same traits hold different meaning depending on where one was in the world? Perhaps it was because the shape of their relationship wasn't predefined. She didn't have to pour herself into the role of a wife or an acquaintance for him, bumping into all the rules and expectations that came with each. Lovers had some leeway, to like each other for one's own sake.

"An army just for me," she said. "Fancy that. The truth is, I would be content with him letting me be when I need it."

He nodded. His thumb was lazily stroking up and down the fragile stem of his goblet. "What else?" he asked. "What else do you need from a husband?"

She was tipsy, and disturbed, because this was no longer a hypothetical discussion, or was it. "I confess I haven't thought too hard about it."

"I have trouble believing it," he said, smiling faintly. "You think hard about everything."

She was struggling to contain a riot, raging right behind her breastbone. Sometimes, she suspected that her rejection of a romantic companion wasn't her actual battle, but only the first line of defense, and that deep down, she wanted love rather too much, with a desperate, grasping passion that scared her witless. When she was under him, open and receptive, the defenses broke down and hope rushed in. But why would she be the exception? Why would it go differently for her, but not the countless others who had dared and failed?

She eyed her empty glass. "Did you know that they give champagne to the debutantes during the London season?" she asked. "As a stimulant?"

"Is that so?" His tone had, thank goodness, returned to conversational.

She nodded. "I had one season. We were expected to socialize five days a week from three o'clock until three in the morning. It's a Darwinian struggle to secure the best mate. They want us to sparkle like a Veuve Clicquot while we do it, and so the glass is never empty. By autumn, I couldn't stand the smell of it."

Elias's eyes were cool. "You could have told me. I'll order something else."

"I'm glad you didn't know." She smiled. "I enjoyed this very much. From now on, champagne shall remind me of our lunch in the oyster bar."

Chapter 25

It was the nights that allowed hidden thoughts to reach the surface. Entwined and drowsy in liminal spaces, they gave voice to the things they usually kept to themselves, until their eyes fell shut or the room filled with light. They drifted over the loss of their mothers, his father's fatal accident at sea; and smaller things, memories of their childhood that somehow seemed relevant again or some wish for the future that sounded too bombastic during the day.

This night was no different, though it was close to the darkest hour and Elias's breathing sounded as if he was already asleep. His head was a dark shape on the pillow, save a thin strip of blue starlight that fell across his face.

"I keep thinking about something Mrs. Weldon said," she whispered.

He gave a sleepy grunt, but he opened an eye.

"She said it wasn't the actual noise that sets me on edge around people, but everything they bring with them. As though we're all surrounded by invisible nuisances."

As though they all had their ghosts trailing along.

He was so silent, she thought he had fallen asleep after all. "It's no trouble for me to stay at the Oxbridge Club," he said at last.

Her heart gave an anxious leap. "Why?"

He rolled onto his back. "We have spent a lot of time together," he said.

"No," she said, quickly. "You don't tire me." She realized this now, as she consciously took stock.

"That's a shame," he said, "because I tried."

Heat suffused her. He did keep her well up at night. "It's just that your presence doesn't seem to count."

He made a low sound of comic exasperation.

She hid her face under the cover. "That came out wrong. You seem to give me more than you take, that's what I mean."

"Ya albi," he said, a cruel note in his tender voice. "My heart. Most would say that I have taken everything."

Most people would say that, she supposed. He had taken her virginity, which greatly reduced her worth on the marriage mart. For a lady, given she cared, it was indeed everything.

She couldn't see the ceiling in the dark, just a faint shimmer of chandelier crystal, and a glimmer of gold from the plaster.

"My husband," she said, "he would have to leave me be, and he must never confine me to the home."

She could sense him smirk. "He wouldn't have to. You are, by nature, a housecat."

"What if I wanted to be outside," she said with some heat. "For my cause. For anything."

He trailed a finger down her cheek. "Do you know why I enjoy watching birds of prey?"

"Tell me?"

"Because they thrill me. How they soar, and swoop at great speed. They are pure freedom. On my life, I would never clip the wings of a falcon."

"A wife is not a bird."

"Indeed," he said. "So imagine how much more I would care for her happiness."

Words, words come easy, she thought, though he sounded rather convincing. There was, of course, the matter of the artifacts between them, which they had managed to ignore in plain sight thus far, such was the power of crazed passion. She would never expect him to give the pieces up, on the contrary, but the situation was the pin waiting to strike their soap bubble. Perhaps she was already dreaming when she had an idea of how to solve that situation. The next morning, the fuzzy plan that had seemed quite brilliant just hours earlier struck her as completely unhinged. By noon, she thought that the line between madness and genius was a fine one, and that she was, possibly, on to something.

During daytime, they played chess, a feeble attempt at maintaining some civility in Cadogan House. For this purpose, they had dragged the round side table from the bedchamber's fainting couch to the middle of the room. Today, the players were in a state of undress, Elias bare-chested and in Ottoman pajama trousers, Catriona in a plain white cotton robe that was missing its cord. Behind them, the bed was rumpled.

I'm not certain I would make that move, Catriona thought as she watched Elias's knight advance.

He looked up with hooded eyes. "If you covered up," he said, "I might be able to hold a thought."

She flushed and made to gather the robe over her exposed breast.

He grabbed her knee below the table. "Don't," he said, and she laughed.

After the lunch at Acton's oyster bar, they had stayed on the District Railway until Charing Cross, which was close to the British Museum. The curator for the Department of Ancient Civilizations of Asia Minor had been away, but his assistant had given Catriona the earliest available appointment for discussing the special exhibition—Saturday morning. In the likely case they secured a transfer date during the meeting, Catriona's official missions in London would be completed.

She let go of the lapels of her robe, and Elias's gaze dropped to her breasts.

"Why did you do this?" he asked, nodding at her piercing while he touched his own chest.

She glanced down. He seemed to like the small barbell well enough; he would gently tug and tongue at it when they were together. This was the first time he asked about it.

"I think at the time, I wanted to impress a German princess," she said.

Elias was quiet. His face underwent various subtle transformations as he processed her statement. Her ears were red, she could feel the tips glow. There had been no need for such honesty, and it was not immediately clear to her why it had been important for her to tell him.

"The chess player," he said at last.

"Yes."

His gaze was very direct. "Do you still want to impress her?"

She did not think so.

"No," she said. "I don't."

Except for the extravagant piece of jewelry, little was left of the girl she had been in the piercing parlor in Paris.

Elias slowly tilted his head, as if to say *Very well, then*.

"Black to move," he said.

She obliged.

Later, when they returned to the bed, she imagined he was holding her hips more firmly and thrusting into her a little harder than usual. He wouldn't suffer jealousy well, she understood, taking in his austere face and black eyes while he moved inside her; no, she couldn't see him with the blasé attitude aristocrats so often displayed toward their spouses' special friends. He was like her, intense in his emotions. She wouldn't share him, either.

Afterward, he sat in the armchair by the open window with his legs stretched out and smoked a cigarette. He was in half profile, and the well-defined curve of his bare shoulder gleamed in the sunlight.

She reclined in the pillows, absently fingering the piercing.

The idea to have it done had been hatched in Bern. It had been winter and the river Aare wound through the city smooth and still like a frozen blue snake. The students' demeanor toward Catriona had been just as frosty, thanks to the stupid chimpanzee incident. Alexandra had still liked her. The night Catriona had learned about nipple piercings, all the girls who shared her dorm except Alex had snuck out to a not-so-secret party in Georgina Rowbotham's room. Catriona had lain next to Alexandra in Alexandra's narrow bed, careful to keep her hip and shoulder from touching her friend's, and they were reading an article about Paris in an American travel magazine. In great detail, a scandalized journalist was warning the reader about a parlor that offered intimate piercings.

"They rub a solution onto the breast that freezes it," Alexandra said. "Then they clamp tongs around the tip. Aua."

She held the magazine in one hand; the other rested on her nightgown over her small breast. Catriona kept her eyes on the page.

"*Then the lady will plunge the piercer through the tubes,*" Alex read out. "*As it passes through the nipple, it is barely felt. The tongs are unscrewed and removed, leaving the piercer still sticking through the nipple.* Oh, I'd give anything to go there and do it."

Catriona blew out a breath.

Alexandra turned her head on the pillow to look at her, gray eyes gleaming with excitement in her kittenish face. In moments like these, it was obvious why the young princess had been sent down from her school in Prussia for bad conduct.

"I tell you a secret," Alex said. "You want to know it?"

When alone, Alex spoke English to her instead of French—"to practice"—and her German accent colored every word.

"I do, yes."

"I have two hundred *Goldmark* in a stocking under this mattress. I think we should take it, and go to Paris, and have our nipples pierced in this parlor." She tapped her finger on the address at the bottom of the page.

That's silly, they won't let us leave the school grounds for even a minute, Catriona thought, but she was learning social graces. "That would be fun," she said. "Ha ha."

"I shall have a ring in each," Alexandra decided. "Then I could connect them with a chain." She traced a path with her fingertip from one breast to the other. The diaphanous nightgown revealed an eyeful, and the thought of a needle maiming the pretty, rosy tips made Catriona want to thrust a protective hand over them. She looked back at the magazine page, her tongue tied, her fingers curled. She had understood the meaning of her feelings for a while now, but after Charlie, she'd rather not have them; besides, she was uncertain what to do. It was ill-advised to make assumptions about a girl, whether she was *one of those*, and it was plain foolish to risk losing her only friend in a hostile environment.

Alexandra took in her red face.

"I shocked you," she said. "How innocent you are."

She sat up and her vanilla-scented hair brushed over Catriona's face.

"Come," she said. "I'll make you a braid for bed."

Her fingers delved in, and the scrape of her nails felt like fire on Catriona's oversensitive scalp. She shot off the mattress. "No, thank you."

"*Wie du willst,*" Alexandra said with a shrug. *As you wish.*

In the end, Catriona had gone to the parlor on her own, a quick stop on her hasty flight back to Scotland with a treacherous Alexandra's *Goldmark* in her satchel. She remembered the room vividly: the gleam of the clean-scrubbed tiled floor, the pungent smell of benzoline and chloride. The "hold her nice and still" from the woman with the piercer to the pretty blond assistant who had put her arm around Catriona's shoulders. It hadn't hurt; all her sensitive parts had been frozen beyond the point of feeling. As usual, the pain had come later. "Bathe it in camphor water whenever it is sore," the blonde had advised, her arm still around Catriona, her voice soft as though she truly cared. Cool-blooded like a reptile then, Catriona had read the girl's eyes and perceived the light press of her body against hers. "Do you know a café nearby?" she had asked, with a knowing emphasis on *café*. "Ah, oui. Venez avec moi! Je finis à cinq heures." *I finish at five.* She went to the women-only café at five, because all the kisses she had saved for Alexandra had wanted to go somewhere, and she had been quite done with placing romantic feelings on a pedestal. No more slinking around like a gloomy young Werther, feeling too much while never actually doing a thing.

"You went far away, in your head," Elias said. He had finished his cigarette and was sprawled in the chair, watching her.

"Just to Paris," she said.

His eyes lit with interest. "Paris."

"It's been years since I went. The government was still in Versailles."

"Let us go there," he said idly. "Perhaps to Provence. I would like to enjoy you in a sunnier place."

The breeze blew through the window, billowing the curtains and ruffling his curls. She watched, transfixed. Everything that was normally unremarkable, love transmuted into something interesting or meaningful. The way his hair moved, how his eyes expressed a range of emotions with just a flick of his lashes, how his laugh began in the right corner of his mouth. What came first: The love that made one person out of millions look perfectly appealing, or a perfectly appealing appearance, which brought on the love? An emotion moved through her, pressing outward; it felt as though her whole body wanted to break into tears for some relief. Had she learned nothing about not feeling too much? How dreamlike the past and life outside this house now seemed to her, and how starkly real she felt in Elias's presence, when it should have been the other way around.

She left the bed, slipped on her robe, and began a circle through the chamber, absently touching the spines of the books on the shelves, the trinkets on the mantelshelf.

"Tell me about Beirut, not France," she said.

He gave an amused huff. "Beirut. Where to begin."

"What do you appreciate most about it?"

His gaze tracked her movements around the room. "The sunsets," he said after a pause. "I have never seen the like anywhere else. The entire horizon is burning, then the sea turns red, but it's deeply peaceful."

"That sounds beautiful."

She could taste salt in the breeze, feel the warmth on her skin, smell the savory fragrance of grilled seafood spritzed with lemon juice. She met her eyes in the mirror over the sink. Her hair looked wild, as though a man had just tossed her around on a mattress.

"It all depends on where you come from, what you will appreciate about Beirut," Elias said. "When you come to it from the East, it probably gives the impression of the West. When you come from the West, like you, it would feel distinctly like the East."

She looked at him. "A moody city, then."

He lifted his chin and glanced down his nose in a gesture she had learned was his way of indicating *no*. "It's a versatile city," he said. "Above all, a resilient city. Old but alive. Every now and then something tries to destroy her, an earthquake, fire, conquest . . . but she keeps rising from the ruins. It's a good time for her now, I think you would enjoy it, there are all sorts of magazines and international literary clubs. The Ottomans invest in her; the streets are modern. The new buildings are built in an ocher stone that appears golden in the sun, or they paint them yellow, or blue. High roofs and arches everywhere and beautiful Baghdadi ceilings. Yalla, you should visit and see for yourself."

"I should, yes." Her hand was limp on the cool ceramic of the sink. Like Paris and Provence, it would likely never happen, not with him by her side. Not unless she recalibrated all the major decisions she had made for her life, decisions she had made with her most persistent needs in mind . . .

"I should like to tell you about Ehden," he said, and now he changed position and leaned forward, his elbows on his thighs.

She wandered toward him. "Ehden?"

He took her by the wrist and pulled her down to sit in his lap. "My family's village."

"I thought that was Zgharta?"

"It's the same—not the same place, but the same people. Ehden used to be the original home, now we only stay there during summer. Every September, we go to Zgharta for the winter months, closer to the sea."

She gripped his arm with some excitement. "The first printing press in the Near East is in Ehden—it's where the first Arabic books in the Levant were printed."

His grin was wide, so wide and dazzling. He gave her waist a squeeze. "Of course you know about it, Professor Campbell."

"Obviously—it's a linguistic milestone. Is it still there, the press? It should be hundreds of years old now."

"Yes. It's still there, still printing. One of our better English imports."

"I should love to see it."

His gaze moved over her glowing face. "Marry me," he said casually. "Marry me, and we could go anywhere, without problems."

She gave a startled little laugh. One of his jokes. Light-headed, she hid her face against his neck, unsettled by the quiet tension that seemed to coil in his muscles. A small pause, then he enfolded her in his arms. One hand slid inside her robe and caressed the sensitive back of her knee. "It's a beautiful place, Ehden," he said, and his low voice pleasantly reverberated through his chest. "Olive tree groves, fruit orchards, and mulberry trees. In spring, the blossoms are white and pink. The mountain water is the cleanest you will ever drink . . ."

The sun-warmed skin of his neck smelled like pine soap and sex. She was growing heavy and relaxed in his arms while he was describing paradise. Her body felt safe in his presence. Her body only cared about the now, and the now was warmth, strength, the pleasure of being held skin to skin by this man. She slept more deeply by his side, too, and felt pleasantly drowsy around him ever since the anxiousness around their scandalous beginnings had faded. Perhaps there could be room for both, the body and the mind, even for someone like her. She closed her eyes, as if to not think of anything at all.

On Friday, Elias rose with the dawn, and it was clear that he was going out to deal with his repatriation business. She sat on the edge of the mattress while he readied himself, her bare feet dangling over the rug. He stopped by the bed on his way out. He smelled of his cologne, and his breath was minty from whatever he used on his teeth.

"I would like a recommendation," he said. "For a church, and a barber."

He rubbed the spot above his ear with his knuckles, where his hair was growing out. The thought of his soft curls landing on a floor, to be swept up and discarded in a dustbin, made her feel very sorry.

"Will a Catholic church do?"

He nodded. She suggested a few places, and he kissed both her hands and left. She sat alone in the bed with a ball of anxiety forming in her chest. A church. Was he eaten by guilt over what they were doing? Would he have a change of heart, and their last time just before dawn had been *the* last time?

She ran herself a hot bath. Her hands were shaking when she uncorked a bottle of lavender essence. An affair was not for the weak; too much second-guessing. While she soaked in the tub, she decided to pull herself together. Remember who she was, what her purpose was beyond this bedroom. *No more fear.*

After she had dried herself off and dressed, she went in search of some of the high-quality stationery she kept in the house, then she sat down at the vanity table and composed a letter to Mrs. Weldon. By the time she put her seal into the wax, it was almost ten o'clock.

The London fog reeked of sulfur this morning—hardly the day for a pleasurable walk. She only briefly diverted from her route and went into the telegraph office near Sloane Square. She sent two telegrams:

One to Hattie in Belgravia.

One to Alexandra.

Alexandra lived close by, in the quarter where European diplomats clustered with their families. It had been a few years, almost eight to be precise, but would she have afternoon tea with her on Monday? Apparently having tea in department stores was all the rage now! Catriona hoped her old friend would bite. Good things had happened ever since she had laid Charlie's ghost to rest the other day. Confronting Alex could do that and more. It might actually help her advance the mad, bad scheme that was brewing at the back of her mind. Feeling quite productive, she boarded the District Railway to Acton with the letter for Mrs. Weldon in her skirt pocket. She kept herself busy afterward, and did not return to Cadogan Place until late afternoon.

Elias arrived late in the evening through the kitchen entrance. She half expected him to stop in the doorway to the drawing room where she was pretending to read, that he would look at her with a noble and severe face and say: *We will not do this again.*

Instead, he came to her, sat down, took her hand, and put it on the back of his freshly shorn head.

"Say na'ymen," he said. He sounded a little tired. The smell of the more wretched parts of the city clung to his navy jacket.

She curved her fingers around his nape. "Naymen?"

He just nodded and placed his hand over hers.

The sense of relief was so forceful, her legs felt weak for a moment. He had come back to her, he was still hers, feeling warm and alive and familiar beneath her palm.

He lifted his head. "I brought you food," he said. "It's in the kitchen."

"Thank you. I don't think I had anything today after breakfast."

I thought so, said his grave, unsurprised expression. "What did you do today?"

A triumphant smile broke over her face. "I went out—I went back to Mrs. Weldon's house."

He sat up straight. "Eywah," he said, looking impressed. "What happened?"

He seemed too interested in her excursion to comment on her cavorting around town on her own.

"I wrote her a letter," she said. "An honest letter. First, I apologized for my sneaky ways. Then I explained that I'm trying to create a legal case Parliament can't ignore." Her gaze slid away. "I suppose I was still a wee bit sneaky; she feels so strongly about spiritualism that I wrote I had felt 'guided' to seek her out, that I sensed she could be the key to a landmark decision that would change the fate of women in Britain. The truth is, though, I do feel it; this . . . buzz right here." She touched her breastbone.

Elias's hand slid over hers again, and their fingers entwined seamlessly. "Did she read it?" he asked.

She grinned. "I think so, yes. Her butler nearly slammed the door into my face, but something rather odd happened—the tabby cat, you know, the one that was sleeping next to the flower pots the last time, this cat got in the way. So, while he was struggling with the tabby around his legs, I just . . . talked at him. Until he took the letter. I said I would wait right there, and if he were so kind to let me know whether Mrs. Weldon accepted it. I waited for half an hour, and the curtains were twitching . . . he came back. He said she will read it."

Elias's smirk looked impressed, proud even. "So now you wait?"

"Aye, now it's out of my power, I have done all I can."

"Then you have done enough," he said. His hand slid up her thigh and curved around her hip with sensual intent.

"You went back to that witch house by yourself," he said.

"I'm afraid I did."

"Brazen woman," he said, leaning over her. "What am I to do with you."

She had a few suggestions.

Chapter 26

Saturday morning. The sky was a mellow blue and a pair of doves cooed in the park across the street. Two empty teacups sat on the round table.

They were expected in the curator's office at ten o'clock. Mrs. Blackstone would meet them at Trafalgar Square; she was a respectable, married woman, and her company would allow Elias to attend the meeting together with Catriona.

Presently, her dark head was bent over his sleeve, her attention focused on slipping his cuff links through his right cuff. He could do it himself, but he enjoyed watching her fingers tending to him. The tip of her right middle finger seemed permanently dyed blue.

She stepped back and looked him up and down before quickly glancing away.

"What?" he asked, glancing between her and his reflection in the mirror.

She moved her lips nervously. "You look handsome," she then said, and blushed, as though she had been the one receiving a compliment.

Her shyness stirred desire low in his body. Not the shyness per se, but that what was between them affected her so. Something was softening in her. Perhaps the heat of passion was melting down her walls.

"It's a good suit," he said. "From a tailor on Savile Row."

She touched his sleeve. "Do you miss your Eastern clothes at all?"

"Yes."

"What do you miss about them?"

"I can wear my boots. The trousers are comfortable. The fabrics are more luxurious, and I can carry my knives in my belt." He could tell his words were painting an image of him in her mind, and he wondered if she liked it. "I can still appreciate a well-made suit," he added. "I practically lived in them in France."

"You wear them well." She leaned back against the dresser, her hands behind her bustle. "Do you ever feel confused?" she asked. "About what you are?"

Had she pried open his skull and looked into his head lately?

He shrugged. "I'm used to it. I'm used to being in between."

"How I admire you for it."

He stepped in front of her and put his hands left and right from her on the dresser. Now she was nicely trapped. The soft smile on her upturned face said she liked it. Her shell-pink lips were still a little swollen from last night's erotic exploits.

"What do you admire about it?" he asked.

"I don't have the constitution for it," she said. "You've met my good friend, Annabelle. Sometimes, when I observe her, how she goes about her days, I feel as though I'm a different species from her entirely. She's a scholar, a wife, a mother, a duchess, a suffragist—everyone wants a slice of her, but she seems to thrive on it. It's as though she receives more from her responsibilities than they cost her."

"You're a scholar, a suffragist, a daughter, a friend."

His lover. She was very good at that, too, unreservedly passionate. In bed, when he embraced her, she trembled and clung to him as though he held her very life in his palm. It disturbed and aroused him on a visceral level. It made him feel like some demigod. Such feelings would come with a price, he was certain of it, he had heard the sermons about hubris.

"I feel I can't be too many things at once," she now said. "It probably means I'm weak, that I can lose myself so easily in the presence of others."

The look on her face was resigned.

"I think you are strong," he said after some thought. "You're from a great, noble clan."

She tilted her head. "But that's my clan. Not me."

"See. You could make the Campbell name your entire identity, but I haven't seen you do it once. Too many people let their family name tell them who they are and what to do." He cupped her silky cheek in his hand. "You . . . you are you."

She focused on his cravat, smoothed it with her fingers. "What about you—is your name telling you how to be?"

"My mother's name could, or the name of her town," he said with a low laugh. "But here it is: my family and the people of Ehden, they call me Ajnabi."

She translated it with a puzzled expression. "The stranger?"

"Yes."

"Your own family," she murmured. "Why?"

"Habit," he said. "My father was not from the village. His ancestors, but not he. His grandparents settled at the coast."

"But—"

"We don't live in the mountains, cut off from the sea and fertile soil, because we enjoy it, Catriona. We retreated there from trouble. Too much trouble makes people cautious."

"Trouble caused by outsiders," she said, nodding.

"Too often, yes. I was born in Jbeil, at the coast," he explained. "But my mother never felt safe when away from the mountains. My father cared for her very much, so they eventually returned to her hometown for the sake of her nerves. Then the war happened, so the mountains no longer felt safe, either. I was their only child. They sent me to an aunt in France, to be safe until the situation became clearer."

"That's when you attended the Jesuit school."

She remembered. Because she listened to everything and forgot nothing.

"Yes," he said.

He slid his arms around her and held her solid, shapely body against his.

"You must have been very young," she said, her face serious.

"Six years old."

"Weren't you terribly homesick?"

His eyes widened sarcastically. "Of course. But when I returned to the mountain a few years later because my mother was gone, I was Ajnabi. Sometimes, I was *Gentleman*—apparently, I was nine years old with the mannerisms of an old Frenchman."

Her fingertips snuck into his collar, the touch gentle on his skin. "Then what are you, Mr. Elias?"

"Hmm." He moved with her in his arms, in slow backsteps across the room to the notes of an inaudible waltz. "I'm many things now. I'm a son of the coast and the mountain. A man of business and a traveler. I read books in three languages, and I had a home in France and studied in Britain. Every book, every country, every new friend, teaches me something, so the old ways, well, you can question them. The trouble is when these different parts jostle against one another, that's when I think, who am I? Can I still call myself Zghartawi when my own people there call me Ajnabi? Am I still from the coast when I have no family left there? Can I be one thing while I'm also another, am I halves of something or am I whole as I am? I could live in France well enough, but I would miss the old country, and the French look at my face and call me a stranger, again."

She had moved with him as one, letting him lead. Now she laid a hand against his cheek. "I like your face."

"Of course," he said, "it's a very handsome face." He laughed out loud and let her go. "The world is changing, amoura. It's moving faster and it's expanding, whether you like it or not. You must weave your own way of being in such a place, with all the different strands you have. Now, hurry. We can't be late to meet this curator."

The office for Ancient Civilizations of Asia Minor was located on the second floor of the British Museum. It was a small room with a large desk. A painting of the ruins of Baalbek hung on the wall behind the desk. Outside the windows, the sunshine had thinned the fog to a diffuse mist and the views were clear; carts, cabs, and pedestrians bustled around the central monument of Trafalgar Square. Two fountains spouted water without sound.

The curator was a lanky, fair-haired Englishman with a kindly face, his age indeterminable thanks to his brown corduroy suit that would have dated anyone to middle age. Both Wester Ross's telegram and Catriona's note were laid out on his desk, along with photographs of the bulls from various angles. The photographs surprised Elias; Catriona hadn't mentioned that she had had them done, nor that she had passed them on.

The museum was enthralled by the idea of a Phoenician special exhibition, the curator assured them. He seemed uncertain whom to address principally, local ladies or a man from Arabia, so his gaze kept darting back and forth between the three of them.

"We could clear out the Assyrian exhibition in the west wing," he said. "The question is, however, whether we find a back room with space for those artifacts currently on display. I'm afraid we are looking at early spring for a date."

Well, that wasn't any good, was it, Elias thought, though he could certainly return sometime next year.

Catriona pushed her glasses up the bridge of her nose. "Are the back rooms truly so crowded?"

A regretful nod. "They are, and more so by the day. The influx of artifacts has in fact forced us to contemplate a costly extension."

"An extension for the display rooms?"

"No, ma'am, an extension for the storage."

Elias frowned. "What share of the artifacts in your collections are actually on display?"

"Round about five percent, sir."

"That means almost everything in the museum's possession is in storage," said Mrs. Blackstone, and she sounded unpleasantly surprised.

The curator coughed softly. "With all due respect, ma'am, five percent on display is plenty. And what we have in our possession, the French don't have."

"Between us, I'm afraid Mr. Leighton's willingness to lend out the artifacts is heavily subjected to his moods," Catriona said. Her cool, flat tone said her head was getting hot. "If you care to have the bulls on display, I advise you to find room sooner rather than later, before he fancies keeping them entirely to himself again."

The curator kneaded his fingers. "Of course. I understand. There is an alternative I have considered."

"Brilliant—I should love to hear it."

"If we were to limit the exhibition to the bulls and selected artifacts from the same period, rather than look at Mr. Leighton's entire collection, I could have a corridor on the first floor available by September."

Catriona glanced at Elias, her eyes asking whether this suited him. He made the decision quickly. The bulls were the crown jewels in the collection. If he took everything but them, it wouldn't feel as though justice had been done, whereas if only the bulls returned to their temple in Sidon, he would still consider it a victory. Also, the sooner he was back home, the sooner he could resume his position in the family business, which was the sensible thing to do. He gave a nod.

"I shall confirm the dates with Mr. Leighton," Catriona said to the curator, "but assume that he shall agree to a first loan in September."

"This is all terribly exciting," chirped Mrs. Blackstone. She pulled a notebook from a large, sparkling reticule. "I should love to share the news in my art circle, perhaps also with our readers of the *Home Counties Weekly*?"

The curator agreed enthusiastically. Catriona and Mrs. Blackstone shared a look.

As they took their leave, they made a detour to see the Parthenon marbles. The frieze and statues were on display in a vast hall on the ground floor where every step echoed on the polished tiles. Two clerks stood guard; voices were hushed. The once brilliant colors of the frieze surrounding them had long faded; the story of gods and humans was told in uniform pale marble now. As for the statues, most had lost a limb, a nose, even a head, under the rough treatment of the Ottomans, or later, when they had been torn from their home in Athens and shipped across a sea. Some had gone down with their ship and the salt had eaten at them before they had been recovered. The broken parts only seemed to edify the bits that had survived the millennia intact, and the battered bodies still told a tale: that people had always been people, that then as now, they had been compelled by valor, worship, and wine-fueled debauchery, and that they had forever felt a keen interest to preserve their stories.

"Have you seen them before?" Catriona was next to him, a little closer than was proper in a public space.

He nodded. "I was here two days ago."

She stilled. "Oh."

He had come here after meeting the next man in the chain of

command, this time in East London. An understanding had been reached, about the type of crew Elias required, which skills, what it would cost him in coin. On his way back to Cadogan Place, he had stopped at the museum. He had craved a reminder why he was doing it, something to substantiate his self-imposed duty to bring home the bulls at all cost. It hadn't helped. Looking at the stories of people who had turned to dust thousands of years ago, only to catch glimpses of familiar needs, brought home the timelessness of the human condition. All lives had been lived before; no triumph or defeat was new. A man might as well make his own choices.

Catriona stood with her head angled back, seemingly absorbed by the display. Her subtle scent still reached him, teased him, made him want to reach out and touch her. Ridiculous, that any one part of her had once seemed plain to him.

Mrs. Blackstone was alternately taking notes in her little book and scrutinizing the marbles. "Does it even have meaning?" she asked as she scribbled. "Displaying them here, with the other half still back at the Acropolis? From an artist's perspective, I daresay it doesn't."

"I imagine seeing them in their original context is a different experience," Catriona replied in a low voice. "Certainly for the visitors whose story they tell."

"The last argument I heard was that the ancient Greeks have little connection to the current Greek people, and if something doesn't clearly belong to one nation, it belongs to anyone," Mrs. Blackstone replied. "What do you say to that, Mr. Khoury? Is it nonsense?"

He exhaled audibly through his nose. "I'd say it's a convenient argument made by nations that managed to formalize their nationhood on time." Which was a bloody enough endeavor without several imperial powers meddling in one's affairs. Just ask Youssef Bek Karam, now in exile as a thanks for his efforts.

The trio eventually parted at the museum's main entrance.

Mrs. Blackstone put her hand on Catriona's sleeve. "I shall see you on Wednesday, then. Suffrage business," she explained to Elias. If it struck her as improper that he and Catriona were leaving the museum together, she didn't let it show.

After the quiet of the museum, London was loud. The sun glared, pedestrians were streaming at them. They shouldn't walk to the underground stop together in such a central place. Catriona moved quickly; the set of her shoulders was rigid.

"Very clever of you to send the curator photographs of the pieces," he said.

"Thank you."

"Now I would like it if you didn't burden yourself with my business any longer," he went on. "You have much to do for your own cause. Your willingness to assist a stranger will not be forgotten."

Her gaze flicked to him from the corner of her eye. "A stranger," she said in an odd voice, and the impression struck him that he had offended her. After a pause, she added: "I'm not doing nearly enough."

Below the brim of her hat, her profile appeared drawn and pale.

"Psst," he said.

She glanced at him again, and her somber expression turned wary.

"You're about to make a joke," she said, "aren't you."

He raised an eyebrow. "Do you know why the Egyptian pyramids are in Egypt?"

"Oh, this is silly."

"Come on, take a guess."

"Pfff." She nestled at her hat. "I suppose you could look at the local availability of—"

"It's because they are too big to fit into the British Museum."

She gasped, then yelped a shocked laugh before she slapped a hand over her mouth.

"What's this," he said, mock amazed, "she's having fun."

She glanced left and right at the people passing them by. "Your sense of humor is awfully dark."

He smiled. "Not as dark as my anger. You laughed, didn't you."

"All right, I did—I'm just as bad."

Looking at each other's grinning faces, they nearly walked into a newspaper cart, which Elias avoided by pulling her with him on a last-second swerve. For a moment, their bodies pressed together, and his hand was on her waist. He released her quickly. Catriona looked up at him, no longer smiling. Her lips had parted, and a loose strand of dark hair clung to her cheek. He focused on the crossing ahead so he would not grip her chin and kiss her in full sight of the world's largest city, in front of the pedestrians and the carriage drivers, the shopkeepers and the flower girl and the policeman at the corner. His chest hurt with the urge to whisk her to the secluded privacy of his home, away from prying eyes and unwanted opinions, to keep her as his well-protected treasure.

"You're staying in town until Wednesday, then," he said, the full heat of his emotions in his voice.

"Aye." She sounded out of breath.

He looked straight ahead at the looming underground sign. "You have any plans?"

Apart from being naked in his arms, under him, on her knees, perhaps on top of him.

Her reply was soft, but it struck through the hum of London clear like a bell.

"You," he heard her say. "You are in my plans."

Chapter 27

On Monday afternoon, Catriona stood in front of the seven-story-high Fortnum & Mason department store on Picca-dilly. She was dressed in sky-blue velvet and had curled her hair. In her reticule was a check, presigned by Wester Ross, worth two hundred *Goldmark*. Around her, the fog hung limp like a damp curtain. The air was still in London today.

Alexandra's reply had been delivered by a messenger boy on Sunday morning, a handwritten note, and the sight of the distinct German Kurrent script had felt like a pinch to Catriona's stomach. *Meine Liebe, it's been too long—we must have afternoon tea at F & Ms.* The pinch had faded quickly. Even now, looking over the store's red-brick façade and knowing she was inside the building, Catriona detected no major disturbance in her pulse. *No more fear.* Besides, she was here to help Elias.

She approached the main doors, and a bellboy held them open for her. The tea salon was located on the ground floor, which was the gourmet floor, and the scent of sugar wafted around her as she walked past honey and jam jar pyramids and shelves stacked with colorful tea and biscuit tin boxes. Hundreds of chocolates were on display on the confectionery counter. When the salon's seating area came into view, she slowed after all. She thought she had seen Alexandra's blond head. Just then, the woman in question turned toward her. When familiar gray eyes met hers, Catriona did feel something, a zing, an echo. A ghost rattling its chain.

Back at the boarding school, Alexandra's arrival had worked like an electric current on her broken heart. The young princess had entered the Common Room slinky like a silverpoint cat; small body, wide-set eyes, heart-shaped face. When their gazes had crossed, something inside Catriona had said *Hello*. Their beds had been next to each other in the dorm, but they hadn't really conversed until Alexandra had walked into Catriona's secret nook in the roped-off turret for a smoke one afternoon.

"Why are you playing alone?" She had nodded at the chessboard where Catriona was practicing her gambits.

"I don't have an opponent here," Catriona muttered.

Alexandra sat on the table, one foot on the floor, the pert curve of her bottom threatening to topple Catriona's right flank on the board.

"Teach me," she said from above. "You scoff? Why?"

Catriona leaned back in her chair, her hands stuffed into her skirt pockets. "I'm sorry."

"You don't think I can learn it?"

Catriona considered it. "I don't know."

"Well, I should like to learn it well enough so that I might impress a gentleman, but not so well that I would beat him."

Catriona frowned. "The point of this game is to win it."

"That may be so," Alexandra allowed, "but the point of the greater game is winning the best possible husband."

"What greater game is that?"

"The game of life, Dummerchen." *Silly one.*

"Ah."

"You are lucky to have met me. You teach me chess, and I teach you how to charm a husband."

"I don't want a husband," she said reflexively, because Charlie would marry someone else.

Alexandra's canine teeth flashed. "You're funny. I like you."

This made no sense as they barely knew each other, but confronted with the girl's cheeky smile, Catriona was tongue-tied. That night, she watched from her bed as Alexandra pulled the pins from her hair, and how the smooth honey-blond locks unfurled down her back. She looked away, quickly, as though she hadn't been supposed to be looking at all. Books knew about such things; schools knew about such things; rigorous daily exercise programs were in place in single-sex institutions to prevent such things. In this case, the matutinal jumping jacks prevented nothing—all the familiar symptoms soon ailed Catriona: the dry mouth, the dreams, the pounding pulse, the impossibility of looking at her new friend while wanting to look at her all the time. She did teach Alex chess, as it involved little talking beyond giving instructions. Meanwhile, especially after the chimpanzee debacle, she had dreamt of moving to Applecross with her friend, to live unencumbered by convention and yet with a romantic companion. Well, that hadn't worked out at all.

Alexandra stood when she approached, her eyes bright with *Wiedersehensfreude*—the pleasure of seeing someone again.

"Catriona," she said. Cheeks were kissed, the smell of sweet powder and Alex briefly went to Catriona's head. Alexandra took both her hands and looked her up and down. "My goodness. You haven't changed."

"Neither have you."

"Oh please," Alex said, amused. She gestured toward her figure, dressed modestly in dark green taffeta silk. "I'm twice the woman I used to be."

"It suits you."

"Do you truly think so?"

Her eyes roamed carefully. "Aye."

They sat. The tables were spread out and busy with ladies taking afternoon tea. As long as one spoke softly, one had some privacy.

Alexandra lifted the gold medallion she wore around her neck. "I have two boys now, can you believe it."

She showed them to Catriona, handsome children with severe side partings.

"Friedrich, and Johannes."

"Lovely."

The elder boy looked at least six years old. They hadn't waited long to marry Alexandra off after she had been caught doing something "unspeakable" with Georgina Rowbotham in the roped-off turret. Mean, uninspiring Georgina, of all people. The betrayal, oh, it could make a girl feel feral. Mrs. Keller had sent the pair home after a night in solitary confinement; their belongings were collected by staff. No one had seemed to know about the stocking with two hundred *Goldmark* under Alexandra's mattress. They vanished with Catriona a few days later.

Alexandra chattered, raised her eyebrows, and made small gestures as she recounted this and that. Her eyes crinkled at the corners now when she smiled. Catriona sipped her tea, and occasionally she nodded or said, "Is that so?" Meanwhile, she was thinking. Did Alex like her husband? Had she liked Georgina? It frightened her, to think about whether people actually lived how they truly thought and felt, or whether they spent their time living two lives: the one they performed, in public and their own homes, and the one that played out in their mind, in parallel to everything they said and did. Neither one, performed or imagined, struck her as more real than the other, so unless the two versions were congruent, one lived only half a life.

"Now I've prattled on and on," Alexandra said. "What about you? Do you still play chess?"

Elias appeared before her mind's eye, bare-chested with a coolly brooding expression as he studied the board. She bit her cheeks to stop herself from grinning stupidly. The last weeks of her life had been near perfect congruency. Every touch, every smile, every minute she had spent in his arms, had been in harmony with her inner desires.

"Yes," she said. "Sometimes, I still play."

"We had such fun playing it."

"Indeed."

Alexandra watched her over the delicate rim of her cup. "You *have* changed," she said. "You shine."

Catriona smiled, embarrassed.

"No, you do," Alexandra said, "you are glowing. That's why I thought you still look seventeen when I first saw you—you're happy." She leaned a little closer. "I'm curious, what was it that made you think of me? To meet me again?"

Catriona nodded. "I owe you this." She took the check from her reticule.

"Goodness?" Alexandra looked at the paper slip with a puzzled frown.

"I took what you left under your bed, back in Bern. I'm sorry."

Her friend's smile was polite and bemused. "How kind of you to think of it." Clearly, she had forgotten all about her stash in her stocking as soon as she had left Switzerland. She made to hand it back to Catriona. "You should keep it."

"Ah, no. I spent it all."

Alexandra shook her head. "What did you spend it on? You never bought anything. I had to force every purchase upon you at the haberdasher."

"I escaped shortly after you left and needed to pay my way."

Alexandra's fine lips formed a scandalized pink O. "You escaped—how?"

"The wagon that brought the milk bottles in the morning."

Alexandra moved her eyes and shook her head as though she was greatly excited by this. "You, a naughty stowaway," she said. "Meine Güte, what fun. I used to have such fun. I used to be fun, too; you know I was."

"You were."

"Now my husband's position is all about protocol. Dreary. Except the parties." A feline smirk curved Alexandra's mouth. "Catriona, you haven't known debauchery unless you have been at an ambassador's ball at two in the morning. Oh, all right, it isn't half as exciting." She laughed softly. "Save me, my scandalous friend."

"Actually," Catriona said, her gaze sliding to the left and then to her right. "I wondered whether you could assist me with something."

They parted a short while later and both women were smiling. The conclusion of their meeting hadn't exactly been a renewal of their friendship but rather the proper closure of it, and they might meet again as the new people they now were. Both were excited by Alexandra's agreement to assist with Catriona's unusual request, which shouldn't cost her much effort but would greatly hurry Catriona's ambitions concerning the artifacts along. Catriona floated around among chocolates and jars of Fortnum & Mason's delicacy section like an escaped balloon at first, free but without direction, adjusting to the sudden absence of a weight that must have dragged on her unconsciously.

Soon she became purposeful and descended the stairs to the Lower Ground Floor, which was effectively a high-end covered market. Voices echoed off the tiled walls here. Strong smells clashed: raw meat, seafood on ice, baked goods, flowers. *Shallow breaths.*

She approached one of the neatly dressed clerks. "Where may I find the cookbooks?"

"What type of cookbook would you be looking for, ma'am?"

"Levantine cuisine."

"We'd have one on Indian cuisine, ma'am."

Noticing her disappointment, the clerk directed her to the manager of the grocery section, who turned out to be a Frenchman.

"They sent you to me because I was a chef at the Midland

Grand Hotel," he said, sounding annoyed, flicking his hand. "*Bon*, I can share some recipes with you. Your cook will not have the spices for them, nor the required techniques, and we don't have the bread on this island, *mais, pas de problème*, you find the spices here in the spice section."

He rapidly dictated four recipes to his assistant, for a salad, a paste, a chicken dish, and a ground beef dish.

"That's rather a lot of parsley," Catriona said doubtfully, skimming the notes.

"Oui, parsley, third aisle. Go and assist the lady, Smith. Pas de problème."

She had help for loading the bags and boxes into a cab, and she managed to unload everything on her own back at Cadogan Place. Elias wasn't home, which suited her just fine. This could be a surprise for him; unlike her, he probably liked surprises. After moving the ingredients to the kitchen, she went upstairs and changed into a loose, old-fashioned morning wrapper. Back in the kitchen, she put on an apron.

"Right," she said, her hands on her hips as she surveyed the pots, the knife block, the stove. She could follow simple, written instructions. She could figure out how to operate a stove.

An hour later, she had a huge, massive, grand *problème*. Her wrist hurt. Her eyes stung. Behind her, steam and smoke welled from the stove. The windows were running with condensation; sweat was running down her back. On the wooden cutting board, one big bushel of parsley after the next seemed to melt to a tiny heap of mush under her knife, but the instruction had underlined the *finely* of *finely chopped*, so she stuck to it. Her heart was pounding because any moment now, Elias would walk in and find her steeped in chaos; there were chicken innards in a bowl, scattered onion peels, a tomato on the floor, dirty spoons everywhere. Something crackled behind her back. The chicken. She dropped the knife and spun around. Slowly now. She put on the large, insulating mitten and carefully lifted the lid of the pot. Heat blasted her face. "Bloody hell," she gasped.

"Hayeti," came a low voice. "What is this?"

She yelped.

"You startled me," she said.

Elias was a blurred, dark shape, leaning with one shoulder against the doorframe. She took off her foggy glasses and rubbed them on her apron; by the time they were back on her nose, he was next to her and lifted the hissing pot by its handles. He put it down on the cast-iron tray that was attached to the side of the stove.

"So that's what this is for," she muttered.

Elias straightened. The starburst pattern around his pupils gleamed golden, and for a beat, she couldn't breathe. Something had grabbed her heart and squeezed.

"I'm sorry," she said without thinking. "I meant for it all to be ready."

She pointed at the mess on the cabinet counter and realized she was still wearing a gigantic mitt.

A popping sound came from the oven, causing her to flinch. Elias grabbed a tea towel, opened the oven flap, and reached into the smoke. The grate and its charred contents landed next to the pot. He flipped down the levers. He picked up the stray tomato, gave it a small toss before he put it on the counter, then turned off the faucet that had been dripping away in the background. He moved between the cabinet, the sink, the stove with ease, and within a minute, the kitchen had fallen silent. Only then, he ran a hand through his hair and glanced around as if to make sense of things. His gaze lingered on the parsley.

"I'm making tabbouleh," she supplied. Parsley salad.

"Inshallah," he murmured.

"All right, it might not turn into tabbouleh, it's not coming together as I had hoped."

His gaze became markedly intense. "You are making tabbouleh."

"I certainly had the intention."

He took in her frizzy hair, the wrapper, the apron. A tingling sensation danced over her skin. His expression was as intent and lustful as though she were spread out naked before him on the bed upstairs.

He hooked a finger into her apron pocket and pulled her against him. "Why are you attempting to cook for me, sweetheart?"

"I thought that perhaps, you miss your home," she said. "You looked as though you were missing home when you told me about Ehden."

The words came haltingly, as though they were part of a much grander confession. Elias lightly touched the back of her head.

"Ta'abrinee," he said, his voice soft and strained.

He shrugged out of his jacket and tossed it over the back of the chair next to the cabinet.

He undid his cuffs and rolled up his sleeves, and he was behind her, his chest against her shoulders, his hands left and right from her on the countertop. The rough beginnings of a beard grazed her cheek when he put his face next to hers to study the disaster on the cutting board.

"You crushed it, rather than sliced it," he said.

His body pressed into hers when he leaned forward to reach a different knife, the largest one. He put her hand on the handle and closed his warm fingers over hers.

"Look, like this."

The sinews in his forearm flexed; his movements were rhythmic and quick. She exhaled. She felt his muscles work against her shoulders as he chopped away, so effortlessly, so innocently, while he had her pinned against the cabinet edge with his hips. The less she tried to keep up, the smoother the knife went about its task. Her hand was loose under his. She turned soft in his embrace. He splayed the fingers of his free hand over her belly and his lips brushed the shell of her ear.

"I would like to have you now," he said, the words humming in his chest.

She nodded, her lower body already painfully heavy with surging desire.

He let go of the knife.

"I have nothing prepared," he added.

"You could—" She turned her face to the side. "You could withdraw."

"If that is what you want, I can do that."

His fingers had undone the apron strings; he was opening the belt of her wrapper. The counter swam before her eyes. When he had said *now*, he had meant now. Would they do it on the floor? Standing up?

"You really liked that I cooked for you," she said, sounding shaky.

A fleeting kiss to the side of her neck. "I like when you show your affection."

He pulled the wrapper over her head and placed it over the back of the chair. She was in her undergarments, tied into her corset. Still dressed, Elias sat on the chair and spread his knees. Like that, then. He took her by the wrist and maneuvered her between his thighs. His eyes were half-closed when he looked up at her and put his hand into the slit of her pantaloons. He touched her carefully, lingered on the soft inside of her thigh, before he went higher. His throat moved when his fingers found her wet. She stared into his face, in an erotic stupor that made her slack and immobile.

He slipped a finger inside her.

"Take me out," he said.

Somehow, she bent down and found the buttons, then the cord of his underwear.

"Yes, like that."

He withdrew from her and pushed down his trousers enough to make a good space for her, then took himself in hand and looked her in the eye. She straddled him and hovered, a last hesitation before meeting him skin to skin. His mouth softened. His other hand rested lightly on her thigh. It hurt, feeling so much for him, and there was only one way to ease it.

When he entered her, she gripped his shoulders.

"Breathe," he said, his tone soothing, his eyes feral.

Her throat was hot. Her thighs were trembling. He held her by the hips, supporting her when she paused.

"I imagined doing it like this," she whispered.

His fingers dug into the soft part of her hips. "How does it feel?"

She closed her eyes. "Very full."

"Does that please you?"

She nodded and sank forward and rested her forehead on his shoulder. She inhaled him through a layer of cotton. He urged her down a little more then, and she made a breathless sound. She felt the fabric of his trousers against her bottom. He held her until he felt her relax. When he finally moved, she understood that sitting on top did not necessarily mean being on top. For a while, they did it fairly quietly, just to the sound of their panting, then the chair began to creak, then it squeaked across the flagstones. She lifted her head and looked around. The setting sun slanted through the window; smoke hung in the air. Chaos on the cabinet.

Elias let go of her hips. He raised his hands to the knot of his cravat and untied it.

"Let me cover your eyes."

The black silk glided through his fingers. His shirt was open now and revealed the V of his chest.

"You may," she said, and touched his throat. He might do anything to her this moment and his small smile said he knew.

Darkness fell, silky smooth on her closed eyelids. His rich scent clung to the fabric. She shivered, and his warm mouth met hers, then she felt his tongue. Now all that existed was him. Until he lifted her and slid from her, leaving her empty and yearning.

"Shh," he said, and turned her around by her shoulders. He walked her a step.

"What are we doing?"

She could hear the smile in his voice: "Bending you over."

It was the cabinet. His hands covered hers, guided them forward over the smooth surface of well-worn wood until they reached the edge. He curled her fingers around it and kept his on top.

His warm, fractured breath brushed over her nape. "Will you hold on to that?"

His thighs were against the back of hers, his chest pressing hers down against the countertop. She nodded, yes, she would hold on. He rose. Behind her, he moved his hips and smoothly slid back into her with a satisfied, drawn-out groan. She arched with a cry of relief. He thrust, once, twice, and then he paused, buried inside her.

His hand was on the small of her back, just holding her there. "The way you feel," he said hoarsely. "I could feel you like this forever."

Forever.

She moaned, more in her chest than out loud. Behind her, his hips drummed as if to drive it home—forever. It broke something open inside her, and a bright, glorious sensation shot through the cracks. Forever. It did not scare her. She was light and air. His hands were gripping her hips, taking more. He was claiming any inch that had been ceded by older preoccupations, until there was only him, him, him. It felt so good, so sublime, that it made her think, why not submit to it, why not ride along it, why not forever, as long as it was with him. When she pulsed around him and cried out, all went black inside her, like an ending.

When she came to, the silk had slipped from her face and fiery red light met her eyes. The sunset glinted off a copper pan.

Elias was resting on top of her, damp and hot, his forearms supporting his weight. They didn't speak, perhaps a little embarrassed at having mated so fiercely next to a pile of tomatoes. In front of them, the stove was perfectly quiet, as if stunned into silence.

He nuzzled her nape, his movements languid with satisfaction.

"What was it," he asked, "what you had baking on the grate?"

"Aubergines," she croaked. "You grill them, then mash them, for . . . baba ghanoush."

"Looks delicious. Congratulations."

"Please."

"Now I know why you train as a firefighter in Oxford."

She tried to struggle up, but he didn't budge and kept her flattened underneath him, his chest shaking with suppressed, evil laughter.

She turned her head sideways and rested her cheek against the careworn wood of the counter.

"The word you said earlier, what did it mean?" she asked.

The way he went quiet said he knew at once what she meant. "Ta'abrinee," he said.

"Yes."

"It means, bury me."

"Isn't that a bit morbid?"

He stroked the back of her hand with his thumb. "We say it to someone we don't want to live without. Hence, we must go first."

I don't want you to go first.

She wanted forever.

She was smiling mindlessly. Perhaps he saw. He very gently kissed her cheek. Her heart kept beating steadily, happily, as though it truly believed that anything was possible for her. For them. Together.

Chapter 28

─────────⊱≈◈≈⊰─────────

She still drifted high and weightless as a cloud to the Blackstone residence in Belgravia two days later. By the time she arrived in Hattie's drawing room, however, she had schooled her expression to neutral. Her newly found hopes still felt tender, like a budding seedling that might be too soft and pale to withstand the full, harsh force of daylight just yet. Secondly, for this meeting, she had a special point on her agenda that would require her friends' help and joint efforts, and if they suspected that she had hatched this mad scheme just because a man had fried her brain with his excellent lovemaking, she'd inspire neither trust nor confidence.

The Blackstone drawing room was grander than the one at the Randolph Hotel, but the arrangement of furniture was quite the same; divans, armchairs, and side tables formed a rectangle with the fireplace, and there were tea cakes. Hattie rested on the divan in a flowing red morning wrapper, a knitting basket at her feet. Annabelle looked a wee bit tired round the eyes, which didn't detract from her beauty. She was comfortable in an armchair next to Catriona.

Lucie, dressed deceptively docile in a soft pastel gown, paced rage-fueled circles on the rug.

"Two weeks," she ground out. "Less than two weeks until the session, and Sir George Campbell and Mr. Warton are on the rise."

"They won back two MPs," Annabelle was saying for the second time. "Only two."

"I mustn't propose violence," Lucie said, having proposed violence minutes earlier.

"What would you actually do," Hattie asked, leaning forward, intrigued.

"Oh, I could think of something," Lucie muttered. "I'm certain I could."

"It's too soon to lose heart," Annabelle said. "We may still win, with a solid margin, too."

"If we don't, I would throw a few stinkpots from the gallery," Lucie said. "There's a nice, lingering stench to go with their rotten politics whenever they reconvene."

Catriona was skeptical. "How would we get a stinkpot through the trellis?"

Lucie frowned in thought. "We could have small ones made; egg-sized ones, they fit."

"We could bring a saw and cut out a piece of the grille," Hattie suggested. "To get a big one through."

Annabelle looked unamused from one to the other. "Are we serious? How will that help?"

"It would help satisfy my spite," Lucie said. She stopped in front of the mirror above the mantelpiece and tucked loose strands of hair behind her ears.

"Catriona," she said. "Have you any news about the writ?"

Catriona changed her position on the armchair. "Aye. I have found our woman."

She recounted the story, starting at the Middleton town house and ending with her having successfully delivered the letter to Mrs. Weldon, without making any mention of Elias. It hurt her throat to leave him out. It felt like a betrayal.

"In conclusion," Lucie said, whose mood looked much improved, "we are currently waiting for Mrs. Weldon to decide whether she's willing to make history?"

"We are, yes."

Hattie and Annabelle saluted her.

Lucie smirked. "Brilliant work, comrade. I believe that is the best we can hope for."

"Thank you." Her pulse picked up. "There is something else," she said. Her tongue felt unwieldy like a brick in her mouth. She folded her hands in her lap. "There is something I must do, and it's outlandish and risky. And I can't do it without you."

Lucie smiled with intrigue. "Tell us everything."

She did not tell them everything, but she told them all about her plan.

Recovering from her surprise, Hattie said: "Is that why you asked me to spread the news about the exhibition through the magazines?"

"Yes."

"Shouldn't you tell Mr. Khoury?" Annabelle asked.

She probably should. Something twisted in her stomach every time she thought of the fact that she was making plans behind Elias's back, but the truth was that knowing as little as possible was for his own good. Or so she thought.

She shook her head at Annabelle. "It would be best if you didn't tell your husband, either knowing nothing might be the one thing to keep them out of trouble."

Annabelle considered this. "I don't usually keep things from Montgomery," she said. "But in this case, you may be right."

In the end, it came as she had hoped: details were discussed, and agreements were made.

The meeting wound down.

Just when they had all readied to leave, Hattie abruptly raised her hand. "I have something to tell you, too."

Chapter 29

⸺⟡⸺

Catriona knew, even before Hattie placed both her hands on her belly and blushed. There was a dreadful shift in the air, a sense of clammy hands reaching for her nape. Lucie's and Annabelle's expressions changed to shocked delight.

She had known for a while. It had been written plainly on Hattie's face since their first meeting in the Randolph in July. Obviously, she ought to be pleased for her friend, now that it was confirmed. She rose from her chair. Lucie and Annabelle had already sat down on the divan to Hattie's left and right, forming a protective semicircle around her.

"Congratulations," Catriona said, and reached down for Hattie's hand, somehow catching only the tips of her fingers. "How are you feeling?"

Hattie's smile was a wee bit toothy. "I'm perfectly well."

Catriona willed her own mouth to smile while images kept flashing: A dark, frightening corridor. A door swinging open, bloodied sheets bunched up in a young MacKenzie's arms; *Who's telling his lordship? Who will tell him?* . . . MacKenzie's shocked face at seeing Catriona standing there, barefoot in the dark, the icy cold of the flagstones seeping into her body, never to leave . . . She turned her head away from her friends. She had been through it when Annabelle had announced that she was with child. It would pass in a moment.

"Oh, Hattie," Annabelle cooed, when she never cooed. "I'm so delighted for you."

"Mr. Blackstone must be over the moon," Lucie said.

"He absolutely is," Hattie said. "Very over the moon."

A pause ensued. Hattie kept her oddly fixed grin on her face. Annabelle and Lucie exchanged a discreet, quizzical glance.

"Hattie," Catriona said cautiously. "Is everything all right?"

Her friend raised her brows. "Of course." It sounded as convincing as a false penny, and Hattie herself noticed. Her insincere smile vanished. "If you must know," she said, "I'm a little worried. About Mr. Blackstone."

They all drew back, surprised.

Hattie made a calming motion with her hand. "It's just that he is rather . . . protective."

Lucie's eyes had turned flinty with suspicion. "Is he confining you?"

"No, no—but, what if he will? What if he insists that I leave London once I show more? What if he keeps me from painting? Or from my photography? Or from my causes."

"Why would he do that, as long as you are feeling well?" Annabelle asked.

"Because the fumes of the paints and turpentine and gelatin plate solutions are probably a little detrimental to my health? The equipment is heavy, too, and I walk long stretches."

Catriona pushed at the armchair to move it closer to the group and sat on its edge.

"Simple," Lucie said to Hattie, "employ someone to carry the equipment and to develop the photographs for you."

"I might do that," Hattie said. "I think it's the fumes he will worry most about; he has a concern for people's lungs."

Come to think of it, Hattie hadn't really talked much about her photography or progress on her paintings in weeks, even though she could have easily pursued all of it at Oxford, away from Mr. Blackstone's potentially disapproving eye.

"Are you worried that Mr. Blackstone will be overly worried," Catriona asked on a hunch, "or is it you who's worried?"

Hattie blinked at her. "What do you mean?"

"If Mr. Blackstone encouraged you to keep painting and photographing, would you?"

Hattie gave her a sullen look, her back very stiff. The next moment, she seemed to fall in on herself like a collapsing soufflé.

"I don't know," she said, and hung her head. "I don't know. One ought to do what is best for the babe."

"Of course," Annabelle said, and reached for Hattie's hand.

Hattie turned her fretful face to her. "What if I don't know what 'best' is?"

"Well—"

"And there is this . . ." She reached into her knitting basket and pulled out a roll of printed pages. They looked as though they had been ripped from a journal haphazardly and had been read and rolled up again many times.

"I came across this article a while ago," she said.

Lucie craned her neck. "What is it?"

"May I read it to you?"

"Go on," Lucie said, her voice already primed for battle.

Hattie smoothed her hand over the first page. *"If the grand essential to a good mother is self-denying, self-effacing love,"* she read out loud, *"this is a bad era for its development. Selfishness and self-seeking is the spirit of the time, and its chilling poison has infected womanhood, and touched even the sacred principle of maternity. In some women it assumes the form of duty. They feel their own mental culture to be of supreme importance, they wish to attend lectures and take lessons, and give themselves to some special study. Or the enslaved condition of their own sex troubles them; they bear in their minds the oppressed shopgirls . . . In these and many ways, they put the natural mission of womanhood aside.*"

She looked up, a hunted expression on her face. "That's us, isn't it? Giving ourselves to special study? Attending lectures? It's me."

"Which crusty creature penned this drivel?" Lucie demanded.

Hattie was flipping through the pages. "*Let any tenderhearted woman go into the parks and watch one of these unhappy children in the care of its nurse,*" she continued in a shaky voice. "*The hot sun beats down on its small, upturned face, and the ignorant creature in charge goes on with her flirtation, or her gossip, or her novel . . . During those awful hours in which its teeth force their way through hot and swollen gums, the forsaken little sufferer is at the mercy of some sleepy, self-indulgent woman who has no love for it . . .* Oh." She looked up with her eyes swimming in misery. "I was fully planning on employing a nanny."

"Of course you will," Lucie said, astonished. "Who doesn't?"

"What about this?" Hattie pointed at the scolding paragraph.

"That's lower-middle-class dross," said Lucie.

"But the poor baby has hot, swollen gums—"

"Hattie. This is your first of likely several children. Will you not make art or help women or properly manage your household until all your offspring have a full set of teeth? You'll be old before you see a camera or a factory meeting again."

Hattie paled. "No. I can't not make art. I mean, I could, but it would be dreadful as it's hardly an urge I can control, is it. The work with the women is even more important."

"Precisely," Lucie said, sounding confident that the problem had been solved.

"What if they leave my baby to fry in its pram," Hattie began again, and Catriona's stomach lurched because tears glistened on Hattie's lashes.

Annabelle put an arm around Hattie's quietly shaking shoulders. "It's all a little frightening, isn't it," she said in the soothing new voice. "A little emotional, too."

"Just a little," Hattie said with a small sob.

"You might feel inclined to listen to all sorts of radical voices in this moment," Annabelle went on.

Hattie gave Annabelle a hopeful look. "How did you know what to do? With Jamie?"

Annabelle tilted her head from side to side. "I confess it was interesting. I was raised by a whole village, and childhood at Claremont is obviously different—I can hardly join the work circles on the farms or in the villages and do my weaving or sewing with the women while the children tumble about. I'd say it's vital that you trust yourself, because, believe me, every baby is different, and the experts differ in their opinions. Remember when opium was all the rage to settle a child? These days, it's whisky. The duke is against potions of any kind going into his son, so some nights no one really sleeps at all. Trust yourself, dear."

Hattie dabbed at the wet corners of her eyes with her fingers. "I know you employed a nanny since the first day."

"Goodness, I employ two—it's hardly a job for just one person. It's the three of us. Mothering is work, Hattie, and you lobby every day for workers to have sufficient rest."

"Of course," Hattie said. "I feel rather silly. I have some lovely memories of my nanny. I have no idea why this article frightens me so, but it's been troubling me for weeks."

Lucie audibly exhaled. "May I." She snatched the pages from Hattie's lap. Her sharp gray eyes flew over the lines. "Ugh. A woman wrote this, a Mrs. Amelia Barr."

"Yes," Hattie said glumly. "She's a successful novelist."

Lucie's lips thinned. "Then she's either not a mother, or she is a hypocrite—clearly, she considers her own mental faculties so supremely important, she must write judgmental articles rather than attend to her children her every waking moment."

"I suppose—"

"And the natural mission of womanhood?" Lucie's eyes were

sparking as though flames were about to shoot out of the side of her head. "Mothers have worked hard for their bread since forever, Hattie. And noblewomen rarely see their children at all, they have castles, if not countries, to run—are they all unnatural? Raising unnatural humans?"

"I—"

"What even is *naturalness?* If it's defined as 'it has always been this way,' then having others care for your children is as natural as breathing. Blimey, most women in Britain work out of the house six days a week to feed their families—have generations of farmers and seamstresses and miners done it wrong all along? Also, why is Mrs. Barr deriding our concerns for shopgirls—what if a shopgirl is a mother, too? How odd that she chooses to decry women who educate themselves rather than the working conditions that keep women from having sufficient time and money for their families."

Hattie touched her temples with her fingertips. "What you say sounds logical."

"Because it is," Lucie snipped. "If I didn't have a bill to push through Parliament, Mrs. Barr would receive a letter from me."

Hattie nodded. "The truth is, though, that I don't have to make art with the same urgency that shopgirls have to work. I'd survive without it. I'm quite free to lavish all my time on the baby."

"You could do that," Lucie said, and returned the article to Hattie with pointy fingers, "if you are so inclined. Just don't be surprised if you lose your mind. Babies are quite dull, if you must know."

Annabelle softly cleared her throat.

"I intend no offense against any particular baby," Lucie amended in a generous tone.

"Babies are wonderful," Annabelle said. "Constantly caring for them without respite, however, might exhaust you. What I have observed, though, is that James doesn't have a preference as to who cares for his needs—he knows I'm his mummy but he's fine with Millie, too. It's fine to lavish time on your own needs, Hattie."

Hattie's hunted expression returned. "I wish my needs were more regular," she said softly. "Mine seem so indulgent."

Something snapped inside Catriona. She felt strangely untethered, on the brink of a cold anger in which people committed foolish acts while fully aware that they were about to commit them.

"Hattie," she said, and the emotion swelled when her friend looked at her with wet brown eyes. "Mrs. Barr writes in a terribly authoritative voice. That doesn't make her opinion a fact. She also makes it sound as though child neglect is a direct consequence of a mother spending time on social issues, when it's in fact the poor choice of caretaker. It just strikes me as yet another trick to direct every moment of a woman's time toward something or someone outside of herself, and to fill her with guilt when she doesn't."

"I'm not surprised it has come to this," Lucie remarked. "A lamentable development of this strange new social class . . . this . . . bizarre, modern place where a woman like Mrs. Barr is kept in the house, perfectly healthy and educated, and yet forbidden to take up most professions, but with no fun parties or proper estate management to distract her. If that happened to me, I would harness my cross as a weapon, too. My babies would teethe in the most perfect manner, they would be the best teethers of them all. If one can't amass glory in business or politics or plant crops that feed the nation, at least we women may outcompete one another in the nursery."

Hattie's eyes were darting back and forth between them. "Don't we welcome modernity, Lucie?" she said. "We have become less barbaric over time because we care more for the weak and helpless— we should be glad for it."

"I don't advocate for less care," Lucie said with a hand on her temple. "I advocate for shared care and perspective."

Annabelle raised her hands between the two. "You're the mistress of your house, Hattie. Choose as you see fit, and your good friends will support you."

Lucie massaged the back of her slender neck. "That's what I said."

"Oh, that's what it was," Annabelle said mildly.

"All right, I ranted," Lucie said with a shrug. "I stand by it, though."

Catriona still felt too icy to speak. Nothing proper would come out of her mouth.

Hattie chewed on her lower lip but her gloomy expression was giving way to tentative determination. "You are both right," she finally said. "I am the mistress of my home. I shall find my own way." Her eyes narrowed. "Here, snubs to you, Amelia Barr."

She crumpled the pages into a ball and leaned forward to toss it into the cold fireplace. It would have been more satisfying to see the ball go up in flames, rather than for it to sit there, slowly unfurling again on the sooty grate, but still a sense of satisfaction filled the room.

Hattie sighed and leaned her head against Annabelle's shoulder. "How I adore you all," she said. "I should have spoken to you much sooner."

She absently stroked her belly, the age-old gesture of expecting mothers everywhere. Catriona glanced away.

Later, she used the moment of goodbyes to furtively pluck the crumpled pages off the grate. She stuffed them deep into her skirt pocket, leaving smudges of ash on her hands. She read while she sat in the cab that carried her back to Cadogan Place.

GOOD AND BAD MOTHERS

BY AMELIA BARR

The world can do without learned women, but it cannot do without good wives and mothers; and when married women prefer to be the social ornaments and intellectual amateurs, they may be called phi-

*lanthropists and scholars, but they are nevertheless moral failures, and
bad mothers . . .*

She folded the pages into a square and forced them back into
her pocket.

At Cadogan House, she set the table for the luncheon food
Elias had procured from the market. Her movements were precise
but slow, as though she were afraid of breaking something.

"You're quiet today," Elias observed during the meal. "You're
usually quiet," he corrected himself, "but today, you're different."

He reached over the table and stroked her cheek with the back
of his fingers. She looked into his darkly tender eyes and anxiety
gushed through her, sudden and deadly like a flash flood. Did he
want children, and if yes, would one be enough for him? What did
he think of women who didn't wish to be swallowed whole by
motherhood? He was her opposite when it came to social aptitude;
he lit up a room when he entered, he exuded a natural personability
that compelled people to seek him out and enjoy his company.
Considering his own large family, he wouldn't just expect children,
he would love on them expressively. She pictured a small child on
his arm, its curly head leaned against his shoulder, a chubby starfish hand on his chest. Something inside her folded into itself until
it was so dense and heavy, she felt it press into her organs. She came
to her feet, and only noticed she had done so when Elias rose, too,
a look of surprise in his eyes.

"I'd like to take a turn around the park," she said in a brittle
voice. "The park across the street."

"Yalla," he said, at once ready. "Let's go."

"Please," she said, holding up her hand. "I need a moment
alone."

She fled.

Chapter 30

Cadogan Park was moderately sized, a rectangle of well-pruned green intended for sitting rather than extensive strolling, and so she kept walking the outer path round and round. Twice she overtook the same young mother who looked perfectly happy pushing a pram along. *I'm the freak*, Catriona thought, *I always have been*. It began with her thoughts on pregnancy, how the very same process in any other context would be the stuff of gothic novels: a woman of sound mind had to watch her belly swell to grotesque proportions, knowing that if all went well, it would merely end in pain. Meanwhile, everyone told the beleaguered woman to be overjoyed. There was a wrongness to this, and a passivity which confirmed for all the world to see that at their most uniquely female activity, women truly were just vessels, to be filled and stretched out by the needs of others. She had enough presence of mind to never share her uncharitable thoughts out loud—not since the chimpanzee incident at the school in Bern.

Bern. The place her father had said would make her a woman. It had certainly taught her what it *meant* to be a woman. At first, it had taught her to do activities she wouldn't have done at home. She had tried to find the good in that. She had soon enjoyed needlework, for example; the precision it required, the meditative effect of the needle darting in and out of the fabric in a lulling rhythm.

But a schedule was in place, and before she could lose herself in a task, a bell would ring, or someone walked in and asked her to start on something else. After a few months, she felt irritable, spread thin, and oddly impaired in her thinking. They didn't let her sink into a book. She couldn't embroider until she felt done. She fell behind on her Arabic and Greek vocabulary. At first, she thought it was lingering heartache over Charles, but the schedule was a culprit, too. It sliced through everything. She complained to Alexandra about it, one of the rare occasions where she emoted rather heatedly.

"Puh, how grim you look," Alexandra said. "Be careful that these wrinkles don't stick."

"Can't you see what is happening?" Catriona shot back. "They are making brilliance impossible for us with these constant interruptions."

Alexandra released a benevolent sigh. "The mistress of a house doesn't have to be brilliant, darling; she has to be functional in the face of constant interruptions."

The other girls in the Common Room were blatantly eavesdropping, and head girl Georgina Rowbotham looked repulsed, so Catriona left. Since her agitation didn't subside, she went to Mrs. Keller's office and shared her worries about the direful consequences of fragmenting a woman's time. Mrs. Keller, young, pretty, and well-liked, nodded along as though she were listening.

The next day, the lovely headmistress betrayed Catriona in front of the entire class.

"A pupil came to my office yesterday," she announced. "I should like to address her grievances in front of all of you, as other girls might have similar feelings. Now, this pupil asked an interesting question: How can we expect 'greatness' from women, when from the very beginning, we organize a woman's time away into 'parcels of meaningless activity'?"

Catriona's face burned as though it had been whacked with a

torch. Everyone who had heard her in the Common Room had turned their heads toward her; everyone was staring.

Mrs. Keller's smile was a little tight. "I propose we ask the question differently: What does 'greatness' mean, for us, as women?"

So began the redefinition of greatness into the act of tirelessly caretaking, organizing transient activities, and brightening people's day. As Mrs. Keller went on about being the beating heart of every home, the social facilitator, the protector of babies and the elderly, a realization dawned on Catriona: that it was all about the body for a woman. Growing a child, birthing it, nursing it; any female body would do for that. Pleasuring a husband, wiping sweaty brows, stirring the stew: any pair of female hands could do it. Whether the head attached to the female had an interest in Arabic or horticulture, whether she was a lady or a peasant, it was irrelevant as long as she provided the body without fuss to those who needed it. As such, a woman's destiny was to react to surroundings, not to actively set her own path. An acute anger merged with months of shattered focus, and Catriona's arm shot up.

Mrs. Keller's brow creased. "Lady Catriona, do you have a question?"

"Yes," Catriona said, her blood pumping in her ears. "Have you ever used an appliance invented by a chimpanzee?"

A shocked laugh came from the back of the room.

"I'm afraid I don't understand your meaning," Mrs. Keller said stiffly.

"Reproduction isn't what sets us apart from animals," Catriona said. "Every wild creature multiplies and raises its young."

The silence was loud. The very air cooled. It dawned on her only slowly that her logic had failed to impress a single person in the room. The faces of the other girls blurred; they were cotton balls on sticks.

Mrs. Keller's mouth was a hyphen. "You are to see me in my office after class," she said.

When the ring of the bell released them from their seats, Alexandra leaned sideways toward Catriona's desk, looking impressed. "Now you have done it," she said. "You called them monkeys—to their faces."

"I didn't," Catriona replied, feeling ill. "Also, chimps are apes, not monkeys."

When Catriona entered Mrs. Keller's study, Mrs. Keller was in the process of writing a letter, which she finished while Catriona stood silently waiting in front of her desk.

Finally, the cap was placed onto the pen and the headmistress lifted her grave eyes.

In an equally grave tone, she asked: "Have you ever heard of a chimpanzee giving their life for a fellow monkey, out of love or duty, Lady Catriona?"

Ape. It's an ape.

"I haven't, no," she said.

"Hm, how about a monkey sharing food with one too weak to gather a meal for itself?"

"That sounds possible."

"Silence," said Mrs. Keller. "What distinguishes us from animals, Lady Catriona, isn't just a bright mind, it is, quite literally, our humanity. The ability to care for our fellow man at the expense of our own selfish needs and desires. This ability expresses differently in the sexes—as we sacrifice ourselves in the home and in support of our husbands' success, our men sacrifice themselves on the battlefield. A civilized society relies on our willingness to offer ourselves up to others—ask yourself why this angers you so."

She thought about it. "I'm selfish?" she suggested. Later, she thought she should have said that not every man enlisted, but every woman was stuck with being a woman.

"Oh, I don't mean for you to think about it here and now," Mrs. Keller said with a frown. "Now, your impertinence ought to merit severe consequences. However, I'm familiar with your file. Your mother passed away in childbed when you were quite young?"

For a moment, Catriona couldn't see very well. "Yes," she said quietly.

Mrs. Keller's face softened. "It must have been hard, growing up without her guidance."

Catriona could think of nothing to say.

"I don't believe confinement would benefit your development," Mrs. Keller continued. "Please, read this letter to your father. Does anything strike you as unfair?"

She handed Catriona the letter she had just finished writing.

Her vision still seemed impaired, and the words on the page were only selectively in focus: *unsociable . . . contrarian . . . impudent . . .*

She handed it back. "It sounds fair enough."

Mrs. Keller had shaken her head slightly, as if to say *What on earth am I to do with you.*

What am I to do? Catriona thought as she now circled the park. Her legs moved steadily and without feeling, as if detached from her body, on and on.

A tall man in a navy blue jacket appeared at the park entrance. Elias. He stood as still as an observing soldier, watching her sharply while she approached.

When she was right within earshot, he addressed her, his voice low but unmistakably steely. "Catriona," he said. "Come home with me."

She walked past him. He stayed put, but soon enough her pace slowed, and the looping thoughts scattered. His commanding tone had tightened around her chest like a rubber sling, its resistance increasing the farther she moved away. She came to a halt with a cynical huff. Until now, she hadn't felt this side of him outside the bedroom. But of course, he could apply it anytime, anywhere. It was probably the bedrock of his jokes and smiles, why his light demeanor struck her as charming rather than silly.

She went home with him. He didn't trouble her with questions, astute enough to not pick losing battles. When he undressed her later, he did ask: *Do you want it?*

She was unexpectedly desperate for him.

Afterward, she gazed at the ceiling, and it felt as though she were up there instead, looking down at their bodies on the bed, next to each other and naked in the sheets like a modern pair of Adam and Eve. The backs of their hands were close to touching.

"I must go back to Oxford tomorrow," she said. The words left her without emotion. They had spent nearly ten days in London now, most of it in bed. Her desires had overruled reason for too long, and she would soon lose her grip entirely. Beyond this chamber, reality awaited, a reality where husbands expected wives to be a certain way and too many women lost themselves in the lives of other people. She'd be as miserable in the role of a wife as she'd be as Elias's long-term lover, meeting up at random to snatch pieces of what could have been until he married someone else. Tears scalded her eyes, and she turned her face away to hide them.

"Heh there, my love, tell me what troubles you," Elias said, rising on his elbow.

For a mad second, she thought about it, why not do it, why not vomit everything ugly and fearful that filled her up inside onto the bedsheet, into the open.

She shook her head. "It's just that we had such a lovely time here, didn't we."

He stared down at her profile for a long minute. Finally, he nodded and said he would stay in London until Monday.

Chapter 31

In the Blackstone drawing room, the clock ticked away at half the normal speed. Hattie, stretched on her side on the fainting couch, kept looking up from her novel and staring at the clock face, then back down at the page. Lucian was late. He wasn't coming home at the regular time these days; ever since he'd known about the baby, he seemed to have doubled the number of his appointments. When he finally entered the drawing room with heavy steps, his jacket gone, his cravat trailing down on either side of his neck, Hattie felt flooded with acute relief. She pushed herself into a sitting position and gazed up at him. Lucian stood in front of her, smelling of remnants of shaving soap and a long day of work. He extended his hand and caressed her cheek, the pad of his thumb rough against her delicate skin.

He smiled. "Hullo, my luscious love."

She stood up abruptly and threw her arms around his neck.

He gave a soft grunt of surprise, but his arms slid around her reflexively. Immediately, she burrowed closer against his broad chest. For a while now, she had guessed that he was working so hard for the same reason she was increasingly fretful about working at all: there was a new life between them that they felt compelled to care for to the best of their abilities. Thank goodness she had somehow understood this before resentment over his absences had set in. She was moody enough as it was these days.

"There now," he said, his hands stroking lightly over her back. "Are you all right? Nervous because of the amendment?"

The session to vote on the Property Act was approaching fast.

"That, too," she said. "But we have done all we can there." She leaned back and met his eyes. "I must ask you something, and please be honest with me," she said.

His brows lowered. "Go on."

"Do you think I should give up my photography, and my painting, and the work for the ethics committee, and the factory workers?"

His skeptical expression deepened. "Why are you asking me?"

"You already hinted that I was overexerting myself."

His broad hand slid over her stomach. "Are you feeling unwell?"

"No, not at all," she said. "But I discussed it all with my friends and it was helpful. So I'd like your opinion, too."

"The situation is new," he said. "Difficult to know what's right."

"The physician would order me to abandon everything: the chemicals in the lab, the bad air in the studio and the poorer parts of town . . . the hurrying from one meeting to the next . . ."

Lucian urged her to sit on the couch again and settled next to her, making the upholstery springs groan under his solid weight.

"*Mo chridhe,*" he said, "my instinct is to wrap you in cotton wool regardless of your condition. But I've grown up watching women doing the washing with the washboard against their bellies, and out came healthy babies, and the mothers seemed to carry on, too. So if you want to keep fulfilling your obligations, I shan't stop you."

She closed her eyes. "Now I feel both reckless as well as spoiled."

"Nah, you just sound like a worried new mum."

She drew back, a terrible understanding dawning. "Is this how it will be from now on? Constant worry?"

He grimaced. "Too late to change your mind now."

"Good grief."

"If it were for me to decide, you'd stay home for a while," he said.

She sat up straighter. "Why?"

"Because you want to," he said. "When I'm around, I always catch you stroking and admiring your belly. And you look so loved up when you do it, it makes me want to put another one in you right away."

She gave a mortified giggle.

He took her small hand in his. "You seem happy with your condition. It's your spreading yourself thin that is putting you in a black mood. There's only so much of you to go around. Everything you do will all be there a year from now; the one thing you cannot do is stop hatching this one. That's only happening now."

Somehow, his words, or was it his low, confident tone, rearranged the disjointed pattern of emotions that had troubled her for weeks and turned it into a clearer picture. With a deep sigh, she leaned her head against his shoulder.

"I love you," she said against his warm neck. "I love hatching our baby."

His lips grazed the crown of her head. "You want me to command you to stop flitting about," he said, "so you don't have to feel guilty for making that choice yourself?"

"I'm a grown woman," she muttered. "I can make that choice. All right. Command me."

"Stay home for a while, wife. Put up your feet, enjoy your belly, and eat biscuits."

She kissed his cheek and greedily inhaled the scent of his skin.

"I love you so," she whispered. "You're the best husband, and the best father."

He remained quite stoic while she scattered heated kisses over his face, but she felt his heart beating fast under her hand.

"Before I forget," she said just when he slipped a hand down into her plunging neckline.

"Mm?"

"I have a favor to ask you. It's Catriona's business, actually—will you help me?"

His eyes were opaque. "Depends on the type of business, my sweet."

She lowered her lashes. "The type I'd rather not know much about."

Chapter 32

Elias's plan to be back in Oxford by Monday had been scuppered by an administrative issue with the bank. It was now sorted: the funds for the bull mission would be released from his account in Beirut. He had also met the man who would lead the crew from the London railway station to the docks, and the fellow seemed professional; sharp, sober, and silent. The plan's execution could still fail, but the planning progressed smoothly like clockwork.

He returned to St. John's on Wednesday, and he spent the remainder of the day unpacking, taking his suits to the dry cleaner on High Street, and organizing his week. It took him by surprise that Nassim's next visit was imminent, but there he was, scribbled into his notebook for Saturday. Time had been meaningless lately. He felt mixed emotions at the prospect of seeing his cousin. He was in dire need of his company, a man close like a brother, but at the same time, Nassim would be able to tell that something was wrong. Elias was not ready to share the details, not while her mood was so cool and strange.

He left a note for Catriona in her pigeonhole, informing her that he had returned.

On Thursday, after waiting in vain for a reply, he decided to seek her out.

He went to the Common Room at one o'clock, without the

chessboard—instinctively, he knew that this phase of their acquaintance where they communicated with the help of a game had
passed; at this point, they needed excruciating honesty. Unsurprisingly, she didn't show. With a dark, annoyed gleam in his eyes, he
strode to her lodgings in the west wing.

His resolute knock at the Campbell door brought him face-to-
face with Wester Ross.

"Mr. Khoury." The professor looked pleasantly surprised to see
him. He clearly had no suspicions that Elias had debauched his
daughter for days on end.

A spasm of guilt tightened Elias's chest. The entire affair had
begun crooked, so naturally it could only grow more twisted as it
went on.

"You are back just in time," Wester Ross said, and stepped aside
as if to usher Elias into the small vestibule. "I had hoped to speak
to you, but I was told you were held up in London."

"My business there took longer than expected," he replied
truthfully.

Catriona's plain blue hat hung on the garderobe. She was at
home.

"I'm meeting a colleague of mine today, Professor Jenkins,
Greek antiquity scholar," the earl said. "I was hoping we could
consult your opinion on the ethics of artifact transferals for academic purposes. For obvious reasons, I have decided to propose an
investigation into our current practices at Oxford . . . but that's not
why you are here, I assume." The earl adjusted his glasses, the gesture eerily like his daughter's. "What can I do for you, Mr. Khoury?"

He put his cards on the table. "I was hoping to take a walk with
Lady Catriona."

Wester Ross's brow pleated slightly. "It's a fine day for a walk,"
he said. "The summer is curiously mild this year, rainy, but mild.
Let me see whether my daughter is at home."

He disappeared into the room at the end of the short corridor. Muffled voices sounded behind the closed door; the low, soft cadence of Catriona's voice was unmistakable. Elias kept flexing and unflexing his hand as the minutes drew out. He could tell that his pulse showed in his throat.

The door opened.

She was pale, and her posture oddly still when they looked at each other. Like a rabbit that was trying to go undetected when the fox was near.

"Mr. Khoury."

His temper simmered. He had been inside her twice a day, rather carelessly, too, toward the end, and she had enjoyed it loud and clear. Now she looked at him as though he were a passing acquaintance.

"Walk with me," he said, his tone even enough.

"MacKenzie has departed to Applecross," she replied. "But my father and Professor Jenkins are going to Christ Church at three o'clock. We may walk with them."

They wouldn't have one, but two chaperones trailing them. Her lashes lowered at his grim little smile.

At shortly past three, they strolled down bustling Magdalen Street at a deceptively leisurely pace. Wester Ross and Professor Jenkins fell so far behind, deep in conversation, it was as though the earl *wanted* Elias to have some privacy with his daughter. The daughter was less enamored of the idea. Catriona's rigid posture radiated cool reserve. Why had she agreed to walk with him, then?

"So," he said. "Is there any news in your life?"

She feigned a smile. "You make it sound as though we haven't seen each other in years."

"The days seem long without you," he replied.

Her gaze flicked sideways, as if to ascertain that her father was indeed far out of earshot.

"I was preoccupied. It seems my father has sold a good chunk of our lands that border Middleton's estate."

An irrational annoyance flashed through him. The land had been her inheritance. He had finished the tome on Scotland; unlike the English, Scottish noble families passed on estates to their daughters.

"I hadn't expected to feel quite so sad about it," she continued. "But I do. Most of the older estates in the north grew wealthy by grabbing the monastic lands after the religious wars. Applecross is one of the few that became comfortable thanks to profitable wool production. I thought those were good conditions for maintaining the business, but over time . . ." She shook her head. "It seems to have fallen apart."

"No business just falls apart," he said with some impatience. "There are always reasons; what you must do is anticipate them, analyze them, find a solution."

"Easy to say, for a man of business."

"A business is in trouble because a change happened to which you couldn't adjust on time. You pay attention and adapt, or you die—that's the nature of it."

Her fingers curled into her shawl. "You're right," she said, matter-of-fact. She gave an unexpectedly helpless little shrug.

He felt a low, hard ache in his stomach. *Let me do it for you*, he thought, *let me look after you and your estate, and you can spend your time on books and science.* He had already thought about Applecross; had tried to assess its easy strengths and weak spots, challenges and opportunities. He had considered the isles near the estate and the great distances to larger trading hubs, and how to deal with the sparse railway infrastructure. His suggestions were the opposite of selling land: he would buy more land, more sheep, and sell a processed product, not just raw material, as this was the same trap that was threatening silk merchants in the East. He'd organize the crofters on the isles as they once were and contract them, exclusively, to produce tweed with Applecross wool. Make a deal with his family to supply her with silk and create a tweed-silk blend, elegant yet robust, the best of East and West entwined in one fabric . . . Look abroad for sales, to America and the East; weave a romantic story around the crofters and the isles that will appeal to wealthy women who dream of quaint and foreign places. A pressure in his jaw said he was gritting his teeth. He had the ideas as well as the entrepreneurial skills to take care of her, and yet he could do exactly nothing. He was not her husband, and he could hardly offer Wester Ross his services while his own business was lingering unattended in Beirut. No, in his current position as her lover, he shouldn't exist in her life by any standards of propriety. He felt it acutely now: his bruised pride, his strained morals, the diffuse but constant resentment haunting someone who had lowered themself to live an untenable compromise.

He moved a little closer to her, his arm an inch from her shoulder. "Let's meet without an audience."

Silence.

He inhaled sharply. "Allow me to make right whatever I have done to cause you such offense."

She shook her head, kept shaking it. "You caused no offense."

Wester Ross was behind him. People were walking toward them. Eyes everywhere. She was right next to him and was as inaccessible as if behind a wall. Their walk was ending, too—the clock tower of Christ Church became visible above the roofs of the houses lining Cornmarket Street.

"Talk to me anyway," he said through smiling lips. "I understand walks are an occasion for conversation."

"I saw Mrs. Weldon on Monday," she said after a pause, an unexpected spark of her usual passion in her voice. She hadn't suddenly turned unfeeling toward the world as a whole, only toward him.

"You came back to London?" he asked.

"No." She hesitated. "I stayed on a little longer than planned, after all."

This took him unawares. "I see."

It meant she had effectively thrown him out of her town house under false pretenses. Oh, he had caused her offense. Perhaps it wasn't something he had done, but rather something he had failed to do, which could be just as injurious to a woman's feelings. Whenever he had made a foray toward a proposal, she had frozen up and he had refrained from pushing the matter. Had she expected him to do it with more force after all, to claim her the old and tested way by going to her father first, or better yet, with an abduction? He wanted to roar his frustration down the busy street.

"How is good old Mrs. Weldon?" he asked idly.

"Her story is bizarre, Elias."

Damn if hearing her say his name didn't ease his displeasure despite himself.

"What is her story," he asked.

"It turned out that Captain Weldon had a mistress," Catriona began. "A few years ago, he decided he wanted to live with the woman, but without the scandal of a divorce. So he tried to have Mrs. Weldon committed to an asylum. He sent two physicians to their home, where they posed as people interested in spiritualism. She engaged with them, suspecting no harm, only for them to declare her insane on the spot. They tried to physically drag her from the house to a carriage, can you believe it?"

He was inclined to believe all sorts of insanity at this point.

"Her butler and her housekeeper intervened," she continued. "It's the only reason she's still free. She's lived in fear ever since, that Captain Weldon could try it again. He attempted it several more times, apparently. It's why she's trying to glean his intentions through séances."

"He's a dog, not a man," he said coolly. "He is no husband."

"Plenty of men are like this, and they are just regular men," came her soft voice.

Did she think he was one of them?

"She wanted to sue him, over the attack on her person," she said and scoffed. "Unfortunately, as per the Married Women's Property Act, a wife can't take such legal action without her husband's explicit consent. Captain Weldon, of course, declined to be brought to justice. However"—and now she turned to him, her eyes brightening—"she can sue for the writ for restitution. And she will do it."

"Anjad? Really?"

She nodded, a smile struggling through as if despite herself, and an echo of their intimacy whispered between them.

"She said she will do it," she said, softer now. "It will take months to see a result, but we have a chance now."

He was proud of her, the clever idea and her tenacity, but less than a week ago, they would have celebrated together. "Meet me," he repeated. "There must be a place where we can see each other."

"I'm going to London tomorrow," she replied, back to looking vaguely in pain.

"Again?"

"The final debate on the MWPA bill is on Tuesday. I'm staying with the Blackstones," she added, as if she had known that he'd go to London, too, to catch her alone.

He didn't ask when she would be back. In the end, it was her prerogative to abandon an ill-advised liaison without an explanation. If that made him feel crazy, then he had himself to blame for taking her to bed without any commitment. One could not force affection from a woman. He couldn't ask her to keep breaking all the rules with him, either; the world had no pity and a man's devotion wasn't enough to compensate a woman for her fall from grace. This was what he had told himself during the year after Nayla, anyway, whenever the infuriating thought had reared its head that he should have just thrown the girl over his shoulder and walked out onto a boat with her. He would speak to Catriona again when she returned from London. Perhaps their backward laws would be changed on Tuesday. Perhaps that would work a change on her.

⁓⁓⁓

"Eli, you look thin," Nassim observed. "Like this." He sucked in his cheeks, making the hollow beneath his strong cheekbones more pronounced. Next to them, a railway station clerk blew a whistle, and the shrill sound cut right into Elias's brain.

"I fucked too much and ate too little," he said to Nassim.

Nassim's brows flew up and he barked a laugh in shocked surprise. "Well done," he said, and slapped Elias's shoulder. "Much better than the other way around."

Their exuberance attracted covert glances from fellow travelers. Elias grabbed Nassim's hand. "Come."

They made their way out of Oxford's railway station, followed by a clerk who pushed Nassim's groaning luggage cart. The small carriage yard was busy and owing to the number of Nassim's suitcases, they would queue awhile for a large enough vehicle.

"What are you taking home?" Elias asked. "Half the port?"

Nassim tilted his head, his expression turning vague. "Gifts." After a pause. "Some pieces for the factory."

"Pieces?"

"A prototype with some of our specifications," Nassim said with a shrug.

"Nassim."

"Fine. A modified steam box that can both steam and then hot-air-dry cocoons. It could save us up to three days in the drying process per batch and raise profits by a few percent."

"By four percent." Elias glared at the luggage cart. "That was my calculation—that box was my suggestion. And it isn't just days saved, it's the improved quality of the cocoon if we dry them that way."

Nassim nodded. "I thought so; it sounded like something you would think about."

Elias's head felt hot. "Yet he wrote to you to bring the prototype. I heard nothing."

Him being Khalo Jabbar.

A four-wheeled carriage with a closed roof pulled up, and Nassim waved at the driver.

"He'll never hear some of us as clearly as he hears some of the others," he said while the luggage was hoisted up onto the carriage roof. "It doesn't mean he doesn't hear you."

Elias shot him a sardonic glance. "He hears me, Nassim. He hears me, and then he uses my suggestions and makes profit with hardly an acknowledgment of my contribution."

Nassim squinted. "But if it's good for the family, isn't it good for you, too?"

It was true, it was why he tolerated it. He didn't like it, though, and it didn't work the other way around, either—when he took a misstep, the shame was squarely his. It wasn't the first time Jabbar had done it, either. A few years ago, Elias had calculated that their competitiveness was hampered by time and quality lost from manually twining ripped silk threads together, and he had suggested an alteration to their reeling technology that had greatly improved their statistics. The alteration had been dismissed at first, then been quietly made after all, months later.

"It won't make a difference, in the end," Elias said after the carriage had pulled away from the station. "We are merely buying time. In ten years, Europe will purchase only Chinese silk, not ours."

"I've heard you say this before," Nassim remarked, and the set of his mouth said he wasn't keen on it.

"Have you seen our forests?" Elias asked.

"No."

"Exactly. Because they are disappearing. They'll be gone. We don't have coal to fuel the boilers. Now make a profit calculation with imported coal, brother, and tell me what you see."

Nassim's hazel eyes sobered. Whatever was on the balance sheet before his mind's eye made him go quiet. "Since when have you known?" he asked.

"A while."

Nassim tutted. "Always three moves ahead, aren't you, Eli. What is your recommendation?"

The carriage parked. Elias looked outside at the ancient wooden doors of St. John's. A group of young women walked past below the carriage window, their heels clacking, their laughter floating in.

"Eli?"

"New horizons."

They stored half of the suitcases behind the desk at the porter's lodge, a favor that porter Clive afforded the foreign visitor as a special courtesy. Elias promised they would be gone on Monday. On the way out, he stole a glance at the Campbell pigeonhole. Empty.

Nassim took a while to refresh himself and change into a day suit. When he emerged from Elias's bedroom, freshly groomed, he drummed a quick rhythm on his stomach with his hands.

"Where are we going for lunch?" He looked at Elias, who lounged on a dining table chair, his long legs stretched out in front of him. "The Lamb and Flag was decent, but perhaps we should try something new, the Eagle and Child, across the road?"

Elias nodded. "We could do that, if you want it."

"Why, what was your plan?"

"I thought we could eat here. Undisturbed."

Nassim glanced at the long dining table. Tested the sturdiness of an ornately carved chair. "All right. Where shall we fetch the food?"

"I befriended the college cook and I gave him some of the jars." Elias pointed at the diminished selection on the mantelpiece. "They'll serve us our plates here."

Nassim's teeth gleamed in a wide smile. "Nice. I like it."

He sat down in a chair and leaned back with a sigh. His hair was cut, no longer overlong like during his last visit. He looked ready to go home.

"You know I am a man of culture," he said to Elias, "but the first thing I will do at home is eat toum with a spoon. Rich, creamy, fluffy toum." He put his fingertips together and kissed them.

Elias could picture it vividly, almost taste it, the garlic paste slathered onto freshly grilled, thinly sliced, well-seasoned chicken, wrapped in hot, soft bread with a tangy pickle . . .

"You look hungry," Nassim said, smiling. "Come home with me. We get a ticket for you at the docks, there's always someone peddling a last-minute ticket."

Tempting. "I have business here."

Nassim made an unwilling sound. "You have business in Beirut, too—if the bulls move at the end of September, what will you do here for another six weeks?"

"Incredible," Elias said. "The operation doesn't happen on its own. I have to practice the moves with the men. The crew needs every detail of the schedule. I haven't yet secured passage on a boat for the pieces because the man I hired to forge the export papers will need at least another week to finish."

And he couldn't leave without having seen her again and making things right—properly.

"All right." Nassim shrugged. "I think it would be a good idea if you came, but it's your decision. You were right about them finding me a wife, by the way. Apparently, Jabbar was busy."

Elias paused. "Is that what you want?"

Another shrug. "Sure. Let's wait and see what he proposes."

Elias looked at him askance. His cousin's face was oddly unreadable, a mix of pleased and yet wary.

"What is it?" Elias asked, because he had known Nassim long enough to know that face. His cousin was keeping something from him. Something other than the prototype.

"Let's eat first," Nassim said.

"Why?"

"You're already in a bad mood, over the steam box."

Elias came to his feet. "Nassim, I swear if you don't tell me, I'll—"

"All right. He's finding you a wife, too."

Chapter 33

⬥

A pressure built behind Elias's eyes. "You are mistaken," he said.

Nassim hunched his shoulders in a disarming manner. "I'm just telling you what I heard."

"What?" Elias ground out. "What did you hear? How?"

"Layal."

"Why is she telling you, not me?"

"She doesn't have your address here. Look." Nassim went to the garderobe, reached inside his jacket pocket, and took out a wad of pound notes and paper slips, among them a telegram.

Elias was next to him with two strides and snatched the telegram from his hand. His brows formed a harsh V while his gaze flew over the lines. At some point, his cousin Layal had had the news dictated to a telegraph officer in Beirut. Black on white, it said *prospective brides . . . let Eli know . . .*

Elias ripped the telegram in half.

"What the hell," said Nassim.

Elias crumpled the bits in his fist and tossed the paper ball onto the table. Shaking from suppressing a great rage, he turned to Nassim.

"Are you not tired of others dictating your life?"

Nassim's eyes were big. "You're angry."

He was incensed. "What are we? Are we eighteen-year-old peasants, having to take the girl our parents pick?"

"Eighteen? No, we're not eighteen," Nassim said, his hands moving, his voice rising. "We're old, you especially, you will be thirty in a few years—what did you expect?"

"To choose my own wife. Jabbar can stay out of it."

"Honestly?" Nassim shot back. "If he finds me a nice woman? I won't cry about it—"

Elias gestured disbelief. "I don't believe that you don't have a preference."

"Damn"—Nassim kept touching Elias's arm now—"damn, I live abroad ten months of the year. How will I find a good wife while I work, work, work, in damn Manchester? Let Jabbar trouble himself with it; if I don't like her, I'll refuse. It's a suggestion, not an order."

Elias stared at his cousin as though he had sprouted a second head. "Refuse? Because it wouldn't cause bad blood at all if Jabbar indicated an interest to a family, and then we decide we don't like the girl. What will they say we said about her—that she's ugly? Has a reputation? Not good enough?"

His very skin burned from the blaze of his temper. Because he had to pack. He had to leave here as soon as possible after all, to stop the unthinkable. It was the one thing he did not want to do, though, leaving her.

"It might be Layal, for you," Nassim said, shaking Elias by the shoulder, as if that would dislodge the fury. "You like each other, it's obvious, so what is your problem?"

"I have someone," Elias said. "That is the problem."

His blood was still pumping behind his eyes, but Nassim's face was in clear view, freezing over with shock.

"You're . . . married?"

"Not yet."

"Who?" cried Nassim. "Who is it?"

Elias clucked his tongue and moved away.

Nassim followed him. "Who? Do we know her?"

"You know nothing about her."

"But—" Nassim stopped, as if hit in the chest. "No," he drawled. "It's the lady, isn't it—the Lady Catriona." When Elias remained quiet, he groaned. "No, you misunderstood the assignment—you were to seduce her, only slightly, not *be* seduced and marry her!"

"Life does not care about our plans."

"She is English!"

"Scottish."

"British, then."

Elias inhaled sharply. "She's from an honorable family. She is highly educated. She speaks our language. She is kind, and wealthy, and she likes our food."

And he loved her, and for none of those things.

Nassim was profoundly disturbed. "She's an outsider."

"Come on, anyone farther than a fifteen-minute walk from the town is an outsider, and you know it."

His cousin locked his gaze to his. "So, she wants to raise her children as Maronites? Her father wouldn't object?"

"A technicality for a Catholic, but let me be very clear," Elias said. "I don't care whether she is from the depths of the sea, or the surface of the moon. It's her, or no one."

"All right, all right." Nassim moved his hands up and down. "Things are changing, we are modern men, we cast a wide net . . . but, my dear, blood of my blood . . . if you must look around abroad, why not pick an Italian. We make decent families with Italians—fine." He threw up his arms. "Just don't say I didn't warn you. People will think you've lost your mind—again."

"At first, they will think that."

Nassim was moving around the room erratically. "Has she

agreed to have you, even though you are taking these pieces from her museum? Will you go on the run with the daughter of a British earl?"

At that, Elias pressed his lips together, as if trying to stay silent through physical pain.

"Damn," said Nassim. "You aren't taking them, are you. You are thinking of giving them up. I can see you thinking it."

"Taking them as planned would make a proposal rather impossible."

His cousin was cussing under his breath. "See," he said, "see. This is only the beginning."

"You carry on as though we have never married outside our province."

"It happens, yes, of course." Nassim sat down heavily on a chair and rubbed his eyes.

"The trouble is," Elias said, "she knows I want to take the artifacts, and if I go to her now and say *I will not take them so you can be my wife*, how does that sound?"

Nassim seemed to give it due consideration even though he was set against the entire idea. "Sounds bad," he said at last. "Like blackmail."

"Exactly."

"You could explain, and she might understand . . ." Nassim groaned again. "How can you change your mind so fast, after all the work you have done to take them back."

"It's not a new idea," Elias said quietly. "It was always there."

Nassim shook his head. "Always?"

"Yes. Like smoke on the back of my mind. I think since the day I first laid eyes on her."

Perhaps even before that, when he had decided as a young man that only a woman who made him feel the way she did would do.

Nassim jumped to his feet, went to the garderobe, and grabbed his hat.

Elias cut him a suspicious look. "Where are you going?"

"Out," said Nassim. "This room is too small."

Shortly after Nassim had stormed off, the kitchen clerk delivered the lunch cart. Elias ate alone, not tasting much but feeling cool and calm in his resolve.

When Nassim returned, his portion of Eastern mezze, grilled chicken, and glazed potatoes had wilted and turned cold. Elias had demolished half a pound of pistachios from Nassim's gift bag, the pale husks piling high on the table.

The cousins looked at each other.

"Come eat," said Elias.

Nassim went to wash his hands. He plonked himself down at the table with a speaking glance and stabbed his fork into a potato.

"You know what it means," he said, "what it will mean for you."

Elias cracked a pistachio between his teeth.

He knew. There was a good chance that it would carve his status of everywhere and nowhere into stone. He couldn't see her navigating the social politics in Mount Lebanon's society successfully; she showed a low aptitude for that even in her own country. As for staying here, he had been treated with great politeness and friendly intrigue at Cambridge, but ultimately, he'd come up against the invisible wall every elite drew around their own. Marrying one of their ladies would not build him a bridge, they were possessive of their women and every time he took her to bed he might as well plant his scimitar into the courtyard of Buckingham Palace. But, in the end, everyone might mellow. He would be successful regardless. The solution was to keep moving, and a loyal wife would transmute the loneliness of building something between worlds into freedom.

"Yeah, I know," he said to Nassim. "I'll encounter donkeys like Mr. Leighton for the rest of my life."

"Tfeh! Men like Leighton should take a shit instead of speaking."

There they agreed.

On Sunday, Elias packed up and inquired about his travel options back east for the end of the week. He expected Catriona to return sometime after Tuesday. They would talk. The potential of a new life was stretching before him, and he spent the days consumed by a burning impatience to begin.

Chapter 34

On the day of the big debate, they took the ducal landau to Parliament, courtesy of Annabelle's husband. It was a dry evening, but the carriage top was up, which provided some much needed privacy for last-minute scheming while they were parked in front of Westminster Palace. Through the large landau windows, they took in the familiar roofline in silence, gothic turrets and looming towers jutting into a hazy sky. The significance of the situation, the possibility of yet another defeat, sat tensely in their midst.

"Now," said Lucie. "Who of you has stink bombs in their reticules?"

Catriona winced. *I knew I had forgotten something.* She hadn't slept. Too much scheming on other fronts.

"I do," said Hattie.

"Me, too," Annabelle said.

"Sorry, I don't," Catriona admitted, feeling sheepish.

Lucie cut them a stern look. "They'll search our belongings at the door. Perhaps not yours," she said to Annabelle, "but let's not be amateurs, shall we." She put her small, booted foot onto the upholstery of the opposite bench and furled up her skirts. A heavy purse hung from her bustle belt. "Hide them."

Hattie shook her head. "I should have thought of that."

Rustling ensued, white underskirts flashed.

Outside, the ducal seal on the carriage door was drawing attention. A small group of onlookers had gathered at a respectful distance, people who hoped to catch a glimpse of the duchess and her outfit.

Annabelle shook out her skirts. "Shall we?" she asked, and reached for the door handle.

Lucie placed her hand over Annabelle's. "Before we go in, I must tell you something."

Her expression was rather grave.

"Uh-oh," said Hattie, apprehension plain on her face.

"I hope you won't be cross with me. But. If our bill is accepted today, Ballentine and I will elope."

Hattie gasped. "What? When?"

"Whenever the chamber closes."

Annabelle looked delighted. "Where will you go?"

"Gretna Green." Lucie smiled wryly. "My life is a romantic novel, can you believe it? Hattie dear, don't look so disappointed. The idea of a grand palaver was utterly tedious, the planning, the . . . everything. This suits us better; Ballentine and I live on our terms, and we shall marry on our terms, which means he, and I, and a Scottish blacksmith."

"I think that's quite romantic," Annabelle said. "Romantic in that it suits you."

Catriona nodded. The idea of loving so vehemently on one's own terms made her too emotional to find the appropriate words, so she just kept nodding.

Hattie released a defeated sigh. "I'm pleased for you. I was just looking forward to seeing you in your full glory and feel moved to tears when two such free spirits who have adored each other for so long finally say their vows." Already her voice was quavering with emotion.

Lucie leaned forward and took Hattie's hand. "You must all come to Ballentine's parliamentary office after this is over tonight, no matter the outcome."

"Why, what's in Ballentine's office?"

"My luggage. Also, I ordered a few buckets of champagne for when we win, and brandy in case we lose."

"We won't lose," Catriona said. The words had come out without her thinking, and she looked as surprised as her friends. "I don't know why I said that," she murmured. "I sounded far too certain."

Lucie smirked. "We appreciate the confidence." She gazed around their small circle, her gray eyes lingering on each of them with an unfamiliar somberness. "Are we ready?" she asked.

Serious nods all around.

"Well, then. Once more unto the breach, dear friends."

The Ladies' Gallery above the chamber was already crowding, and judging by the variety of hats and dresses, the debate had drawn spectators from lady to office girl, all trying to cram into the limited space. They had to make do with five rows of chairs behind windows barred by ornate metal grilles. The air was turning thick from too many people breathing together, lukewarm condensation would soon drip off the fixtures. Voices from the floor below drifted up in a muffled hum. Lucie insisted that the poor acoustics had been designed this way on purpose.

A soft whistle directed Catriona's attention to a slim woman with cropped hair at the front row of chairs. Aoife Byrne. Sure enough, there was the blond head of her bosom friend Susan Patterson, a few chairs down.

"We've reserved the whole row for you," Aoife announced. "Susan brought toffees for sustenance; the tin is making the rounds. Don't be shy, grab a handful."

Lucie walked right up to the loathsome metal grille and pressed her face to it. Judging by the angle, she was trying to peer down into the Strangers' Gallery where the men sat, just below their caged section.

"I can't see Ballentine," she said. "Nor Wester Ross. They must be right below us."

"What about Blackstone?" Hattie asked, sitting down but craning her neck.

Lucie shook her head. "Can't see him, dear. Ah, there's the duke."

Catriona sat down between Hattie and Aoife.

"How do you think it'll go?" Aoife asked, licking toffee off her teeth.

"Lucie thinks our bill will come last," Catriona said. "Our opposition, likely Mr. Warton, will try to push our point off the agenda entirely by drawing out the other points; that's what he's been doing during the previous sessions. The speaker won't let it stand today. We will have our reading and a decision."

Aoife's lips curved down. "We'll starve up here. It'll be hours."

"Probably."

More women arrived, filling the gallery antechamber and the corridor where they could neither hear nor see anything except for the reactions of the women at the front. Below the gallery, the speaker, out of their field of vision, opened the session.

Hours did pass. The ventilation shafts sluggishly turned over exhausted air. As dusk dimmed the natural light from the chamber windows, the subdued gaslight in the Ladies' Gallery strained the eyes. Heads were drooping, some were snoozing, by the time Mr. Morgan Osborne tabled the motion of the amendment.

"The honorable Member for Kirkcaldy," the speaker announced.

A burst of energy made Catriona sit up straight and blink to clear her eyes.

Heckling ensued, and oh-ohs rose from the benches of the House.

Lucie pressed her forehead back to the screen. "Ugh. It's Sir George."

Catriona rose and put her face to the grille, too. There was enough space for one eye to have a clear view. In a sea of heads, the Scotsman's stern visage stood out, looking red even from a distance.

"I suggest any honorable members who say 'oh-oh' might leave the House," he bellowed. "Mr. Speaker, if you believe that I shall let this bill pass without a reasonable discussion—"

"Hmm," said Lucie, "almost thirty years of discussion are unreasonable, then?"

". . . this bill is as important as all the other bills that passed the House since this Parliament began."

Someone laughed.

"Aye, the honorable members might laugh, but this bill created a social revolution that affected almost every family in this country and was being passed through the House without one man or woman in a million having any idea of what was being done."

"What?" Hattie squeezed her head next to Catriona's, her cheek radiating indignant heat. "Lucie, is he serious? We have spent years on educating people about the bill—So. Many. Years . . ."

"Shh," hissed Lucie. "Your feather is in my face."

"Whoops." Hattie took off her hat.

". . . The Christian form of marriage, under which there was complete community between the married parties for life, is the best form of marriage!" Sir George proclaimed. "However, the 'women's righters' have been exceedingly energetic—" Here, he shot a glare at the gallery, causing some of the women to shrink back. Lucie bared her teeth. ". . . *Exceedingly* energetic, whilst the friends of the poor married man have been indolent. I can sense the mood of this House, so I wish to stand here today and be eternalized in the records as one of the few who fought to obtain a small measure of justice for the poor, unfortunate married man."

Another MP rose from the bench, his bald pate shiny in the gaslight. Catriona recognized the lilt of his voice from one of her countless petition meetings, a Mr. Fowler.

"Mr. Speaker," Mr. Fowler said, "I should like to know how fair is it, that the honorable Member for Kirkcaldy, a Scotchman, should interpose to prevent the English women having what the Scotch women got last year?"

There were sounds of approval; ask a room full of Englishmen whether they hold with an Englishwoman or a Scotsman, and enough discovered that their local patriotism outranked sentiments of brotherhood.

Sir George raised his hands. "To spare you the trouble," he said in a tone that barely repressed the indignity of having to speak to idiots. "No man would marry a woman with property, knowing that she could set him at defiance so long as the marriage continued. It would change the position of the sexes, and make the woman, instead of a kind and loving wife, a domestic tyrant. Scripture was opposed to the bill—"

The speaker's voice came from under the gallery: "The honorable and learned Member's speech is certainly very discursive, and I must invite him to address himself to the question."

Sir George snarled something that sounded like "buffoons" as he sat back down again.

"That didn't go too well for him," Catriona said with cold glee.

"Serves him right, silly lad," said Lucie. "Oh, here comes Mr. Warton. Boo, hiss."

She must have said it too loudly because Catriona saw the Duke of Montgomery turn his head their way. His cool, pale gaze glided over the gallery in a gentle warning.

Mr. Warton, meanwhile, was imploring the House to stop and think; after all, the bill had been "rushed" through the House of Lords.

Morgan Osborne reminded everyone in a deeply tired tone that the bill had been practically discussed to death and was already approved by the Lord Chancellor, and only Warton and Campbell were really blocking it now.

"It's obstruction," someone cried.

"Order!"

Unperturbed, Mr. Warton took offense at the wording in almost every line of the bill. Hot air rose from the chamber while his finicky analyses dragged on; the collective mood was stewing like a pot left too long over the fire, any minute now it would boil over.

Mr. Warton charged ahead undeterred. "Consider this— consider that the way this bill is amended as is presently proposed, it backdates its effects. As of the passing of this bill, every husband in Britain who entered marriage under the old conditions shall find himself trapped in a legal situation he never chose . . ."

Shouting ensued. It took a moment to realize that the committee members on the government side had come to their feet in protest.

Hattie curled her hands around the trellis and peered at the teeming scene. "This will go badly again, won't it," she said, sounding shaken. "Won't it?"

"No," Catriona said thickly. "No, Hattie, for once, this is going rather well for us."

"You are imposing social revolution on us," Mr. Warton yelled at no one in particular. "It is a post facto social revolution!"

"Ordaahh!" The speaker was joining the fray, shouting like the referee of a boxing match. "Ordaahh. Question negatived."

When the clock ticked past one o'clock in the morning and the count was read at once, the result was clear: after four-and-twenty years, a decision was made in favor of women. Above the uproar, in their ornate cage, women fell into one another's arms with incoherent cries of joy.

Still breathless and flushed with triumph, they crammed into Ballentine's office half an hour later. Dripping ice buckets with champagne bottles and piles of sandwiches on silver platters waited on the viscount's desk; in the aftermath of battle, the rules of formality were suspended. Lucie herself was serving, handing out overflowing goblets and laughing with her head thrown back. Aoife and Susan had joined them along with two ladies from the London Print investment consortium. The energy in the small space buzzed, the excited voices blended to an indistinct chatter. Lady Salisbury, consortium chair, thumped the floor with her cane whenever she wanted to emphasize a point. Catriona retreated into the corner next to the door. She kept the cool, sticky rim of the glass against her bottom lip and focused on breathing. A pleasant masculine scent lingered in Ballentine's room, not exactly tailored to her palate but enough to push the constant presence at the back of her mind to the fore. Elias. She gulped the champagne. The taste held memories, too. Her lungs constricted, turning her cold on the inside, detached from her surroundings.

The door opened and the men walked in, Ballentine, Blackstone, Wester Ross. The duke was last. His normally sleek blond hair had curled in the damp air.

"Hullo there," Lucie hollered, one fist waving in the air, and judging by Ballentine's smirk, he approved. Blackstone put an arm around Hattie's waist, and she placed a hand on his chest. The duke kept his hands to himself, but his sharp gaze was riveted on Annabelle's beaming face as though she were the only person in existence. In a room filled with people she loved, Catriona's chest hollowed with crushing emptiness. *He should have been here.* She bore it quietly, this agony of two vast and opposite emotions, victory and loss, trying to exist in her body at the same time.

"Are you all right, my dear?" Wester Ross stood next to her, a Scotch in hand. "You look a little peaked."

"It was a long day," she said vaguely.

"Quite," her father replied, amused. "Well done. Here, have a sandwich."

Somehow, she made it through eating sandwiches, and chitchatted with whoever intruded into her corner.

When the platters and bottles had been emptied for a while and the atmosphere naturally transitioned to drowsy, Lucie and Aoife stuck their heads together and a moment later, they disappeared into the antechamber. Eventually, Aoife emerged again and looked at Ballentine. "She asks that you leave the room for a moment," she said. "In fact, why don't all the gentlemen wait outside for a bit."

The gentlemen exchanged bemused glances but obliged.

Aoife knocked on the antechamber door. "The air's clear."

The door opened.

Catriona nearly dropped her glass.

A vision of a bride had appeared on the doorstep.

"Lucie," Hattie cried. "You are stunning!"

Lucie wore white. Gleaming, uncompromising white and . . . she sparkled. The gauzy layers of tulle and the delicate scalloped lace veil were shot through with tiny diamonds. Silver thread embroidery trimmed the skirt and snug satin sleeves.

"Feast your eyes," Lucie said, and swished her skirts. "Since you will miss the ceremony." She turned back and forth. "Do you think Ballentine will like it?"

"He will adore you," Hattie said and furiously dabbed at her wet cheeks.

Annabelle grinned. "You will have to tell us what it looks like, when a reformed rake cries."

It wasn't the grand dress that took Catriona's breath away, it was the look on her friend's face. Lucie's usually hawkish eyes were glowing with a deeply private excitement. A month ago, Catriona would have simply felt satisfied that her dear friend was very much in love with her betrothed. Now she recognized the emotion beyond the abstract, and it ripped her heart in half like a paper shape.

When they parted for the night, Hattie took her hand in both of hers. "Remember," she said, "there's a proper celebration in the Randolph for the Oxford chapter on Thursday. Be there at noon."

Catriona nodded. On Thursday, she would be packing for Applecross.

By the time she was in her father's carriage to the Campbell town house, her watch showed the witching hour, three o'clock in the morning. She was in an odd state of lethargy, her body exhausted, her mind still rushing with thoughts. Images of the chamber, broiling with their hard-won victory, and of Lucie, dressed like a fairy queen, kept looping past.

Wester Ross sat opposite her, his face turned to the window. The lenses of his spectacles reflected the light of the street lanterns, and it wasn't possible to tell whether his eyes were open or closed.

"Sir," she said softly.

"Yes, my dear?"

"I wondered . . . why have you never prevailed on me to marry?"

He looked at her with mild surprise. "Is marriage on your mind now? Has the change in the law worked a change on you?"

"I have wondered why you never remarried," she admitted. "And a good match for either of us could have fixed our purse."

Wester Ross remained quiet for so long, looking out into the night with such an absent-minded expression, Catriona suspected he had considered and then forgotten his answer, when he turned to her and said: "I loved your mother."

A lump formed in her throat. "Of course you did."

"Not everyone up in Applecross approved of our match." The earl nodded, as if to himself. "Her father was an Englishman and she had roots in Sussex. It didn't stop us."

He had never shared of himself like this before. So much was left unsaid, deterred by the gulf between the generations or the walls of grief.

She seized the opportunity. "Were you worried the disapproval would drive you apart?"

He chuckled. "Oh no. I knew my mind. So did she. Sometimes, the unions that don't fit the mold are the strongest. You only choose something complicated over a more conventional, and as such, convenient option . . . funny how these words are related, isn't it, convenient, conventional . . . anyway, you only brave it when you feel very certain about it indeed." He seemed to look far back in time now. Whatever he saw was making him smile softly in a way that took years off his face. "In Emilia, I had a companion," he said. "A friend. A clever counsel. And so much joy. We were separate creatures, of course, but from the beginning, we were also extensions of each other." He looked at her quite sharply then. "Let me be clear: if you found a love like that, I would expect you to marry. I would expect it for your own good. But as long as our finances permit it, I could never ask you to yoke yourself to a pale imitation of what your mother and I had. I don't expect it of myself, either. Certainly not when we could be writing books instead."

Her eyes stung. She exhaled slowly, scared that she would let out an ugly sob.

"She'd be very proud of you today," said her father, "how much work and time you have dedicated to changing the course of history—child, what is wrong?"

Catriona pressed her fist to her mouth. "Papa," she croaked. "I'm sorry. I have done something . . . I have kept something from you. I have caused trouble for you."

She confessed what she had done about the artifacts.

Chapter 35

On Monday, after a quick lunch at the Lamb and Flag, Elias accompanied Nassim to the railway station. It was a pleasant enough day, so he decided to return to St. John's in a roundabout way. On a whim, he let his walk take him past the Ashmolean Museum. He contemplated the charming building with narrowed eyes. He had made up his mind to let it go; there was no reason to go in and have a last look. He had decided to prioritize his woman over this, and he knew what it would cost him.

Still, he went ahead and entered. He greeted the clerk at the desk and wrote his name and the time in the ledger, ten minutes past one o'clock. The airy hall was largely abandoned; few people visited what still felt like a museum in progress.

He slid the key into the door lock at the Leighton room. His first warning should have been that the room was not, in fact, locked.

The room was empty.

A spot of nothing yawned under the skylight. The shelves were bare.

Elias stared at the situation in silence.

The clerk at the desk watched him approach with some alarm. "How may I help you—"

"Where are the artifacts from Mr. Leighton's room?"

The young man looked up at him with wide eyes.

"They were picked up for transfer quite early this morning," he said.

"Transfer to where?"

"To the British Museum."

"No," said Elias. "No, that's not possible."

"It's quite possible, sir. They had been packed up overnight."

Elias leaned over the desk. "The transfer was planned for September."

The clerk brushed his fingers over his blond mustache and picked up the ledger. "A change in schedule, perhaps?"

"I would know about that," said Elias, "I work on these pieces, I would have been informed." She would have told him; it made no sense that she wouldn't.

As the clerk became more nervous, Elias became proportionally more impatient.

"Where's the curator?" he demanded.

The blood was slowly leaving the clerk's face. "He's taking a sabbatical today. He . . . he hadn't informed me about the pickup, come to think of it. But they presented official documents . . . signed and stamped . . ."

"Well, when were you informed about the change?"

"This morning?"

"By the crew itself?"

His voice sounded far too harsh to his own ears. As if his body already knew something his heart hadn't the capacity to admit. It was well possible that she hadn't told him. On purpose. It felt as though the ground moved under his feet.

The clerk met his eyes. "I think we may have a situation," he said.

Chapter 36

The interview with Scotland Yard had been brief, though they had questioned Elias for longer than the clerk. Neither he nor the clerk had had much to say about the unexpected disappearance of Leighton's entire haul; they provided dates, names, unusual observations or rather, the lack thereof, and the officers who took their statements had seemed satisfied for the time being and let them go. Elias had walked away from the museum with his senses primed for defense; the quaint, leafy surroundings had turned menacing and glared back at him like drawn blades. Something sharp had kept slicing into his chest with every beat of his heart.

She did not return on Tuesday. Nor on Wednesday. He knew because he watched the quadrangle from an upper-floor corridor window. Thursday morning, he sat up straighter in his nook, because the familiar upright figure, dressed in dark blue, appeared in the archway. She was accompanied by her father, so he remained put. An hour later, she left, alone, without luggage, so he expected her to return. As the minutes ticked past, the icy flame of his restrained fury licked higher. Things became interesting when Wester Ross left. When Catriona returned while her father was still gone, Elias pushed away from the wall.

The door to the Campbell flat was unlocked. He crossed the

vestibule without making a sound. He knew she was home; his body was still attuned to her presence. In the study, he paused. A suspicious silence lurked in the adjacent room. The door was ajar.

It was a bedchamber. Catriona was on the other side of the bed, frozen in a hunch over an open valise, her blue gaze flickering over him warily. And knowingly. There was a pile of clothes on the counterpane. She was packing up her things. He gripped the door-frame with one hand, his lips white with a terrible emotion, the sickening gut punch of betrayal.

"You lied to me, my heart," he said. "You lied, and now you're running, too?"

She straightened. "I should have told you," she said in a flat voice. "I realize that it was a mistake to keep it from you. I imagine you are displeased."

Now, that was the understatement of the century.

"Why?" he asked. "You could have just reported me. Why the charade in London? For weeks?"

Her throat moved nervously. "The artifacts are on their way to your family's warehouse in Beirut Port."

Her meaning did not filter through the heat of his temper at once.

"I had the pieces shipped back to the Levant," she said again.

His mind fell silent.

She writhed under his quiet stare. "I thought it best to not tell you, in case there was an investigation," she said. "I understand Scotland Yard has already taken your statement?"

"Oh yes. I called them to the scene."

She nodded. "Good. I doubt they will take a closer look at you again before this is taken care of." She couldn't look at him. She kept looking everywhere but at him. "I thought the more genuinely confused you appeared, the lower the risk . . . the less you knew, the better. Their interrogation techniques are ghastly once they smell blood. They won't look at me too closely again, I hope; ladies are rarely prime suspects. Everyone else who's involved is in a position to make this go away."

His chest burned like a fire pit. "La tifzaii illa min al naher al hedi," he said, shaking his head. *Fear only the quiet river.* "Has it occurred to you, my lady, that since I did plan to take the artifacts, I might have roused their suspicions during their interview anyway?"

"There was a risk," she conceded. "But they would have asked the clerk about you, too. I imagine you were convincing in your initial surprise."

Yes, he had been that.

He had no idea how she had accomplished this operation. He simply hated that it had happened. She had deceived him. She had been in his bed, soft and clinging, making him envision a future . . . no, he had envisioned that all by himself, he had needed no encouragement.

"You shouldn't have done it," he said. "It's a shame that you have done this."

She twisted her hands. "I thought it was the most effective—"

"You had no right," he burst out. "You had no right to take this from me."

"Take?"

"It was my right to execute that man's comeuppance. I swore I would have those pieces back, you heard me say it."

Her eyes were changing, from guilty to realizing the full extent of the damage she had caused.

"Yes," she stammered, "but you said 'one way or another' . . ."

"Why don't you keep semantics out of this, my dear," he said so quietly, she fell silent.

Never mind that he had already decided to humble himself and let it all go anyway. His hand on the door was hurting; either the oak or his bones would give. He abruptly released his grip.

She was deathly pale. "I apologize," she said mechanically. "I hadn't thought of that. I never intended to offend you."

"You had this planned from the beginning—it's why you suggested the transfer in the first place, hm?"

A barely perceptible nod. "I didn't know how exactly, then. Just that it was a chance."

He bit his lip. "Your mind is so bright," he said, "so bright that it's blinding you to certain realities."

"I'm sorry," she repeated.

He took a step into the room. "Why did you do it?"

She wrapped her arms around herself as though his presence brought an icy wind. "It was the right thing to do," she said. "The pieces don't belong here, not if they are wanted where they came from."

"You would have put your name and your father's name at risk for anyone in my position?"

"I should have," she said. "I hope that I would have, yes. At least there's a good chance now that you remain a free man here—free to visit Britain or do business here."

"Why is that important to you?" *Tell me you have done it for us,* he thought; *tell me you have done it out of mindless love for me and a hope for a future,* because then he would dig deep and forgive her.

She looked away. "Why, because it's the right—"

"How reticent you are," he said under his breath. "You can't say it, can you?"

The silence drew out.

"I wouldn't have taken them," he finally said. "I was prepared to leave them here, and you know why, don't you."

She shook her head, and kept shaking it, eyes frozen, like someone who was losing their mind.

"My train is leaving." She closed the lid of her valise.

"Where are you going?"

"Applecross."

"Ah," he said hotly. "Back to your windy castle . . . What is your plan, Catriona? Becoming Miss Havisham?"

She flinched. "Don't be cruel, I beg you."

He gave an ugly laugh. "It's a waste."

At that, something sparked in her face. "I know I may be a woman—"

"It's a waste of love," he cut her off. "I have seen the things people die for, what they kill for, and this, this is one of the few things worth fighting for, and you are turning away from it without even a struggle."

Her lips were clamped tight, she was a fragile thing barely held together by misguided, infuriating stubbornness. He could persist and force some admission from her, but he'd be damned before he laid himself at a woman's feet like a twenty-year-old fool in a warehouse once again. If there had been any truth in their nights in London, then she could own it. If she couldn't, then her feelings were too weak; they lacked the substance required to weather the storms that would batter them from the outside. Her head was bowed now, but there was some emotion; her poor, ink-stained hands were trembling so badly, her efforts to close the latches on her valise kept failing. The pathetic attempts went on for a minute, so eventually, he went to her, round the bed, and wordlessly took over the latches.

He closed the left latch, then the right.

Behind her spectacles, her eyes looked vacant. She had already gone somewhere; there was no point in staying and prolonging the torture.

"Here, allow me." He lifted the valise off the bed. "Where do you want it?"

"In the corridor," she whispered. "Thank you."

She followed him to the door. When he put down the valise and turned back round to her, she stood at a little distance, misery dripping off her hunched form.

"I'm leaving, too," he said. "I'm urgently needed back home." He cocked his head. "You're quite safe from the awkwardness of tiptoeing around our situation, whenever you return from Scotland."

She tensed around her mouth at hearing her own words repeated back at her. The day in the sheep stable seemed a lifetime ago.

"It's nothing serious, I hope," she said. "Back home."

His smile was faintly ironic. "I believe some would call it a joyful occasion."

A last glance at her lovely, deceiving, shuttered face.

"May God keep you," he said, and here his voice turned scratchy. "May you have a long life in good health."

He didn't permit himself to look at her any longer and left.

Chapter 37

Instead of going to the railway station, Catriona found that she had walked back to the Randolph Hotel. Hattie, Annabelle, and Aoife were still in the drawing room, finishing up a pot of tea amid the debris of the victory party for the Oxford chapter.

They fell silent when she appeared in the doorframe.

Annabelle took a closer look at her and quickly rose. "What happened?"

"Mr. Khoury is gone."

Hattie's eyes were wide. "What? Why?"

Catriona swallowed hard. "He's gone home."

"Are you certain?"

She nodded.

Annabelle was next to her. "Here, sit down."

She seemed to stand and watch from outside her body while the others moved around her: Aoife softly excused herself and left, Annabelle ushered her into an armchair, and then Hattie was smoothing her plaid over her shoulders.

"Why did he leave?" Hattie asked. "It seems so hasty."

"He found out about the artifacts, and he was rather angry. He had to go home anyway—he said it was urgent."

Annabelle took her cold hand in hers. "You were fond of him, weren't you?"

She made to say something, and then she just slightly shook her head. Paused. Shook her head again. "It's for the best," she said thinly. "Nothing could have come from it, right?"

"Did he not say anything to you?" Hattie demanded, indignation reddening her face. "Nothing at all? He just"—she flicked her hand—"walked away, after everything?"

"After *everything*?" Annabelle asked, her tone suspicious.

Catriona looked away.

"Oh," Annabelle breathed. Her hand went slack around Catriona's. Then she gripped it more tightly than before.

"I should have told him," Catriona whispered. Sweat stood hot on her brow. "I should have told him everything. I hadn't thought it through from a manly perspective. I hurt his pride."

"You did whatever was necessary to give him what he really wanted—the artifacts—and at the lowest possible risk to him."

Only that it was more complicated. He had wanted something more and now he felt fooled. She should have told him that he had managed to make her dream of a forever. Words, letters, scraps of sentences flew at her from every direction, a mass of sounds; her head was imploding.

She pressed her hands to the sides of her face. "He's not coming back, is he."

"Don't go anywhere," said Hattie. She rushed into the side chamber that led to her bedroom, and when she returned, she held a large envelope in her hand. "I had meant to give him these for a while," she said. "My brain is much more scrambled than usual these days, so I kept forgetting to give them to him."

She handed Catriona the envelope. It contained a set of photography plates, and there was Elias, cast in matte sepia. A scalding devastation spread through her chest.

"These are from the fire drill."

Hattie nodded. "Post them to him—he was quite keen on having the ones with the equipment. It's innocent enough, and any gentleman would feel compelled to reply, regardless of how you parted."

Elias, with his hand on the water wagon. Elias, standing a head taller than the proud fire brigades in front of the dorm. Elias in portrait. He held his head at a proud angle and wore a serious expression for a sharp image, but he seemed distracted, with his eyes privately smiling at something or someone beyond the camera lens.

Silence filled her head like water. She was submerged in it, but she wasn't weightless, she was drowning.

She closed the envelope with numb fingers. "I have properly messed up, haven't I? I really loved him—I love him, and now it feels as though nothing will ever be good again."

"Oh, my dear," Annabelle said with a worried frown, "try to breathe."

She rose. "He might still be at St. John's. Perhaps I can still—perhaps he's still here."

She hurried from the room, her friends' voices a distorted echo in her ears.

The door to his flat at St. John's was locked. She rushed back to the lodge and asked porter Clive for the spare key, desperately trying to suppress her panting. She could not bring herself to ask: *Has Mr. Khoury left?* A few minutes later, his room spoke for itself. Everything was gone: his shoes, hat, coat. Glaring emptiness on the mantelshelf; he had packed up his jars. She leaned against the doorframe, a hand on her throat, feeling panic surge and drum under her fingers . . . A small figurine on the dining table caught her eye. A chess piece.

Her heart leapt sharply—he would return. He wouldn't leave one of his precious chess pieces behind; at the very least she had a reason now to send him a note, and Hattie was right, he was a gentleman, and he would reply. They hadn't yet exchanged their last word, not yet . . . She went and grabbed the piece, clutched it in her hand.

It dawned on her then that she was holding the white king.

He had surrendered the one piece that had to remain standing for there to be a game.

Checkmate.

A low, keening sound came from her throat, more animal than human.

The abyss of loss inside her cracked open so wide that for a moment, all went black.

Somehow, she was in his bedchamber. She went to the wardrobe and yanked open the doors. Empty. She pulled out drawers, looked under the bed. Empty, empty, empty. Her heart pounded faster than a rushing train, and she stopped whirling and pressed her hands over her ribs. Her gaze jumped around the abandoned room, hunting for any sign of him, any reminder that he had been real. There was something in the bin, next to his desk. Here she was, clawing through his rubbish with a feverish face. It was a telegram, torn in half. She put the torn edges together. . . . *let Eli know . . .*

"No," she said out loud.

She was still a ball on the floor when the door opened, hasty footsteps neared, and her friends rushed into the room.

"All right," Hattie said. "All right, so we have a bit of a boggle-debotch situation. But! It can be fixed."

Catriona gave her a red-eyed look. "How."

The three women were sitting at the long dining table in Elias's former reception room. Elias was probably on a boat by now, leaving Europe.

"You must be brave and lay yourself bare to him," Hattie said. "I know it isn't the proper thing to do, to wear one's heart on one's sleeve, but this is an emergency. You'll feel much better, regardless of whether you marry him or forget him or just carry on a torrid, secret affair for decades."

As if she'd ever forget him. "I think he has been wooing me for weeks."

Hattie wrinkled her nose. "He probably was. You're a hard nut to crack."

"He said *marry me*, but I thought it was a joke."

"Oh, Catriona, do be serious," said Annabelle.

Catriona massaged her throat. "Do you know the saying *Beware the fury of a patient man*?"

"Oh no," Annabelle said quickly, "no, you don't owe a man a yes or even your affection just because he wooed you. Your apprehensions are entirely justified, marriage can make or break a woman. Second, Hattie is right—if you truly love each other, then it can be fixed. Remember, I was in your position just a few years ago over Montgomery."

Her head heated as the thought carousel spun again. "I should have told him that I love him."

"Why didn't you?" asked Hattie, sounding curious rather than judgmental.

"If only I knew," she said. "Every time the words were forming, I became utterly paralyzed. As if something terrible would happen if I said it out loud."

She knocked her knuckles against her forehead, and it made a dull sound.

Annabelle grabbed her hand. "Stop that, that's of no use. Just think of what to do now."

"If he's being matched with someone, whatever you do, you have to do it quickly," Hattie remarked, eyeing the smoothed halves of the telegram.

"Be honest with me," Catriona said, looking at Hattie, then at Annabelle. "Is a month enough to know? Can one month make you want to change your life?"

Annabelle's green eyes were soft with compassion. "My dear," she said, "a single moment is enough—if it's a moment that you have been waiting for all along."

Goose bumps spread up her spine. She jumped to her feet. "I have to go," she said. "To Beirut."

They talked over one another—How would she travel: by boat. When: as soon as possible. With whom? She couldn't go to the Levant alone; they needed a man to escort her.

"Your father!" Hattie cried.

Catriona shook her head. "No, he would never understand the urgency, not unless I . . ." *Told him about my scandalous weeks in London and broke his heart and made him look at Elias askance for the rest of our lives* . . . If there was to be a rest of their lives. She might well be too late.

"I should love to accompany you," Hattie said, "but I don't dare, not in my condition."

"You mustn't," Catriona said quickly, and to Annabelle, "and neither would I ever expect you to leave Jamie for goodness knows how long."

Her stomach roiled with nerves. She would arrive too late.

"Ha," said Annabelle with a rare, triumphant smirk. "I know someone."

Hattie and Catriona leaned toward her as one. "Who?"

Annabelle's eyes narrowed. "Someone who owes you." She flicked the artfully twisted coil of her hair back over her shoulder. "Let's pay a visit to my brother-in-law, shall we."

Minutes later, on the ground floor, three hands knocked frantically on the door to Peregrin's lodgings.

"What if he isn't in?" Hattie whispered, still rapping away.

"We'll find him," Annabelle said with scary cheer.

"Hold it," came a muffled voice from inside the beleaguered flat.

Catriona's nerves buzzed at the sound of the door bolt sliding back.

Peregrin appeared, tall and lanky, his blond hair obviously combed with five fingers and his jacket slightly askew as though he had put it on in haste. He looked back and forth between them, baffled.

"Ladies. What an unexpected pleasure. Sister." He dipped his head to Annabelle.

His unruffled drawl was a constant; not even when Catriona had first discovered him in his hideout in St. John's wine cellar had his voice betrayed his distress. How charmingly he had asked for her assistance, whether she would please not rat him out, and oh, whether she'd be inclined to smuggle some bread and cheese his way? For weeks, she had kept his secret and supplied him with oil for his lamp and nourishing meals from the college kitchen.

"Lady Catriona requires an escort," Annabelle informed the young lord. "After due consideration, we agreed you are the most suitable gentleman available."

His brows flew up. "Am I?" he asked. "Available? Where are we going?"

"You are going to Beirut," said Annabelle. "Tomorrow."

"Erm—"

"Actually," Catriona said, "I would stay in Beirut, and you would go to a place in the northern mountains, called Ehden."

Peregrin leaned a little closer and gave a discreet sniff.

"We're not intoxicated," Annabelle said calmly.

He drew back. "Very well," he muttered, "but—why? Why me?"

"Because you have experience with traveling in the east, and because you owe Lady Catriona," Annabelle said with a small smile. "A Devereux settles his debts."

Peregrin cleared his throat. "Right. Who else is part of this merry excursion?"

"It's just the two of you."

His hazel eyes widened. "Are you certain you haven't ingested something, accidentally, perhaps—"

"You will have to exercise discretion at all times," Annabelle said as if he hadn't spoken. "For the duration of the journey, I recommend you travel under a false name and pretend to be husband and wife."

Catriona went stiff. She didn't want to pretend any such thing with anyone other than Elias, nor run the risk of a scandal with another man. Peregrin seemed equally unimpressed; a rare frown furrowed his brow. It sobered her fast; his cooperation was crucial for this madcap undertaking.

"Please," she said quietly. "My happiness depends upon it."

She'd beg if need be.

He did not let it come to that; Peregrin's expression soon became resigned. He pulled his cravat away from his throat with his thumb.

"Very well," he muttered. "Wife." And, under his breath: "Montgomery will kill me."

Chapter 38

Sebastian Devereux, nineteenth Duke of Montgomery, was presiding over his morning correspondence when a hectic knock on his study door disturbed his peace.

His valet entered with a wary look in his eyes.

"Ramsey," said Sebastian, and put down his fountain pen. "What is it."

"Your Grace, you have a visitor."

"I'm not expecting anyone."

"It's Mr. Leighton, Your Grace," Ramsey said. "He's quite adamant that you receive him. Bonville is having trouble containing him."

"Containing him?"

"I'm afraid so."

Leighton. He had no direct connection to the textile merchant. His only lingering impression of the man was that he always spat a little when he spoke.

"Admit him."

Five minutes later, Leighton marched in, his chest puffed out and his eyes ablaze beneath bushy brows.

"I want them back," he said, and thrust a finger at Sebastian. Both Bonville and Ramsey hovered at the study door. Sebastian waved them away while boring his cool gaze into Leighton's. The man's advance on the ducal desk slowed. With a jerky movement, he took off his hat.

"Your Grace." It scraped out with reluctance.

"Mr. Leighton." Sebastian watched him over steepled fingers. "There appears to be an urgency. What can I do for you."

Leighton's fingertips crushed the crimp of his hat. "I demand the return of my bulls."

Sebastian was genuinely baffled. "I don't recall having any dealings with your cattle."

Leighton threw up his hands. "Not livestock," he cried, looking like an enraged bovine himself with his flaring nostrils. "Sculptures. Phoenician ones. Big, antique marbles," he added while windmilling his arms in a circle to indicate just how big they were.

"Right," Sebastian said blandly. It was a possibility that Leighton was not in good health.

"I am *bewildered*, Your Grace, that a gentleman in your position would act like . . . like an outlaw."

"I understand that you have lost your marbles," Sebastian drawled, "and I gather you suspect me of having a hand in their disappearance. A rather bold proposition, sir."

Leighton glared quietly, but his back teeth were grinding.

Sebastian rose and went to the nearby drinks cabinet. "Have a drink."

"Absolutely not," Leighton huffed, and, upon catching the warning glint in Sebastian's eyes, he said: "A brandy, thank you."

Sebastian poured. He prepared himself a drink, too, because it was the polite thing to do. He would set it aside untouched later, it was barely nine o'clock.

Leighton finished his glass in one gulp. "If you—if the pieces were returned to me," he then said, "I shall never mention it again, Your Grace. No offense taken. I can see why a man would be tempted to have them at all costs."

Sebastian looked him directly in the eye, and as expected, Leighton squirmed a little on the spot.

"Tell me," Sebastian said as he stared, "am I known for collecting Phoenician marbles?"

Squirm. "Not exactly."

"Or any marbles."

"Not to my knowledge," Leighton admitted, "but, since they disappeared on your train, the conclusion drew itself."

"My train?" Sebastian said sharply. "The ducal train?"

Leighton narrowed his eyes, clearly surprised by Sebastian's sudden alertness. "Indeed."

Sebastian turned the tumbler in his hand. He had not sanctioned the use of his train.

"Start at the beginning, please."

Leighton's gaze flickered with uncertainty for the first time. "The pieces were scheduled for transfer from the Ashmolean in Oxford to the British Museum, in September. Curiously, someone issued the marching orders a few days ago, and your train was used for transport, well, until it went astray—"

"Astray—the whole thing?"

"Apparently, it went to Southampton. The sheriff says the crates were loaded onto a ship that promptly left port."

"What about my train?"

"What about it? It returned to whence it came, but a train is quite replaceable, with one being quite like the next—but my bulls, they are unique, priceless . . ."

"What of the ship, was it mine, too?" Sebastian asked with some impatience.

Leighton ran his tongue over his teeth. "No. Apparently, it sails under the royal standard of the German Emperor and the load had diplomatic immunity—God knows where it's going!"

Germany. He hadn't engaged with German affairs in months, and the only way his train moved was by way of a written order that bore his signature and seal. Whoever had given the order, it hadn't been him. A suspicion crossed his mind like a strike of lightning. He flung back his drink after all.

"Mr. Leighton," he said, "I give you my word that if I ever felt inclined to nab your antiques, I wouldn't collude with the Prussians to do it and I'd certainly not leave an evidence trail the size of a train."

Leighton's chest was deflating. "Well," he said. "When one puts it like that . . ."

Sebastian nodded sympathetically. "Sounds absurd, doesn't it. Hardly worth a diplomatic incident, either."

"No, of course not." Leighton looked around the study, only now realizing his surroundings fully. He scratched his head. He cleared his throat with an awkward cough. "You might wish to look into the matter, Your Grace," he said at last. "There appears to be a forger at large who sets your trains in motion."

Indeed. Sebastian suspected the culprit was in the nursery upstairs.

When the crazed man of business had gone, Sebastian pulled the bell string on the wall behind his desk.

Bonville reappeared at the study door a few minutes later.

"Where is the duchess?" Sebastian asked. His wife had kept on celebrating the MWPA victory last night long after Sebastian had gone to bed. He hardly expected her to be up.

"I shall find out at once," said Bonville.

When he returned, he confirmed that Her Grace was in the nursery.

It was a long walk across two floors of Claremont, but by the time Sebastian arrived at the door, he still hadn't found an explanation for Annabelle's behavior.

He opened the door with caution. The only thing worse than waking sleeping dogs was waking sleeping babies.

His son was wide awake, in his day dress, and attached to his mother's side with the stubborn clasp of a koala bear. Annabelle stood at the window, pointing out things in the courtyard below. She glanced back over her shoulder and upon seeing Sebastian, a smile broke over her face. It heated his blood more quickly than the brandy. He approached her, transfixed by how beautiful she looked in her flowing morning robe and her tumbling hair held back with a simple ribbon . . .

"Where is the nanny?" he asked.

She tilted her face up at him. "I told Millie to take a good long nap. Apparently, your son was up all night, trying to grow a tooth. Weren't you," she cooed at the baby.

"Good morning, James," murmured Sebastian.

James stared at him with eerily deep indigo eyes. At ten months old, he had developed a habit of fixating on people and objects he found interesting with all-absorbing intensity. A smile broke over his round face, revealing the culpable little rice grain teeth.

"Say good morning to your father, Jamie," Annabelle said, and the featherlight weight of the Earl of Wiltshire promptly settled against Sebastian's chest. Sebastian glanced at Annabelle over James's ruffled lace cap and met sparkling green eyes. She was always handing him the child matter-of-factly, even when James had been a freshly hatched red-faced creature; tiny, twisty, and awfully breakable. Sebastian had felt terror when holding him, half of his heart, his whole future, literally in his hands. Ten months on, it felt natural. That had to have been Annabelle's intention all along, in her quest to ward off the thoroughly distanced mannerisms that had marred his own upbringing. He slid his free arm around his wife's shoulders and pulled her close, so he held both her and his son.

"My love," he said. "Have you any knowledge of a pair of marble sculptures? Bulls from the Near East, I understand."

She stilled against him. There was his answer.

When she faced him, her expression was serious. "It was for a just cause," she said.

"That should satisfy the foreign office, then," he said dryly.

He had gifted her blank sheets of the ducal correspondence paper on their first wedding anniversary, already signed and with a replica of his signet ring. "I don't need to know when you use them," he had told her in a declaration of unconditional trust. To his knowledge, this was the first time she had made use of her proxy power.

Annabelle smoothed the already perfectly smooth lapel of his jacket. "I didn't tell you beforehand because there was a risk someone would confront you, and I assumed you'd rather not feign ignorance," she explained. "In any case, your innocence would appear more authentic if you truly didn't know."

"This is outrageous," he remarked.

"Did it work?"

He bounced the wiggling baby. "Perfectly. But the whole train . . . and the German Emperor, Annabelle?"

She had the decency to look apologetic. "It was Catriona's plan. She involved someone at the German embassy—to smudge the tracks, as she put it."

"Well, it did that. No one is particularly keen on investigating the Kaiser."

"I only supplied the train," Annabelle said. "Blackstone supplied the crew, and the German contact the ship. Lucie's magazine at London Print shared news about the pieces with tens of thousands of households, good luck with interviewing all possible suspects. Before this goes any further at all, however, I was hoping you could take care of the sheriff."

Her confidence in him warmed his chest despite himself. No, he didn't like being left in the dark, but he very much liked that she thought he could fix anything.

"When does the day nanny arrive?" he asked. It came out clipped.

What she saw in his eyes made her blush. "At ten o'clock," she supplied.

He wanted to pull the ribbon from her hair. He wanted to part her robe . . . James squirmed and plucked Sebastian's cravat pin loose with astounding dexterity. Sebastian returned him into Annabelle's waiting arms.

"Whatever you have scheduled from ten o'clock, can you reschedule it?"

Her plush lips curved into a smile. "To what time?"

"Lunch."

They made thorough use of those two hours.

Chapter 39

The breeze blew freely through the high arches of the mansion's balcony and carried the rich, warm fragrance of a summer afternoon in the mountains. A drowsy atmosphere lay over the family drawing room. Aunt Georgette was lounging on the striped silk divan, snoozing after a smoke. Charbel and Layal were playing Dama on the floor, next to the table that was cluttered with empty coffee cups and platters with leftover fruit. Elias was sprawled on a sofa, sharing an argileh with Nassim. Behind a veil of curling white smoke, his face was deceptively still, as if carved in stone.

Hana, the doorman, entered the room, his house shoes soundless on the marble floor.

"Mr. Elias. A gentleman is here to see you."

Elias's dispassionate gaze moved in the man's direction. "Who is it?"

"A gentleman from abroad."

He sat up, slowly. "Describe him."

It was an older, dark-haired Scotsman, wasn't it, keen on avenging his daughter's honor.

"He is a young, fair-haired Englishman," said Hana. "His name was unintelligible."

A tiny spark glimmering in Elias's gut extinguished back to black.

"He asked me to give you this," Hana said, and held up an object. Elias waved him closer. "Show me."

The object was the size of a small pinecone, wrapped in fabric and tied with string. The fabric was, in fact, a handkerchief. Embroidered like a woman's. Premonition struck his chest like lightning, making all the fine hairs on his arms stand on end. He felt Nassim's alert gaze on him.

Layal craned her graceful neck. "What is it?"

She wasn't the only one encroaching with a curious look in her eyes.

Elias rose and left the room with long strides.

He unwrapped the mysterious object on his way out the door into the front yard. The sunlight gleamed off polished ivory. The white king had returned. His head jerked up.

A man stood near the bottom of the stairs, evidently a guide. He held two disgruntled mules on their reins. Next to him, the English visitor. The young man looked red and quite miserable, Elias thought as he approached them; the foreigner had eaten dust during his ride up the mountains. The cut of the man's suit, the high forehead, and raffish blond hair suggested an aristocrat.

Elias planted himself in front of him. "Ahlan wa sahlan. Welcome to my family's home. I'm Elias Iskander Khoury, how can I help you?"

"Salam . . ." the cultured voice floundered. "Good day, sir." A hand was offered, and hazel eyes met his. "Lord Peregrin Devereux. I'm a friend of Wester Ross."

The chess piece bit into Elias's palm. "Where is his lordship?"

"*Her lady*ship," the lordling corrected. "She took a room at the Hotel Allemand Blaich, near the port."

Catriona.

His body had reflexively angled west, toward the coastline. His heart was pounding, his muscles readied for a dash down the road. He shook himself. In the distance, the sun was already descending over the sea. It was half a day's ride to reach the port town of Chekka, and several hours on a sailboat that took people from Chekka to Beirut. He'd have to ride into the night only to miss the last departure of the boat.

"Who is with her now?" he asked the Englishman.

"She's keeping her own company," came the hesitant reply.

Displeasure ripped through Elias like a shooting flame. "You traveled with her, alone?"

Lord Peregrin Devereux flinched, and Elias realized he had taken a step toward the young man. Who was, on all accounts, a traveler, and his guest. His jaw clenched with the vain effort to rein in his temper. "You traveled with her, alone," he repeated, "and you abandoned her in a foreign city?"

Lord Peregrin's chin rose. "I doubt it will improve your opinion of me, sir, but for what it's worth, I was forced into this appalling scheme by the lady herself."

What kind of man are you, Elias thought, *to allow yourself to be forced into idiotic, improper acts that endanger a woman's name and safety?* As he stared into Lord Peregrin's perspiring face, he felt supremely annoyed because he himself had been exactly that kind of man.

"The lady knows her own mind," he said curtly.

Lord Peregrin's alert posture relaxed a fraction. "Indeed."

Elias clapped him on the shoulder and left his hand there. "Lord Peregrin. It would be our honor to have you as our guest. Our house is your house, rest, join us for the evening meal. Have a room for the night." He cast a last glance at the horizon. "I shall leave for Beirut shortly before dawn."

"Gladly, sir. I appreciate it."

Elias gestured one of their guards closer and instructed him to provide the guide and his mules with rest and refreshments. Activity broke out at the entrance to the main house; his family was gathering. The women were absent, probably supervising the preparations for the guest, coffee, sweets, and the sitting room reserved for visitors. He turned back to the English lord. His mouth was smiling but his voice had an edge when he leaned in close. "I shall introduce you to my family as a fellow student from Cambridge days. You happen to be in Beirut for pleasure and came to see me on a whim. You don't mention the lady. Not a word."

Lord Peregrin squirmed a little, possibly perturbed at a stranger claiming his personal space and whispering threats into his ear, but when Elias's fingers tightened slightly on his shoulder, he peered sideways at Elias's face and nodded. "Very well, I don't mention the lady."

When they ascended the stairs, Lord Peregrin fell into step with Elias.

"What was our college?" he asked from the corner of his mouth. "Did we row together? You have a good height for rowing. So do I, but I'm more of a cricket man myself . . ."

The next few hours would feel like years.

The sea of Zaitounay Bay reflected the sun like a metal sheet, and the glare blinded Catriona through the flimsy screen of her travel veil. For a while, she had shielded her eyes with her hand, but eventually her arm had grown tired. Waves crashed ceaselessly against the wall of the promenade, salt coated her lips. Sensations of home, of Applecross, though notably warmer and brighter; still, she clung to this vague sense of familiarity to keep calm. Peregrin had left the hotel yesterday morning, now it was afternoon and there was still no sign of him. It had been impossible to stay indoors, trapped with vivid mental scenarios of Elias married to someone else, of Elias disliking her, of him scratching her from his memory. The hotel was behind her, a few hundred yards to the left. She might have to return for a drink of water soon, the glass of sweet lemonade she had bought from a street vendor earlier seemed a distant dream. Her posture was beginning to sag, her tongue stuck to the roof of her mouth; she had been out under the sun for hours.

A man approached the hotel. He drew her attention as if he had called her name. He wore Ottoman clothes: a cropped, intricately embroidered velvet jacket, and the sherwal, baggy trousers that disappeared into knee-high leather boots. A brown, conical cap covered his hair, and a white scarf, tied around the cap, concealed half of his face. Her knees sagged. She would have recognized him in any attire, with his face fully covered. She would know him by the set of his shoulders, the tilt of his head, his smooth walk that was half grace, half purpose.

He had recognized her, too, shrouded as she was in dark lace from head to toe. He changed course, coming right toward her. She turned back to the sea, her shaking fingers curling around the railing, and focused on breathing in and out.

She inhaled dust and male sweat and him, and, faintly, something warm and smoky, the smell of leather. Her chest contracted with a bittersweet pang of yearning. He was growing a beard, looking handsome but different. Already his life was moving on without her. But he had a rifle and a knapsack slung over his shoulders, the various straps crisscrossing over his chest; he must have come to her straight from the mountains, and it fanned her flicker of hope.

"You're here," he said. His voice was gravelly, assessing rather than pleased. A wary tension hummed in his body and his gaze was gliding over her quickly.

Her heart sank. "I am," she said. "I arrived two days ago."

He pulled his scarf forward, creating a screen between his profile and people walking past him from his left. She flipped her travel veil back from her face and hung it over her right shoulder, helping form a makeshift cocoon around them. Appreciation for her presence of mind briefly lit Elias's eyes. Perhaps it was just a reflection of the sun. The blood seemed to drain from her face and pooled heavily in her feet.

Elias muttered something under his breath and he detached a flask from his belt. "Here."

She gulped down the lukewarm water. "Thank you."

"You ought to sit, I shall find us a bench."

"I'm fine right here, thanks."

He arched a brow but didn't insist. His gaze furtively ran over their surroundings, then penetrated her with a grave intensity.

"Are you . . ." He leaned closer. "Are we in trouble?"

The meaning of his question evaded her at first. The penny dropped when his eyes moved over her belly.

She bit back a hysterical little laugh.

In her darkest moment, after she had found him gone, she had briefly hoped for it, that sort of trouble, as it would have allowed her to keep a piece of him. The scathing irony of that thought had not been lost on her.

"No," she said, "that's not why I came."

His expression didn't much change, no sigh of relief, no prayer of thanks, just a nondescript flicker in the depths of his eyes and a slight twist of his lips.

"You came here," he said. "With only a young man for company."

"Lord Peregrin was the only experienced, trustworthy traveler available at short notice."

He rubbed his temples, looked over the sea, then back at her. His handsome face was set in hard lines.

"Has anyone seen you?"

"Here? The hotel staff."

"If anyone asks," he said, "say that he's your brother."

"Yes," she agreed. "It's how we registered at the hotel."

"That's good," Elias said. His shoulders were relaxing, his mouth softened. His voice was soft now, too: "How are you?"

A flash of numbness.

She shook her head. Rallied. Tried again. "Ana bhebak," she said. "I love you."

He went very still.

In the bright light, the blues and greens of his eyes were entrancing, vivid, an irresistible lure. She had a sensation of slowly falling forward, of sinking into him until the rest of the world had gone out of focus and she wasn't certain where he began, and she ended.

"Tell me," she said, her lips barely moving. "Am I too late?"

He moved his hand toward hers on the railing. "No," he said. "Not too late."

She exhaled, a long, shaky breath, until no air was left.

"My darling," he murmured. "You could have told me sooner. We could have saved ourselves angry feelings."

"No," she said. "I couldn't."

It had taken crashing down to the bottom of her own abyss to shake the words loose, to show her that a lifetime without him felt worse than whatever fears were swirling in that pit. Fears that were so bound up with her mother, death, a brother she had never met, a cold, empty castle, and other terrors, such as the never-ending stream of sorry fates like Mrs. Weldon's. All that fearful scrambling to keep herself safe, to keep history from repeating itself, to keep distance from danger because her skin was too unbetterable porous. It was Elias who had called her sensitivity a gift, it was his lips and hands that had shown her the full glory of the other side of the coin.

"I was afraid," she said.

His brows swooped. "Of me?"

"Of everything." Her palms were damp inside the gloves. She took the gloves off, the caress of the wind and Elias's stealthy gaze over her bare fingers providing instant relief.

"I was afraid to tell you that I love you. And I didn't tell you about my artifact scheme—it was for your protection, of course, but it also would have told you more than words ever could."

He gestured, seemingly at a loss. "What did you think would happen?"

Something diffuse but terrible. "That you might propose in earnest. That you might want a dozen children, that you'd resent me for my aspirations, and ask me to leave my father and all my friends forever and I'd be trapped in a marriage where I could never leave, nor remain myself . . . that one day, I would lose you."

Elias had paled under his tan. "A dozen children?"

"Or three, or four—I don't know, too many for someone like me."

He sucked in a breath. "Catriona. My grandmother was a midwife."

"I recall."

"We don't work the land, why would we need so many sons?" His eyebrows were still touching his hairline. "I've heard enough to know that a man who loves his wife wouldn't do that to her."

"I thought you would decide we didn't suit at all, and that you would leave me, forever."

He blinked. "So you said nothing—which made me leave."

"Quite."

"Ya salame." He massaged his forehead, looking incredulous even with his eyes closed.

"Is it the number of children?" he asked after a pause. "Or do you want none at all? You don't want them on principle?"

The look on his face was serious, bone-deep apprehension.

A curly head, leaned against his shoulder, a small starfish hand on his chest.

She scoffed with mild self-deprecation. "It's become clear to me rather recently that I wouldn't mind one. I don't object on principle. I object to this notion that it would be my highest purpose, or my only purpose. Because I don't think it is. I think that I . . . I matter. A woman matters, married or not, children or no children. I matter, just as I am, right now. I'm a whole human being."

He smiled; relieved but bemused. "Of course you matter."

Her heart was heated and drumming too quickly, like pistons in an out-of-control machine. The words had poured out; outrageous, frightful words, and yet here he was, smiling.

"I still need my brain for thinking coherent thoughts, at least until I have made a proper name for myself," she said. "I don't *want* my mind crammed with worries over someone else's teething. I don't want to feel guilt-ridden, either, if I don't worry about their teeth as much as we are told we should."

"Who," he asked, spinning his hand, "who is telling you that?"

She opened her mouth, then she frowned. "Everyone?"

"Twelve babies." He was laughing, very softly. "You know, I thought, perhaps you ran away from us because we are from different families, different cultures."

"What?"

He nodded.

"Goodness. I don't care about that," she said with a dismissive grimace. "Society will, for a bit, but I'm rarely out in society anyway."

He tsked. "Then why do you care about the other things they say?"

"I . . . I don't know."

"I tell you why, habibti, it's because you are very soft inside. You are caring, always doing things for your friends, for other women, even for strangers who show up at your castle. It's easy to make you give too much."

He sighed and put his hand over his nape. A sleek, small gull swooped past, and he watched the bird, followed it as it balanced in the air with its yellow feet neatly tucked back against its belly.

"It appears we have much to discuss," he finally said. "Can you ride astride?"

She shook herself out of her little daze. "Aye, though I haven't in a while."

"We ride slowly. I'd like you to come on an excursion with me. We leave tomorrow morning."

"All right?"

"Good. Where is your shawl? The old one?"

She raised her shoulders, reflexively searching for the weight of the protective covering.

"I forgot it at home; I packed rather hastily."

He made to take off his scarf, loosely slung, airy cotton with white and blue stripes.

"Thank you," she said. "But I think I'm fine."

His Beiruti lodgings were in another district, and he did not invite her to join him. At night, she tossed around alone in the pillows, in turns overwhelmed and ecstatic from the ebbs and flows of pure emotions, and the entire time she was missing his warm, supple body next to her in the foreign bed.

The pale-yellow gleam of the morning sun spread east over the sea when she took breakfast, a small cup of syrupy Turkish coffee. A sleepy-looking Peregrin joined her at the table. He set down a tray in front of her, small plates with olives, slices of grilled white cheese, yogurt garnished with swirls of oil, and some of the local bread, soft and thin as a crêpe.

"Trust me," he said, his eyebrows moving meaningfully. "You will need the sustenance."

He would know, her itinerary was the reverse of his tour de force earlier: first, a sailboat journey to the old port town Chekka, where Elias had left his horses, then a ride up into the mountains, beyond Ehden to Bsharri, a Maronite town which seemed of importance to Elias.

"It will be fine," she said, trying to force a slice of cheese down her nervous throat.

"I hope so," Peregrin said, his gaze narrowing. "Otherwise, Montgomery and Annabelle will take turns to end me."

The three met at Beirut Port, where the boat was readying for departure, sails clanging against the mast. Elias's lean figure slipped through the crowd toward them, his hand outstretched to

Peregrin. The white scarf was twisted round his cap in a neat coil. His boots were freshly polished, and he wore a crisp new shirt under his buttoned velvet vest. A shiver went through Catriona when he dipped his head to her, so formal, but she knew the look in his eyes, languid and full of indecent promises. She could smell him, summer and salt. She wanted to press up against his chest and lick his neck. A heavy, damning heat sank through her belly. Would they be alone together sometime soon? Would they be alone at all?

On the deck, he kept an appropriate distance from her, but their bodies kept angling toward each other, drawn by the same center of gravity between them that had inexorably pulled them into bed together before. They stood at the bow now where the turquoise waves parted into foaming trails, and she turned her face into the headwind to let the cool sea spray hit her face. The ride would take five hours. Five hours of Elias with no touching.

He purchased drinking water from the boat vendor and handed her a bottle. His fingertips brushed against hers, his bare, hers gloved, and the fleeting contact prickled through far more delicate places.

Elias watched her raise the trembling bottle to her lips with hooded eyes.

"It is clear, then," he said. "We love each other."

She swallowed her drink without choking. "Indeed."

"And we have forgiven each other."

"Have you?" she asked, carefully.

He did not reply immediately. "I wanted to stay angry with you," he then said. A shrug. "I couldn't. You weren't in front of my eyes, but you were the only thing I could see all week. I still don't like being made a fool of, my dear. You may keep secrets; however, if you were mine, you couldn't keep secrets that involve me. I would need you to be honest. I need to be able to trust you. If I don't know something, I can't fix it."

If you were mine.

A wedding was not a foregone conclusion, then. She clasped the water bottle, nodding. "What else?" she asked. "What else do you need in a wife?"

That earned her a lazy grin. They both remembered cold champagne in Acton Town.

"Go look into a mirror," he said. "And you will see."

She flushed with pleasure. "I found your telegram, in St. John's," she blurted. "I thought perhaps, you are engaged by the time I arrive here."

"Ah."

A lock of her hair, tugged loose by gusts of wind, glued itself to her lips. Elias looked at it keenly for a moment, but he closed his fingers over the strap of his knapsack instead of brushing it away.

"I'm not engaged," he replied. "But I am leaving the family business." He hesitated. "And I'm leaving Mount Lebanon."

Perceiving her shocked silence, he gave her a moment to recover, idly leaning against the railing, his eyes half-closed against the mist and sunshine.

"What happened?" she dared to ask. *And what does it mean for us?*

A muscle worked in his jaw. "Wallahi, I love my family, but there's not enough room for both my uncle and me in the business," he said. "And outside of that, I have a feeling the Ottomans will make it rough for us. Their control over this region is slipping, there's something in the air in the cities on the coast. They can't really fight us in the mountains, but they can cut us off, the supply routes . . ." With a glance at her perturbed face, his voice trailed off. "If there's a war, I will come back here to fight with Zgharta," he said brusquely, "but as long as all remains as it is, quite stable, quite good, I'll just start building my business elsewhere."

She took a fortifying breath. "Where will you go?"

"London. I might expand to America."

"London."

"It's the largest city," he said, "but terrible weather."

"I suppose," she said, feeling a little faint.

"I own a property in my father's hometown here, in Jbeil. We'll pass it soon, I'll point it out to you. I'll build a larger house and spend the winters there, once the company is running well."

"London," she repeated, her heart thumping wildly in her throat now. She could see him do it. He had the brains, the optimism, the fortitude, and adaptability to make a success of himself, she would put connections at disposal. She felt fiercely possessive of him that moment, of his capability and competence, and envious of anyone lucky enough to walk through life by his side. It made her long to be in his arms, naked, her skin desiring the feel of his with an urge akin to hunger. Of course, he noticed. He made a soft, clucking sound of disapproval, but then a smug smile curved his mouth. That smile vanished rather fast when she looked him in the eye and slowly licked the salty spray off her bottom lip.

The hunger beat through her body when they arrived in Chekka and had lunch by the sea; when they picked up the horses; when Elias pointed her toward a cluttered little garment shop and told her to change her skirt into a pair of billowing cotton trousers for the ride. They would have company during the journey, one of Elias's family guards had stayed with the horses and would travel with them.

Heat, dust, thyme-scented air, and striking views over forested mountain slopes registered on the periphery of her perception. His V-shaped back, right ahead of her, took up most of her focus. Occasionally, her thoughts circled the fact that he would have come to London, independently of whatever was between them, and that one day she could have bumped into him while walking down a street in Chelsea unawares. Perhaps he'd have had a wife on his arm. The mere vision twisted her gut, sickened her, yes, she'd have perished right there on the pavement. If there had been any doubts left whether jumping onto a boat to Greater Syria had been the correct decision, here was her answer.

When the sun was descending toward the sea behind them,

they stopped in the small mountain town of Chira to take rooms for the night in an inn.

"I will sign us in as husband and wife," Elias said. "Any objections?"

No. No, she had no objections.

"Will we ride through Ehden tomorrow?" she asked.

He waved his hand in dismissal. "We're taking the road on the other side of the gorge."

She suspected he wanted to avoid crossing paths with his family. It was sensible; it saved him a slew of pressures and complications given their unorthodox situation, and a part of her appreciated his caution.

Their chamber was small, though the bed would fit two. The window front revealed a large balcony and sweeping views over yellow-green slopes rolling to the sea. A mezze dinner was served on the balcony, and she rather gorged herself on the variety of flavorful dishes. Elias was watching her quietly, evidently pleased with her appetite. In the distance, the setting sun lit the strip of sea on fire. *We could be on that beach every winter*, she thought. She was testing the possibility, listening into her body as she turned it over in her mind.

The table was cleared, and she was served a drink. Across her on the pillowed bench, Elias was smoking a water pipe and the sweet smoke and soft gurgle of water lulled her yearning tension.

"I had an idea for a book," she said, sipping cold white wine. "It occurred to me somewhere between Marseille and Beirut. Odd what a few days at sea can do."

Elias's eyes were half-lidded, he seemed fabulously relaxed. "What will you do?"

"I'll finish the anthology, about powerful women," she said. "But I will add another part—about remarkable women today, who stand on these bygone women's shoulders, who are leading, influencing, and most importantly, thriving. If academia doesn't want it, a commercial printing press might."

Elias exhaled a slow stream of smoke. "It's very good," he said. "May you write it quickly."

She wondered whether he was thinking of her schedule, first acclaim, then family. It steered her thoughts back to the bedroom.

Her disappointment when Elias grabbed a pillow to make a bed for himself on the floor plummeted through her body like lead. He went out onto the dark balcony while she changed into her nightgown in the washroom, and he didn't come inside until she had slipped under the covers. Fine. He was being a gentleman. Then it was his turn to come from the washroom, and her toes curled under the blanket. He was trying to torment her. He wore familiar low-slung pajama trousers and nothing else, strode carelessly right past her bed with his muscles sliding enticingly under his skin and his chain gleaming softly on his bare chest.

He leaned over the nightstand, wrapping her in his clean scent.

"May I," he asked, looking at her, brows raised, his fingers on the valve of the gas lamp.

"Of course."

She would not travel for a few thousand miles and then beg for it. She did have some dignity.

He stretched out on the floor with a low sigh.

The moon was out and coated the room in silver.

His breathing was light and slow.

Neither of them moved.

In the tense silence, she heard him swallow.

She turned her head on the pillow.

"Elias." A whisper, trembling under the weight of her longing.

She held her breath.

A rustle.

He was sitting up, and his bare torso appeared next to the bed.

His eyes glittered from the shadows, filled with a hunger that was matching hers.

"I told myself I wouldn't do this again unless you were mine," he said darkly. "Properly mine."

The muscled curve of his shoulder looked smooth like marble in the moonlight. She wanted to press her mouth to it, bite it, claim it, with a visceral urgency.

"I am yours," she whispered.

He rose. The sheet was drawn away from her. She shivered under his perusal, felt his attention linger on the dips and valleys of her body beneath the gauzy nightgown. His strong hand pushed down his trousers, exposing him. He stood proud and ready for her, and her knees fell apart in response. He made a soft sound of approval and came over her while drawing her nightgown up to her waist. Already her breathing came in little gasps. The heat of his bare skin scorched her to the core, softened and readied her for him. Above her, the left side of his face was cast in light; something like pain twisted his features when he settled against her.

"It seems I'm still weak for you," he murmured. "Whatever is beating inside my chest is not my heart, because you have taken it from me."

His lips brushed her mouth in the dark, opening her, finding her tongue. Below, he slipped in slowly, with an exquisite care that said he was savoring every yielding inch. Her last conscious thought was *Thank you*, a powerful, humbling swell of gratitude that they had been granted a second chance, that she was back in his arms, that she could feel him again, and again.

Ghosts could be laid to rest. Patterns could be reversed. One could cross out *The End* and add another paragraph. And occasionally, one had to let go of a good thing to make room for a potentially better thing. It was a risk. But life, just by way of passing, eventually caused a change of circumstances anyway, so a woman might as well make the decision to be brave, and trust in her ability to navigate the unknown.

She slept through the sunrise. When she woke, she was alone in a warm circle of morning light, but the sound of a pitcher pouring water suggested that Elias was in the washroom. She slipped into her nightgown and went out onto the balcony. The sea was a hazy blue shimmer on the horizon, the sun diffuse like gold dust in the air. She stretched, arms open wide. The gentle summer wind brushing up the mountain felt like uplift for her new wings.

A pair of strong hands slid around her middle from behind, then spun her around for a kiss.

Elias was in a playful mood this morning, exuding a bouncing energy, like he was moving in a shower of sparks.

"Katinka," he crooned, and grabbed at her. "Cattoush, my little falcon."

He twirled her back to the view.

"Are you happy?" He held her from behind, his hands wrapped over her belly.

"Very happy."

"You know what would make me happy?"

She nestled more snugly against his chest. "Tell me."

His cheek grazed against hers, pleasantly, because his beard was already turning silky. "Let me learn your heart," he said. "Let me woo you when I'm in London. Let me show you that I want to love you right. If you need time for your thoughts, I'll let you stay in your tower of ivory every winter." He nuzzled her ear, teasingly, softly. "Let me court you, ya roohi," he whispered, "and if you're not convinced, I will leave you be and you can keep my heart as a memory."

Ya roohi. *My soul.* She turned in his arms and took his face in her hands. She had never said *yes* faster.

When she detangled herself, she was dizzy and breathless from kissing too hard and she laughed for no particular reason.

"I should like to go for a swim," she said, pointing to where the sky blended into the sea.

Elias kissed the top of her head. "We shall do that," he said. "Later."

Half a day's ride was left to Bsharri. At this altitude, the wind was lovely and cool, taking the sting out of the sun. The horses moved carefully on the uneven dirt road, the repetitive sway of their warm big bodies could put a rider into a meditative state. With her heart and mind appeased, Catriona's eyes were wide open to the landscape this time. The cragged rock faces of the gorge plunged hundreds of feet into the Kadisha Valley. Elias claimed that miracles happened here, but to her, it seemed like a stronghold created by nature herself, seemingly hostile to life. Eventually, little by little, the marks humans had left on the steep slopes over the millennia became visible to the naked eye. Monasteries clung to vertical rock like beehives to the walls of a giant porch, blending into the pale stone to the point of near invisibility. Crosses were chiseled into rocks to indicate the dwellings of hermits and entries to monastic caves. It suddenly struck her as absurd that she hadn't spent more time tracing her beloved languages in the wild instead of dissecting them in her study.

It turned out that Elias hadn't been as interested in the town of Bsharri—*they don't much like us here*—as much as in an ancient cedar forest that covered the nearby slope.

He eventually halted their little convoy to point out the sprawling canopies.

"Arz al-Rabb," he said. "The Cedars of God."

Already the warm air was pungent with the fragrance of cedar wood. They rode closer until the man-high drystone wall snaking around the grove stopped their advance.

Elias unmounted and patted the neck of his horse. He handed

the reins to the guard, then came to Catriona and lifted her from the saddle.

"Guess who paid for this wall," he asked, steering her toward it with his hand on the small of her back. She wondered how much he was paying the guard to keep their secrets.

"I haven't a clue," she said, eyeing the lichen-covered stones.

He tipped his head to the side. "Your Queen Victoria."

"How curious."

"It's true," he said earnestly. "She heard that the trees that built the temple of Solomon were dying out because the Turks cut the timber, and the goats eat the saplings. It offended her, that goats should be the reason for the demise of biblical trees. Her wall protects a hundred hectares." Now he cracked a grin. "Bsharri rifles protect the wall."

The wall posed no obstacle to him. He helped her climb it, her foot on his thigh, and then he scaled it by himself, smoothly like a mountain lion, to assist her down on the other side.

For a while, she wandered among the trees in silence. They were not particularly tall, but remarkably wide, the branches spreading horizontally as though they grew with providing shade in mind. The powerful trunks seemed to emanate a calm warmth.

"They don't rot," Elias said. "They don't burn. They need little. Unless you cut them down, they grow for thousands of years."

He surprised her by stepping off the path and kneeling in the dirt, next to a sapling, perhaps ten inches tall.

He looked up at her with an apologetic shrug. "Now I do something forbidden."

He pulled the knife from his belt and stabbed the wide blade into the ground. He moved the knife around, back and forth, loosening the soil in a generous circle around the small cedar.

"I shouldn't mind living in two places," he said, his attention on the digging. "Home can be many things, a life's work, or a person." The blade went deeper, exposing tree roots, intricate and fragile like a network of veins. "What troubles me is that I might not always come back here as planned, every winter, for reasons we can't yet envision. You know what will happen then? I've seen it happen to others: two versions of my homeland will begin to exist, one that is built on the myths of my memories, and the real place, which keeps moving forward without me. One day, I might not recognize it anymore when I return. It might not recognize me."

His fingers worked diligently now, carefully removing clinging stones and lumps of soil from the sapling's pale tendrils. She'd never tire of looking at him, she realized; she could stand right here for the rest of the days and gaze at the strong, tanned curve of his neck, how his back muscles worked under his vest, how gentle his hands could be and how his hair curled out from under his cap. *I will love you with all that I have*, she vowed. Love could not fix everything, but it could be a strength, a shield, and a comfort.

"You will always have a home here," she said quietly. "And wherever you go, you carry the mountains with you and will leave an imprint."

He looked back at her over his shoulder, his expression softening. He sheathed the knife and stood up, cradling the cedar sapling to his chest with the care one would afford a newborn.

"It's coming with us," he said. "The roots are good. They will grow again."

Waves washed over the sandy shore of the small island. A sailboat bobbed gently in place, anchored in shallow waters. A man and a woman floated on their backs, their hands entwined, their faces upturned to the blue expanse of sky above. Now and then a wave lapped over the woman's face and left a salty taste on her lips. Her eyes were peaceful. She was smiling.

Epilogue

─────◆────◆─────

December 14th, 1918

The general election fell on a wet Saturday. Newspapers prophesied doom—no woman would turn up to cast her vote in the rain, in winter. *We shall see about that*, Lucie had said, *we shall see.* For the past four years, women had driven ambulances to the front lines, flown aircraft, served as spies, and replaced millions of absent men in factories, schools, hospitals, and office buildings. They might just dare to get their feet wet for an afternoon.

A convoy of three Rolls-Royces moved slowly through the drizzle toward Westminster Palace. Annabelle sat in the backseat of the first vehicle, protected from the cold by an elegant winter coat and with her granddaughter nestled comfortably against her side. She had cast her ballot in Belgravia this morning and had stayed on to assist first-time women voters. Since leaving, she had had Jamie stop the car twice, in Chelsea, and in St. James, to collect Hattie, Catriona, Lucie, and various offspring from their respective voting booths.

For the last hour, she had sent the convoy through the London districts, pointing out different polling stations to Aurelia, and they had tried to count the women in the queues as they passed.

Annabelle glanced down at Aurelia's small face and watched the girl's quiet green eyes take in the history being made. She tried to remember her life when she had been Aurelia's age, ten years old. This close to Christmas, she would have been helping her mother and the maid in their small country kitchen, eager to sneak raisins and bits of dough.

They passed Parliament Square. Westminster Palace looked blurry behind its thin veil of brown fog. Annabelle leaned forward and placed her hand on the upholstery of the driver's seat. "Stop right here, darling."

"We are meeting Father at the Old Palace Yard," Jamie replied, his eyes on the road. "It's coming up in a minute."

"I know. Stop here."

"Mummy, this street is not for parking," he remarked, but he pulled over and stepped on the brake.

The wide pavement was busy with pedestrians. Straight ahead, a queue of voters ran past St. Margaret's Church and disappeared into a building on the corner of Broad Sanctuary.

"So many have come," Annabelle said, not for the first time. "Lucie was right."

Jamie looked back over his shoulder, his faintly amused expression a copy of his father's.

"How could you have doubted Lucinda?"

"Frankly, I hadn't known what to expect."

The war effort aside, the Representation of the People Act that granted women over the age of thirty and all men in Britain the vote had only just come into effect; it was so new, it was barely real. The suffrage cause itself had been dormant throughout four years of war. Even the militant suffragettes had laid down their weapons and dedicated their efforts to supporting the nation. The world was still in turmoil. The armistice had been called a month ago, but peace returned only slowly; Claremont's west wing was still a makeshift hospital and convalescing soldiers were wandering around the grounds at all hours. Here in London, motorized omnibuses with American flags hanging from the windows pushed through the traffic.

"I should like to get out for a moment," Annabelle said.

Jamie glanced at the rear mirror. The automobiles behind them had come to a halt, forming a haphazard line along the curb. Annabelle could see Lucie gesticulating quizzically from behind her wheel. Next to her, their granddaughter Josephine was making faces. That girl. *She takes after you*, Annabelle would tell her friend; *No, she very much takes after you*, Lucie would reply, *and thank goodness for that*. As long as she doesn't take after Ballentine, was all Sebastian ever said to that. To this day, the duke was baffled to find himself tied to a once-notorious lothario by way of his elder daughter's marriage to said lothario's son, and that his and Ballentine's heritage would mix so well in two delightful grandchildren.

"Very well." Jamie switched off the engine. He opened his door and Annabelle watched as he carefully climbed down the step, then limped alongside the automobile to assist with her and Aurelia's descent. Ever since shrapnel had taken the proper mobility of his legs, her son had forgone a chauffeur and driven the Silver Ghost himself. She took his arm because she wanted to be close to him, not because she would have required assistance. Once safely on the pavement, she glanced up at his stoic profile.

"I'm glad you are by my side today," she said.

He gave a nod. "Of course," he said. "It's your victory day."

Indeed, but not all children cared to understand their mother's battles.

People walked around her, breathing in fog and exhaling white clouds. Engines rumbled and hooves clopped past. Just a little farther down the street was the Old Palace Yard that fronted the House of Lords. She had stood in this spot here before, clutching a woolen scarf against her chest in chilly autumn air. She remembered a tall man in a top hat seeming to materialize from the fog.

"Jamie," she said absently. "Why don't you walk ahead. I should like to stay here awhile."

Jamie gave her an odd look. "Aurelia, sweet," he said, "come with Papa."

Aurelia looked like a doll on his hand, in her small blue coat and with her honey-blond braids lying neatly on her shoulders. *How strange life is*, Annabelle thought. Had Lucie not ordered her to hand out pamphlets in this very spot forty years ago, had Sebastian not walked toward her at that minute, this perfect little girl would not exist. Either all existence was frightfully fragile, a result of infinite, random chances, or it was preordained in every detail.

Lucie's voice came from behind: "My lovelies, what are we doing?"

She was approaching with Josephine and Josi's brother, their mutual grandson, Alexander. A sour-faced Charlotte stomped behind the trio in her sturdy old boots. Annabelle's second-eldest daughter had shared a ride with Lucie, not wanting to squeeze herself into the space next to Jamie while he was driving. Farther behind, at the curb, Hattie and Catriona seemed to struggle with closing their vehicle doors properly, until their chauffeur set himself to the task. Elyssa, Catriona's only child, stood aside and covered her eyes with her hands, clearly unimpressed by the collective practical incompetence on display. Like Charlotte, Elyssa's patience seemed to wear a little thin today. At one-and-twenty years old, she wasn't qualified to vote during this or even the next election.

"Aunty Elyssa wanted to vote, and Aunty Charlie is cross because not a single woman has been elected, and she thinks Aunt Lucie should have run for MP," Josephine announced in her bright voice when their group had caught up.

"It is a sad thing," Charlotte remarked, looking down her proud nose.

"According to poll estimates, Constance Markievicz ought to win her seat," Elyssa pointed out.

"Indeed; if only she weren't currently in prison for anti-conscriptionist activities," Charlotte snipped. "Or were not a member of Sinn Féin and as such can't take her seat anyway."

"A clever choice, to vote in a convict bound by abstentionism," remarked Alexander, his hazel gaze flicking back and forth between his aunties.

"Young man, at your age, you ought to refrain from sarcasm entirely," Lucie scolded him, as though he had had a choice in the matter with all the Ballentine blood in his veins.

"Why didn't you run for MP, Aunt Lucie?" Josephine asked.

"Ah well." Lucie gave her a lopsided smile. "Because, my dear, I'm tired."

This confused the children, who only knew the kind of tired that took place shortly before bed.

"You could have done it for just one term," Charlie said, her blue eyes flashing, "to make a point . . . to set an example. I thought that was what you fought for."

"Charlotte," Annabelle said quietly.

Her daughter pressed her lips together and ducked her head.

Lucie sighed. "Charlie, child," she said. "I have fought for this day today since 1868. How many years is that? Fifty years? Yes, fifty."

"Half a century," muttered Alexander.

"Am I that old?" Lucie asked mildly. "So it seems that for half a century, seven days a week, I rose to a list of tasks I had to accomplish for the Cause, and I went to bed knowing I still hadn't done enough. Does this not sound tiring to you?"

A contrite expression came over Charlotte's face. "I didn't mean to—"

"When we pioneered this cause," Lucie broke in, "we knew very well that it was for the benefit of those who were to come after us. Had I hoped to see this day today? Absolutely. But I had never expected it. This fight began before I was born. I recall too many women who dedicated their lives to the Cause, and they passed on decades ago. Most of you won't ever know their names. Don't mistake me, there is still work to be done; the wheel of human inanity will undoubtedly keep turning. However, my ride on it ends here, today. This is your cause now, if you want it—pick up the torch. See that the right to vote extends to women in their twenties, and the penniless. Help women put themselves up for every election. See to it that Oxford will finally give its women proper degrees. Support your sisters, regardless of their position in life, and tell them to use their rights—to receive an education, to keep their earnings, to find a husband who treats them as an equal, or to remain single. As for me, I desire no thanks for helping you get those rights, but don't begrudge me my rest. I shall spend the next part of my life napping, going to pretty places, and making my husband happy. Ah. Speaking of the devil."

Jamie and Aurelia were returning to their group, and they brought company: Sebastian's erect figure in a dark austere winter coat was easily spotted, standing out in any crowd. His once wintry blond hair had lightened to the color of snow. The duke's eldest daughter, Artemis, mother of Josi and Alex, had her hand tucked into the crook of his arm. Next to Artemis was her husband, Lucie's son Henry, whose auburn hair and tall frame were so like his father's that Annabelle sometimes had to look twice, thinking she had spotted a young Ballentine. The actual Ballentine, now the Earl of Rochester, was presently in animated discussion with Aurelia. In ten days' time, their group would be complete at Claremont for a Christmas house party: Jamie's wife and son would join, the Campbell-Khourys, the Ballentines, the Blackstones and their four redheaded daughters, Peregrin and his wife, old friends like Aoife Byrne and her companion Susan. Charlotte would bring her friend, a pretty physician she had met during her medical studies at London University and with whom she had gone to the front with the medical corps. A sudden pressure swelled in Annabelle's throat, and she turned away to hide her crumpling expression. It was a miracle that all her loved ones had come home. Some days, it still felt unreal.

While greetings were exchanged behind her back and they obstructed the pavement with their large group, the wind turned, and the drizzle turned to sleet. In the queue of voters moving past St. Margaret's Church, umbrellas popped up quick like mushrooms.

Hattie appeared by Annabelle's side, the tip of her upturned nose pink from the cold. "That's snow, isn't it?" she asked, and squinted at the gray sky.

Catriona joined them. "Only if one possesses vast quantities of optimism."

"She has that," remarked Lucie as she fell in line next to Annabelle.

Annabelle smiled. "And we adore her for it."

Shoulder to shoulder with her friends, the familiar scents of their perfumes in her nose, she felt the pressure ease behind her eyes. Sebastian's presence was there, too; warm and gentle like a shielding blanket against her back. The coil of tension in her chest unspooled. Nothing was normal these days, but there was love surrounding her. One could master new shores.

The great clash of empires, over a century in the making, had left once-powerful old institutions across Europe broken beyond repair. The Russian royal family was wiped out, the German monarchy abolished, Austria-Hungary had split, and the Ottoman Empire had fallen. While the United States had begun her rise as a new global power on the other side of the Atlantic, Britain had been badly battered, and even its insulated, glacially slow-moving world of the aristocracy was facing change. Annabelle did not fear change as such; here, it could be a good thing. She was, however, apprehensive about the chaos that so often erupted into the voids of power. Sometimes, of course, something new had long been preparing in the wings, raring to claim its rightful place should the opportunity arise. On the other side of the street, the women moved slowly, patiently, toward the ballot box. The hats in the queue ranged from fashionably large flower-laden ones to the now bygone smaller models of her youth. Her nose stung with tears, after all. She felt Hattie's hand in hers and clasped it tightly.

"This is a new dawn," she said.

"It's rising over ruins, though," Hattie murmured.

"Yes," said Annabelle, "but we are looking at the silver lining."

Author's Note

Inspiration for Elias's story

In 2017, the FBI raided the Metropolitan Museum of Art in New York to collect a Phoenician marble bull head from Lebanon's Temple of Eshmun. The sculpture had been stolen from its safe-keeping location during Lebanon's civil war in the 1980s and had ended up in the hands of an American art collector couple. Legal action was required to have the piece returned.

Artifact theft is an old story. In the Victorian era, the rulers of China, Persia, and the Ottoman Empire designed legislation to limit the outflow of local heritage into the hands of foreign collectors. A 2017 *Washington Post* article ("Indiana Jones and the Big Lie") highlights reactions to these measures at the time: *In the 1870s, an American consul . . . advised Heinrich Schliemann, a German-American tycoon who had smuggled valuable treasures out of the Ottoman Empire, that permitting "any part of them to go into the absurd collection of rubbish which the Turks call their 'Museum,' would be worse than throwing them away."*

The history of Lebanon is long, fractured, and complex, and I only capture a small slice of its rich tapestry in this novel. For those interested in reading more on the themes mentioned, I recommend the works of Ussama Samir Makdisi and Akram Fouad Khater. As for Elias, it hurt to make him leave the mountain, but it is representative of the Lebanese experience throughout the centuries—about forty percent of Mount Lebanon's population left between the 1860s and the end of World War I. Today, more Lebanese people live outside Lebanon than in Lebanon.

Artistic license

I merged "A man goes on a journey, or a stranger comes to town" (John Gardner) with Richard Skinner's "boy meets girl; boy loses girl; man hunts whale."

The Phoenician wine press in Tell el-Burak was discovered in 2020.

The Married Women's Property Act (MWPA)

The MWPA amendment was not sponsored by the Duke of Montgomery—who is a work of fiction—but by the man who inspired his character, Lord Selborne. Selborne was a conservative peer who eventually changed his mind and supported women's rights, and he successfully introduced the bill to the House of Lords on February 14, 1882. It passed into the House of Commons later that year and was passed with amendments on August 15. To better convey the tone of the debate surrounding the bill, I merged the statements made by Sir George Campbell, Mr. Warton, and Mr. Fowler during an MWPA committee meeting on August 11 with the August 15 sitting; see the minutes for August 11, 1882, Hansard 1604.

The Writ for Restitution of Conjugal Rights

In 1884, Parliament abolished the jail penalty for noncompliance thanks to *Weldon v. Weldon*, an 1883 divorce court decision. Mrs.

Weldon had sued her husband for restitution, which was highly unusual. Previously, Captain Weldon had tried to commit Mrs. Weldon to an asylum on grounds of her spiritualism, because he wanted to live with his mistress. When the court granted Mrs. Weldon's plea, the law was swiftly changed to spare other men Captain Weldon's fate. For this story, I changed the timeline of this event to 1882.

Gifted women in the Victorian era

Today, Catriona would probably be classed as gifted, with giftedness being a form of neurodiversity. Giftedness is traditionally perceived as positive, but the inherent overexcitability may express as impaired executive function, intense emotions, sensory issues, and anxiety. Some traits, such as valuing content over presentation, continue to be coded as "typically male," which makes it more challenging for gifted girls to feel they belong. I imagined such a woman in late Victorian Britain. As a working-class woman, she would have had little time or energy left to apply herself after work, childcare, and chores. In the middle and upper classes, the new cult of domesticity sidelined women who refused to fulfill an increasingly narrow role. "Good and Bad Mothers" is an actual article, reflective of attitudes at the time, and I imagine a thick skin was required to ignore the shaming. We will never know how many female contributions are missing from science, the arts, and politics, just because rigid gender norms forced women to choose between sharing their gift or being socially accepted. I'm forever grateful to the women who came before me who found the strength to be true to themselves under such circumstances. We stand on their shoulders when we choose who and where we want to be today.

Acknowledgments

To my readers—I want to thank you for your patience. While I began writing in 2020, various grievous events converged and it took me a year longer than planned to finish this novel.

Throughout, I received an incredible amount of support. Here I want to thank Matthias—being partnered with a writer can be rough at the best of times, and it's your encouragement and understanding that allows me to have it all. To Montse: it's you who makes me finish a chapter, and this book wouldn't have gotten done without you. Mama and Micha, thank you for letting me boomerang and for giving me the nineteenth-century gentleman treatment so I could focus entirely on writing for a bit. I would like to thank my father for helping me access historical sources about Mount Lebanon, and my sister Josiane, who took the time to spar with me despite her looming bar exam. I'm grateful to Melanie and Jemima, for their fierce enthusiasm and input.

To the brilliant Roshani Chokshi and Christine Wells, I can hardly thank you enough for wading through the first ten chapters of draftiest draft and making them so much better with your suggestions. I also owe the Lyonesses, for bearing with me, always ready with advice; I'm lucky to be part of such a talented and supportive group of women. Much love to my fellow authors who add my work to their towering reading lists and let their light shine on it; in particular Kate Quinn, Jodi Picoult, Mimi Matthews, Chanel Cleeton, Julia Quinn, and Beth O'Leary. Dr. Mira Assaf Kafantaris, I'm hugely grateful that you took the time to share your thoughtful perspective on the historical aspects of this novel (though any errors or oversights are of course mine and Elias's).

Finally, I owe a debt of gratitude to my editor, Sarah Blumenstock, and my agent, Kevan Lyon—your professional acclaim is out there for everyone to see, so here I wish to highlight the great kindness, tremendous patience, and unwavering positivity that you have shown me from start to finish.

The Gentleman's Gambit

EVIE DUNMORE

READERS GUIDE

Discussion Questions

1. Who owns history?

2. Why did Elias feel so drawn to someone like Catriona, whom he considered well-rooted both within herself and in her homeland? Did you see his perception change toward the end?

3. Can you relate to Catriona's idea that her love-at-first-sight moments were an indication of the attributes she was missing in herself? Why or why not?

4. What challenges do you see for Elias and Catriona as a couple down the road?

5. Do you feel that Elias's anger over Catriona's maneuver to send him the artifacts was justified? Why or why not? Would you have approached either of their positions differently?

6. As an introvert, Catriona rightly worries about losing herself in a relationship, which was particularly demanding on women during the Victorian era. What has and hasn't changed in regard to the expectation that a "good" woman's time and purpose should be subsumed by her relationships?

7. The concepts of motherhood, childhood, and housewife as we know them were constructed in the Victorian era—can you see how they have carried over to contemporary society? Why or why not?

8. After women in Britain won the right to own property and retain legal personhood in a marriage, it still took another fifty years before they could vote on equal terms with men. Can you imagine why legislators kept denying women the right to vote, and why did their position change only after a world war?

9. The long power struggle between the five empires dominated nineteenth-century politics—can you think of examples of how the repercussions are still showing up in today's politics?

10. Catriona frequently turns to past patterns to help her navigate her present. At what point does the past turn from a useful source of information for making better choices into a prison instead? Do you have any events in your life where you chose based on the past rather than the now?

Photograph by the author

Evie Dunmore is the *USA Today* bestselling author of the League of Extraordinary Women series, which is inspired by her passion for romance, women pioneers, and all things Victorian. In her civilian life, she is a consultant with a MSc in diplomacy from Oxford. Evie lives in Berlin and pours her fascination with nineteenth-century Britain into her writing. She is a member of the British Romantic Novelists' Association (RNA).

Learn more about this book and other titles from *USA Today* bestselling author

EVIE DUNMORE

SCAN ME
or visit
prh.com/eviedunmore